About the Author

MARY KAY ANDREWS is a former journalist for the *Atlanta Journal-Constitution* and the national bestselling author of *Savannah Blues*, *Little Bitty Lies*, and *Hissy Fit*. She lives in Raleigh, North Carolina.

Savannah Breeze

Mary Kay Andrews

HARPER

NEW YORK • LONDON • TORONTO • SYDNEY

HARPER

A hardcover edition of this book was published in 2006 by HarperCollins Publishers.

HarperCollins books may be purchased for educational, business, or sales promotional use. For information please write: Special Markets Department, HarperCollins Publishers, 10 East 53rd Street, New York, NY 10022.

FIRST HARPER PAPERBACK PUBLISHED 2007.

The Library of Congress has catalogued the hardcover edition as follows:
Andrews, Mary Kay
    savannah breeze / Mary Kay Andrews.—1st ed.
      p. cm.
     1.Savannah (Ga.)—Fiction. I. Title.
  PS3570.R587B74 2006
  813'.6—dc22   2005046251

ISBN: 978-0-06-056467-4 (pbk.)
ISBN-10: 0-06-056467-9 (pbk.)

07 08 09 10 11 ❖/RRD 10 9 8 7 6 5 4 3 2 1

For Patti Hogan Coyle, "She ain't heavy, she's my sister!" With love.

Acknowledgments

As always, I'm indebted to the kindnesses of friends—and strangers, who helped with the research for *Savannah Breeze*. Anne Landers shared innkeeping secrets; Bob Dykema and Jeff Johnston of Thunderbolt Yacht Sales told me about yacht shopping; Jimmy Marsden helped with boat stuff. Junking buddies Polly Powers Stram and Jacky Yglesias shared their love and knowledge of Savannah and Tybee, and Oline Cogdill helped out with Fort Lauderdale info. Thanks also to Virginia Reeve and Ron and Leuveda Garner for sharing their corner of Tybee with me. Any errors or misstatements of fact are my own fault and not theirs. Of course, I owe everything to the love and support of my family, Tom, Katie, and Andy Trocheck, who keep me sane and never fail to remind me that I'm nothing without them! I'm also deeply indebted to my HarperCollins family, especially Carolyn Marino, Jennifer Civiletto, Leslie Cohen and Elly Weisenberg, and the SKLA team, Stuart Krichevsky, Shana Cohen, and Liz Coen. I really *am* nothing without them.

I

He was introduced to me as "Reddy"—short for Ryan Edward Millbanks III. And I should have known better. He was younger. Too young. Sexy. Too sexy. Dead sexy. Exquisite manners. And as he leaned in, kissing me lightly on the cheek, I nearly fainted from the pheromones the man emitted. "I've heard so much about you from your ex-husband," he whispered, his mustache tickling my ear.

Alarms should have gone off. Sirens, blinking lights. Robotic voices should have warned me away. But the band was playing something Gershwinish, and I wouldn't have listened anyway. I only heard what I wanted to hear.

At the mention of my ex, I looked around the tightly packed ballroom with alarm. "Richard? What's Richard doing here? They were supposed to notify me when he was released."

Reddy looked confused and laughed to cover up his embarrassment. "Richard? But . . . Sandy Thayer told me, I mean, well, Sandy said you were his ex-wife. That is, he pointed in this direction and suggested I come talk to you. In fact, he suggested you might need rescuing from your date. You are BeBe Loudermilk, have I got that right?"

Now it was my turn to laugh. "Oh, Sandy. Yes, you've got that right. Sandy is my ex. Or I'm his. Twice, in fact. Sorry, I've been drinking wine all night. As for my date, I'm not sure he remembers he brought me." I grimaced in the direction of Tater Love, my so-called date, who'd spent most of the evening drooling down the front of my ball gown, and who was now draped over the bar, consuming one beer after another.

Tater was a last-minute fix-up, and I should have known better, but it was the Telfair Ball, which was the social event of the year in Savannah, and I'd already paid for the tickets, and it wasn't as though my former fiancé, Emery Cooper, would be joining me.

Emery, one of the Cooper-Hale Mortuary Coopers, had called long distance, the previous week, to let me know that he and his ex-wife were on their way to Jamaica, to be remarried on the beach, which was the site of their first wedding. And their second honeymoon.

I thought I handled the news rather well. I took the salmon steaks I'd bought for our dinner that evening, drove over to his town house on Lafayette Square, and slid them through the mail slot in the door. That way, when Emery and his new bride returned home in a week, they'd have something to remember me by.

There was no way I was going to skip the Telfair Ball. For one thing, I was on the host committee. For another, by now, everybody in town knew that Emery had thrown me over for Cissy Drobish, the bucktoothed millionairess mother of his three children. It wouldn't do to have people talking about me behind my back. If they were going to talk, by God, they could just do it to my face.

"Hold your head up high, girl," I could hear my late father saying to me, nudging me as I slumped down in the pew in church. So I did as I was taught. I'd spent the whole day of the ball getting ready for battle: manicure, pedicure, facial, herbal massage, and new honey-blond highlights in my hair. I'd gotten all my big-girl jewelry out of the safe-deposit box, and had Roi, my hairdresser, pile my hair on top of my head so everybody could see that I hadn't returned Emery's diamond earrings.

However fabulous I looked, however, did not change the fact that I was stuck for the evening with Tater Love, friend of a friend of a friend, confirmed bachelor, who'd been too cheap to rent the evening shoes to go with his tux. Scuffed-black-loafer Tater Love. Cocktail-sauce-on-his-shirtfront Tater Love. It was going to be a very long evening. Which was why I'd decided to anesthetize myself with chardonnay as soon as we arrived at the dance.

Reddy took my elbow and guided me firmly from the dance floor to a remote corner of the ballroom occupied only by a grotesque marble statue of an unidentified Greek goddess and a large potted palm.

"About my exes—" I started to explain.

"Shhh," Reddy said, putting a finger to my lips. "Be right back," he promised. And when he reappeared, he had a plate of lobster in one hand and a pair of crystal flutes in the other. He lifted the front of his dinner jacket—it looked Armani, but I couldn't be sure—and extracted an unopened bottle of Moët & Chandon from the waistband of his trousers.

Which should have signaled another set of alarms—beware of men bearing gifts in their pants.

He popped the champagne cork with one smooth, expert motion—I was soon to learn that he was an expert on many, many things—and poured a glass for each of us.

Reddy clinked his flute lightly against mine. "To new beginnings," he said, and he smiled that rogue smile.

And that was the end of all my good intentions.

We ditched Tater and the Telfair Ball without another thought. I wrapped myself in my grandmother Lorena's long, sable coat, and as I stepped out of the museum and onto the moonlit pavement of Barnard Street, Reddy came roaring up in a dusty silver Jaguar. Getting into a sports car in a skintight sheath with thigh-high slits isn't the easiest thing to do in this world, but somehow I managed to get myself almost seated before Reddy floored the accelerator. As we rounded the corner of Telfair Square on two tires, I caught a glimpse of a white-jacketed man standing forlornly on the curb, a bottle of Old Milwaukee clutched in his hand.

I felt only a very faint spasm of guilt. Not for Tater. Tater still had his open bar and two more free meals ahead of him that night. He wouldn't miss me at all. No, I felt guilty about my mother.

She'd been dead and in the grave for five years. But I could hear her tsk-tsking. "Really, BeBe! I have never *heard* of such insupportable behavior."

Lately, I've been seeing those bumper stickers asking "What Would Jesus Do?" Never mind Jesus, I always think.

What Would Mama Say?

Mama was a stickler for doing the right thing. She would have been appalled by my behavior that night. Or any other night during the past five years since we'd buried her over at Bonaventure Cemetery, come to think of it.

I quickly put Tater and Mama out of my mind, and devoted all my powers of concentration on the man sitting next to me in that Jaguar.

He was tall, of course, but then I'm only five foot three, so everybody seems tall to me. In reality, he was probably a shade short of six feet tall. His eyes were a pale blue and were a startling contrast to his deeply tanned face. His hair was brownish-blondish and wavy, and already starting to recede a little in front, although the back brushed over the collar of his dress shirt. I gave him extra points for not resorting to one of those hideous comb-over tricks, and more points for the tiny diamond stud earring he wore in his left earlobe. An earring! *Quel* scandal! And anyway, I'd never dated a man with jewelry as nice as mine. But the clincher was the cleft in his chin. I had to fold my hands in my lap to keep from reaching over there and tracing that cleft with my finger.

"Are you gonna be warm enough in that skimpy little dress of yours?" he asked, glancing over at me as we raced down Victory Drive in the direction of the beach. It was February, and forty degrees that night, practically glacial weather in Savannah.

I snuggled my chin deep into the folds of the fur coat's shawl collar, and got a whiff of Lorena's Chanel No. 5 perfume. "Depends on where we're going," I said. "I'm not exactly dressed for Tybee."

"Not the beach," he assured me. "But I'll have to ask you to leave those shoes on the dock. Those heels of yours would work hell on my teak decking."

"A boat?" I grinned. Reddy grinned right back.

"But this is a yacht," I said when I saw the gleaming white craft tied up at the Wilmington Island Yacht Club slip. *Blue Moon* was painted on the stern in flowing gold-tipped blue lettering. "It's huge."

Reddy stepped nimbly aboard and turned to give me a hand. He yanked on the mooring lines to rock the boat closer to the dock, and got a devilish glint in his eye when I had to hike my skirt even higher to make the jump to the deck. He caught me expertly and held me briefly in his arms. "Not a yacht technically," he whispered in my ear. "It's only forty-eight feet."

"Only."

He laughed at himself then. "Well, maybe you could call it a baby yacht."

Half an hour later we were sitting in deck chairs on the bow of the *Blue Moon*, sipping champagne and watching the stars as tiny little wavelets slapped gently against the boat's hull.

A CD player in the cabin was playing soft jazz, and we'd scooted our chairs as close together as possible. "Tell me about you, BeBe Loudermilk," Reddy said, squeezing my hand.

I sighed. "Not much to tell. I've lived in Savannah my whole life. Everybody in my family has always lived in Savannah their whole lives. I have some business investments. I'm a natural blonde. Mostly. And I am currently a single-type person."

"Currently," he said. "Why do I get the feeling there's a story there?"

"Not much of a story," I said. "You might as well know, I was recently jilted. Not quite at the altar, but near enough to it that it still hurts."

He shook his head in wonder. "What kind of moron would let somebody like you slip through his fingers?"

I shrugged. "It's probably all for the best. He eloped last week with his ex-wife. And I did get to keep some very presentable jewelry."

He leaned over and nibbled my earlobe. "Including these earrings. Which you wore tonight to show everybody in town that you don't give a damn."

I giggled. "Am I that transparent?"

"Not transparent. Fascinating," he said. "I love a lady with a past."

"That's not how my mother would put it," I said, giving him a wry smile. "Mama never got over the fact that mine was the first divorce in our family."

"My mother never got over the fact that I dropped out of law school a semester short of getting my degree," Reddy said. "I'm the only male Millbanks in four generations not to graduate from Duke."

"Ooh," I said, getting a shiver up my spine. "Another black sheep."

"Another? What's that supposed to mean?"

The wind was picking up, and despite the multiple layers of hair spray Roi had spritzed me with, I could feel my updo coming undone.

"You have a thing for ladies with a past," I said, pushing a strand of hair out of my eyes. "Unfortunately, I seem to have a predilection for bad boys."

"Hey. I object," he said. "I never said I was bad."

"You don't have to say it," I told him, turning up the collar of the fur. "You just are. It's not your fault. And it's not mine either."

"You're cold," he said, looking over at me. He patted his lap. "Come here, BeBe. I'll show you I'm not bad at all."

His kisses certainly weren't anything like bad. They were long and sweet and tender. And dangerous. And delicious. I don't think I'd ever been kissed quite that nicely or thoroughly before.

"Just what kind of past do you have?" he asked once, when we'd both come up for air.

"I'm a divorcée," I said. "Three times over. Does that shock you?"

He laughed. "Divorcée! Nobody uses that word anymore. But really? Three times?"

"Technically. But really, I've only ever been married to two men. And I was only nineteen when I married Sandy Thayer, the man you met earlier tonight? He was my older brother's best friend. We ran off to Myrtle Beach and got married over spring break my freshman year at St. Mary's. My parents were horrified. They had it annulled right away. They told St. Mary's I was home sick with mononucleosis, and I went back and finished school like nothing had ever happened."

Reddy held up one finger. "Okay, technically, that marriage was annulled, so it never really happened. What about husband number two?"

"Richard Hodges." I shuddered as I said it. "What a nightmare. My last blind date. Ever. I was twenty-eight, running my first little restaurant, so busy I didn't have time to meet anybody, let alone date. Richard seemed like such a great guy. Very successful stockbroker, from a nice family. We dated for a year, and I was absolutely smitten with the guy. Even my mother loved him. Which should have been some kind of signal."

"Why do you say that?" Reddy asked.

"Richard," I said succinctly, "turned out to be a perv. A world-class pervert. We'd been married two months before I found the phone bills. He'd managed to spend $12,000 from our joint checking account. For phone sex. I didn't find out about the computer porn until after I kicked him out." I made a face. "When I found it, I took his laptop outside and ran it over with my car, then tossed it in a Dumpster. Which was a mistake, because my lawyer said we could have used it in court. But I didn't care. I just wanted him out of my life. And he is. Way out. He's doing ten to twelve in a minimum-security prison."

Reddy winced. "You poor kid." He kissed me again. "Darlin', your past is in the past. I'm only interested in your future."

I kissed him back. "I'm almost done now. Husband number three was Sandy."

"Again?"

"Yup. I was on the rebound from Richard. My sister-in-law had a surprise fortieth birthday party for my brother Arch, and Sandy was there. It was the first time I'd seen him in ten years. He was so sweet, so thoughtful. So un-Richard. I fell for him all over again."

"We only talked for a few minutes, but he seems like a decent guy."

"He is," I agreed. "Sandy is a total sweetheart. But he took a job in Chicago months after we got married. It was January. Have you ever been in Chicago in January?"

"No."

"Good for you," I said. "It wasn't anybody's fault, what happened between us. Sandy was on the road all the time for his job, and I was stuck out in this snooty Chicago suburb, miserable as mud. All I did was eat and cry and watch daytime television. I gained thirty pounds in eighteen months. And when that first snowstorm hit, that second year, I made up my mind. Packed my bags and caught a cab. I called Sandy from O'Hare. He was a good sport about it, but that's Sandy. And he's never held a grudge. He'd do anything for me, and I'd do the same for him."

I sighed. "So that's it. That's my big, bad past. But what about you? What makes you so bad, Ryan Edward Millbanks?"

"You're cold," he said suddenly. And he stood up, cradling me in his arms like a big fur-wrapped baby. "Come on," he said. "Let's go inside the cabin before you catch pneumonia out here."

I twisted the face of his watch until I could see the luminous dial. It was late. Nearly two A.M. "What's in that cabin of yours?" I asked.

"The usual. There's a nifty little galley. Are you hungry, sugar? I feel bad that I made you skip out of your party without any supper. I could cook us something. Warm up some chili, something like that?"

I shook my head. "Not hungry. Just a little sleepy."

There was that grin again. "Well, why didn't you say so? The owner's quarters are pretty special, if I do say so myself. And I'd be delighted to show them to you."

I shook my head. "That's *not* what I meant. It's late. I've had a long day, and I've got to be at work in the morning." I kissed him lightly. "It's been a lovely night, Reddy. But I think you'd better take me home."

He kissed me back. "Home? But I thought we were getting along so well. You're a lady with a past, and I'm a bad boy. We were meant to be."

It was tempting. I was so sleepy. And his arms felt so right, wrapped around me that way. I felt safe. And happy. And yes, I'll admit it, more than a little horny.

"Stay," he whispered in my ear.

But then it occurred to me. This was a man I'd met only a few hours earlier. And here I was, ready to jump into bed without another thought.

What Would Mama Say?

3

"About time," Daniel said when I strolled into the kitchen at Guale at four o'clock Sunday afternoon. I yawned and stretched and made a point of ignoring my chef. It was true that I'd slept through brunch and was now perilously close to missing our busy dinner trade too, but damnit, what's the point of owning your own restaurant if you can't sleep late once in a while?

I flipped the pages of the reservation book to see what kind of night to expect. Not too shabby. I recognized the names of some of our regulars, and was glad to see that the new concierge at the Westin had booked four different parties in for the evening.

"How was brunch?" I asked.

"A little slow," he admitted. "But up from last week."

"The dogwood in my front yard is loaded with buds," I said. "Pretty soon the azaleas in Forsyth Park will be in full bloom. Before you know it, we'll be packed with tourists. Enjoy the quiet while you can, my friend."

He nodded agreement. We were both native Savannahians, which meant we were both old enough to remember the days when the town was just another beautiful, if sleepy, Southern port. For as long as we could remember, shipping and paper mills were the industries that paid the bills in Savannah. When I grew up, in the seventies, there had been just one good hotel in town, the DeSoto Hilton, and only a handful of what anybody would call fine restaurants. But all that had changed in the nineties, with the publication of a book, and a movie by the same title, that had portrayed Savannah as a steamy hotbed of voodoo, sex, drag queens, and scandal.

These days, tourism pumps millions every year into our economy. Whole blocks of formerly squalid businesses and houses in the historic district have been restored to pristine condition, and new luxury hotels line the riverfront. Tour buses and trolleys clog the moss-draped old squares, and if you take a seat in any of the dozens of new restaurants that have opened downtown, you're as likely to hear Japanese or German being spoken at the next table as you are a Southen drawl.

But some things hadn't changed. High season—and spring—in Savannah starts officially on St. Patrick's Day, which is when the city throws a celebration they claim is second only to New York's for bluster and blarney. As usual, we were already booked solid with private dinners and parties for the entire week before St. Patrick's Day, and barring any unforeseen natural disasters, our business would stay strong right through till Christmas.

Daniel lifted the lid from a pot of simmering veal stock, dipped in a spoon, and tasted. He tossed his head in the direction of the tiny closet I call my office. "Guy came by earlier today and left something for you," he said, adding a couple of grinds of pepper to the pot.

"Hmm. Did he leave a name?"

"I didn't ask," Daniel said. "I was busy trying to keep us in business, you know?"

I flipped him the bird and hurried across the kitchen to my office.

A huge arrangement of pale pink roses in a cut-glass vase was centered on top of a pile of junk mail on my desk. A business card was Scotch-taped to the vase. The card was made of thick vellum. "Ryan Edward Millbanks III," it said. "Asset Management." There was no address, just a telephone number. I flipped it over. There were only two words on the back. "Dinner, tonight?"

I smiled to myself. "Definitely dinner tonight."

"New boyfriend?"

I whirled around, my face scarlet with embarrassment at being caught all moony-faced. Daniel leaned on the door frame.

"New friend," I said. With my foot I kicked the door shut, and sat down and dialed the number on the card.

The phone rang four times before a recording advised me to leave a message. "Steady, girl," I told myself. It wouldn't do to appear too eager. I hung up without leaving a message. Time to get to work. I plucked Reddy's card from the vase and tucked it into the pocket of my slacks. And I took the flowers and placed them on the pine console table at the front of the house.

The next few hours were a blur. Around five, just as the first early birds were coming through the door, both Kevin, our bartender, and Rikki, one of the waitresses, called in sick. It wasn't the first time the two of them had bailed on me on the same night, and I had my suspicions about the nature of their sickness, but shorthanded as we were, there was no time to conduct an inquisition.

Most people think the restaurant business is the epitome of hip and happenin', but the truth of the business is, it's mostly just dog-hard work. For every hour I spend exchanging air kisses with local celebrities, I spend another three in a sweltering kitchen, up to my elbows in dirty pans, irate chefs, and incompetent help. When the ladies' room commode backs up, I'm the one mopping the floor and cursing the plumber. When my local supplier sends whipping cream instead of crème fraiche or grouper instead of snapper, I'm the one who has to break the news to Daniel that the catch of the day has suddenly changed. And when the help bails out, I have to pitch in.

It was true that I'd arrived fashionably late at my restaurant in a chic black pantsuit and high-heeled black slingbacks, but I spent the rest of the evening racing from the maître d' stand to the bar to the kitchen, greeting customers, fixing drinks, and urging Daniel and his assistants to get the food out with a minimum of fuss.

By ten o'clock, when the last of the stragglers, a hard-drinking party of six, were pushing back from their white-clothed table, I was ready to drop dead from exhaustion, and my toes were screaming in pain.

"Great dinner, BeBe," exclaimed Preston Conover, the florid-faced vice president of Coastal Trust Bank, as he slung an arm around my shoulder and kissed me a little too close to my mouth. "Great little place you got here." Over his shoulder, his wife rolled her eyes. I managed to shrug his arm away and thanked him with as much sincerity as I could muster. After all, he wasn't just a banker. He was *my* banker, and he'd personally approved a half-a-million-dollar loan that had allowed me to expand my lounge into the vacant space next to mine there on Barnard Street.

Preston thrust his check and his platinum American Express card toward me, and I demurely thrust the credit card back at him.

"Aw, BeBe," he protested weakly. This was a game he liked to play to impress his friends. Big-shot Preston would insist on picking up the dinner check at the fanciest restaurants in town, knowing that owners like me would insist on comping him. In truth, I wouldn't have minded comping just Preston and Jeanine, but this was a party of six, and they'd all ordered the most expensive appetizers, entrées, and wine from our menu. Their bar bill alone came to $300, which I knew because I'd been the one fetching their drinks all night.

"Run along, Preston," I said, easing him toward the door. As soon as he was clear of it, I bolted the lock and sank down onto a seat at the bar.

"Owww," I moaned, sliding my feet out of my shoes. "Eeeww," I added, catching a glimpse of myself in the back-bar mirror. My hair was limp and drenched with perspiration, what was left of my lipstick was smeared, and I was missing an earring.

Suddenly there was somebody pounding on the door.

"We're closed," I hollered, too tired to stand up.

More pounding.

"Try the Marriott," I hollered. "They don't close till eleven."

More pounding.

I got up and hobbled, barefoot, to the door. I snapped the lock and flung the door open wide. "Get the fu—"

I managed to swallow the rest of the obscenity I'd been about to utter. The door pounder was Ryan Edward Millbanks III.

"Hey there," he said, taking a step back. "Did I catch you at a bad moment?"

I snatched off the apron, and tucked a damp strand of hair behind my ear.

"Long night," I said.

He gazed past me into the foyer, and I saw him looking at the arrangement of roses on the console table. "The flowers are beautiful," I said, gesturing toward them. "My favorite color rose. I didn't get a chance to call and thank you properly because we've been slammed all night. My bartender and one of my waitresses are shacked up somewhere, so I had to fill in, plus hostess. And then—"

He put a finger across my lips. "Shh," he said. "Doesn't matter. I just stopped by to see if you wanted to go get a bite to eat."

"Right now?" I said. "I can't go anywhere like this. Look at me. I'm a wreck."

"You look fine to me. And it doesn't have to be anyplace fancy," Reddy said amiably. "I'm mostly just interested in the company."

"It's Sunday night, and it's nearly eleven," I reminded him. "This is Savannah, not New York. There isn't anyplace decent open this late."

"I know a place," he said, extending a hand to me. "Come on. You're the boss. You don't have to clock out, do you?"

I laughed despite my tiredness. "No. Just let me tell Daniel I'm leaving."

"That's the chef?"

"Yeah. I guess you met him when you came by earlier."

"Technically, we didn't meet," Reddy said. "I dropped the flowers by and left. I got the impression he doesn't appreciate having strangers messing around in his kitchen."

"His bark's worse than his bite," I said. "He's really a sweetie. I'd introduce you properly, but it's been a long night for all of us."

"Another time, then," Reddy said.

Out in the kitchen, Daniel was just putting away his knives, which meant he too was getting ready to leave.

"I'm toast," I told him.

"How'd it go out front?" he asked. "Anybody bitch about the fact that we ran out of the scallops?"

"They did," I admitted, "but I was so busy I didn't pay any attention. That new oyster appetizer of yours was a big hit. But I noticed a couple of people didn't seem too thrilled with the seared tuna."

"That's because they ordered it cooked to death. This is sashimi-grade tuna, BeBe. It's no good unless you order it rare," Daniel groused. "We've got to educate these people's palates."

"No. We've got to serve them food they like," I corrected him. "Let's think about taking the tuna off the menu for a while. Maybe substitute flounder."

"Flounder!" Daniel slapped the stainless-steel prep table with the flat of his hand. "Why don't we just do fried catfish and hush puppies?"

"We'll talk about it Tuesday," I said, turning my back to him. "See you then."

"Hey," he said, sounding surprised. "Where are you going? It's Sunday night. Weezie's expecting us."

Most Sunday nights for the past couple of years, my best friend, Weezie Foley, and I have had a standing dinner date.

The dinners had started as a girl's-only affair, when we were both in deepest, darkest, divorce recovery. We'd meet at Weezie's for drinks and dinner, and usually watch some old chick flick and fantasize about what it would be like to live in the moment of our favorite movies. Daniel had been added to the equation after he and Weezie became an item, and our number had since grown to five, with the addition of Weezie's uncle James, and Jonathan McDowell, his significant other.

The men were a great addition to the mix, because Daniel, after all, cooked like a dream, and James and Jonathan were gay men, so they liked everything we liked, plus they were both lawyers, which always comes in handy.

"Damn," I said, slapping my thigh. "I completely forgot. I've kind of got a date."

"So bring him," Daniel said.

"No," I said quickly. "It's not that kind of date. I mean, well, it's complicated. Anyway, Weezie'll understand. Tell her I'll call her tomorrow."

"A date?" Daniel raised one eyebrow. "The guy with the flowers?"

"None of your business," I said. "See you Tuesday."

He shook his head, telegraphing his disapproval. "Has Weezie met this Ryan Edward Millbanks the third character?"

"You read the card? My private mail?"

"Sure," Daniel said. "Some guy busts in my kitchen, wants to know where you are, and how business is, damn straight I read the card. Not that there was much on it. Who ever heard of a business card without an address?"

"Reddy is in asset management," I said. "He's from one of the finest old families in Charleston. He doesn't *need* a business card to tell people what he does or where he lives. And I don't need you checking up on my personal business."

"Right," Daniel said sourly. "Because you have such good judgment where men are concerned."

"I hired you," I reminded him. And I was tempted to add that I could fire him too if the need arose. But I wasn't that stupid. And anyway, there was a very attractive man waiting out front to take me to dinner.

"Give the gang my regrets," I said, pushing open the swinging door to the dining room. "And from now on, stay out of my office."

4

On Mondays, my only real day off from the restaurant, I visit the home. Technically, Magnolia Manor Assisted Living is a "managed-care community," but in reality, it's an old folks' home. A very fancy, very expensive old folks' home, where my grandparents, Spencer and Lorena Loudermilk, have been living for the past three years.

Granddaddy met me at the door to the trim little stucco cottage he and my grandmother share. He wore a pair of faded red sweatpants, a plaid flannel work shirt, and a Georgia Tech golf visor. His huge feet were stuffed, sockless, into unlaced work boots. He peered down at me for a moment through thick bifocals, his clear blue eyes sparkling once he realized who I was.

"Sugarpie!" he exclaimed, folding his long, thin arms around me. "When did you get back?"

"Back?" I blinked. "Granddaddy, I haven't been anywhere to come back from."

"Europe," he said. "Your brother told me you were in Europe for two weeks."

"Which brother?" I asked.

"You know," he said. "The one with the hair."

I have six brothers, and the last time I checked, they all had hair. Granddaddy was terrible with names. But my oldest brother is the only one of the whole useless bunch who ever bothers to call or visit my grandparents, so it was a good guess that was who he was referring to.

"Arch? Did Arch come to visit? How nice!"

"Arch," Granddaddy said, nodding happily. "He's a hairy sumbitch, isn't he?"

"Granddaddy! I think Arch is very nice looking. His beard makes him look distinguished."

"Hairy like an ape," Granddaddy insisted. "He doesn't get that from the Loudermilk side of the family. Your mother's people were a hairy bunch though. There was an uncle of hers I met one time looked just like that Rasputin fella over there in Russia. But Ellen didn't have hair like that. Or maybe she just shaved, and I never noticed."

"No," I said, giggling. "I don't think Mama had an unusual amount of hair." We'd been talking as I followed him into the abbreviated living room, which was crammed with dark, ornate mahogany furniture, an overstuffed sofa, and a huge console television set, which, as far as I knew, was only ever turned to the weather channel or the stock market channel, with the volume cranked up high.

I grabbed the remote control from the armrest of Granddaddy's BarcaLounger, and ratcheted the volume way, way down.

"Where's Grandmama?" I asked, peeking around the corner into the kitchenette. An open jar of peanut butter was sitting on the dinette table, with a huge serving spoon stuck into it. The table was littered with candy wrappers and dirty plates and cups. "She's not napping this early in the day, is she?"

"Who?" Granddaddy asked, plopping down into his chair.

"Grandmama," I said, trying to be patient. "Your wife, Lorena. Is she asleep?"

"How should I know?" he said, looking annoyed. "Ask the nurse."

"Nurse?" I pushed open the door to the bedroom, but the bed, though slightly rumpled, was made, and empty. "What nurse? Granddaddy, where's Lorena?"

He made a vague jabbing gesture with his finger. "Over there."

"Where over there?" I sat down on the arm of his chair and grasped his hand.

"You know," he said, leaning forward to get a better view of the television, which I was blocking. "Over there in the building."

I took the remote control and snapped off the television. "Granddaddy! Please. What building? Where did Lorena go? Can you tell me?"

"Hell, yes, I can tell you," he exploded. "Think I'm senile? Like I said, she's over there in that big building, over yonder. You know. The place. The doctor says she can't come home until she pees better."

"The hospital?" I asked, still groping for understanding. "Are you telling me Grandmama is in the hospital? When did this happen?"

"How should I know?" Granddaddy said. "I can't keep track of all the comings and goings around here. All I know is, I ain't had a hot meal since who knows when."

I took my cell phone out of my purse and called my brother Arch, praying that he would be at his desk.

"Arch? It's BeBe. I'm at the home with Granddaddy. Do you know anything about Grandmama going into the hospital?"

"Nooo," he said cautiously. "I saw her last week, Sunday maybe. She seemed fine. A little ditsy, but no more than usual. Is that what Granddaddy is telling you?"

"I think so," I said with a sigh. "She's definitely not here. The bed hasn't been slept in, the kitchen's a mess, and I think he's been living off peanut butter and Kit Kat bars."

"Christ," Arch said. "What are you going to do?"

I bit my lip. What was I going to do? What was he going to do? For that matter, what was anybody else in the family going to do? Who died and left me in charge?

"I'm here," I said finally. "I'll call over to the infirmary and see if they have her there."

"Fine," Arch said. "Look, I'm sorry, but I've got a meeting in five. Call me and let me know if you find her."

I hung up, found the number for the Magnolia Manor infirmary, and after fifteen minutes on hold, ascertained that yes, indeed, Mrs.

Lorena Loudermilk had been admitted to the infirmary three days ago, with a bladder infection.

"This is her granddaughter," I said, letting my voice go deliberately cold and imperious. "I had no idea she was ill. My grandfather has been living alone for the past three days, not eating, and probably not sleeping, either. Why wasn't the family informed that she was being admitted to the hospital?"

"Can't say," the woman said. And she clearly didn't care that she couldn't say, either. "You'd have to ask her doctor."

"I'll do just that," I said grimly.

"Granddaddy," I said brightly. "Let's go visit Grandmama in the hospital, want to?"

"Maybe later," he said, glancing up at the clock on the living-room wall. "It's time for the Rukeyser report."

"I think we'd better go now," I said, tugging gently on his arm. "You can watch television later."

I dug the key to the bungalow out of my purse and locked the door behind us. "It's too cold to walk over to the main building," I told my grandfather. I pointed toward the white Lexus parked in the visitor's slot. "I'm parked right there."

"And I'm parked right there," Granddaddy said, pointing proudly to a white Lincoln Town Car parked beside mine.

He took a set of keys from the pocket of the red sweatpants and jingled them excitedly. "After the hospital, we can go get some ice cream. Just like when you were a little girl."

I walked over to the driver's side of the Lincoln and gazed, speechlessly, at the sticker pasted to the window. I was looking at a brand-new top-of-the-line car, for which somebody had paid $42,698.

Granddaddy mashed the automatic lock button on the car, and held open the passenger door. "After you," he said proudly.

The paper mats were still on the floor of the car, and the leatherette owner's manual was sitting on the seat. I glanced over at the odometer, which read 14.7 miles.

"Granddaddy," I said, when he got in. "Where did you get this car?"

"Mitchell Motors, same as always," he said, running his hands over the smooth leather upholstery. "I been trading with the Mitchells since 1964. Nice folks."

"This car cost nearly $43,000," I said, my voice shaking. "How did you pay for it?"

"Cash money," Granddaddy said. "Same as always."

"But, where did you get the cash?" I asked, trying to stay calm. I'd been taking care of my grandparents' financial affairs ever since they'd moved into Magnolia Manor. We had a joint custodial checking account, and I paid all their monthly bills, leaving them with a monthly stipend of cash to pay for groceries and miscellaneous items like Grandmama's hairdresser and the occasional bottle of Scotch for Granddaddy. As far as I knew, there was never any more than a couple hundred dollars in cash around the house.

He waved his hand. "Oh, I wrote one of them checks you left in the bureau drawer."

I felt the blood drain from my face. The previous month, I'd left the checkbook for their money-market account in a bureau drawer in the bedroom, after paying all their bills. I had no idea Granddaddy was aware the checkbook was there.

"You wrote a check for $43,000," I said flatly.

"Yes, ma'am," he said happily. He poked aimlessly at the Lincoln's console with the key, trying to find the ignition.

"Damnit," he said. "Gotta have a college degree to start these new cars."

With one poke, the Lincoln's moon roof slid silently open. Another poke and our seat slid into a nearly reclining position. With another poke, an unseen voice filled the car's pristine white interior.

"OnStar," a silky woman's voice said.

"What?" Granddaddy said, whipping his head around to find the source of the voice. "What's that?"

"OnStar," the woman repeated.

"Who are you?" Granddaddy demanded.

"OnStar Roadside Assistance," she said calmly. "Sir, are you all right?"

He considered the question for a few seconds.

"I'm okay," he said finally. "But Lorena's having female problems."

"Sir?" the woman said blankly.

"He's fine," I said. "False alarm." I leaned over and mashed the OnStar button.

"She sounds nice," Granddaddy said. He started the ignition and beamed with pride. "Where to, sugarpie?"

It took my grandfather approximately fifteen minutes to back up the boat-size Lincoln and maneuver it the half block to Magnolia Manor's administration building. We took the elevator up to the third floor and wound through a white-tiled corridor and through a set of double doors marked INFIRMARY.

"She's sleeping," said the nurse at the infirmary desk. "Mrs. Loudermilk likes her nap in the afternoon."

"I'm sure she does," I said. "But I need to see her and talk to her. We won't take long."

A wall-mounted television droned from the tiny waiting area near the desk. Granddaddy sank down into a chair with his eyes riveted on the set. "I'll wait here," he said happily.

The nurse pulled back the curtains surrounding the last of three cubicles in the ward. My grandmother was curled up on her side, eyes closed, her toothless mouth agape. A pale blue sheet was pulled up around her neck, and a thin plastic tube ran from an IV stand beside the bed to her toothpick-thin arm, and another tube ran from beneath the sheet to a catheter bag on the lower rung of the stand.

"Antibiotics," the nurse whispered. "Her urine output is much better. The doctor thinks he can remove the catheter by the weekend."

I curled my fingers around my grandmother's blue-tinged wrist. It was so thin I could have wrapped them around twice, I thought. I felt hot tears on my cheeks.

I'd seen my grandmother only a week ago, but in that time, it seemed Lorena Loudermilk had abandoned the body I'd known and loved all my life. This shrunken wisp was nobody I recognized.

"What else?" I asked, turning to the nurse. "What else is wrong with her? She wasn't this bad a week ago. I just saw her. We played Parcheesi, and she beat me, same as always. She fixed me soup for lunch."

The nurse shrugged. "Bladder infection is all I know about. She's a sweet little lady. Never complains."

I stared at her. Sweet? Never complains? There was something very, very wrong here. My grandmother was a pistol. She and my grandfather had been married fifty-seven years, and she had complained about something every day of her life. Lorena Loudermilk was a complicated, wonderful, exasperating presence. Sweet little lady my ass.

5

I had a pad of paper and a basket of pill bottles I'd gathered from around my grandparents' cottage, and I was jotting down the names of all my grandmother's prescriptions. Digoxin. Lasix. Flagyl. Cipro. Vicodin. Atavan. Ambien. "Does Grandmama take all of these pills every day?" I asked my grandfather, squinting at the expiration date on the Digoxin bottle.

"How the hell do I know?" he asked, involved in a swirling white mass on the weather channel, which indicated some kind of storm in Minnesota.

I sighed. With my grandmother in the hospital, and granddaddy apparently subsisting on peanut butter and Kit Kat bars, it was clear that it was time for an intervention.

"Would it be all right if I stayed over here for a couple of days?" I asked meekly.

He shrugged, not taking his eyes off the television. "Suit yourself. Don't see why you'd want to, when you got that nice house one of those husbands of yours bought you."

"Right," I said slowly. It would do no good to point out to him that I'd bought the town house on West Jones Street, as well as three other downtown rental properties, all by myself.

My parents had started their own real estate agency, Loudermilk & Associates, in the 1970s, and Mama, especially, had always preached the value of home ownership. With her scouting out properties for me before they were even listed, I'd managed to buy my first house, at the age of twenty-two, a hideous red brick two-bedroom ranch house on the Southside that had been repossessed by the bank, for $48,000.

Mama had fronted me $5,000 for the down payment, and cosigned the mortgage on that first house, but after that, I'd flown solo as far as home buying went. I'd fixed up the ranch—doing most of the work myself—and flipped it two years later, making a tidy $30,000 profit, and immediately plowed that money into my next project—a dilapidated wood-frame bungalow on East Sixty-seventh Street.

Since that initial ugly-duckling ranch, I'd bought and sold nearly a dozen houses, and each house had been more desirable—and expensive, and successively closer to the downtown historic district, where it had been my goal to live ever since I was a little girl.

The West Jones Street town house was actually one of a pair of mirror-image row houses, built of beautiful old Savannah gray bricks in 1853 by a wealthy local cotton merchant for his twin sons. When Mama had first spotted my house, it was so dilapidated that a ten-foot-tall mimosa tree was growing through the roof of what had once been the kitchen. I'd hated the house at first sight, but Mama had insisted it was a diamond in the rough—not to mention the cheapest house in the historic district, priced at $450,000.

Jones Street was a money pit. It had taken me five years to make it the showplace it now was, and during that time I had survived two divorces and more heartaches than I cared to remember.

Still, it was the last house Mama had found for me. I could still hear her voice echoing in the high-ceilinged marble entryway the day she'd first taken me through it. "BeBe—look at this staircase. Look at this cast-iron mantelpiece. This place will be fabulous. You will make it fabulous." And I had, but she hadn't lived long enough to see the house finished.

Despite all my successful real estate wheeling and dealing, as far as my grandfather was concerned, I was still just a poor, dim-witted divorcée, depending on the kindness of strangers to get along in the world.

"I'm going to the grocery store. Wanna come along?"

"Nope."

I picked up the keys to the Lincoln from the kitchen table. "Okay if I take that pretty new car of yours to the store?"

That got me his full attention.

"It's got a lot more horsepower than you're used to," he said, looking dubious.

"I'll take it slow," I promised.

He nodded and reached down into the pocket of the red sweatpants.

"Here," he said, bringing out a ten-dollar bill and handing it to me.

"What's this for?" I asked.

"For my best sugarpie," he said, smiling. "Top off the gas tank, and buy yourself some ice cream while you're at it."

I planted a kiss on his liver-spotted forehead. "Thanks, sport. I'll be right back."

Backing the Lincoln out of the parking spot proved to be somewhat like steering a sofa. I'd never driven such a huge car before. I drove very, very carefully over to Mitchell Motors on Victory Drive.

It was four in the afternoon, and a low, gray sky hovered overhead, denouncing the existence of spring in Savannah. The glass-walled showroom was quiet except for the drone of a huge plasma-screen television showing all the handling attributes of the latest model of Lincoln Navigator. It was a slow day for luxury American sedans, I guessed.

A pink-faced kid in a blue suit that looked a size too large sat at the raised mahogany reception desk in the front of the showroom, leafing through the March issue of *Maxim* magazine.

"Hi!" he said, shoving the magazine under the desk blotter and standing up. "Can I show you a new Navigator?"

"No thanks," I said. "I actually have all the automobiles I need. My name is BeBe Loudermilk. I've come about my grandfather's new Town Car."

"Oh?" He sat back down. I noticed the nameplate on the desk. It said "Tyler Mitchell."

"My grandfather is Spencer Loudermilk," I continued. "Somebody here sold him a brand-new car last week. To the tune of $43,000. He apparently paid sticker price."

Young Tyler nodded. "I remember Mr. Loudermilk. My uncle Ray sold him that car. Sweet ride, huh?"

I leaned forward on the desk. "The thing is, Tyler, my grandfather is eighty-two years old. He has glaucoma and high blood pressure. He lives in a nursing home, and rarely drives farther than the Piggly Wiggly. His 1986 Buick Electra only had 28,000 miles on it. But your uncle Ray sold him this gigantic new Lincoln. It has a moon roof and high-performance Michelin tires and satellite radio."

"And GPS," Tyler said helpfully. "That's one bad ride."

"But he's eighty-two," I repeated. "He lives on a fixed income." I felt my face becoming flushed, now that we were discussing finances. "See, Tyler, senior citizens don't need a bad ride. What they need is a low-mileage Buick that they can figure out how to start and stop. And money to pay for medicine and doctors' bills and a nursing home. Not to mention Kit Kat bars and Scotch."

"Is there a problem with the Lincoln? Because we have an awesome DVD we can give him that shows how to operate all the electronics." Tyler slid open the top drawer of the desk and produced a DVD in a handsomely wrapped plastic jewel box.

"DVD?" I put my face very close to Tyler's. His cheeks were the texture of milk. I don't think he'd started to shave yet. "He's eighty-friggin'-two! He probably thinks a DVD is the place you get your driver's license. What I'm trying to say here, Tyler, is, I want you to take back the Lincoln. I want you people to refund the full $43,000 purchase price, and I want you to sell me back the 1986 Buick."

Tyler blinked and backed his chair away from me.

"I don't think so," he said, shaking his head back and forth. "No, I don't think my uncle Ray would go for something like that."

I tapped the telephone sitting on the reception desk. "Call him. Tell him you have a customer out front who needs to talk to him. You might mention that I have anger issues. And I'm currently off my meds."

Tyler shook his head some more. He was starting to remind me of one of those stuffed dogs you see in the rear window of some people's cars. Granddaddy's Buick had one of those dogs in it. "But, Uncle Ray's not here," he said. "He's at the NADA convention."

"All right. Get me another manager."

"I can't. They're all down at the NADA convention. In Palm Beach. Uncle Ray is up for dealer of the year."

I pushed the Lincoln's keys across the desk at him. "Fine. I'm assuming that you're capable of making decisions, since they left you in charge. You give me the refund. And the Electra."

Tyler shoved the keys back toward me. "Sorry. Can't do it."

"There must be somebody here who can help me," I said, raising my voice. "The Lincoln only has fifteen miles on it. It still has the paper floor mats. My grandfather can't afford that car. You've got to give me the money back."

The phone on the desk rang, and Tyler grabbed for it. "Mitchell Motors," he said breathlessly. "Come in today and test-drive the new Lincoln Navigator and win a chance at a weekend for two in Montego Bay, Jamaica."

I snatched the phone out of his hand and slammed the receiver down. "Tyler! Pay attention here. I want my $43,000. And the Buick."

His neck flushed red. His eyes narrowed. "What's the matter, *Bee-Bee*, are you worried that the old man's blowing your inheritance?"

Without thinking, I reached out and slapped the smirk off his face. I grabbed the keys and flounced out of the Mitchell Motors showroom. And I laid rubber as I peeled off onto Victory Drive.

6

My hands shook with anger and frustration as I unlocked the front door of my town house. I picked up the mail that had been slid through the mail slot and sorted it aimlessly.

The phone rang in the kitchen, and I sprinted toward it, hoping it would be one of my grandmother's doctors.

But the caller ID digital readout told me I was being called from a Budget Inn in Daytona Beach, Florida.

"BeBe? Hey. It's Rikki." My missing-in-action waitress sounded as though she'd been gargling with gravel.

"Hi, Rikki," I said coolly. "How are you?"

I was answered by a series of racking coughs. "Not so good," she rasped. "I'm coughing up a lot of green goo. And I've had a fever of 102 all day. My doctor says there's something going around. He says I should stay in bed. Because I'm probably contagious."

"You poor thing," I cooed. "That's terrible. Listen, you stay right there in bed. I'm going to bring over some of Daniel's chicken soup and some cough drops."

Rikki coughed violently. "No! Don't do that. I'll be fine in a couple of days. Anyway, I don't want you to catch this crud."

"That's so thoughtful of you," I said. "And how about Kevin? How's he feeling?"

"Kevin?" Her voice was cautious. "I, I don't really know."

"Really?" I said. "Why don't you lean over in the bed there in the Budget Inn in Daytona Beach and ask him how he feels?"

"Huh?"

"You're busted, Rikki," I said. "So don't give me any more of that calling-in-sick crap. In fact, I don't want any more of your crap again, ever. But I do appreciate your calling. That way, I can fire both you and Kevin at the same time. And the beauty of it is, you're paying for the long-distance phone call. 'Bye now."

I slammed the phone down, but it gave me little pleasure. Kevin and Rikki weren't exactly employee-of-the-month material, but Rikki was a shapely blonde who was great at selling our customers on expensive wine, and Kevin, who was tall, dark, and shallow, was a big draw for our women customers who liked to fantasize about making it with a bartender.

A wave of depression washed over me. Our busiest season was just around the corner and I was suddenly short two experienced, if unreliable, employees.

I continued going through the mail, and slammed down the stack of junk mail in anger when it didn't contain a rent check from my deadbeat tenant Brenna. No surprise there. Brenna, who was the niece of an old friend, had been late with her rent for the past three months, sometimes as much as ten days late.

Time to get tough, I decided. The carriage house on West Gordon Street rented for $800 a month, and if Brenna, a film major at Savannah College of Art and Design, didn't want to pay the rent on time, I could find any number of tenants who could and would.

After I'd called both Brenna's cell phone and house phone, I decided to pay her a visit, maybe even check out how she was keeping the place up. I had a strict no-pet policy for all my rental properties, but the last time I'd gone by the carriage house, I thought I'd heard a dog barking from inside.

I grabbed a jacket and scarf and decided it would be simplest to just walk the six blocks to West Gordon.

When I got to the 300 block of West Gordon, where the carriage house was located, I noticed something strange. The sidewalk was wet. The street was wet too. And it hadn't rained in two days. I got a sinking feeling in the pit of my stomach.

"No," I said, moaning, when I saw the front door of the carriage house. Water was sluicing out from under it.

"Brenna!" I screamed, pounding on the door.

I sorted through the knot of keys on my key ring until I found the right one, and fit it into the lock. The knob turned, but the door wouldn't budge. The wood, I knew, was probably swollen from moisture.

Giving up on the front door, I sprinted around to the back. No water here, thank God. And the back-door key worked fine. I pulled on the door, stepped inside, and instantly wished I hadn't.

The smell of mildew nearly knocked me down. The kitchen's linoleum floor was covered with half an inch of water. I glanced around. The sink was overflowing with dirty dishes. A plastic trash can lay on its side, with soda bottles and sodden fast-food wrappers spilled onto the floor.

I looked down at my $350 suede high-heeled boots. Ruined.

It wasn't hard to find the source of the water. The bathroom was just steps from the kitchenette. The black-and-white octagon-tile floor was barely visible under an inch of dirty water, which was overflowing from the pedestal sink.

I could have cried. I twisted the knobs, but the cold-water faucet seemed to have been stripped. I squatted down on the floor and searched for the cutoff valve, but it was frozen stuck.

"Damnit," I cried. My pants were soaked, my boots were ruined. I peeked into the living room to confirm what I already knew. Brenna had flown the coop. I didn't have the stomach to see what other nasty surprises my missing tenant had left for me. I trudged back home, threw the boots in the trash, and sat down by the fireplace to cry and feel sorry for myself.

The doorbell rang, but I stayed in my easy chair. I had endured my full quota of shit for the day. No more, I decided. No more sick relatives, sleazy car salesmen, slacker employees, or sorry-ass tenants.

But the doorbell kept ringing.

"Go away," I hollered. "We don't want any."

"BeBe?" It was a man's voice. "It's me, Reddy. I left my wristwatch here last night. But, are you all right?"

My shoulders sagged. I didn't want Reddy to see me this way. Our relationship was too shiny and new to expose him to the nuttiness that was my life. And besides, I had black ribbons of melted mascara trailing down both sides of my face.

"I'm all right," I called back. "Just having a really bad day. I'll call you later, okay?"

"Can I get my watch?"

"I'll slide it under the door."

"Maybe I can help," he answered. "Let me in, sweetheart, please?"

I sighed, but trudged to the door. I opened it, turned around, and trudged back to my easy chair.

But before I got there, Reddy had folded me into his arms. Which was bad. Because I started to cry again. And it wasn't just crying. It was full-out caterwauling. Weeping, sobbing, chest-heaving hysteria, accompanied by double-barreled snot rockets. Not a pretty sight.

But Reddy didn't seem to notice any of that. "Hey," he said softly, stroking my hair. "Hey, what's wrong, pretty lady?"

"Everything," I wailed. "My life sucks. My grandmother's sick and Granddaddy bought a Lincoln and that little shit Tyler at the car lot won't give me back the money, and I had to fire Rikki and Kevin . . ." I was gulping for air in between sobs.

"Man," he said, taking his forefinger and wiping away a streak of mascara. "You have had a rotten day."

"I know!" I wailed. "And the tenant at West Gordon ran off without paying her rent and the bathroom sink is busted and it's flooded everything out . . ."

He dug a handkerchief out of the pocket of his neatly pressed navy slacks and handed it to me. "Blow," he instructed.

So I did.

He pushed me gently down into the chair. "Sit."

And I did.

Then he went into the kitchen, and when he came back it was with a tray holding two glasses of red wine and a plate with cheese and crackers.

"I bet you haven't eaten today, have you?" he said sternly.

I shook my head. "Not hungry." I reached for the goblet. "Just thirsty."

He pushed my hand away. "Eat something first or you'll give yourself a wine headache."

"Hey," I said, amazed. "How did you know red wine gives me a headache if I drink it without eating?"

He raised an eyebrow. "I know these kinds of things."

So I nibbled at a cracker with some cheese, and eventually, I was able to stop sniffling and drink a full glass of wine.

"Now," Reddy said, sipping his own wine. "Start at the beginning, and tell me everything."

So I did. I told him about my grandmother's alarming decline, and the Lincoln, and the trouble with my employees, and the disaster at West Gordon.

He nodded thoughtfully, not interrupting or offering advice, but just listening.

It was a new experience, having a man just listen.

When I was done telling my tale of woe, he leaned over and kissed me softly on the lips.

"All right, then," he said, squaring his shoulders. "I'm afraid I can't do anything about your grandmother's condition. It sounds like you'll have to talk to her doctors to get a handle on that. But I do have some experience with car dealers, and I should be able to help with the Lincoln situation. This salesman obviously took advantage of your grandfather. And since he's only had the car for less than a week, there's no reason they shouldn't take the car back and refund the money."

"I don't know," I said. "The little shit was pretty adamant. Did I mention I slapped him?"

Reddy winced.

"I know, but he started it," I said.

He held out his hand, palm up. "Keys, please. I should be back in less than an hour. Will that give you time to get cleaned up and ready for dinner?"

"Yes, but—"

"No buts," he said, leaning down to give me a kiss. "And no more wine. At least not until I get back to drink it with you."

He let himself out the front door, and I leaned back in my armchair and smiled. It was the first thing I'd had to smile about all day.

7

It started so innocently, with those keys. My hair was still wet from the shower by the time Reddy got back to my place. The cuffs of his pants were soaked, as were his formerly immaculate white tennis shoes.

"Done," he said lightly, handing over a cashier's check for the entire $43,000 purchase price of the Lincoln, plus a set of keys I didn't recognize.

"How?"

He waved off my questions. "Those are the keys to your grandfather's Buick Electra. And listen. It's probably best if you don't go back to Mitchell Motors any time soon. Tyler Mitchell is not your biggest fan."

"But—"

He put his forefinger across my lips. "No big deal. Oh yeah," he added casually. "I stopped by the carriage house and shut off the water at the street."

"Thank God," I said. "I called the plumber, but he wasn't going to be able to get over there until tomorrow at the earliest."

"It's all fixed," Reddy repeated. "I took a shop vac over and siphoned off most of the water, and opened a window to air the place out. But the hardwood floors are ruined. And you're going to need paint and wallpaper in all those flooded-out downstairs rooms. That place was a pigsty," he said, making a face. "How'd you hook up with her in the first place?"

Now I was the one making the face. "She's the niece of an old school friend. I made an exception to my 'no-students' rule for her, and that's the thanks I get."

"Don't you check your tenants' references before you rent to them?" Reddy asked.

"No." I sighed. "I guess I'm not that organized. Usually, I just find tenants through word of mouth, the Savannah way. I've been lucky up to now. Never been burned before."

"But you make your tenants give you a deposit of first and last month's rent—right?"

"No," I said meekly. "I've always been a trusting soul. Dumb, huh?"

He shrugged. "Not the best property-management policy I've ever heard of."

"I know. I just stay so busy with the restaurant, and the rentals take up so much of my time and energy. I've thought seriously about turning them over to an agency, but I've never quite gotten around to it."

"How many units do you have?" Reddy asked.

"Besides West Gordon, there's the town house on East Liberty—which has three units, counting a studio over the garage; the little house on President—that's two units; and then the house on Gwinnett, in the Victorian district, that's just one unit, but it's empty right now."

"How come?" he asked, sipping his wine.

"I've got electrical problems," I said. "The last tenant in there was a self-styled electrician. He decided to rewire the kitchen and damn near burned the place down."

"How long has it been empty?"

"Since November," I admitted. "I'm terrible at this, aren't I?"

He kissed me. "Not terrible. Just over-committed. Where shall we go for dinner?"

I glanced at my watch and shook my head. "I can't. I've got to take some groceries over to Granddaddy's and fix him supper."

"Afterward?" Reddy asked. "It's early yet, and I had a late lunch."

"Afraid not," I said reluctantly. "I'm going to sleep over there tonight, at the very least, to make sure he takes his medicine and goes to bed. With Grandmama in the hospital, he hasn't been taking care of himself. He stays up all night tracking storms and eating Kit Kat bars."

"I thought you had family here in town," Reddy said, sounding exasperated.

"I do. Three of my brothers live right here in Savannah. Another lives in Hilton Head, one's in Atlanta, and the other's in Jacksonville."

"So? Can't one of them step up to the plate?"

"They could, but they're probably not going to," I said. "Arch, at least, helps out sometimes. But Bert has four kids, a wife who's manic-depressive, and he travels all the time."

"Brother number three?"

"Carlton. Don't remind me. He thinks of himself as an only child."

"Which leaves BeBe," he observed.

"I don't mind," I said, and I thought I meant it. "I'm the only one who's single. I don't have kids, and just between us, I've always been Granddaddy's favorite. And the boys know it too."

"Still, it's a lot of responsibility, and you're already running full tilt with the restaurant and the rentals and your own life."

"What life?" I asked gloomily. "I work. I eat. I sleep. And sometimes," I said, giving him a wicked grin, "I play."

"That's what we have to make more time for," Reddy said. "The play part."

"You'll get no argument from me there," I said. "I know I'm doing a lousy job of juggling everything, but I just don't know how else to keep all my bases covered."

"I do," he said.

"Yeah?"

We were standing by my front door, and I was wrapping my scarf around my neck because I could hear the wind whipping around outside. So much for spring.

"Let me help out," Reddy said. "At least with some of the business stuff. I'm pretty damned good at it, you know."

"I couldn't," I said quickly. "You don't have any idea how much is involved. And I wouldn't begin to know how to explain everything to you. My files are in a mess, and I won't know how much time I'll be spending at my grandparents' until I talk to the doctors."

I kissed him warmly. "You really and truly are an angel to suggest it. But I couldn't take advantage of you like that. I really couldn't."

He kissed me back. "Take advantage of me, please."

The phone rang then. "Hold that thought," I told him, and I dashed for the kitchen.

"Miss Loudermilk? This is Robert Walker. Dr. Walker. I'm your grandmother's internist. I understand you were trying to reach me?"

"Yes," I said eagerly. "I saw my grandmother in the infirmary at Magnolia Manor today, and I was shocked by her condition. She's lost so much weight, and the nurses say she sleeps most of the time."

"Well, she was in a good bit of pain from the urinary-tract infection, so we've been giving her something for that, and to help her sleep."

"I counted seven different kinds of pills she's taking," I said. "All that medicine can't be a good thing."

"Seven?" he said, his voice sharp. "I've got her on Flagyl and Cipro, for the bladder infection, Vicodin for the pain, and Ambien to sleep. That's only four. Plus, of course, we're treating her now for a kidney infection."

"Kidney infection?" I yelped. "Since when? Nobody said anything about a kidney infection to me when I was over there today."

"I stopped by to see her on rounds at four, and didn't like the look of her blood levels," Dr. Walker said. "So we got her started on something for that right away."

"God," I groaned. "But there were two other medicine bottles at the apartment. My grandfather said she's also been taking Lasix and Digoxin, and Atavan."

"Oh?" he said.

"You didn't know?" Could things have gotten any worse? I glanced up at the kitchen ceiling, wondering when it would fall in on me.

We hung up, and I went back to the front door, where Reddy was patiently waiting for me.

"Sorry," I said. It seemed as though I'd been saying that all day. And it had really been a very sorry day. "I had to take that call. It was Grandmama's doctor. Now she's got something else wrong with her. He says there's something going on with her kidneys."

"Anything I can do?" Reddy asked. "I told you before, I'm good at a lot of different things. Except hospitals and sick people. That I'm not too good at."

"Nothing," I said. But then I remembered.

"Wait. There is something." I rummaged around in the big copper dish I keep on the table in the foyer. It was where I kept all the keys to the rentals, plus the extra keys to my own town house.

"I want to be at the hospital in the morning, to talk to the doctor, but in the meantime, the insurance adjuster is supposed to meet me over at West Gordon at ten. And the bug guy is supposed to be here at noon to spray. I've got silverfish. I hate to ask, but you've been so sweet to offer. Would you?"

He held out his hand, and I gave him the keys. "This one with the red tag is for here, and the green one is for West Gordon. Tell Jerry, the bug guy, to be sure and spray the attic this time."

Reddy nodded. "I'm on it. See you tomorrow?"

"I hope so," I said. "Things can't get any worse between now and then, can they?"

8

"Grandmama?" I'd been sitting at my grandmother's bedside for more than two hours. She hadn't stirred in all that time, except for the intermittent buzz of snoring. And the doctor still hadn't shown.

Her eyes fluttered open at the sound of my voice. She squeezed my hand.

"How are you feeling? Any better?"

She grimaced. "Tubes. I hate all these tubes." Her voice was weak, barely audible, but if she was complaining, she was definitely feeling better.

"I know," I said. "You've had a bad time of it this week."

She struggled to sit upright. "Where's Spencer?"

"He's at home, still sleeping," I said. "He had a late night. Flash floods in northern California, mud slides, and a tropical disturbance in the Azores."

"Old fool," she muttered. "What day is it?"

"It's Tuesday."

My grandmother shrugged but said nothing.

There was a short knock on the door. Dr. Walker, a big, white-haired bear of a man, strode over and took Grandmama's hand in his, giving me a polite nod.

"Mrs. Loudermilk?" he said, softly. "I hear you had a bad night last night?"

"So-so," Grandmama said meekly. "Some problems breathing."

"We're going to move you over to Memorial Hospital, to do some more tests on you. There's an ambulance waiting right downstairs. Would that be all right?"

"More tests?" she said, her voice suddenly sharper. "And how much is all that gonna cost?"

Dr. Walker grinned. "I don't want you to have a heart attack on me."

"It's all right," I assured her, standing at the side of her bed. "You've got good insurance. You can afford all the tests they want to run."

I glanced down at my watch. It was after eleven. I'd already fielded several phone calls from the restaurant, and I still had to figure out how to replace the two employees I'd fired over the weekend.

"She'll be fine," Dr. Walker said quickly. "I'll meet her over there in an hour. I've called ahead and let them know which tests I want run. You won't really be able to see her until she's back from X-ray anyway, and that'll be around four."

"You're sure?" I asked. "I can shuffle my schedule if I need to."

"Positive," he said.

"Go on about your business," Grandmama said imperiously. "And don't tell Spencer about all these tests. You know how he gets himself all worked up over nothing."

"I'll bring him when I come this afternoon," I promised. "You sure you don't need me to help you move?"

She waved me away. "Go."

It was closer to five by the time I left the restaurant, went back to Magnolia Manor to pick up my grandfather, and then over to Memorial Hospital.

Granddaddy paused outside the door to her room. His face was pale. "She's bad, isn't she?" For the first time, he looked really scared.

"Not that bad," I said. "They're just being cautious. Just in case. You'll see. She's going to be fine. Just make sure you tell her I'm feeding you good, so she doesn't give me fits about not taking care of you."

I waited outside in the hallway to give them some privacy. After fifteen minutes, I went inside. Grandmama had a clear plastic mask over her face, with a hose hooked up to a humming machine. Granddaddy was sitting on a chair beside her hospital bed, holding his wife's hand in his, staring raptly up at the television, watching what looked like a thirty-year-old rerun of *Hollywood Squares*.

He looked up when I came in, and pointed at the television. "They got the Game Show Channel. Paul Lynde! We don't get that at our place."

Grandmama pushed her mask aside. "I told this old fool to cut it off. I'm not paying for deluxe cable. They probably charge you double in a place like this." She would have said more too, but her tirade was interrupted by a fit of coughing.

A nurse came in then, looked at one of the monitors at her bedside, and shooed us back out into the hallway.

My cell phone rang, and I walked rapidly to the visitors' waiting area to take the call.

It was Reddy. "Hey, BeBe," he said. "How's it going at your end?"

I sighed. "Not so good. They've moved my grandmother over to Memorial Hospital, and they're running a bunch of tests. I don't really understand any of it."

"Hang in there," Reddy said. "Who's her doctor?"

"Robert Walker," I said.

"I know Robert," Reddy said. "One of my sisters was in his class at Emory. He's the best."

"Hope so," I said fervently. "Did you see the insurance adjuster?"

"It's all taken care of," Reddy said. "They're cutting you a check for $18,000 today. I called a floor guy I know, and he says he can do the job for a lot less than that. And the bug guy was here. He sprayed the attic, like you asked. I gave him a check, and he said to tell you he'll see you next month."

"You're the best," I said, meaning it. "But you didn't need to pay him. He usually just sends a bill."

"It was a new guy," Reddy said. "Your regular guy is on vacation or something. Don't worry about it, I took care of it."

"All right," I said

At eleven that night, I was finally able to ferry Granddaddy home. We were both exhausted. As soon as his head hit the pillow, he was fast asleep.

I got a blanket and pillow of my own, and tried to make myself comfortable on the sofa bed, which felt as if it had been designed specifically as an instrument of torture. I closed my eyes and waited for sleep. Which never came.

What did come was waves of anxiety. My grandmother was ill, her diagnosis uncertain. Granddaddy's snores reverberated off the walls of the small apartment. He'd been worried about Lorena's condition, but on the trip home he'd blithely assured me that the pills she'd been given would make her "right as rain."

Rain. Once it started, it never seemed to let up.

9

"BeBe?"

"Hmm?"

I was right on the edge of sleep. Not awake really, not asleep, just in that delicious twilight place between the two.

We were aboard the *Blue Moon*, in the stateroom. I'd arrived late, and exhausted after a long night at Guale, and two glasses of Reddy's champagne, along with the gentle rocking of the boat at its moorings, had the combined effect of knocking me out almost instantaneously.

For more than a week, I'd been racing back and forth between my house, the restaurant, the hospital, and Magnolia Manor. My grandmother had finally been moved to a rehab ward, but on the other hand, Granddaddy, without his wife of fifty-two years, was like a ship adrift at sea. He ate only when I insisted, slept mostly, sitting up in front of television. I was already feeling guilt gnawing at the edges of my pleasure at being with Reddy.

Between the demands of taking care of each of my grandparents, I'd given up trying to make it in to work on a daily basis. My erratic schedule irritated Daniel, as it did me, but I was all out of options.

Reddy, bless him, had turned into my hero. He had a knack for knowing what needed to be done, and a gift for doing it with a minimum of fuss. In the short time we'd been together, he'd gotten the West Gordon apartment fixed up and rented out again—at a $150 a month increase in rent—gotten the wiring fixed in the Victorian district house, and had even found me a great little bungalow on East

Forty-eighth Street to buy for a steal—and cut me in as a full partner on the deal. We sold it a week later, and split a $20,000 profit for a week's work. He'd even taken to going into my office at Guale, to take a look at our books for me, a situation Daniel really resented.

"Who *is* this guy?" Daniel asked—more than once. "He doesn't know squat about the restaurant business, yet he's trying to tell me we need to switch produce vendors, and he brought in this cheap-ass coffee, which he claims you approved."

"I did approve it," I said sharply, looking up from a stack of bills on my desk. "We were paying an insane price for those Kona blue beans of yours. The new coffee is fine—and it's half the price."

"It tastes like sludge," Daniel muttered. "But hey, I'm just the chef here. Don't go by my opinion."

"Fine. I won't."

Tension between us was high, and it didn't help that Weezie was down in Florida on a buying trip for her antiques shop. Daniel could be really moody on the best of days, but without Weezie's softening influence, he'd accelerated from moody to downright cranky.

I missed Weezie too. She was my sounding board, somebody to laugh with, shop with, and bitch to. Besides, I couldn't wait for her to meet Reddy.

Who was, in the meantime, nibbling at my ear and rubbing my back and just generally making himself indispensable.

"Mmm," I sighed. "Don't stop. Okay? I'll give you a million dollars if you'll promise to never stop doing that."

"Throw in another million and I'll do this too," he whispered. And for what he did next, a million was definitely a bargain.

"Mmm." I kissed him lazily. "But I've got to get some sleep now. I promised Granddad I'd pick him up at eight for his appointment with the eye doctor, which means if I'm not there by seven-thirty, he'll be calling the cops to report me missing."

Reddy got up and brought a sheaf of papers back to bed. "I just need you to sign some stuff for me," he said, nuzzling my neck and handing me a pen. "We're going to make an offer on the house next to the one you already own on Huntingdon Street."

"Now?" I yawned and squinted at the tiny type. "My reading glasses are up on deck. Can't it wait till morning?"

"I've got an early meeting too," Reddy said. "Some investors are coming in from Oklahoma, and I'm picking them up at the airport. I want to drop the contract by the broker's office first thing. If that house gets on multiple listing, it'll sell in a skinny minute."

"Okay," I relented. He put his finger on a line, and I signed there, and three or four more places, and then I couldn't keep my eyes open for another minute. "Get some sleep," Reddy said.

In the morning, he was gone, but he'd made a fresh pot of coffee, and a banana muffin sat on a plate next to a paper napkin. I smiled as I sipped my coffee and nibbled at my breakfast. This one, I told myself, was a keeper. The sun shone weakly on the gray-blue waters of the yacht basin. A single seagull perched on the mast of a sailboat tied two slips over, squawked noisily as I stepped from the deck of the *Blue Moon*.

I'd overslept, so there was no time to run home and change clothes. Instead, I raced over to Magnolia Manor, where my grandfather was busily pacing back and forth on the sidewalk in front of his unit. He was dressed in his best: neatly pressed dark slacks, a white shirt, wide-striped tie, and straw fedora.

"Where were you last night? I was worried when you didn't come home."

I'd called him from the restaurant to tell him I wasn't coming, but obviously, he'd forgotten as soon as he'd hung up the phone. "Remember, I called to tell you I had a late night at work? I was so beat I just went straight home to bed." I crossed my fingers mentally at the lie, at the same time chiding myself for not having the nerve to admit to my grandfather that, at thirty-five, and thrice married, I was no longer a virgin.

"Sorry!" I said, coming around the car to open the door for him.

He tapped the face of his wristwatch and frowned at me.

"It'll only take me five minutes to get to the doctor's office," I said, deliberately underestimating.

"Time is money," Granddaddy said pointedly, fumbling for the seat belt. I leaned over and fastened it for him, and bussed him on the cheek.

While he was in with the doctor, I went outside and called the hospital to check on my grandmother, as I did every morning. The unit's visiting hours didn't start until three o'clock, but Granddaddy insisted on getting a progress report first thing every day.

I dialed the extension for my grandmother's room. She picked up on the fourth ring.

"Spencer?" Her voice was a whimper. "I want you to come get me right this minute. These waitresses here are terrible. I never been to a hotel as sorry as this one."

"Grandmama, it's me, BeBe."

"Who? What'd you say?"

"It's BeBe," I said loudly.

"Put Spencer on the line," she demanded.

"I can't right now. He's with the eye doctor," I said. "Grandmama, do you know that you're in the hospital? You're in the rehab unit at Memorial. Remember?"

"I want to check out of this hotel," she said, her voice weak. "Right now. Tell Spencer."

And then she hung up.

When we left the doctor's office, I took my grandfather through the drive-in window at McDonald's for his favorite breakfast, hotcakes and sausage. "Doctor says I've got the eyes of a young kid," he reported in between chews. "You know why that is?"

"No," I said. "Why?"

"Good genes," he said. "All the Loudermilks have great eyesight. My grandfather? He lived to be ninety, and he never did need eyeglasses. It's the genes. And buttermilk."

"Really?"

He glanced over at me, and pointed at the reading glasses I'd pushed on top of my head. "You never did drink any buttermilk, did you?"

"Not much," I admitted.

He nodded thoughtfully. "Explains a lot. Plus, your mother's people were weak-eyed. Nice enough, but weak-eyed, the whole lot of 'em."

We pulled up in front of Magnolia Manor. "I better get going," he said as I unlocked the door to his villa. "Got a lot to do this morning. It's Thursday, you know. Grocery coupons." He made a scissoring motion with his hand. "I gotta get my coupons clipped. Thursday is double-coupon day for seniors at the Kroger." He glanced around the parking lot and frowned at the sight of his old Buick Electra, parked where the Lincoln had been parked only a few days earlier.

"What did you say happened to my new white Lincoln?"

"I told you. Remember? The, uh, Lincoln was recalled, Grand-daddy. Yeah. The dealership called me and said that the new models had faulty, uh, defibrillators and the government was making them take them all back. See, if you accelerated too quickly, with that doohickey thing, you could have spontaneous combustion."

Granddaddy took off his fedora and ran his fingers through his thinning white hair. "That's a bunch of bull hockey, young lady. You telling me somebody called you up and handed you that line and you believed it?"

"Yes, sir," I said meekly. I was afraid to look him in the eye. "I didn't want to worry you over it, with Grandmama sick and all. So I just took the Lincoln in and they gave me back your old car."

He thought about that for a while. "Defibrillator, huh?"

"Something like that."

He sighed. "All right then. You get my money back?"

"Yes, sir."

"Damn shame," he said, shaking his head. "The American automobile industry ain't what it used to be. I'll tell you that right now."

"Yes, sir. I'll pick you up at six to go to the hospital. Don't forget to take your pills this afternoon."

But I didn't make it back at six. Guale was packed with lunch business, and at four that afternoon, when we should have been breaking down the kitchen to get ready for dinner, a tour bus from Milwaukee rolled up and disgorged sixty-eight starving Rotarians. Their lunch reservation had been for one o'clock, but their bus driver had gotten lost somewhere north of Charleston. By the time we got the group fed and out the door and I got back to Magnolia Manor to shower, it was more like seven-thirty.

Granddaddy glowered at me the whole way up in the hospital elevator. "Lorena likes me to have dinner with her," he said accusingly. "Now we've missed *Wheel of Fortune* and *Jeopardy*."

The two of them watched television together, and after I dropped Granddaddy off at the home, I tried Reddy's cell phone number again, but there was still no answer, and unlike the other times I'd called him in the past, I didn't get a recording directing me to leave a voice-mail message.

This was not like Reddy. He was never without his cell phone, and was constantly checking voice-mail messages. I was starting to worry. Maybe he was in trouble. Maybe he was sick. I'd been so overwhelmed with my own problems lately, I'd barely paid any attention to this new, wonderful man in my life.

I sped down Victory Drive, toward the yacht club, even tempting fate by running the red light in Thunderbolt, where there was nearly always a traffic cop lurking nearby. I parked the Lexus and trotted out to the end of the dock where the *Blue Moon* was tied up. I breathed a sigh of relief when I saw that the lights were on in the master stateroom and on deck. But as I walked alongside the yacht's port side, I noticed for the first time a sign tacked to the bow. FOR SALE: AVAILABLE IMMEDIATELY. And there was a phone number I didn't know listed below.

Available? Had Reddy decided to sell the *Blue Moon*? Impossible.

He adored the yacht. Spent every Saturday polishing and washing it, like a teenager with his first car. I pulled on the bowline as he'd shown me, kicked off my shoes, and stepped lightly onto the deck.

"Reddy?" I called. "Permission to come aboard?"

The boat rocked from side to side. A man's head popped out of the pilothouse. Not Reddy. Not even close. He looked to be in his late fifties, balding, with only a fringe of snow-white hair around the ears. Although it was dark out, he wore gold-rimmed sunglasses, and a frown.

"Ma'am? Can I help you?"

He took a step closer. I took one backward. "Who are you?" I demanded, feeling my scalp prickle. I'd read about people hijacking boats, about modern-day pirates, violent criminals who stole yachts to use in drug-running schemes. "Where's Reddy?"

"Who?" He pushed his sunglasses to the top of his head. He was wearing a faded Hawaiian shirt and baggy white shorts. He was barefoot, and probably unarmed. On closer inspection, I had to admit to myself that he didn't look much like a drug runner. But then again, maybe he'd aged out.

"Reddy. Reddy Millbanks," I said loudly. "He owns the *Blue Moon*."

The man chuckled softly, but he didn't seem all that amused. "That what he told you?"

"Of course," I said. "What did you say your name was? And what did you say you were doing here?" I took my cell phone out of my pocketbook. "I'm just going to check with my friend to see if you have permission to be aboard this boat tonight."

"Check away," the man said. He turned to go back into the cabin. "The police should be here pretty soon. Then we'll get this all sorted out."

10

The cop arrived in a white-and-blue-striped Thunderbolt Police Department cruiser, lights flashing and siren blaring. He bounded out of the car with his radio clasped in one hand and his nightstick in the other, ready to wage war against whatever crime wave was afoot in the marina.

"Oh, hey, man, that ain't necessary," called out my would-be pirate, who'd introduced himself to me as Jimmy Yglesias, still insisting that he was the *Blue Moon*'s rightful owner. Yglesias set his beer down on the deck table and stood up. "It ain't like somebody was killed or anything."

The cop blushed, but holstered his nightstick and clambered aboard the yacht. He was slightly built, in his mid-twenties, with a scraggly mouse-colored mustache and small brown eyes that blinked nervously as he asked his questions. His official badge indicated that he was "D. Stonecipher."

Yglesias told his story, and I told mine, and the cop still wasn't getting it.

"Tell me again how you met the suspect," he urged, leaning forward in the deck chair, the red-and-white-striped canvas one where Reddy had held me on his lap the night we met. But now Reddy was gone, and this kiddie cop sat there instead, pen poised over his spiral-bound notebook.

"He's not a suspect," I said, bristling. "That's what I keep trying to explain. His name is Ryan Edward Millbanks the third. We met at the

Telfair Ball. He's a financial consultant. From Charleston. Very successful."

"Successful con artist," said Yglesias. "He fooled me, and I don't fool easy."

I glared at Yglesias, then back at Stonecipher. "I'm sure this is all some kind of misunderstanding."

"No misunderstanding," Yglesias said, taking a long pull on his beer. "You say your boyfriend's name is Millbanks. He told me his name was Mariani. Joe Mariani. Joe Scumbag is more like it. He was leasing the *Blue Moon*, with an option to buy. His rent was two weeks overdue. I called him about it, but he kept ducking me. I finally drove out here early yesterday. He was just leaving in that fancy Jag of his. I told him then, pony up my money or get the hell off my boat. He gave me some song and dance about an important business meeting, and like a jackass, I let him off the hook. Later on, I got to thinking about it, and I decided the whole thing was fishy. So I came right over, and took some precautions."

"Precautions?" the cop said, stroking the end of his mustache.

Yglesias grinned, showing even, white teeth that glowed against his deep tan. "I disabled the engine. There's a manual stop switch that supplies air to the diesels, so I pulled that. Figured if he tried to take off, that would slow him down some. I would have waited around for him to come back, but I had to drive over to Hilton Head early this morning for a golf tournament I was playing in. I came straight over here as soon as the banquet was over. Good thing I did. Mariani, or whatever his name is, had cleared out. And this lady came looking for him. That's when we called you."

The cop nodded gravely. "Good thinking. How much money did the suspect owe you?"

"He's not a sus—" I started.

"I hate to say," Yglesias said, shaking his head. "Thirty-six hundred in back rent to start. And he ripped off all my electronics. We're talking about a Furuno model 962 split-screen GPS plotter, with radar, autopilot, and color depth finder. That's another thirty thousand, easy. I could kick myself in the goddamned head for letting him get away with this stunt. I knew there was something wrong about the guy."

"You said he was fishy?" Stonecipher said, looking up from his scribbles. "What was so fishy?"

Yglesias looked pained. "He, uh, paid in cash. Both months. All twenties."

"You said the rent was thirty-six hundred? That's a lot of twenties. Did he say why?" Stonecipher asked.

"Said his ex-wife was squeezing his balls for alimony. So he did everything on a cash-and-carry basis. Hey, I been there myself. At the time, it sounded reasonable. But then, things got a little weird. See, when he first approached me about leasing the boat, I wasn't even interested. I was down here on a Sunday afternoon, piddling around up here on deck, and he came over, introduced himself, told me we had a mutual acquaintance. Somebody he'd met at a bar down in Lauderdale. Only he couldn't think of the guy's name. Hell, he knew the bar. The Compass Rose. Local dive. All the boaters hang out there at one time or another. I been there dozens of times. He described the guy. Late forties, thinning gray hair, real lady's man. 'Spoony?' I say. 'Bert Spoonmaker? Has a seventy-two-foot Hatteras?' And Mariani, he says, 'Yeah, Spoony. That's the guy. I mentioned to him that I was thinking of relocating to Savannah, and he suggested I look you up. So here I am. And I'm looking to buy a yacht. You looking to sell?'"

Yglesias took another long pull on the beer, then crushed the can with his bare heel. "I just laughed him off. Told him I wasn't looking to sell. He took it pretty well, gave me his card, asked me to call if I changed my mind. I never had any intention of selling the *Blue Moon*. Not at first. But then, I got stupid. Greedy. I called Mariani back, asked him, just out of curiosity, what he had in mind. The price he offered me was ridiculous, $900,000. I told him you could get a new boat for that. This one's got a couple hundred hours on it. But he said no, he liked the *Blue Moon*. He met me for dinner at Elizabeth's on Thirty-Seventh. Made me this lease-to-buy offer. We had a great dinner. Lot of wine. The guy threw money around like it was water. And at the end of the night, I thought, What the hell. I had a knee replacement last March, didn't take the boat out more than half a dozen times last summer. So maybe this was meant to be."

Yglesias spat over the side of the railing. "So much for intuition. I ran into Spoony down in Jacksonville a couple of weeks ago. Told him thanks for the referral. You know, from Mariani. He looked at me like I was crazy. He'd never heard of a guy named Mariani."

Stonecipher looked at me. "Ma'am? How about you? Did the suspect steal anything from you?"

My mouth was dry, but my hands were wringing wet. I felt sick. "He's . . . it's the wrong man. It must be."

"Good-looking guy, am I right?" Yglesias said. "Five-ten, maybe five-eleven? Pale blue eyes, mustache, brown hair, fading at the front? And a diamond earring. Jesus! What was I thinking? The guy had a diamond earring, for Christ's sake."

A cement-blocklike weight crushed my chest. I couldn't breathe. I stood up so quickly the boat pitched violently beneath me, and I had to grab hold of the brass handrail to steady myself.

"Ma'am?" Stonecipher said. "Did this individual steal anything from you? Are you okay?"

"No," I said finally. "I have to go."

All the way into town I told myself what I had told that cop and Yglesias. It was a mistake. A misunderstanding. This was not Reddy. Not my Reddy. I had heard all about identity theft. One of our customers at the restaurant had had his identity stolen and it had been a nightmare. That's what must have happened to Reddy. Some scumbag was passing himself off as Reddy Millbanks, committing crimes under Reddy's name. I tried calling his cell phone again, but now the recording said the number was no longer in service.

Where was he? I was past frantic. West Jones Street, I told myself.

He was probably at West Jones Street. It was after midnight. He'd be fast asleep in my bed on West Jones Street. Nude, turned on his left side, with his right arm thrown across to my pillow, his clothes folded neatly on the Chippendale chair by the door. I felt a twinge of panic when I pulled into my parking slot in the lane behind the house. No sign of the Jag. But there was a battered, rusted-out blue pickup parked in Reddy's usual slot. I cursed in annoyance. The Arrendales, a pushy Yankee couple who'd made a killing on dot-coms had bought the town house next to mine a year ago. They had a bad habit of allowing their guests to park in my slot when they thought I'd be away. And I'd been away so much lately, they'd probably just assumed I was out of town. Reddy had probably been forced to park somewhere on the street out front.

Fuming, I banged open the wrought-iron gate to the courtyard. First thing tomorrow, I promised myself, I would let the Arrendales know in no uncertain terms that I didn't appreciate them poaching on my parking slot.

The courtyard was dark. I'd been meaning to replace the bulb in the light fixture over the door, but things had been so hectic lately that the burned-out bulb was only one thing on my long to-do list. I bumped my shins against something hard and metallic and cursed out loud. "Shit!" I groped the item with my hands and finally concluded that it must be my wheelbarrow. Which should have been in the tool-shed.

I picked my way carefully to the back door, groped for the door-knob, and fiddled around with my keys for a minute. But the doorknob wouldn't turn. "Shit," I muttered. Add another item to my to-do list.

I tried banging on the door, to see if I could rouse Reddy from his sleep. But after knocking and calling his name in a low voice, I gave up and walked down the lane and around to the front of the house.

The light was out on my front stoop too. But the streetlight bathed the street and the front of my brick town house in a cold, un-forgiving light. What I saw then froze me in my tracks. A heavy multilock box was threaded through the polished brass door handle. A small but tasteful sign was perched in my front bay window, which should have been draped in the swagged and fringed sea foam green damask drapes I'd paid a small fortune to have made six months ago. But the windows were bare. And the sign said it all: SOLD.

In a minute, I forgot all propriety. I banged the brass door knocker as hard as I could, then gave that up to pound on the heavy wooden door. "Reddy!" I shrieked. "Reddy! Reddy! Reddy!"

The Arrendales' Pekingese started barking next door. I saw lights snap on in their upstairs window. I didn't care if I woke up the whole damned block.

"Reddy!" I screamed, over and over, pounding and kicking at the door. I didn't stop kicking until Steve Arrendale came over, bare-legged, barefoot, wrapped only in a terry-cloth robe, shivering in the cold, with the Pekingese clutched in his arms.

"BeBe! For the love of God, be quiet," he urged, setting the dog down on the sidewalk and climbing up my stoop to join me. "What's wrong? Got seller's remorse?"

"My house," I screamed. "This is my house."

Arrendale ran his hands through his dark, thinning hair and pointed at the sign in the window of my town house.

"But you sold it. Your boyfriend told us you'd decided to buy something closer to your grandparents. We didn't even know it was on the market," he added petulantly. "If you'd told us, we would have made you an offer. Gretchen's pregnant, and we need more room, and if we bought your place, we could break through that common wall and—"

"I didn't sell my house!" I screeched. "I would never sell my house."

"But you did," he said stupidly. "Your boyfriend told us. I've never seen movers pack a house that fast."

"Movers!" I turned and pressed my face against the parlor window, but it was too dark to see anything inside.

"Three of 'em," Steve Arrendale said. "Mexican, by the looks of them. I didn't know those fellas moved that fast. Usually, you see them lolling around on a job site, leaning on shovels, eating their tacos or whatever, but these guys really hustled. In and out in three hours, and I told Gretchen maybe we should get their number, because—"

I grabbed Arrendale by the collar of his bathrobe. "What did they take? Did they take my furniture?"

He brushed me away. "Hey. That's uncalled for. I was just telling you. Of course they took your furniture. That's what movers do. As far as I know, they took everything. Except for that painting over your mantel. And I have to tell you, Gretchen was so thrilled that you would sell it to us. We've always wanted a Maybelle Johns. Have you any idea what her paintings will be worth once she's dead? Gretchen's already planning to paint the front parlor . . ."

He prattled on like that. I sat down on the steps. My steps. I didn't care what anybody said, these were my damn steps and nobody could sell them without my permission. This was all a horrible mistake, I told myself.

"Wait," I said, looking up at him. "Did you say you bought one of my paintings? The one over my mantel? Which mantel?"

"The Maybelle Johns portrait over your living-room mantel," Arrendale said. He was hopping up and down, trying to keep warm, and he looked so comical there, with his skinny bare legs, so pale against the black of the night. "The painting of the little red-headed girl in the blue dress? Gretchen saw it listed in a book about Savannah artists. But I told your boyfriend, just because a painting has been appraised for a price doesn't mean anybody will pay that price."

"The Maybelle Johns painting. Of my aunt Alice. He sold that to you?"

"Oh, the little girl was your aunt?" Arrendale said, looking fascinated. "Wait till Gretchen hears. She's been wondering about its provenance. She says that's really important for resale value. Not that we'd sell it. Not until Maybelle Johns dies. I heard she's in a nursing home. After she dies, the value will really skyrocket."

I leaped up and grabbed him again. "That painting is of my mother's baby sister, Alice. She died two years after it was painted. She was only eight. You can't buy that painting. He had no right to sell it to you. It's a family heirloom. It's the most valuable thing I own. It isn't for sale."

Arrendale backed away quickly. "Not anymore it's not."

And he shot inside his own front door and I heard the bolt slide shut.

That night, I slept in the Lexus, parked outside the town house. At first light, I got up and peered in the front window of my town house. Steve Arrendale hadn't exaggerated. From what I could see, Reddy's movers had taken everything. My oriental carpets, paintings, furniture, everything, down to the chandelier that had once hung over the dining-room table. I tried all the ground-floor windows and doors, but they were all locked tight, and my keys no longer worked.

I drove over to my rental properties: West Gordon Street, East Liberty, President Street, and Gwinnett. Each had the same discreet little SOLD sign in the window. The keys to all my houses should have been back in my desk at West Jones Street. But I had to keep reminding myself that the desk was gone, and so were those keys. Not that they would have worked. Reddy would have taken care of that too.

11

Weezie

I was standing in the checkout line at an estate sale in a cramped 1930s bungalow in St. Petersburg when my cell phone rang. I had to put down the heavy wicker rocker I had lugged all the way in from the garage. As soon as I did so, a heavyset woman with a tangle of wild, bleached-blond hair and heavily rouged cheeks sprang at it from out of nowhere, snatching at the arm, which had one of those magazine racks built into it.

"Hey!" I told the woman, my voice sharp, my instincts territorial. I plopped myself down into the chair. "Don't even think about it."

The woman backed away, muttering something about pushy dealers. I flipped the phone open. "Hello?"

"Oh, Weezie." It was BeBe. "I need you," she whispered. "Can you come home?"

"Just as soon as I load the truck," I told her. "Six hours, babe. I'll be there in six hours."

BeBe Loudermilk was my best friend. I'd known her since Hector was a pup, and in all the years we'd been friends, even with everything we'd been through together, which included the death of both her parents and all three of her divorces, she had never asked for my help. So she didn't need to tell me what was wrong. I knew, from the pleading in her voice, that something was bad wrong. It was just understood that if she called, I would answer.

Of course, it was also understood that I would finish my negotiations first. I'm an antiques dealer, and junk, literally, is my life as well as my living. Even my own mother is aware that if, in the event of her untimely death, her funeral procession passes an estate sale on the way from the church to the cemetery, that limo will have to make an unplanned detour.

I'd been an antiques picker for years before finally opening my own shop a year ago. The shop is called Maisie's Daisy, and I named it after my grandmother Maisie, whom I called Meemaw. It's in the carriage house beside my town house on Charlton Street, which is on Troup Square, in the historic district. I've loved playing store, painting each room of the shop, arranging vignettes, and finally meeting the people who give my treasures a home, but the downside of playing store is that you have to have inventory to sell.

After only three weeks into what I'd planned as a month-long buying trip to Florida, my tail was already starting to drag. With the advent of eBay and HGTV and shows like *Antiques Roadshow*, everybody and their dog is suddenly hot to buy and sell antiques. Choice junk is even scarcer than it was when I started picking as an eighteen-year-old, and prices have gone through the roof. A scarred oak dresser I could have picked up at a yard sale for $30 three years ago would now be tarted up with a distressed white paint "shabby chic" finish and sold in junk stores for $150. Good smalls were sky high too, and you could almost forget about finding decent affordable wicker anymore. I'd scoured every inch of Florida, stopping at thrift stores, flea markets, junk stores, and estate sales, and my seventeen-foot U-Haul wasn't even half full yet.

Still, I'd had a good morning at the estate sale. On the way to breakfast at the Seahorse, my favorite restaurant at my favorite Gulf beach, Pass-A-Grille, I'd spied the handwritten sign tacked to a Sabal palm. I'd veered the truck so sharply off the road that two cars behind me blared their horns in protest. Breakfast could wait.

My pulse had raced as I backed the truck up to the curb in front of the weatherbeaten little bungalow. Joy of joys, I knew instinctively that I'd hit the macdaddy fantasy of junkers—a real, true, amateur estate sale. All the signs were promising. The sale had not been advertised, I knew, because the first thing I'd done when I'd hit town was to buy a copy of the *St. Petersburg Times*, along with neighborhood "shopper papers" to look for sales. It was only Wednesday. Professionals never have sales midweek. Best of all, a frowsy woman in a flowered muumuu had set up a card table beside the front door. CASH ONLY said the sign scrawled on a piece of cardboard duct-taped to her table.

Within one frantic fifteen-minute sweep of the stifling little house, I'd scored big. The wicker chair had been hidden behind the garage, by the garbage cans. I always check garbage cans at sales like this because amateurs nearly always toss out anything they consider too old, damaged, or embarrassing to sell. I turn up lots of plastic hospital urinals, yellowed lingerie, and broken aluminum yard chairs in this kind of Dumpster diving, but just as often as not, I find wicker or rattan needing only minor repair, wonderful vintage children's books and games, orphaned sets of china dishes, and even whole sets of pots and pans. I can't sell pots and pans, of course, but most people aren't aware how collectible—and pricey—things like a marked Griswold cast-iron skillet can be.

Back inside the house, I'd found a four-place green depression-glass luncheon set for $15, a cardboard beer box full of vintage Florida road maps and old postcards for a buck, some ugly Royal Hager fifties flower vases in maroon, gray, and chartreuse for 25 cents apiece, a boxful of stained women's hankies for a nickel apiece, and another box jammed full of old Florida souvenirware from the twenties to the sixties. The Floridiana stuff was the best I'd found on the trip. There were a dozen old state plates with scalloped edges, all depicting different pre–Disney Florida tourist spots like Cypress Gardens, the Bok Singing Tower, Silver Springs, Weeki Wachee Springs, Monkey Jungle, and Gatorland. There was wonderfully hideous shell art too: a lamp depicting a Southern belle made entirely of coquina and scallop shells, and shell-encrusted bookends and picture frames and even a naughty mermaid statuette with exposed coquina-shell nipples. I'd surreptitiously opened a closet door in one of the two tiny bedrooms and squealed with delight at what I found there: a gigantic stuffed and mounted tarpon.

To finish off the collection, I found a hand-painted juice set with a pitcher and six glasses, marked $5. I'd seen the pitcher by itself, priced at $35, in a vintage kitchenware price guide. And I'd never seen one with all six glasses intact.

I left the house with regret. It was the kind of old-timey beach shack you almost never see anymore. The front screen door had a stylized wrought-iron heron motif, the floors were varnish-darkened heart pine, and window fans had been jammed into all the open windows. If my best friend hadn't been in dire need, I could have spent another hour browsing. But time was short, and I still had to check out of my motel.

I hauled everything out to the pay table and wrapped it with my "Sold to Foley" masking tape. The muumuu-clad cashier didn't bat an eyelash when she saw the stuffed tarpon. "My daddy caught that in the Manatee River in 1968," she said. "Mama raised hell when she found out what he spent having that thing stuffed."

"How much?" I asked.

"Gimme five," she said. "Thing stinks."

She flicked her cigarette ash on the sandy yard and punched numbers nimbly on her tiny adding machine, pausing only when she came to the wicker chair. "Where'd you find that thing?" she asked, her eyes narrowed.

"In the garbage pile," I said blithely. "How much?"

"That's real old wicker," she said, realizing she had a live prospect. "It was in this house when my mama bought it, and that was 1962."

"Fine," I said cheerfully. "How much?"

"I'd need to get twenty-five," she said, sizing me up.

"Fine." I was reaching for my cash stash when I noticed the chair she was sitting on. It was heavy old wrought iron, with a scroll-and-grape motif. There was a matching chair sitting off to the side too. It looked like it had come from a set of fifties garden furniture, the kind with the glass-topped table.

"Is your chair for sale too?" I inquired politely. "That and the one beside you?"

"I dunno. What'd you give for 'em?"

"Ten apiece," I said quickly. "More if you have any matching pieces."

"Ten apiece!" She laughed. "Lady, there's four more of these over at my sister's house sitting there rusting in the carport. Plus a table, but the glass top is broke, and a settee and a couple of armchair-type things. You want that stuff too?"

"Sure," I said jovially. "I'll take all you want to sell. How's a hundred, even, for all of it?"

"Done," she said. She picked up a cell phone that was sitting on top of her pack of Kools. "Let me just call my nephew and get him to haul it over here."

"I've got a truck and I can pick it up, if you'll just give me directions," I said.

An hour later, I was dripping wet with sweat, but the rest of the truck was now filled up. The garden furniture had been an unexpected bonanza. There were two chaises longues, a three-seater settee, a love seat, two armchairs, the glass-topped coffee table, and two end tables, not to mention the rest of the dining-room set and a planter. There were no cushions, and everything was crusted with corrosion, but I loved the set on the spot. It would furnish somebody's beach cottage out at Tybee Island, and once I wire-brushed it, spray-painted it, and had my friend Tacky Jacky make new cushions for everything, I could easily ask $2,500 for the whole set. Turquoise, I decided, heading my U-Haul toward I-75 and Savannah. All the pieces would be painted beach-house turquoise. I would have to find the perfect replica bark cloth for upholstering the cushions, but I knew of an online place called Repro-Depot that had amazing reproduction fabrics.

As I was planning the fabulous window I would design around all the Floridiana, with the stuffed tarpon as its centerpiece, my cell phone rang, and at a glance I saw it was Daniel calling. Daniel. I hadn't thought of him all day. Or of BeBe, come to think of it, not since her panicky phone call two hours earlier.

Junk would have to wait. I had a love life to attend to, and a best friend to rescue.

12

Weezie's uncle James has the kindest eyes I've ever seen. They're a dark blue-gray, and when he smiles, the crinkles reach all the way to his ears, and when he doesn't smile, his eyes still seem to say, "There, there. It'll be all right."

Today wasn't one of those smiling days. We were sitting in his law office, which was in an old cotton-broker's loft on Factor's Walk, overlooking the river. A heavy gray rain was falling, and outside, on the river, the shadow of a freighter loomed ghostly in the mist, as though it were peeking inside the window at us. James Foley looked worried. He had a yellow legal pad on the desk in front of him, covered with scribbles, and a file folder full of official-looking documents. "You don't look so hot," he told me. "When was the last time you slept?"

I looked down at my wrinkled corduroy slacks, at the sweater with the coffee stain at the neck, and the grungy sneakers I'd tossed months ago into the trunk of my car. These were the only clothes I had now other than what I'd been wearing when my life fell apart. I knew without looking that my hair was a wild tangle of curls, and that my nails were bitten down to the quick. I wore no makeup.

"I go to bed," I told James truthfully. "But I don't sleep. I can't."

James sighed. "I don't have much in the way of good news."

"Tell me anyway," I said, sitting up straight in the chair, the way my mother taught me to. I folded my hands in my lap and kept my chin up. *What would mama say?* I kept thinking. What would she say if she knew what I'd gotten myself into?

"Ryan Edward Millbanks the third doesn't exist," James began. "Of course, you already knew that much. There is a Ryan Edward Millbanks Junior, as you know. He has some official-sounding title at the family's business in Charleston, but he doesn't actually work there. He's never married and he's certainly never had any children. He's what people of my generation would call a 'confirmed bachelor.' Or, as my sister-in-law Marian would put it, 'He's gay as a goose.' "

We both had a good laugh at that one, considering that James is gay. I was out of practice with laughing, but it felt okay, considering. And I got to see James's eyes crinkle, which was worth a lot that gray, awful day.

"I've been talking to Jay Bradley. Remember him? The Savannah police detective? And he's done some checking around. Unofficially. The man you knew as Reddy is actually named Roy Eugene Moseley. Born in Hardeeville, South Carolina. He's twenty-eight years old. Never married, that we know of. Previous convictions for bank fraud, forgery, theft by deceiving. He gets around, but up until this year, he was mostly a small-time crook. Jay talked to a police detective in . . ."

James peered down at his scribbled notes. "Vero Beach, Florida. They'd like to catch up with Roy Eugene Moseley and talk to him about some questionable business transactions he entered into down there. They figure he stole $300,000 from a fifty-four-year-old widow who winters in Vero. But the victim has refused to press charges."

Victim. I winced at the word. I'd never been a victim before. Never allowed myself to think of the word "victim." But I sure as hell felt like one today, sitting there in clothes I'd meant to donate to the Junior League thrift shop, living day to day out of the backseat of my car, sleeping on the sofa at my grandparents' apartment.

My car and the clothes on my back were virtually all I had left, except for Guale, which I'd had to shutter because I couldn't afford to pay my staff. Reddy had taken everything else. There was no palatable, socially acceptable word for me. I was a victim, all right.

"He used the same approach with the Florida woman that he used with you," James went on. "He scammed his way into some charity function, introduced himself, and very quickly charmed his way into her life."

"And her bed," I said.

James blushed and looked away. He'd been a priest for a long time before becoming a lawyer, and he was still pretty old fashioned. I guess he's not used to women talking about their sex lives.

I leaned over and patted his hand. "It's all right, James. I'm embarrassed. Humiliated. I slept with the guy, and he turned around and swindled me out of my life's savings. I'm a big girl. I'll get over the sex part of it. But I'll never get over how pissed off I feel about the rest of it. Pissed off at him. And at myself."

He took a sip of coffee.

"In Florida, Moseley called himself Randall Munoz. There is a real Munoz family living down there. They're old-time sugar barons from Belle Glade. Moseley was passing himself off as a dot-com boy genius who'd made a killing on tech stocks before cashing out to live the good life. He somehow talked this woman into allowing him to 'look over' her investment portfolio. Before she knew it, he'd liquidated everything, taken the money, and left town. This was in late January."

"And he met me just a few weeks later," I said. "The guy doesn't let any grass grow under his feet, does he?"

James shook his head. "Bradley says that's how these con men operate. They work fast so that the victim doesn't have time to ask questions or check up on their claims. You shouldn't feel so bad, BeBe. You're not his first victim."

"Just his most generous," I said bitterly. "And the stupidest. So don't bother trying to make me feel better about myself, James, because it won't work. Just tell me what my legal situation is. Bottom line."

James shuffled the documents on his desktop until he had the one he wanted.

"These," he said, patting the file folder on his desk, "are copies of the bills of sale for your home on West Jones, as well as your other real-estate holdings. According to the clerk's office, all the sales were executed three days ago. Apparently, you gave this Reddy person a power of attorney to allow him to make the sales."

"No!" I exclaimed. "I never did anything of the sort."

James held up his hand. "We'll get to that part later. The buyer of all the properties is a single entity, a corporation called St. Andrews Holdings."

"I've never heard of them," I said, near tears again.

"I've got Janet doing some research on them," James said. "But the court documents look genuine. St. Andrews Holdings paid a little over two million for the entire package." He looked over his glasses at me. "Cash."

"The paper he had you sign that last night aboard the *Blue Moon*, the one he told you was a purchase agreement for the house on Huntingdon Street, was actually a power of attorney," James went on.

He held the document up. "Does this look familiar? Is it your signature?"

I put on my reading glasses and scanned the document, paying particular attention to the bottom of the document where "BeBe N. Loudermilk" was signed with its familiar loops and whorls. Too damned flamboyant for my own good, I reflected now, too late.

"This is my signature, all right," I said. "But I couldn't tell you whether this is the paper I signed that night. It was late. I'd been drinking champagne and I was dead on my feet. And I wasn't wearing my glasses. Reddy, I mean, Roy, or whatever his real name is, had to show me where to sign. I did it, I fell asleep, and the next thing I knew, he was gone."

James nodded unhappily. "It could be that he slipped some kind of drug into your drink. We don't know, because he cleaned everything on the boat very thoroughly. But that's what Bradley thinks happened."

"What about this paper?" I asked, flicking it with my fingertips. "It's not legal, right? I mean, he had me sign it under false pretenses."

"But it's your signature," James pointed out. "There's no question about that. And the thing is, you gave him power of attorney, which allowed him to legally sell your house on West Jones, as well as the other properties."

"He lied to me!" I cried. "I never would have sold my house. Or the other houses. And what about all my stuff? My furniture, my paintings, my great-grandmother's silver? And all my clothes. James, all my good jewelry was in the little safe in the floor of my bedroom closet. My mother's engagement ring was in there. And her mother's engagement ring, and oh God, Grandmama's rings. And her earrings and the pearls Granddaddy brought her back from Korea."

Despite all my promises to myself, I broke down in tears again. When I found out that Grandmama had gone into the hospital, I'd talked my grandfather into letting me put all her jewelry in my safe. With the strain of her illness, I'd worried that he might hide her jewelry in the same "safe" place he'd hidden the Buick spare keys, which we still couldn't find. And now it was all gone. Along with everything else.

James stood up, walked around the desk and stood there, awkwardly thumping my back. "It's not your fault," he kept saying. "Don't blame yourself. You couldn't have known."

But we both knew it was *all* my fault. If I hadn't been so blazing mad at Emery Cooper for dumping me, if I hadn't been so eager to jump into bed with the first man to give me a friendly nod, if I hadn't been such a blind, stupid idiot, none of this would have happened.

It had been three days since I'd discovered the truth about Reddy Millbanks. Three days since I'd gone home and discovered that I no longer had a home.

I felt numb all over. So tired. My eyes burned and my head throbbed. I was cold. I looked out the window at the long, gray freighter that seemed suspended on a bank of fog.

"Did you hear me, BeBe?" James leaned across his desk. "Can I get you anything?

"We'll find out who this St. Andrews Holdings is," James said. "We'll explain what happened. Tell them you were victimized. It should be obvious that they bought the properties at a fire-sale price. If they're a reputable outfit, they'll understand that you've been defrauded, and they'll nullify the deal."

"And if they're not reputable?"

"We can take them to court. This was not a good-faith transaction. You've signed a complaint with the police, and Jay Bradley says there will be an investigation. I talked to Jonathan about it . . ."

He blushed again. Jonathan McDowell was the chief assistant in the Chatham County district attorney's office. He was also James's significant other. I would have enjoyed James's discomfort, if at that moment I'd been capable of enjoying anything.

"And Jonathan's going to have somebody from the DA's white-collar crime unit contact you."

"What about my house?" I asked dully. "When can I get back into my house?"

James sighed. "You can't. Not for a while yet. I'm sorry, BeBe. But until I track down somebody with St. Andrews Holdings, I don't have any way to get you into that house. Or any of the others. They've been sold."

"And my stuff? The furniture? My jewelry?"

"Bradley will be calling you. You need to give him an inventory of everything that was taken. If you have any photos, that would be really helpful. The police can check pawnshops and places like that. Bradley will be calling your neighbor to see if he can give a better description of that moving truck."

"Steve Arrendale," I said, my eyes blazing. "That pretentious prick. Reddy sold him the Maybelle Johns portrait of my aunt Alice. He won't return my phone calls. He won't even come to the door when I knock. Can you get my painting back, James?"

"Probably, but we'll have to take him to court," James said. He coughed and stared out the window. "Look, BeBe. The thing is, Arrendale has already filed a complaint against you for harassment."

"Me! Harassment? He doesn't know what harassment is. He stole my painting. He's lucky I haven't had him arrested."

"Stop calling," James said flatly. "Stay away from his house. You're not helping matters. We'll deal with Arrendale when things calm down."

"And when will that be?" I asked, sinking down into the chair. "James, this sucks so bad. And it just keeps sucking. It doesn't get any better. I've lost everything."

"Well," he said, looking down at his notepad again. "Actually, not everything."

"Yeah," I said, gesturing toward myself. "I've still got my looks. Right?"

"That and the Breeze Inn," James said.

"Say what?"

"The Breeze Inn. From the legal descriptions it appears to be a fifteen-unit motel on Tybee Island. Which you bought last week."

"I never bought anything out at Tybee," I said. "I haven't been out there in years. I hate the beach. And Tybee." I shuddered. "Talk about tacky."

"All I know is, the deed to the place is in your name. You, or somebody representing you, paid $650,000 for the Breeze Inn. Actually, this could be a blessing, BeBe. Tybee real estate prices have gone through the roof in the past few years. Even if this Breeze Inn place is a falling-down roach motel, it's got to be worth a lot more than $650,000." He looked down at the pad again. "It's on 1.6 acres. On Chatham at Seventeenth Street. That's the south end of the island." He smiled. "Maybe, just maybe, you're back in business."

"I'll never be back in business," I said glumly. "I've had to close the restaurant. I don't have the money to keep it open and make payroll. That's sixteen people who are out of work. Because I couldn't keep my britches up."

James winced, but then he smiled that smile of his. "You know what my mother used to say?"

"Something relentlessly cheerful, I'm sure. But I don't need cheer right now. I need my painting back. I need my house back. I need my life back."

James rocked back in his chair. "Still. She used to say, 'God never closes a door that he doesn't open a window.'"

"And my mother used to tell me, 'Vulgarity is the crutch of the weak and the ignorant,'" I snapped. "But what the fuck did she know?"

13

Rain flattened the expanses of gray-green marsh grass on either side of Tybee Road, and I had to grip the Lexus's steering wheel with both hands to keep from being blown into the other lane. Not that it would have mattered. In such cold, wet weather, late in the afternoon, nearly six, traffic to the beach was nonexistent.

I scowled down at the water below as I crossed the humpbacked bridge over Lazaretto Creek, and wrinkled my nose at the dank musk of saltwater and marsh mud. This was a fool's errand, I was sure. Despite James's nauseatingly optimistic tendency to look for a silver lining in the thunderclouds hovering over my financial horizon, I had no hope for what I'd find out at Tybee Island. Reddy had been ruthlessly efficient in selling off all my other assets. Why would he have left behind a piece of valuable beach property when he'd gone to such lengths to liquidate everything else?

As the highway followed the bend in the island, I slowed to get my bearings. When had I last been out to Tybee? Not since my college days, I decided. Even back then, in the late eighties, Tybee had been a last-ditch destination. If my friends and I had any choice in the matter, we went south, to St. Simons, or north, to Hilton Head, or even west, to the Gulf beaches on the Florida panhandle, Destin or Panama City. Never Tybee, with its depressing collection of cracker-box cottages, cheap motels, and sleazy bars. As far as I knew, there was not a single white-tablecloth restaurant, tennis court, or golf course on Tybee.

Of course, I knew people who'd bought and even restored beach cottages at Tybee. They called Tybee quaint, genuine, even charming. Daniel, for one, insisted that there was nowhere else he'd rather live.

Fine. If real estate prices at the beach really had escalated as much as James claimed, maybe, just maybe, there was something worth salvaging at the Breeze Inn. Although I very much doubted it.

I swiveled my head back and forth as I headed south on Butler Avenue. Tybee had definitely changed. There was a new brick city hall building and YMCA, and new hotels and midrise condo buildings blocked the view of the ocean. Some things hadn't changed though. Every other block seemed to hold a convenience store. The island's only grocery store, the Tybee Market, was still there, and as I got closer to the cluster of faded concrete-block buildings that made up the commercial district, I saw that the cheesy bars and tourist traps were still there too, though most had probably changed hands and names a dozen times since I'd last seen them.

When Butler Avenue played out, I turned onto Seventeenth Street, and found my way to the address James had given me.

A faded billboard in the crushed-oyster-shell parking lot had an arrow pointing to the left. BREEZE INN, it said, with stylized white palm trees swaying to some unseen ocean breeze. It was almost dark, and the neon VACANCY light was lit.

No surprise there. I turned into the parking lot, and even though I had absolutely no expectations for what I would find there, I was still disappointed. Eight squat buildings were scattered around a central building that was—incongruously—built to look like a log cabin. A whitewashed log cabin at that, one that leaned precariously to the left, and whose rusted tin roof looked as though a puff of breath could send it flying off into the ocean, which was presumably just over the nearest sand dune. A small, hand-lettered sign proclaimed this the manager's office.

A tattered and faded American flag flew from a pole tacked to the cabin's front porch, and there was but one car in the parking lot, an old wood-sided seventies-era Vista Cruiser station wagon that looked like the ones my parents used to load us up in for summer vacation trips.

I parked beside the Vista Cruiser and got out and walked around. The buildings were actually duplexes of a sort, with two units to a building. The numbers were missing from most of the doors. All of the windows were dirt streaked and fly specked. Each unit had a modest, covered porch furnished with a couple of rickety aluminum lawn chairs and cheap plastic tables. None of the cabins was lit up.

"It's the Bates sur la Beach," I muttered under my breath, turning toward the log cabin. I could see the blue glow of a television from the front window. Somebody was home. "Meet the Manager," I muttered, tromping up the front steps and pressing on the door buzzer mounted on the door frame. From inside I could hear the voice of a television announcer, calling what sounded like football plays. Odd, since it was February.

Footsteps clomped toward the door, but it didn't open. I pressed the buzzer again.

"Hello?" I called. "Anybody there?"

"Go away," called a man's raspy voice. "We're closed."

I took a step away from the door and looked back at the Breeze Inn sign.

"Hey," I called back. "There's a vacancy sign out front. So you can't be closed."

More footsteps, retreating, and then returning to the door. I glanced over at the billboard and saw the NO part of the VACANCY sign light up.

"Cute. Really cute," I called. "But there are no other cars in the parking lot. None of these units is occupied. Anyway, you're a motel. You can't be closed. Open up, damnit."

"Damnit," I heard the man on the other side of the door echo softly. I heard the click of a lock, and then the squeak of rusty door hinges. A bearish man with a deep tan and a half-inch of stubble on his face peered out at me from behind a chain security lock.

"Listen," he said, frowning, "I'm busy in here. If you want a room, try the Holiday Inn, or the Days Inn. They're open. And their toilets actually flush."

He started to close the door, but I wedged the toe of my sneaker in the opening.

"I don't want the Days Inn," I said. "I want this motel."

"Why?" he asked, his chin jutting out belligerently. I saw him looking in the direction of my Lexus. "You can afford something a lot better than this dump."

Little did he know. I took a deep breath. "I happen to own this dump. Now can I come in?"

"Since when? Johnny Reese owns the Breeze."

"Not since last week, when I bought the place."

He unlatched the lock and swung the door wide. "By all means, do come in."

The inside of the log cabin was as depressing as the outside. We were standing in a long, narrow room. A huge fireplace covered with what looked like millions of seashells randomly plastered into place had a hideous kerosene stove sticking out of what should have been the wood box. The floors were painted battleship gray, and the furniture looked like rejects from the Salvation Army. A wide-screen television set took up most of the far wall of the room, and a beat-up kitchen table held a partially disassembled outboard-boat motor. One glance confirmed what I'd already guessed—that this place, and the rest of the Breeze Inn, was a prime candidate for a total teardown.

My host crossed his arms over his burly chest and watched me warily. He wore a faded Hawaiian shirt, baggy khaki shorts with cargo pockets, and was barefoot. He had wiry brown hair, a weather-beaten face, and gray-green eyes. His age was hard to guess. Maybe forties? And pissed. He looked pissed.

"And you would be . . . ," I asked, staring him down with my own version of pissed off.

"I would be watching the fourth quarter of the Notre Dame and Michigan game if you hadn't busted your way in here," he snapped. "But if you're looking for a name, mine is Harry Sorrentino. I'm the manager. Now. How about you?"

"BeBe Loudermilk," I said. "Isn't football season over?"

"Not for me," he said. "It's ESPN Classic. Any other questions?"

"How, uh, long have you been working here?"

He ignored my question. "The Reeses didn't say anything to me about selling out."

"It was a surprise to me too," I said. There was no way I was going to admit the circumstances of the sale to this stranger. "Now, how long did you say you'd been here?"

"About three months," he said. "Johnny Reese hired me on after his dad died."

"I take it you live here?" I asked, gesturing toward the television, the outboard motor, and the makeshift shelves of paperback novels on either side of the fireplace.

"That's right," Sorrentino said. "Rent free. I was supposed to get paid a hundred bucks a week too, but business has been slow, so the pay deal kinda went by the wayside."

"Slow," I said, deliberately drawing out the word. "As in . . . non-existent?"

"It's off-season," Sorrentino said, his face reddening. "Check the other hotels on the beach. Nothing going on this time of year."

"Especially if you refuse to rent rooms to anybody who happens to knock on the door," I pointed out.

"Screw that," Sorrentino said. "I'm doing work on all the units. Paint, plumbing, that kind of thing. Johnny knew that. That's what you do in the off-season. Maintenance. It's part of my deal."

I walked around the room to get a better look at it. There was a small kitchen just off the main living/dining room. It had ancient red

Formica countertops, and rusting white metal cabinets, and one of those old round-shouldered refrigerators just like the one my dad used to keep beer in out in the garage. For a man's kitchen, it was surprisingly neat. No dirty dishes in the sink, or grunge on the floor. Just off the kitchen was a large utility room with two huge commercial washers and dryers, white-painted shelves full of neatly folded bed and bath linens, rolls of toilet paper, and stacks of hotel-size shampoos and soaps.

Sorrentino caught up with me at the kitchen doorway. "Anything in particular you're looking for here?" he asked.

"Just getting a look at my investment," I said airily. "You don't mind, do you?"

"A phone call would have been nice," he said. "To let me know you were on the way. I would have straightened up the place."

"I didn't have a phone number," I said evenly. "Anyway, it looks all right to me. Is there a bedroom?"

"There is," he said. "But these are my private living quarters. Johnny never came poking around in my apartment. And I'd appreciate it if you'd do the same."

"Fine," I said. But secretly, I was dying to see what the bedroom looked like. And why didn't he want me looking around in there?

"So," Sorrentino said. "What's the deal?"

"Deal?"

"With you. And me. Do I keep my job? And the apartment? Johnny and I had an understanding. That I would stay here and work through the end of the summer, till I get my boat going again."

"Which boat is that?" I asked.

"The *Jitterbug*," he said proudly. "A thirty-foot T-Craft. I run a charter-fishing business. She's, uh, in dry dock over at Marsden Marina. Soon as I get her up and running again, I'll be out of here. Say, September, probably." He gave me a grudging smile. His teeth were big and white and even. "So, is it a deal?"

"Harry," I said. "Let's be square with each other. You know, and I know, that the Breeze Inn has seen better days. This place is a derelict. To be frank, it's a teardown."

"Some painting. And plumbing," he protested. "I finished the roofing last week. Got toilets on order at Lowes. Two weeks, tops, we'll be booked nonstop."

"No," I said. "We won't. How much does one of these units rent for, anyway?"

"High season? The one-bedrooms bring $750 a week, the efficiencies $500. Johnny says business is real steady. Same families come back year after year. I got a phone call from some folks in Tifton, just yesterday. They want unit six the week of July the Fourth."

I shook my head again. "Not enough. I haven't seen the tax assessment for the Breeze Inn yet, but I know it'll be a killer. The real value in this place, as far as I can see, is the location. I've got a little over one and a half acres here. Technically, it's ocean-view property. And those are the magic words, Harry. 'Ocean view.'"

"Shit," he said, turning his back to me. "You too?"

"What's that supposed to mean?"

"Look around the island," he said bitterly. "Goddamn developers are ruining the place. Anything with any age, any character, they tear down and put up a damned high-rise. The Breeze is the last of the old-time motels. My folks brought us here for a week every June when I was a kid. And you wanna tear that down to make a fast buck."

I bit my tongue. He had no idea just how fast a buck I needed to make. I wanted my house back. I wanted my restaurant open and running again. And if it meant bulldozing this place, well, that was just too bad.

"I'm a businesswoman," I said. "And to stay in business, I have to make a profit. As far as I can see, the only way to do that is to rethink this business for the highest and best use."

"Yeah, whatever," Sorrentino said. "Are we done here? 'Cause I got a game to watch, and a motor to rewind."

"I'm done," I said. "And I'm sorry about the Breeze. I'm going to make some phone calls tomorrow and get the ball rolling. I'll try to give you advance warning so you can find another place to live, but that's about all I can promise."

"Swell," he said. He slumped down into an armchair facing the television and cranked up the volume. I was dismissed.

14

Weezie

Daniel was standing at my stove, sautéing onions when I walked in the back door. He turned and gave me a big grin. Jethro jumped up from his hiding place under the kitchen table and put his big paws on my chest, slathering my face with adoring slurps. Ah, the rewards of home.

When Jethro was done with his welcome, Daniel gave me his. Not nearly as sloppy, but just as deeply felt, I thought.

I stretched and yawned, then sank down onto one of the stripped pine chairs. "I'm whipped," I said. "What's for supper?"

"Meat loaf with garlic mashed potatoes, green beans, and squash casserole," he said, switching off the heat under the frying pan. "I was just making some tomato gravy, so we should be ready to eat in fifteen minutes."

"Perfect," I said. "I've been living off fast food for weeks. I'd kill for some fresh vegetables and anything that's not fried or supersized. I leaned over and scratched Jethro behind the ears. "Not that I don't love having my own private chef, but how come you're in my kitchen instead of Guale's?"

He sat down in the chair beside mine, then poured me a glass of cabernet. "Have you talked to BeBe yet?"

"Yeah," I said. "That's why I shot back here in such a hurry. She sounded desperate. When I tried calling the house, I got a recording saying the number had been disconnected. What's going on?"

"It's a disaster," Daniel said. "That new boyfriend of hers? Reddy, the playboy of the western world? Turns out he was a total fraud. Fake name, fake everything. He's ripped her off, Weeze. Big-time. Sold her house, all her rental properties, cleaned out her bank account. Everything. She's closed Guale because she can't even make payroll."

"Oh my God," I said, rubbing my eyes. "How? I've only been gone two weeks. How could this happen? BeBe's no dummy. How in the world?"

"Long story," Daniel said, taking a sip of his own wine. "But the short answer is, she fell hard for this guy. And I met him. He's slick. Real slick. I guess he sort of came to BeBe's rescue when she was having problems with her rental properties, and she was so distracted with everything going on with her grandmother, she was grateful for his help. Your uncle James says the guy tricked her into signing a power-of-attorney document, and once he had that, he sold everything out from underneath her. Including the West Jones house and everything in it."

"Oh my God." It was boring and unimaginative, but I couldn't think of anything else to say. "Not her house. After she held on to it through both divorces. That house is everything to her. I can't believe it. And the rental properties too? Is everything gone?"

"James says it's pretty bad," Daniel told me. "All the properties were sold to an out-of-town holding company. The bad thing is, James thinks they're a legitimate company, and with BeBe's signature on that power of attorney, the sale looks legal. He's working on it, but in the meantime, I think she's been sleeping in her car."

"Daniel! What about her grandparents?"

"That's the only good news. Her grandmother was released from the hospital yesterday. And they've got nurses coming in to look after her. I guess there really wasn't any room over there."

I gave his arm a not-so-playful punch. "Why didn't you make her come over here?"

He shook his head. "I tried. You know BeBe. Hates to impose. Hates to ask for a favor. And she's embarrassed as all get-out, especially since I tried to warn her about the guy but she wouldn't listen. Basically told me to butt out."

"What about the restaurant? He didn't sell it too, did he?"

"He would have if he'd had the chance. As it is, BeBe closed down Guale the other night. Temporarily, she hopes. We all got our paychecks, but most of us aren't cashing 'em. Everybody's just kind of waiting around, to see if she can pull things back together again."

"Can she? What'll you do?" I asked. "I mean, your house and truck are paid for, I know. But what about long-term?"

He shrugged. "The news is on the street. Everybody in Savannah knows BeBe's in trouble. I've had three or four phone calls already, offering jobs. I hate to take on anything permanent. Guale's where I want to be. I've lined up some catering jobs, and BeBe says I can use the kitchen at Guale, so I'll be all right for money. And a couple of the girls are going to waitress for me at the bigger parties. It's BeBe I'm worried about."

The oven timer buzzed, and he leaped up, potholder in hand. He took the still-sizzling meat loaf out of the oven and nimbly lifted it out of the pan and onto a waiting platter, pouring the tomato gravy over it.

Jethro stood up and poked his muzzle over the edge of the table. I didn't blame him. The smells of home-cooked dinner filled the small kitchen and fogged the windows, and I was suddenly near tears, my emotions mixed up at being glad to be home, here, with this man, and this dog, who both loved me, and being distressed by my best friend's plight.

I set the table for two, and Daniel poured more wine.

"Have you seen her today?" I asked.

He shook his head. "I think she's avoiding me."

I took my fork and laid it sideways on the mound of mashed potatoes on my plate, allowing a river of tomato gravy to flow onto it from the slab of meat loaf. I nearly swooned after the first taste. When Daniel wasn't looking, I snuck a chunk of meat to Jethro, who did the dog version of a swoon, flopping onto his back and rolling around on the floor in utter ecstasy.

"Well, she can't avoid me," I said, tucking into my meal. "I'm gonna track her down and drag her back here if it kills me. Right after I finish my supper."

"Right after?" Daniel said, lifting one eyebrow. "I haven't seen you in two weeks." He put his hand on my thigh, under the table. Jethro licked his hand and my thigh.

"Well, maybe after that," I said.

Daniel smiled.

"And after you help me unload the U-Haul and get everything into the carriage house," I added. "Wait till you see all the stuff I bought in St. Pete. And since you're not really working, maybe you can help me repaint the window backdrop tomorrow, after we get BeBe squared away. I'm doing vintage Florida, and I've got it all planned out. . . ."

15

The good news was that Grandmama was out of the hospital and back at their cottage at the retirement home. The bad news was that I was living there too, and with no job to go to, no home of my own, I was slowly going stark, raving bonkers.

The doorbell rang, and I jumped up to get it, happy for any distraction.

"Babe!" Weezie stepped inside and folded me into a hug.

"Are you all right?" she asked.

I gave my head a slight warning shake.

"Who's that at the door?" Grandmama asked, craning her neck. "If it's that kid selling magazines, run him off. I don't need no more magazines."

"It's me, Weezie, Mrs. Loudermilk," Weezie said, holding out a small, prettily wrapped package. "I'm sorry I didn't get over to see you in the hospital, but I've been out of town."

Grandmama smiled angelically up at Weezie, and tore the wrapping from the package, revealing a box of Russell Stover milk chocolates. "Isn't that nice?" she said, patting Weezie's hand. "If I wadn't diabetic, these would sure taste good."

Weezie's face fell so fast, I had to laugh. "It's okay, Weezie," I told her. "Granddaddy loves chocolate. He'll take care of these."

"I forgot," Weezie said. "I'm so sorry, Mrs. Loudermilk. I'll bring you another present, I promise."

"Never mind," I told Weezie. "It's awful hot in here. Let's go outside for a walk."

"But—" Weezie started to protest.

I took her by the arm and guided her outside. The sun was shining, and the fresh air felt wonderful after days of being cooped up in that apartment with the smell of Granddaddy's Wild Root Oil and Grandmama's creamed tuna on toast, which was all she claimed she could eat after her hospital stay.

I sat on the bumper of my Lexus and leaned back, letting the sun beat down on my face.

"Thank God you came over," I told Weezie, closing my eyes. "Those two are driving me nuts with their bickering. I love 'em to pieces, but I don't know how much longer I can stay here. That sofa bed has springs sticking up out of it, and the mattress is all mildewy. Granddaddy clears his throat for twenty minutes every morning and night, and it sounds like he's goin' to cough up a big old hairball or something. And she's just as bad. She hums! All the time. Off-key humming. It's like Chinese water torture, Weezie."

"I know what you mean," Weezie said. "My daddy jingles the change in his pocket until I think I'll lose my mind. And Mama reads everything out loud. Every story in the paper. Every sign you pass in the car."

I nodded agreement. "I'm going stir crazy without something to do. I'm seriously thinking about taking a job at McDonald's, just to get away from Ma and Pa Kettle in there."

"It's bad, I know," Weezie said, leaning back on the hood beside me. "I talked to Uncle James this morning. He told me about Reddy and everything."

"Some shit, huh?"

"It sucks," Weezie said. "You should have called me sooner, BeBe."

"Nothing you could do," I said. "Nothing anybody can do until I track the bastard down and get my money back."

"I've got a little money," Weezie said. "The shop's doing really well now, and it's all because of you."

"No," I said flatly. "Don't even start. I am not taking money from you. I got myself into this, and I'll get myself out."

"How?" Weezie asked. "James says the company that bought your houses is being a total prick."

"He'll figure that part out," I said, sounding more confident than I really felt. "Anyway, I've still got the Breeze Inn."

"That motel out at Tybee?" Weezie sounded dubious.

"It's a wreck," I agreed. "But I've checked around. Land prices out there have skyrocketed. The motel sits on more than an acre. The lot alone should bring way over a million."

"Daniel says there's somebody living there," Weezie said. "A charter-boat captain. He used to buy fish from him sometimes, for Guale. Harry something?"

"Sorrentino. Harry Sorrentino. He reminds me of Cap'n Crunch," I said dismissively. "He says he had a deal with the previous owner. Supposed to be the resident manager and caretaker. But he's been living there rent free for three months, and the place is in terrible shape, as far as I can tell. I've told him he can stay until I sell the place, but that shouldn't take long."

"You're really going to tear it down?" Weezie asked, her voice wistful. I knew that tone of voice. Weezie thinks anything that's old and run-down is a treasure beyond price. "Daniel and I ride our bikes past the Breeze Inn sometimes. It could be awful cute, fixed up. You could do it totally retro, with old rattan furniture—"

"Don't start," I warned her. "It's just awful, period. Anyway, I don't have the money to fix it up. And I have no interest in Tybee Island. Besides, it's not as if I have a choice. The sooner I sell the Breeze Inn, the sooner I can reopen Guale and get my life back on track."

"I've always wanted to see what the units look like inside. Hey," she said, brightening. "Maybe there's some stuff you could salvage and sell. Like old pedestal sinks or tubs or kitchen cabinets. I've always got customers looking for that kind of stuff."

"Doubtful," I said. "I've seen the inside of the manager's unit. It's tacky as hell."

"We should take a look," Weezie insisted. "Come on. Let's ride out to Tybee and take a look."

"Why not?" I said, though still unconvinced. "It's not like I've got anything else to do around here. The visiting nurse should be over in a little while to help Grandmama with her bath and meds. And Granddaddy's glued to the television. What the hell. Let's go."

We took Weezie's truck, at her insistence. "Just in case there's something worth salvaging now," she reasoned.

I was in a much better mood on this trip to Tybee. For one thing, the sun was shining and I wasn't locked in that tiny apartment with my crazy grandparents. But mostly, it was good just to be riding shotgun in that beat-up old truck with my best friend, who almost had me believing things were looking up. Weezie popped a disc in the CD player, and we left the windows down, singing along with Sheryl Crow and bopping along without a care in the world.

My good mood lasted only about thirty minutes, the time it took to drive out to Tybee Island, and to pull up to the parking lot at the Breeze Inn, which was all but obliterated from view by a huge new billboard.

COMING SOON!
THE SANDCASTLE
14 LUXURY OCEANFRONT VILLAS
Pre-construction Prices Starting at $600,000
Listed Exclusively by Sandcastle Realty Associates

My mouth literally hung open in dumb surprise.

"Hey!" Weezie said. "You didn't tell me you'd already made a deal to sell the place."

"I haven't," I said, staring up at the sign. I pulled out my cell phone and started to dial the number listed at the bottom of the billboard. "I don't know anything about this."

The phone rang, and an answering machine picked up. I left a message saying only that it was urgent I talk to somebody about the new Sandcastle villas. Then I called James Foley. While I waited for his assistant, Janet, to put him on the line, Weezie and I got out of the truck and started walking toward the manager's office.

Harry Sorrentino met us halfway there, his eyes blazing.

"Hey!" he shouted at me. "What's the fuckin' idea?"

"Excuse me?" I said. "I'm on the phone here, as you can see."

"What? Selling off one of your exclusive oceanfront villas? You are some piece of work, lady, you know that?"

Weezie blushed and turned away.

"BeBe?" James came on the line. "Janet says you've got an emergency. What's the problem?"

I covered the phone with my hand and stared Sorrentino down. "Just a minute."

"James, I'm out at the Breeze Inn. There's a huge billboard out in front of it for something called the Sandcastle. It's offering oceanfront villas starting at $600,000."

"Christ," James said softly. "What else does the sign say?"

"Just something about exclusive listings by Sandcastle Realty. There's a phone number. I called it, but I got an answering machine. I left a message, telling them it was urgent that they call me back."

"Give me the number," James said. "I'll have Janet look into it. And I'll call you as soon as I know something."

"How can this happen?" I asked, getting panicky. "I mean, you said I own the place, free and clear. So how can something like this happen?"

"I don't know," James said. "But calm down. We'll get it straightened out."

I flipped the phone shut.

Harry Sorrentino stood defiantly in front of me, his arms crossed over his chest. "Well?"

I sighed. "That was my lawyer. There's been some kind of misunderstanding. He's going to figure out what's going on. But I have no idea who these Sandcastle people are, or how they think they can just put up a sign on my property."

"Right," Sorrentino said. "Some jackleg just showed up here and nailed up a sign without your permission. After you swore you'd give me plenty of notice and time to find a new place and a new job. You expect me to believe that?"

"It's true," Weezie said, butting in. "She had no idea this was going to happen. We were just coming out today to look around the place. BeBe hasn't made any kind of deal yet. She wouldn't lie about something like that."

"The guys that put up that sign told me they expect to start demolition early next week," Sorrentino said. "How the hell am I going to find a place to live that soon?"

"Listen, Harry," I said. "Watch my lips. Nobody is tearing anything down until I say so. Just chill out, will you?"

"Easy for you to say," Sorrentino muttered, turning to walk back toward the motel. "You've got a place to stay. Nobody jerking you around."

"Like hell," I said, but softly, under my breath. "Hey," I called after him.

"What now?" He didn't even turn around.

"I need the keys to the other units. I want to check out the whole property."

He disappeared inside the manager's office, and a minute later came out with a huge, old-fashioned ring of keys, which he tossed in my direction.

I leaped forward to make the catch, but missed by a country mile. The keys landed in the oyster-shell lot, sending up a puff of sand.

He allowed himself a small smirk of satisfaction at seeing me bend down to pick them up.

"I'm going over to the marina," Sorrentino said. "Be back this evening. The door to unit seven is warped. You gotta really yank on it. I haven't gotten to the roof on nine and ten yet, so there's probably still some water on the floor in there. Lock up when you leave, okay?"

"Sure thing," I said through gritted teeth. I wanted to pick up something heavy and chunk it at him, but there wasn't anything handy to throw, and anyway, I hated to give him the satisfaction of seeing my klutziness a second time.

He walked toward the battered station wagon, but paused as he opened the door. "So you really haven't made a deal yet to sell the place?"

This was getting old. "No," I said. "Not yet."

He whistled then, and a tiny white ball of fur came hurtling through the open door of the manager's unit. It was a dog, some kind of terrier, but since I'm not an authority on dogs, I couldn't be certain of the breed.

"Come on, Jeeves," Harry called, stepping away from the driver's-side door to allow the dog to jump into the front seat. He was smiling for the first time since I'd met him. "Let's go for a boat ride."

"Jeeves?" I turned to Weezie with a raised eyebrow. Sorrentino caught the look, and his smile was gone.

"I happen to like Wodehouse," he said. "You got a problem with that?"

I had no idea who Wodehouse was, but I wasn't about to admit that to Sorrentino. "I didn't know you had a dog living here."

"Well, now you do," he said. And he got into the car, slammed the door, and drove off in a cloud of oyster dust.

Weezie grinned. "He seems nice."

My hands were covered in dust. I wiped them on the seat of my pants and headed toward the manager's unit. "He's history," I said. "Just as soon as I sell this place."

16

Weezie

BeBe turned the key in the lock and leaned against the door. Nothing. "I have a bad feeling about this," she said, grimacing.

"Let me try," I said, shoving her aside ever so gently. I turned the key and slammed my hip—much more substantial than hers—against the door. A moment later I was inside—sprawled out on the floor.

"Eeeewww," BeBe said, sticking her head inside the door. "You're going to have to burn those jeans."

I stood up and wiped my hands on the seat of my jeans, which were, admittedly, now caked in some kind of unspecified crud, and took a look around.

The room was small, maybe fourteen by sixteen feet. The walls were pine paneled and crusted in sixty-year-old grime. Two big picture windows should have looked out on sand dunes, but they too were coated with dust and dirt. A naked lightbulb swung from a fraying cord in the middle of the ceiling, and underfoot was the gnarliest avocado shag carpet I'd ever seen.

"Come on," BeBe said, grabbing my hand and pulling me toward the door. "We're out of here. The only thing that's gonna help this place is a can of kerosene and a big box of matches."

"Hang on," I said, yanking her back inside. "Don't be such a pessimist. It's not that bad."

The far end of the room had a kitchenette, with a green Formica countertop over built-in metal cabinets, an ancient under-the-counter refrigerator, a tiny stainless-steel sink, even a two-burner stove. An abbreviated countertop had two old faux-bamboo bar stools pulled up to it, their green vinyl seats cracked and patched with duct tape.

"It's an efficiency," I said, turning the handle of the sink faucet. A groaning noise came forth from the wall, and dark brown water trickled into the sink. "Plumbing works," I announced.

"Yippee," BeBe muttered, nevertheless coming over to take a look. "We'll just check you right into Motel Hell."

I ignored her, flipping the dial on the stove top. Within minutes, the burner glowed orange, and an incredible stink filled the room.

"Jeezo-Pete," BeBe said, gasping for air. "Turn it off before the place explodes."

I'd already turned it off, and was trying to crank open the tiny jalousie window in the kitchen area.

"This is great," I said, fanning in fresh air. "The plumbing works, and the stove works. That means you won't have to look for a replacement. I doubt anybody makes this small a unit anymore. Look at how cute this thing is. All this old chrome and stuff. It looks like something Donna Reed might have cooked on."

"If Donna Reed lived in a crack house," BeBe said, shaking her head in disgust. "Honestly, Weezie, look at this place. Not even you can think it's worth saving."

"This must be the bathroom," I said, turning toward the doorway on the long wall of the kitchen area.

BeBe clasped her hands over her eyes. Always the drama queen. "I can't look," she said. "You know I have a weak stomach."

I switched over to mouth breathing. You never know, you know. The bathroom door swung open on creaky hinges. Rusty water dribbled into a filthy pink porcelain sink. A naked hole in the pink and turquoise tiled floor showed the spot where the commode had once been. The pink bathtub showed multiple rust rings. There was a window above the tub, but it had been boarded over. The walls were painted a garish hot pink, with turquoise dolphin decals pasted around the ceiling line.

I took a deep breath. "Okay. It has potential. Definite potential."

BeBe peeked from between her fingers. "Sick." She groaned, backing away.

I closed the bathroom door behind me and caught up with her outside as she locked up.

"There is no way," she said, shaking her head as she tried to extricate the key from the lock. "No way in hell this place could ever be made livable. I'm sorry, Weezie, but you saw for yourself. If nothing else, it's a health hazard."

"It's not," I insisted, following her across the parking lot. "Let's take a look at the other units."

"No," she said, marching toward my truck. "I've seen enough. As soon as your uncle gets this Sandcastle thing straightened out, I'm putting the place on the market."

I grabbed her arm and spun her around to face me. "It's not that bad," I insisted. "It's dirty, that's all. Run down. But believe me, this place could be a gold mine."

"You're nuts," she said flatly. "I know you know a lot about antiques and stuff like that, but, Weezie, I happen to know a little bit about real estate. And the land under this motel is worth far more than I can ever make by running a motel."

"Nuh-uh," I told her. "Look. You know I just got back from a buying trip down in Florida. And there's nothing like this left down there. It's all high-rise hotels and condo towers, all up and down the beaches. Except for one place. One of my antiques dealer friends took me to see it. It's down in Sarasota. Called The High Tide. It's little dinky concrete-block cottages, just like these. And it's not even on the beach. It's across the street. But a couple of gay guys bought it four years ago and fixed it up. Babe, I wish you could see the place. Each of the units is painted a different pastel color—from the street it looks like a box of dinner mints. The units are arranged in kind of a horseshoe shape, around a little swimming pool, and they've turned the old coffee shop into an espresso bar. It's the hottest place on the beach. Linda, my dealer friend, says they have an eighteen-month waiting list for the units—summer and winter. It's been in *Southern Living*, and they shoot television commercials there all the time."

"That's Florida," Bebe pointed out. "Hip. Trendy. This is Tybee. Tacky. Worn-out. The only thing anybody would ever shoot here is one of the roaches."

"You don't even know Tybee," I protested. "It's changed. There's stuff happening out here. And the Breeze Inn is unique. There's no other place like it left."

Bebe leaned up against the bed of my pickup truck and crossed her arms over her chest. "You're not listening, Weezie. I can't do it. I just can't. Not even if I wanted to. I am dead broke. I don't have any money to fix up this place. The only way out of the mess I'm in is if I sell it." She pushed a strand of blond hair off her forehead and smiled grimly. "And once I've sold it, I'm going after Roy Eugene Moseley."

"Who?" I opened the door of the truck and got in.

"Roy Eugene Moseley," she said, hopping up onto the passenger's seat. "Of course, he told me his name was Ryan Edward Millbanks III. Can you believe I fell for that?"

"Reddy," I said.

"Reddy," she agreed. "I'm going to hunt him down like a dog. And I'm going to get my money back. And my house. And my granny's pearls. And the painting of my aunt, and every other damn thing he stole from me."

"Oh-kay," I said slowly, starting the truck. "Can we go get a drink first, before we start hunting him down? And maybe a sandwich? I didn't have lunch."

She turned toward me with a sad little smile. "Can't."

"I'm buying," I assured her.

Fifteen minutes later we were seated at the bar at the North Beach Grille. The place was nearly deserted, and the guy at the bar was too busy watching a golf tournament on the wall-mounted television to pay us much attention. I ordered for both of us, crab-cake sandwiches and a couple of iced teas.

BeBe nibbled warily at her sandwich. "Not bad."

"It's great, and you know it," I said, taking a forkful of coleslaw. "What's up with you and Tybee? What have you got against it?"

"Nothing," she said, wiping her fingers on her paper napkin. "I've got nothing against Tybee. I just don't happen to think it's as swell as you do. Is that a sin? You know me. I'm a downtown girl."

"Living in a white-bread world," I agreed.

Her cell phone rang then, and she snapped it open.

"Hey, James," she said. "What did you find out?"

She listened intently. "You're kidding. Steve Arrendale? As in the Steve Arrendale who lives next door to me? You're absolutely sure it's the same guy? Unbelievable. I'll kill him. I really will. Well, no, not literally, but he's going to be sorry he messed with me."

She listened for a while, swore, peppered my uncle with questions, and then, finally, snapped the phone shut. The bartender gave her an annoyed look, which she pretended not to notice.

I ate my sandwich and waited for her to fill me in. She took a long sip of tea and finally pushed her plate away, her lunch barely touched.

"Sandcastle Realty," BeBe said, "is Steve Arrendale."

"Your neighbor," I said helpfully.

"Ex-neighbor. I no longer own a house on West Jones."

"This is the same guy who bought your Maybelle Johns painting?"

"Yankee scum," she said, nodding. "Devious, social-climbing, name-dropping Yankee scum. It turns out that the painting isn't the only thing Reddy sold him."

"I don't understand," I said.

"It's complicated. According to your uncle James, this was just another of Reddy's rip-off schemes. He bought the Breeze Inn, at a fire-sale price, using my money. Then, before the ink was even dry on the sales contract from the Breeze Inn, he turned around and sold a three-month option on the property to Steve Arrendale for three hundred thousand against a three-million dollar purchase price."

"Why an option?" I asked. "Why not just sell it outright?"

"James doesn't really know," BeBe said, shrugging. "He thinks maybe Reddy planned to sell options to more than one person, but just didn't get around to it before he skipped town with my money."

"Is that legal?" I wanted to know.

"Hopefully, not," BeBe said. "James is going to file an injunction against Arrendale and Sandcastle Realty in superior court. He'll claim fraud, which is what it is, and ask that Arrendale be enjoined from selling units in his so-called town-home community."

"Which is good, right?"

"James hopes to get a temporary restraining order," BeBe said. "But it's just that, temporary. He says if the judge grants it, which he probably will, it'll keep Arrendale from selling the units. But James says it also means, for the time being, that I can't sell the Breeze Inn either. Not until the whole thing is ironed out in court."

I had to duck my head to keep her from seeing my smile.

"Shit," BeBe said. I looked up quickly. Her eyes were filling with tears.

"Shit," she said again, dabbing at her eyes with her paper napkin. "I can't believe this is happening to me."

I reached over to the dispenser and grabbed a thick wad of napkins, which I handed to her.

"I *hate* this," she said fiercely, swiveling around on the bar stool so that her back was to the bartender, who'd suddenly found our conversation entirely too fascinating. "I can't go back to my grandparents', Weezie. I can't face them."

"Why not?" I asked. "They don't care if you're broke. They love you, BeBe. They're your family. And they need you too."

"You don't understand," she whispered. "It's not just my money that's gone. It's theirs too. Reddy took it. He took all of it."

"How?" Lorena and Spencer Loudermilk were old-time, old-money Savannah. They were as close as it came to local aristocracy. They had once owned the ritziest furniture store in town. It had been closed for at least twenty years, but I was sure that their family fortune was intact. BeBe's grandfather might have driven a beat-up old hoopdie of a car, but I knew for a fact that he was a member of the Oglethorpe Club, and that most of the exquisite furniture and paintings in BeBe's West Jones Street house had been on loan to her from her grandparents since their move into an assisted-living cottage.

BeBe bit her lip. "Stupid. I was so goddamned stupid. You know I took care of their finances, right?"

I nodded.

"Granddaddy's not senile. Not at all. He's just gotten so forgetful. And it upsets him when he finds out he forgot to pay a bill or something. He's still so old-fashioned. He can't stand the idea that somebody would think he was a deadbeat. So he had my name put on all their accounts. My brothers couldn't be bothered with that kind of thing. And I was happy to be able to do such a little thing for them. And now . . ."

She sobbed and buried her head in her hands. The bartender turned away, embarrassed by such a naked display of emotion. I reached over and stroked BeBe's arm, at a loss for words.

She sat up finally and straightened her shoulders. "It's my own fault. After Granddaddy bought that stupid new Lincoln, I tried to get the dealership to take it back. Only they wouldn't. And Grandmama was in the hospital, and she was so sick, and I don't know, it was like everything was so *overwhelming*. And Reddy was right there. He said he'd take care of things, and he did. He made them give us back the old Buick, and they refunded the price of the Lincoln. And he offered to deal with my rental properties, and I let him. He said he wanted to take care of me. You know?"

We exchanged sad, knowing smiles.

"Nobody ever did that for me before," BeBe said. "I always took care of myself. Even when I was a little girl, Mama said that even though I was the youngest, I was the only one she could trust to do things the way they ought to be done."

"You're the strongest woman I know," I offered. "And the smartest."

"No," she said, shaking her head vehemently. "I'm a fraud. Look at me. Three marriages. Twice to the same guy! I never learn. And now it's too late. Reddy didn't miss a trick. After that thing with the car, he knew where I kept my grandparents' bank book. He emptied out their money-market account. Every last dime."

"Oh, Bebe," I said, blinking back tears of my own. "I didn't know."

She blew her nose on the wadded-up paper napkins. "They don't know either. I can't bear to tell them. I can't bear to look them in the face. They trusted me. And look what happened."

"What'll you do?" I asked.

She shrugged. "They're all right for the short term. They own the cottage, outright, and they actually have meals paid for in the center's dining room, although Granddaddy insists all their food tastes like boiled brussels sprouts. They have hospitalization, so I'm not too worried about the medical bills. It's the other things. Walking-around money. I used to dole it out to them. But now I just don't have it. They don't have it."

"What about your brothers? Can't they help out?"

"They don't know. And I intend to keep it that way. They'd never let me live it down if they knew. And anyway, I'm not so sure any of them are in a position to help out, financially."

"So now what?"

"I find a buyer for the Breeze Inn," she said, hopping down from the bar stool. "And then I find Reddy Millbanks and get my money back."

17

Restaurant life usually means freakish hours. In the past, I'd get home from Guale around twelve-thirty, or sometimes one A.M. But most nights I was too keyed up from work to go right to bed. I'd stay up, have a glass of wine, read, or watch old movies, and turn in around two. And head back to the restaurant by ten the next morning.

But my old life was gone, as I was reminded in countless ways, every day. In its place, I was left in a kind of twilight zone, trying to figure out how to piece together a new existence.

Not everything was awful. Grandmama was getting stronger every day. She insisted on taking short walks, and was even fixing breakfast some mornings. I knew she was truly on the mend when she reinstated her standing Friday beauty shop appointment. And Granddaddy was better too. He drove her to her doctors' appointments, took her grocery shopping, even met his old buddies for lunch again.

I was the one who was a pity case. I was still camping out on the sofa at their apartment. I made endless clandestine phone calls to James Foley, checking on the progress of my legal action, and took catnaps at odd hours because I still wasn't getting much sleep at night. Just the previous evening, for example, the lake effect was doing something in the Midwest, and between that and a nasty wildfire in the Sierra Madres, Granddaddy sat up watching television until nearly three A.M. After he finally did go to bed, Grandmama was up and down at least half a dozen more times, going to the bathroom.

Finally, one sunny afternoon, Grandmama shook me awake gently.

"Huh?" I said, rolling over groggily.

"BeBe, sweetheart," she said. "Your granddaddy and I need to have a talk with you."

"Are you all right?" I asked, suddenly alert.

"I'm fine," she said, perching on the sofa arm.

I sat up, yawned, and rubbed the sleep from my eyes. "What time is it?"

"Nearly two o'clock," she said, her lips slightly pursed.

"Yes," chimed in Granddaddy. "And here you are, sleeping the day away." He frowned. "That's what we want to talk to you about. Things can't go on like this, young lady."

"Spencer!" Grandmama exclaimed. "Hush." Her face flushed slightly.

"Sweetheart," she said slowly, taking my hand in hers, "your granddaddy and I have been talking. And we are just so proud and grateful for the way you've pitched in and helped out while I was ailing. You've been a godsend."

"Mostly," Granddaddy said. "But now it's time—"

"Spencer!" Grandmama snapped. "We agreed that I would do the talking."

"Beating around the bush," Granddaddy muttered. "Just tell her flat out."

"Tell me what?" I asked, glancing from one to the other.

"Well . . . it's just that, um, I'm feeling much better now. And the doctor says if I'm careful, I can do pretty much whatever I want. And we thought . . ."

"We think it's time you moved back home," Granddaddy put in. "High time. You can't just lay around on this sofa all day long."

"Spencer, for heaven's sakes!" Grandmama exclaimed.

"Wait a minute," I said. "Let me get this straight. You're kicking me out? That's what you wanted to talk to me about?"

"Well," Grandmama said, "I wouldn't say we were kicking you out. But we do agree that I'm well enough for you to go home now."

"Yeah," Granddaddy said. "I even packed your stuff. Not that there's very much of it. Traveling kind of light these days, ain't you?"

I blinked. "You've already packed for me. And you want me to leave."

"Lorena's got her bridge club girls coming over here at four o'clock," Granddaddy said. "And she's been after me to Swiffter the living room. Can't hardly do that with you underfoot."

Grandmama stood up and punched Granddaddy hard on the arm. "Spencer Loudermilk! I swear to goodness I don't know what to do with you." But then she tucked an arm around his waist, and he kissed the top of her head. And for a minute there, the two of them looked like a couple of lovelorn teenagers.

"Okay," I said, looking around the room for my aforementioned luggage, which consisted of a brown paper sack from the Winn-Dixie. "I guess I'll be going, uh, home. I'm sorry, guys, if I've been underfoot. I didn't realize I've been cramping your style."

"You haven't been underfoot," Grandmama said. "Just ignore your grandfather. He's an old fool. He's just cuttin' up because his poker buddies are supposed to come over here tomorrow night, and he knows you'll fuss at them for smoking cigars."

"It's all right," I said, gathering up the paper sack and my pocket-book. "He's perfectly right. You're much better now, and you two need your privacy. So I'll just be heading home, unless you need anything else."

"Not a thing," Granddaddy said, a little too heartily. He slung an arm around my shoulder and basically force-marched me to the front door. Then he kissed me on the head, and tucked something in the back pocket of my jeans.

"What's that?" I asked.

"Just some folding money," Granddaddy said. "The least we could do after all the baby-sitting you've been doing around here."

I pulled out the wad of folding money. It was five crisp one-hundred-dollar bills.

"Where'd you get this?" I asked, alarmed. Had he been withdrawing money from an account that was riding on empty?

"Don't you worry about that," he said airily. "I have my resources."

"No, really," I said. "I know you didn't take it out of the money-market account, because the checkbook isn't here. Where did this money come from, Granddaddy? I need to know, to keep all your accounts straight."

"You don't know about *all* our accounts, young lady," he said. "I've got money squirreled away. And that's all you have to know about that."

I was starting to panic. "You don't have cash hidden around here, do you? That's not really a good idea. If there was a fire or something—"

Grandmama laughed. "Don't worry. It's not like he's got a fruit jar full of hundred-dollar bills hidden under the bed, if that's what you mean. Your grandfather still has a very good head for numbers. Always has had. We're nicely fixed. And you children will be too, when we've passed. So you go on home now. Maybe take a shower and fix your hair. And put on some of those pretty clothes you used to wear."

"Yeah," I said dully, heading for the door. "I'll do that. I'll drop by later in the week to check on you."

"Be sure and call first," Granddaddy said.

I could have sworn I heard the lock click behind me as I headed for the Lexus.

For an hour, I drove aimlessly around town. It was one of those nasty, bitter-cold days when you could almost see the blooming azaleas and dogwoods shivering in the wind whipping through Forsyth Park. Because of course, I wasn't really driving aimlessly. I drove straight downtown, past the park, and circled my block of West Jones three times, praying for a sighting of Steve Arrendale. I wanted to run him down, or at the very least maim him. But it was late afternoon, and the street was deserted. I scowled every time I saw the SOLD sign posted in my front parlor window.

Already the town house was looking forlorn and bedraggled. The boxwoods in their antique cast-iron urns by the front door had big brown splotches, and the ivy cascading around them had died, leaving a windswept carpet of dead leaves on the front stoop. Pigeons had taken up residence under the front portico, and there was a nasty mound of droppings on the sidewalk.

Stop this! I finally told myself. I drove over to Weezie's house on Charlton Street. I was tired, I was depressed, I hadn't had any food all day. I needed sympathy. And hard liquor. And my best friend.

I tucked my Winn-Dixie luggage under my arm and rang the front doorbell.

"Oh!" Marian Foley wore a pale pink polyester jogging suit and a look of surprise. "Why, BeBe," she said. "How nice to see you. Does Eloise expect you?"

"Hi, Mrs. Foley." I gave her a dutiful peck on the cheek. Weezie's mother was big on proprieties. "No, Weezie's not expecting me. I just decided to drop by on the spur of the moment. Is this a bad time?"

"Not at all," she said. "We were just sitting in the kitchen with a cup of tea, having a little mother-and-daughter chat. I'm sure she'll be thrilled to see you." But her look said otherwise.

I followed Marian to the back of the house, to Weezie's kitchen, where she was sitting at her oak table looking deeply unhappy. There was a pot of tea on the table, two mugs, and a plate of lumpy, misshapen neon-orange muffins.

"BeBe!" Weezie said, brightening, and at the same time instantly taking in the grocery sack.

"Hey," I said wanly. "I didn't know your mom was here. I can come back later. Just call me. On my cell," I said, knowing she'd get my meaning.

"Oh, Mom doesn't mind, do you?" she asked, looking from me to Marian.

Marian's shrug said she actually minded very much.

"BeBe was just dropping by some of her grandmother's old handkerchiefs for me to sell in the shop," Weezie said, brazenly lying. "I'm making little flower boutonnieres out of them to sell in Maisie's Daisy."

"Other people's used hankies," Marian said, shuddering. "Why on earth would anybody pay good money for something like that?"

"Just another wacky trend, I guess," Weezie said glibly. She grabbed me by the elbow and headed me out the back door, in the direction of the shop. "We'll be back in a minute, Mama. Go ahead and pour yourself another cup of tea."

"I'll save you a muffin, BeBe," Marian said. "They're orange-pistachio. It's a new recipe. You use a bottle of Nehi Orange Crush soda, a box of orange Jell-O, and a can of those mandarin oranges, and—"

"Later, Mama," Weezie said, rolling her eyes once her back was turned to her mother. Marian Foley is a very nice lady, I suppose. She'd been a lifelong closet drinker up until a few years ago, when she went through rehab and took up cooking as therapy. The problem was, she was a much better drinker than cooker.

"I'm gonna kill myself," Weezie said under her breath. "Or her."

She unlocked the door to the antiques shop and snapped on the lights as we stepped inside. Quiet classical music flowed from hidden speakers, and she sank down onto a funky wrought-iron chair and patted the seat of its mate opposite her.

"What's really in the sack?" she asked, getting right down to business.

"Money. Half a million. I hit the lottery last night. Didn't you hear?"

"No," she said, arching one eyebrow. "Mama watches the Food Channel nonstop. This whole town could burn to the ground and I wouldn't know a thing about it."

"What's she doing here?"

"Their hot-water heater exploded. The whole house flooded. Their carpet's ruined, and they can't move back in until everything dries out."

"And they're staying with you?"

"Mama is. And that's the problem. Daddy just turned right around and went down to South Carolina to go hunting. So it's just Mama and me."

"And the muffins," I added.

"Have you ever seen anything so hideous? I shouldn't be like this," Weezie said, shaking her head. "I'm *ashamed* of myself for being like this. But she makes me . . ."

"Crazy," I said.

"Exactly. I can't be in the same room with her for more than an hour at a time. She sucks up all the oxygen in the atmosphere."

"I know," I agreed. "She's a wonderful woman, but . . ."

"Impossible," Weezie finished. "But I'll get through it. Somehow. But enough about me and my troubles. What's going on with you? What's really in that sack?"

"I'm homeless," I said, blurting it out. "My grandparents kicked me out of the house."

"For real?"

"'Fraid so," I said. "Here I thought I was being so noble, sacrificing myself to help take care of them, and it turns out they've been plotting to get rid of me."

"Why?"

"I don't blame 'em," I said. "They don't need me anymore. Grandmama is feeling much better. They've got their own life. And they don't need me underfoot."

"You can stay here, of course," Weezie said. "Mama can move into my room with me, and you can have the guest room."

"No 'effin way," I said. "To tell you the truth, I came over here intending to ask if I could bunk with you for a while. But there's no way I'd move in now. You've got enough to deal with."

"I'm begging you," Weezie said, grasping my hand. "Please. I just want another sane human being to talk to."

But I shook my head and stood up. "Can't do it."

"But where'll you go?" she asked.

"A motel," I said, and the answer surprised even me. "I'm thinking of checking into the owner's quarters at the Breeze Inn. Tybee's supposed to be lovely this time of year."

Weezie grinned. "Save me a room. If they don't get that carpet replaced soon, I'm outta here too."

18

Harry Sorrentino's station wagon was missing from the parking lot at the Breeze Inn. I frowned and fidgeted with the ring of keys in my lap. I had practiced my speech all the way out to Tybee. I would tell Harry in a calm, reasonable way that he would have to vacate the manager's quarters because I needed to move in. Immediately. It was the only way, I would say, that I could protect my property rights from developers who were trying to swoop in and steal the place out from under me. And him. I had decided, in a magnanimous gesture of goodwill, to allow Harry to stay on, rent free, as long as he moved into one of the vacant motel units and stepped up his efforts at renovating the rest of them. If I couldn't sell the motel immediately, as originally planned, I could at least get the Breeze Inn ready to start renting rooms and become a paying proposition.

A seagull skimmed past the windshield of the Lexus and left an ugly greenish-white splatter as a souvenir. I swear, the motley creature laughed as it soared off on a gust of wind and I hit the power-wash button for the windshield wipers.

I knocked hard on the door of the manager's unit, to no avail. I jiggled the key ring some more, then walked around to the back of the log cabin, where I remembered seeing a set of French doors. Maybe Harry was home, but napping. Or maybe he was just being obstinate and refusing to open up, as he had the first night I'd laid eyes on him and the Breeze Inn.

The French doors, salt misted, revealed no sign of my motel manager. In the dim light from a single table lamp, I saw that the room looked much the same as it had before, except now the outboard engine was missing from the table, and in its place was a huge cast net, which was draped over the table and three chairs.

I rapped on the glass panes of the door. "Harry!" I called. "It's me. BeBe Loudermilk. Harry, are you home?"

No answer. I sighed and walked around to the front. I glanced at my watch. It was starting to get dark, nearly five-thirty now, and it was getting colder too. I thought longingly of that ugly woodstove inside the log cabin. Then I thought about my favorite winter coat, the soft, camel-colored quilted jacket with the Burberry lining, and the cashmere Burberry scarf I always wore with it. The jacket and the scarf had been in my bedroom closet in the West Jones Street house. My house. My home. Gone, all of it. I shivered and pulled up the collar of the worn red sweater Weezie had donated to my clothing cause.

Damn Harry Sorrentino. Where was the man? I didn't want to just move in and kick him out without giving him the benefit of my speech. But really, enough was enough. I was cold and tired, and come to think of it, hungry too. For a moment, I regretted not sampling one of Marian Foley's weird orange Nehi muffins. But only for a moment.

Suddenly, I remembered the money Granddaddy had given me, and patted the pocket of my jeans just to reassure myself that the money was still there. I could leave this godforsaken place, check into the Holiday Inn down the street, go out and have a nice seafood dinner someplace, then go back and go to sleep on a real bed, without the Weather Channel droning in my ear, without listening to people shuffling to and from the bathroom, without the springs of my grandparents' Hide-A-Bed poking me in the ribs.

I got back behind the wheel of the Lexus, and even started to back out of the parking lot before changing my mind.

No, I thought. Hell no. Sure, I could check into a motel, and the money would last for a few days, but what would I do when the money ran out? Go sniveling back to my grandparents for another handout? Admit to them that I was homeless and penniless, and worse, that they were probably well on their way to the poor farm too, thanks to my stupidity?

Oh no. For better or worse, I was now the owner and sole proprietor of the Breeze Inn. And Harry Sorrentino could just get used to it. Whenever he showed up again. *If* he ever showed up again.

I made a quick trip to the Tybee Market for dinner supplies. I'd resigned myself to finding only the barest of necessities in the old-timey grocery store, but was amazed by what I found. A full-service deli, baked goods, even fresh seafood and decent produce. I paused in front of the meat case and drooled over a display of fresh-made crab cakes, and a display of iced-down, fresh-caught shrimp, but steeled myself against such profligate spending and settled instead for dinner makings consisting of a can of tomato soup, a box of crackers, and for a splurge, a bottle of California chardonnay and a chunk of aged cheddar cheese.

When I got back to the Breeze there was still no sign of Harry. Which was a good sign, I told myself. Still, after I unlocked the front door of the log cabin, I stood for a long time before stepping over the threshold.

"Harry?" My voice cracked a little, with unaccustomed uncertainty. I gave it one more try. "Harry?"

I set my grocery sack on the kitchen counter, and my Winn-Dixie luggage on the wing chair facing the television set. I had to unload half a case of Heineken just to put my groceries in the small refrigerator. In the kitchen, pots and pans were stacked neatly in a wooden cupboard beside the stove, and I felt a small involuntary twinge of guilt as I dumped a can of soup into a small copper-bottomed saucepan, then put it on the stove to heat.

Another twinge hit me as I went to open what must surely have been the bedroom door. During my first visit here, Harry had been distinctly territorial about his private quarters.

I shrugged and opened the door anyway. *His* quarters were now *mine*. The room was larger than I'd expected, although still only half the size of my bedroom on West Jones Street. An old iron bed with a sagging mattress, covered with a faded, though neatly arranged pink chenille bedspread, took up the wall facing a bank of three windows. Old wooden fruit crates stood on end for nightstands on both sides of the bed. A wooden splat-back chair and cheap Formica-topped dresser were the only other pieces of furniture in the room. The linoleum floor, although bare, was swept clean.

I opened a narrow door and found the closet. It was the size of my broom closet at home, and the single wooden rod held a few cotton dress shirts and some khaki slacks. I checked the shirt labels, feeling guilty again. Polo by Ralph Lauren. What was this beach-bum type doing with dress shirts that retailed for seventy bucks apiece? I wondered. I ran my hand across the rest of the clothes and was surprised to see a navy wool blazer hanging at the end of the clothes rod. The wool was dove soft, good quality, so I felt no compunction at all about checking the label. Hmm. The satin label was from J. Parker's, the nicest men's store in Savannah.

The top shelf of the closet held a single suitcase. Good. I lifted the suitcase down and set it on the bed. I took my time folding the clothes neatly and stacking them in the suitcase. I hesitated as I turned to face the dresser, and caught a glimpse of myself in the wavy glass of the mirror. Who was this person? What was she doing here?

Shirts, trousers, and jackets were one thing. But that dresser probably held everything Harry Sorrentino owned. Personal things. It was one thing to pack up the closet. But it was another thing altogether to delve into a stranger's dresser drawers. I thought about how I'd felt that awful morning I'd peered through the windows of the West Jones Street house and seen the bare floors where my carpets had once lain, the naked walls and windows where my paintings and drapes had once hung. I thought about how I'd felt when I'd discovered that everything, absolutely *everything* I owned that was not on my back or in my car had been packed up and hauled off by strangers.

I shivered again as I thought about strange men running their hands through my lingerie, dumping my shirts and dresses and sweaters and shoes into cardboard cartons. I could hear them talking about me, about my things, feel their sweaty hands on the flesh of my neck. I sank down onto the bed and sighed. This I could not do to Harry Sorrentino.

Yes, Harry would have to move out. There was no other way. But I wouldn't take from Harry Sorrentino what Reddy Millbanks—or whatever his name was—had taken from me. I unpacked the suitcase, hung the clothes where I'd found them, and went out to the kitchen to eat my soup and wait for Harry to come home.

I gingerly folded back one corner of the cast net and ate my supper with the television on, nibbling slowly at the cheese and crackers, keeping one ear cocked for the sound of a car in the parking lot. I felt like Goldilocks, waiting for the three bears to return home.

It was cold in the little cabin. I looked around vainly for a thermostat and finally, glumly, conceded that my new home's only heat was that potbellied stove in the main room. Damn. The West Jones Street house had four fireplaces, but I'd long ago had them all retrofitted with gas logs. The closest I ever came to fire building these days was to push the remote-control button that ignited them.

I sighed and got up to fetch wood, but shrank back when I opened the front door and a gust of wind blew it back in my face. I went into the bedroom, opened the closet doors, and helped myself to a heavy wool-plaid shirt I'd seen there. It was Pendleton. Whoever had bought it the first time around had paid a lot for this shirt. The sleeves hung down to my knees, but I rolled them to my wrists, turned up the collar, and went out to face the elements again in my borrowed finery. At least there was wood. I'd seen it on the porch of the cabin earlier, a tall stack of it, the edge peeking out from a blue tarp. I fetched an armload of logs, topped it with a handful of kindling from an old iron kettle near the door, and went back inside to try and remember my Girl Scout training. Crouching in front of the iron stove, I arranged the wood as our scout leader, Miss Betsy, had instructed all those years ago, in a sort of tepee affair, with the kindling at the bottom, and then crumpled and twisted a sheet of newspaper to act as a torch, holding my breath as I watched the little orange flames lick at the edges of the kindling.

"Come on, baby," I whispered, unable to take my eyes from my creation. "Burn, baby, burn."

When the sticks of kindling flared up, I clapped my hands in delight. "Merit badge!" To celebrate my new survival prowess, I opened the bottle of chardonnay, and sat cross-legged on the floor, sipping wine and watching my fire catch and burn. I found the television's remote control wedged into the arm of the recliner, but there was nothing on except reality shows and bad sitcoms. Annoyed, I shut the television off and went roaming around the room looking for something to read to kill the time.

Harry's taste in reading was definitely different. I found what looked to be a complete set of first-edition P. G. Wodehouse, as well as what was probably the definitive body of John D. MacDonald's life's work, not to mention at least two dozen books about the history of Cuba, one whole shelf of law-school textbooks, and a new-looking autographed copy of *The Perfect Storm*. Odd. I picked up one of the law books, a torts case study, and found it dog-eared and heavily underlined with green highlighter.

I picked out a Travis McGee paperback with a particularly garish illustration of a raven-haired woman staring down the barrel of a snub-nosed pistol, sat down in the recliner, and slowly immersed myself in the world of the Bahia Mar marina, a place where the gin was cold, the women hot, the steaks rare, and valor even rarer. Now that I thought about it, I remembered that my father had a collection of ratty paperback books like these, which he kept behind closed doors in his den. Boy books. I'd never read a single one, but maybe tonight was the night to give old John D. a try.

The language was so archaic, so politically incorrect, I had to laugh. Travis McGee's various women were described as cookies, bunnies, beach kittens, hotsies, or broads. He'd never get away with that crap today. Still, there was something to the storytelling, to the honest, unapologetic, yet incredibly evocative way McGee captured pre-Disney Florida, that reminded me of Savannah, way back when. I found myself turning pages eagerly, immersing myself in the world of the *Busted Flush*. I could taste the humidity of a cypress swamp, hear the buzz of gnats, see the golden sunlight filtering through a curtain of Spanish moss.

Finally, between the heat from the fire and the chardonnay, I started to feel warmth seeping into my body. I leaned the recliner back a little and closed my eyes, suddenly, unavoidably drowsy. At some point, I heard the book fall to the floor. I should pick it up, I thought. Wash out my dinner dishes. Brush my teeth. Floss. Moisturize. Ah, the hell with it. That was my last conscious thought.

Now I was in dreamland, a bikini-clad beach kitten, snuggled up in the stateroom of the *Busted Flush*, admiring the bronzed brute that was Travis McGee, who'd just saved me from a vicious pack of greedy real estate developers. I tossed my long mane of platinum hair and demurely began to unfasten my bikini top, letting my sun-ripened breasts spill—

"Hey!"

The voice was loud, obnoxious, right in my ear. "What the hell? What the hell do you think you're doing here?"

"Trav?"

"What the hell?"

It was Harry Sorrentino, not Travis McGee, standing there, eyes blazing with righteous indignation, glaring daggers at me. I sat upright, confused, disoriented. Where was I? Who was I?

I rubbed the sleep out of my eyes, trying to make sense of things.

Ah yes, now it came to me. I was BeBe Loudermilk. Failed deb, failed divorcée, penniless, homeless. And about to disenfranchise the wild-eyed maniac standing before me.

"So you're back," I said, struggling for my dignity.

"Obviously," he said. "I live here, remember?"

"Yes," I said. "I'm aware of that."

"So. What the hell are you doing here, at midnight, wearing my shirt, asleep in my chair? And more to the point, what the hell did you do with my beer?"

"Beer?" I said, blinking rapidly, trying to think back. "I didn't drink any beer."

He held up the half bottle of chardonnay. "No. You were drinking this. But you took all my beer out of my refrigerator."

"Yes," I said, again. "I did."

He ran his fingers through his hair, leaving a crop of brown spikes standing on end. "Let me ask you again. What the hell are you doing here?"

I pushed the recliner upright. "I came to tell you something. But you weren't here. I waited a long time, but it got late, and I was tired, so I fell asleep."

"What gives you the right to just walk right in here?" he demanded. "What gives you the right to rifle through my belongings, help yourself to my clothes, and by God, what gives you the *right* to let all my beer get warm?"

I stood up and looked him right in the eye. "Not all of it," I said. "There are still two bottles in the refrigerator. On the bottom shelf. Behind the soy milk."

He turned abruptly and stalked into the kitchen. I heard things being shoved aside, and then the sound of clinking bottles, and then the pop and soft fizz of a bottle being opened.

And then he was right back in my face. He had a finger laced around the neck of one bottle. It was half empty. And he had the other bottle in his other hand.

"Let's try this again," he said, taking a long pull from the bottle. "What the *fuck* do you think you're doing here?"

I was trying hard to remember the salient points of the speech I'd composed on the drive out to Tybee. But it was late, and I was woozy.

"I own this place," I said.

"Unfortunately, I'm aware of that fact," he said. He glanced at the half-empty wine bottle. "Are you drunk?" He frowned. "Oh. I get it. You're one of those downtown designer-drug types, right? Is that it? Well, I suggest you don't try to drive back to town, because the Thunderbolt cops will stop you, sure as hell, and throw your cute little ass in the clink. They just love catching drugged-out debs like you."

"No!" I said, shrilly. "I don't do drugs. I had two glasses of wine. Hours ago. I'm just tired, that's all. I haven't been sleeping very well lately."

"Boo-hoo," he said. "Now, could you please go home? It's been a long night. I'm tired myself, and I've got a long day tomorrow."

"I *am* home," I said. "That's why I came out here. To tell you the situation. And explain my plan."

"Plan?" He raised one eyebrow. The dog—Jeeves? The same furry white terrier type I'd seen the other day came trotting into the room. He barked one short, indignant bark, baring his teeth at me momentarily, before jumping into the recliner I'd just vacated. The dog turned once, twice, then snuggled itself down into the faded green upholstery, tucking its muzzle down into its paws with a sigh.

"Plan?" Harry leaned over and scratched the dog between its ears. "Why do I need to hear your plan, at midnight, in my living room?"

It was my turn to sigh. Clearly, he wasn't going to make this any easier for me.

"Look," I started. "This is not how I wanted to do this. I came out here this afternoon, to tell you. Explain, really, why things have to change."

He crossed his arms over his chest. "And why do they have to change?"

"Because this is about business," I said, my face flushing, feeling myself going on the defensive. "The Breeze Inn is a business. It may not be a going concern right now. It may, in fact, be a piece-of-crap investment. But, nevertheless, this motel is sitting on a very valuable piece of oceanfront real estate."

"I'm aware of that," he said testily.

"Then you must also be aware of the situation I'm in. Through no fault of mine, some real estate developer has bought an option to develop this property. As I told you before, I had nothing to do with that. My lawyer is working to rectify the situation."

"Your lawyer," he said, smirking. "Why doesn't that make me feel any better?"

"The point is, until we straighten out that situation, I need to make the Breeze Inn into a profitable business."

"And?"

I straightened my shoulders, suddenly aware that they were clad in *his* shirt. "I feel I need to live on-site. And supervise the renovations. Hands on. As it were."

"Here?" He gestured around the room. "You think you're going to live here?"

"Well," I hesitated. "Yes. That's why I came out here today. To tell you that I'll be moving in. And you'll be, um, moving out."

He ran his fingers through his hair again, flattening out what he'd previously uprooted. He chewed the side of his jaw while he thought about things.

"The hell you say."

"Yes."

"Just like that."

"Well, yes. I'm sorry. But there it is. I was thinking, you could move into another unit. Maybe number seven, the one I looked at yesterday. It's a little primitive, I'll admit. But you did say you had the toilets ordered, and the roof is done."

"Are you nuts? I can't get that unit ready in less than a week. Anyway, what's your hurry? I told you, I've got things under control. Some plumbing, some roofing, paint. Ten days, it'll be ready to rent. Okay? Ten days. I swear." He managed a lopsided grin.

"Hmmpph." We both turned to stare at the recliner. Jeeves was sound asleep, sighing in his sleep. The sleep of the innocent, I thought.

"The thing is," I said. "I'm moving in here. Right away."

He stared at me, still not comprehending. "Here?"

"Right here," I said. "Right now."

19

Harry's eyes narrowed. "You can't do that. You can't just stroll in here, unannounced, and toss me out. In the middle of the night."

"It wasn't the middle of the night when I got here. It was still daylight. And you weren't around. I had no idea where you were."

"It's none of your *business* where I was," he said, his voice low. "I don't have to answer to you."

The dog sat up suddenly, sniffing the air. Maybe he smelled blood.

"Look," I said. "This is getting us nowhere. It's late. I'm tired, you're tired. Why don't you just go bunk with a friend tonight, and then tomorrow, you can start getting unit seven ready to move into."

"No way," he said, turning on his heel and heading for the kitchen. I watched him, speechless. Was he going to get another beer? A knife maybe?

"You can't bully me, you know," I called after him. "Better men than you have tried, and failed. So just face it. I'm here, and I'm staying."

He clomped back across the room toward me, his arms loaded with folded sheets, a pillow, and a blanket, which he thrust, unceremoniously, into my arms.

"You wanna stay, fine," he said. "The bedroom's taken. I see you figured out how to work the woodstove. If I were you, I'd stoke it up a little more before turning in. It's supposed to get down to forty tonight, and there's no insulation in these walls. See you in the morning."

Before I could say anything, he was gone, slamming the bedroom door behind him. Moments later I heard the rasp of a bolt sliding into place.

"Hey!" I called after him. "We're not done here."

"I am."

I wouldn't give him the satisfaction of hammering on the bedroom door, demanding that he vacate it. For tonight, and tonight only, I would sleep out here. I turned toward the recliner.

Jeeves sat straight up and bared his teeth, a low growl emanating from the back of his throat. "Okay," I said, backing away. "I get the message. I'll try the sofa."

After shoving as many logs into the stove as I could, I spread the sheets and blankets out on the sofa and tried to make myself comfortable, which was a laugh. The sofa looked like something Weezie would have put in a beach house, one of those three-seater rattan numbers, with a narrow seat and three pitifully thin foam-rubber cushions. I turned this way and that, wedged myself against the back, and, finally, exhausted, fell asleep.

Minutes later, it seemed, I heard water running. I opened one eye, then closed it again. It was still pitch-black outside. I'd taken off my watch, but surely it couldn't be much more than two in the morning. Cold. It was cold as a tomb in the room. I pulled the thin woolen blanket over my head and tried to burrow down into the sheets for warmth. I prayed that Harry Sorrentino would come out and stoke up the fire again. Or offer me another blanket. Or better yet, the bedroom. I'd seen a small kerosene heater in there the night before. That bedroom would be toasty warm by now.

I sat up and pulled the blanket around my shoulders. The bedroom door was ajar, and the bathroom door was closed. Puffs of steam escaped under the door. Pale purple light struggled through the glass panes of the French doors. Could it be sunrise, already? I got up, wrapped the blanket around myself, papoose style, then padded over to the doors to look outside.

A stand of beach myrtles, palmettos, and wind-sculpted pines stood out in sharp contrast to the white of the dunes beyond. Off in the distance, I could see the silver of the Atlantic, through a fringe of waving sea oats, illuminated by the slowly rising sun.

I stared out at the peaceful scene. Could this be Tybee? Standing here, staring out at that small, barren stretch of seascape, I could have been on my own private island.

As I watched, a small, stooped figure came marching rapidly down the beach. His bare, bony brown chest gleamed in the gathering sunlight, as did his completely bald head. Long, bony arms pumped at his sides. He wore a skimpy blue Speedo bathing suit, and nothing else except for a set of headphones. I shivered involuntarily. As the old man jogged, his head swung from side to side, and now, an ancient black Labrador retriever came bounding along behind him, crashing joyfully through the surf.

The bathroom door opened then, and Harry Sorrentino emerged in a cloud of steam. His hair was damp, he wore weathered blue jeans and a plaid flannel shirt. His face was red and I could see a place on his chin where he'd nicked himself shaving.

"So you're up," he said, nodding in my direction. He strode over to the front door, held it ajar, and gave a sharp whistle. "Jeeves!" he called.

The terrier sat up, blinked, and stretched.

"Come on, boy," Harry called. "Let's go pee."

I hurried in the direction of the vacated bathroom, thinking it was the first good idea I'd heard from him.

By the time I'd showered and changed, it was fully daylight. The worn wooden walls of the cabin were bathed in the morning sun, and the fire in the little woodstove was crackling merrily. The scent of fresh-brewed coffee and frying bacon wafted from the kitchen. Harry stood at the stove, his back to me, and Jeeves beside him, tail thumping on the floor, obviously waiting for breakfast to be served.

The sheets and blankets on the rattan sofa had disappeared. It was as if he'd deliberately obliterated any sign of my existence there the night before.

I stowed my stuff back in the Winn-Dixie bag, which he'd pointedly set beside the front door.

"Coffee?" He slid a full mug down the kitchen counter in my general direction.

I wasn't too proud to take it, seizing it eagerly between my hands and inhaling the rich smell.

"We need to talk," I said, between sips.

"I've said what I need to say," he said, flipping strips of bacon onto a paper-towel-covered platter. "I had a deal. I've put in hundreds of hours on this place and not been paid a damn dime. It may not look like much to you, but when I moved in over here, there was no hot-water heater. The roof leaked like a sieve, the foundation was about to cave in, the wiring was shot, and all the plumbing was rusted through. I've fixed all that and more. Now you waltz in here, say the deal's off. New owner, new plan. Your new plan leaves me out in the cold and I don't like it worth a damn."

"I said you could stay on here," I started.

"No. You said I had to move out. As of last night. Offered to let me live in one of the other units, when I've already told you it'll take me at least a week to get one of 'em ready to move into." He turned and gave me a sardonic smile. "Mighty white of you."

He flipped a piece of bacon in the dog's direction and Jeeves leaped up and caught it in midair.

I frowned. "That can't be good for him."

"You let me worry about what's good for my dog," Harry snapped. "We were getting along fine until you showed up here."

I started to say something, but thought better of it.

"Anyway, as you say, you do own the place now. And if you want to move in out here, although I don't understand why you'd want to, there's nothing I can do to stop you. Which leaves me and Jeeves here out in the cold. Nothing I can do about it. The Reeses and I didn't have any kind of a contract, just an oral agreement, which we both know isn't binding in any kind of court of law."

He turned the burner off and pushed the frying pan to the back of the stove, then walked over to the table and got a piece of paper, which he brusquely handed me.

"What's this?"

"Just a statement of what I'm owed," he said, going back to the stove to pour himself a mug of coffee. "Skilled workmen get fourteen dollars an hour, anyplace out here they want to work. I only billed you for ten an hour. The difference is what I'd have paid in rent to stay here. The way I figure it, with what I've paid out for materials and what I'm owed for labor, figure twenty hours a week, for six months, it comes out to around $4,800."

I stared down at the piece of paper and then up at him.

"This is the way you figure it," I said, taking a deep breath.

"That's right," he said. "Pay me what I'm owed and I'm out of here."

"Forty-eight hundred dollars," I repeated.

"Might not be a lot to you, but it's a living wage to me," he said, sipping his coffee. "Moving into a new place, I'll have to pay first and last month's rent, utility deposits. Have to get somebody to help me move all my furniture."

I raised an eyebrow and looked around. "Your furniture?"

"Yes, ma'am. All this stuff is mine. The place was empty when I moved in. Except for the pigeons." He gave me a malicious grin then. "And the mice."

"Mice?"

"Mostly. Jeeves here took care of the one rat we saw." He slid two pieces of whole-wheat bread into the toaster and pushed down the lever.

I was trying hard to keep a poker face. I would not give him the satisfaction of screaming, "*Eek!* a mouse," and heading for the hills. "I'm glad Jeeves was on the job. I think mice are kinda cute, but it would be bad for business if word got out on the island that we had a rat problem."

"We?"

I sighed. His poker face was at least as good as mine. I was fairly sure the Savannah gossip mill was already churning with stories of BeBe Loudermilk's comeuppance. After all, Guale was closed, and my house had been sold. But this was Tybee, after all, and with any luck, Harry Sorrentino didn't know anybody in my rarified social circle. Still, I didn't know how much he knew about me, or about my dire financial straits. I had no intention of telling him that I didn't have $4,800 to pay him in back wages. And I certainly didn't intend to let him know that the Breeze Inn was truly my last resort.

"Good help's hard to get, I know," I said. "I'm not disputing that you've done the work, and you're owed compensation. And maybe I've been unreasonable about the living arrangement here. Surely we can come up with some kind of compromise. One that would allow you to continue living here on the property, and getting on with the repairs, but at the same time allow me to put all my capital into completing the repairs so we can start getting this business in the black."

He picked up a piece of bacon with his fingers, broke off a piece and flipped it to Jeeves, then ate the other half. My stomach growled. I was starving.

"What kind of compromise did you have in mind?" he asked.

I shrugged. "Which of the units is the closest to being ready to occupy?"

"Number two's pretty far along," he admitted. "The roof's done. Wiring's sound. Have to get the new hot-water heater hooked up. All those units have the old-timey built-in space heaters, but they're pretty simple, so I'm assuming it'll work. Other than that, it's just a matter of a lot of elbow grease."

"Fine," I said, finishing my coffee. "I've got elbow grease to spare. I'll get started this morning. How soon can you get the hot-water heater hooked up?"

"Soon as you buy one," he said. The toast popped up then. He folded a piece in half and slid in a couple of slices of bacon, then extended the sandwich toward me. "Breakfast, ma'am?"

He made himself a sandwich too, and we stood there in the kitchen, with our backs against the counter, chewing in companionable silence.

When we were done, I took some paper towels and wiped out the cast-iron skillet, then set it on the back burner. There was one slice of bacon on the platter. I looked at Sorrentino, and at Jeeves, who was sniffing around on the floor in hopes of seconds.

"Just one more piece," Harry said, nodding approval. "Bacon makes him fart."

I made a face, but knelt down and fed the dog the last bits of our breakfast. He nearly licked the skin off my fingertips in appreciation.

"All right," I said, after I'd wiped down the countertops and stove. "Guess you'd better give me a look at unit two."

"In a minute," he said, digging in his pocket. He brought out a penny and held it up for me to see.

"What's that for?"

"I'll flip you for it," he announced. "Heads I stay here, tails I move into unit two."

"No deal."

He pocketed the coin and headed for the door. "See you around."

I knew when I was beaten. "Never mind."

He made a big show of producing the coin again and flipping it into the air, then slapping it on the backside of his left hand.

I made a mental note to call Weezie as soon as possible. I was going to need some furniture in a hurry to move into unit two.

20

Three hours and $1,600 later, I stood in the checkout line at Home Depot and handed over my Visa card to the cashier with a trembling heart and shaking hands. I'd always been conservative with my credit, scrupulously paying off bank card balances every month, but as I stood in that line, it suddenly occurred to me that I had no idea whether or not Reddy had thought to help himself to my credit cards while he was looting the rest of my personal finances.

I was standing very still as the computer digested my credit card, just waiting for a big net to drop down over my head and a huge neon arrow to start flashing "Credit Declined." But nothing happened. The cashier handed back my Visa card, I signed the receipt, then bolted for the parking lot, just in case the credit gods changed their minds at the last minute.

By noon, nearly every inch of my being was covered with dirt, grease, or paint spatters. Unit two, it turned out, was a long way from being habitable. It did, as Harry had promised, have working plumbing and wiring. And a roof. But the rest of the place was a shambles.

"Home sweet hovel," I mumbled, standing in the middle of my new residence, taking stock. To call the space a cottage would have been charitable. It was a smallish, rectangular room. There was a stunted, fly-specked picture window that looked out on a sand dune, which could, I supposed, count as a beach view. The wind whistled through gaps in the window frame.

"A little caulk will take care of that," Harry noted as he saw me stuffing newspaper in the cracks.

The wall opposite the window had been designed as a sleeping alcove, with built-in shelves for lamps and a bookshelf headboard. The whole unit was covered with forties vintage knotty-pine paneling, gone nearly black with age.

Another alcove held the abbreviated kitchen, which was identical to the one in unit seven—the one Weezie had found so charming. I opened the tiny refrigerator door and gasped at the stench that flowed out. But Harry patted the door lovingly. "Works great," he said. "Feel that cold air? A little bleach and it'll be good as new."

He knelt down in front of the wall heater, fiddled with a knob, and after five minutes, of ominous metallic banging noises, the exposed heating coils glowed red with heat. In another five minutes, we had to open the door and all the windows to cool things down a little. "Heat's fine," he pronounced.

The bathroom was, as far as I was concerned, a total loss. The porcelain coating of the cast-iron tub was pitted and gray, the tile floors chipped and stained, and the pedestal sink had a bowl but no faucets.

My face went pale as I stood there, wondering what I'd gotten myself into.

What would Mama say?

Maybe, I thought, it was time to let my grandparents in on my situation. Once I explained, they would welcome me back to the sofa bed at Magnolia Manor. And I'd be grateful, this time around. At least at my grandparents' house, I'd had indoor plumbing, heat, and some sort of amenities for basic hygiene. This, I thought, was worse than the worst public bathroom I'd ever experienced in my youthful backpacking days in Europe.

"Okay," Harry said cheerfully. "Better get cracking if you're planning on moving in tonight."

I spent the next two hours with a crowbar, pry bar, and blowtorch, peeling back and ripping up layers of disintegrating carpet and crumbling linoleum tiles, only to find underneath not the heart-pine floors I'd secretly anticipated, but instead, deeply scarred floors that were a patchwork combination of oak, pine, and some other, unidentified kind of wood. Trailer siding, maybe.

"Oh God," I said, moaning. "This is useless."

"Now what?" Harry asked, looking in from the bathroom, where he'd been installing the hot-water heater and the new toilet. I pointed at the floor.

"We could put down some new carpet, but that's going to eat into your budget."

"No more carpet. I've got a better idea. Have we got any white enamel?"

"Sure," he said. "Gallons of it. Out in the toolshed. You're gonna paint the floor?"

"The floor, the walls, the trim, anything that doesn't move," I said.

I found a long-handled extension for the paint roller, a five-gallon bucket of white latex enamel, and reserves of energy I didn't know I possessed. I tackled the walls first.

"Hey," Harry protested, looking in again from the bathroom. "That's authentic pine. You're ruining it."

"Stick to the plumbing," I advised him. "And I'll stick to the design decisions."

The old paneling seemed to suck up every drop of paint in my bucket, but within an hour, I had the walls covered.

"Not bad," Harry decided, tracking through the room with some faucets he'd salvaged from the toolshed. He pointed to a corner near the sleeping alcove. "But you missed a spot." I took the roller and promptly painted it, and then added a stripe to the front of his gray T-shirt.

"You were warned," I said.

He just shook his head and walked away.

At three, I took a lunch break, and called Weezie to report in.

"How's it going?" she asked.

"It's going," I said.

"I told Mama about your little project," Weezie said.

"She knows? About Reddy, and all that?"

"No! I just told her that you've bought the Breeze Inn and have moved out there," Weezie assured me. "She said she and Daddy spent a weekend out at the Breeze Inn when they were first married. Called it her little honeymoon cottage. She's dying to come take a look. She wants to know how she can help out."

"I don't know," I said dubiously. "It's pretty awful."

"Why don't you just plan to come into town and spend tonight with us?" Weezie asked. She lowered her voice to a whisper. "She's in the other room, making tuna-noodle casserole. If our friendship ever really meant anything to you, you'd come over here and help me flush that slop down the commode."

"As alluring as that invitation is," I said, "I'm gonna take a rain check. I really just wanted to know if you can put some furniture together for me."

"Furniture?" Weezie laughed. "Does Ethel Kennedy have a black dress? Honey, I have been mentally decorating that whole motel ever since I laid eyes on it. You just tell me what time you want me there with the truck."

"I can't pay you anything," I warned. "Not right now. I just loaded up my Visa card at the Home Depot today, and there's no telling how much more I'm going to have to spend to get the rest of these units whipped into shape."

"Pay me?" Weezie hooted. "Are you forgetting the interest-free loan you made me when I was starting up Maisie's Daisy? How you bailed me out of jail after that awful night out at Beaulieu, when the cops were sure I'd killed Caroline DeSantos?"

"That's ancient history," I pointed out. "You paid me back as soon as you got on your feet. But I don't honestly know when or if I'll be able to pay you back."

"You let me worry about that," Weezie scolded. "Just tell me what all you need."

"There's not room for much. A bed, for sure. Dresser, table, and a couple of chairs. Something else to sit on. And a big bottle of ibuprofen. Every muscle in my body is screaming for mercy, and I haven't even gotten to the kitchen or the bathroom yet."

"Consider it done," Weezie said. "Want me to bring the furniture out tonight?"

"Doubtful," I said. "The paint won't be dry enough. I'll call you tomorrow."

"Wait," Weezie said. "God, I almost forgot. James called. He needs to talk to you and your cell phone isn't working."

"I turned it off. Can't pay the bill. Did James say what he wanted to tell me?"

"Sorry. He just said to tell you to give him a call."

I was dialing James when Harry walked in. I hurriedly put down the receiver.

"Your toilet's hooked up. And you've got hot water," he announced. He washed his hands at the kitchen sink, grabbed the keys to his station wagon, and whistled for Jeeves, who'd been napping in his recliner.

"See you later," he said, heading for the door with Jeeves hot on his heels.

"Wait." I followed him to the door. "You're leaving? What about all the work we've got to do yet in unit two?"

"It'll get there," he said. "There's more paint out in the shed. And when you quit for the night, make sure you lock it up. All my power tools and fishing gear's out there, and I don't want anybody walking off with it. Stuff's expensive."

"Where are you going?" I demanded. "It's only three o'clock. I can't fix that place up all by myself. I thought we had a deal."

"We do," Harry said, getting into the station wagon and starting the engine. "My part's done. The rest is up to you. Guess you've got the sofa for at least another night. And don't forget to bring in enough firewood. See you."

He spun out of the parking lot in a cloud of dust.

I stood there cussing him for a minute, then went back to the manager's office to call my lawyer.

"Please tell me you've got some good news," I said when James Foley came on the line.

"All right," he said amicably. "I just got back from the doctor's office. My cholesterol's down. And I've lost two pounds since my last checkup. Jonathan has been making me walk almost every day in Forsyth Park."

"I'm glad," I said. "But I was hoping for some good news that concerned me."

"Oh," he said. "Well, sure. Jay Bradley thinks he may have a line on Reddy."

"Where is he? Have they arrested him?"

"Not even close," James said with a little too much cheer. "Jay's pretty sure he's down in Florida somewhere. But it's a big state."

"I know you said the cops think he ripped off another woman down there, but wouldn't he have left the state after that? Like he did with me?"

"If he had any sense, he would have left," James agreed. "But Florida's nice in the wintertime. All that sunshine. And ocean. And all those big, beautiful boats."

"Boats? What's that got to do with anything?"

"Jay Bradley went back to talk to Jimmy Yglesias, the owner of the *Blue Moon*, the yacht Roy 'borrowed' while he was living in Savannah," James said. "And while he was sitting in the yacht's wheelhouse, he happened to notice a little brass plaque on the yacht's steering console. 'Sea Urchin.' So he asked about the meaning of that, and Yglesias told him that's the name of the *Blue Moon*'s manufacturer. It's kind of an unusual company name. Sea Urchin. The Sea Urchin Corporation of Charlevoix, Michigan. And that's when Bradley remembered that woman down in Vero Beach. So he called the detective who'd worked that case to see if there'd been any new developments."

"Had there been?"

"There weren't any new developments. But Bradley asked the detective if the Vero Beach victim owned a boat. Why, yes, the detective said, as a matter of fact, the victim's late husband owned a seventy-two-foot yacht called *Polly's Folly*. Polly Findley is the woman's name. And that's how the woman came to meet Moseley. She and some friends were having lunch aboard the *Folly* one day at the marina when Moseley pulled alongside in another boat, and struck up a conversation with her. One thing led to another, and pretty soon they were 'keeping company.'"

"Screwing, you mean," I said bitterly.

"If you say so," James said. "Now here's the interesting part, BeBe. *Polly's Folly* was manufactured by the Sea Urchin Corporation of Charlevoix, Michigan."

"I guess it's interesting if you say so," I said. "So Roy likes yachts. And wealthy women. We already knew that much."

"We didn't know how much he likes this one specific kind of yacht," James said.

"Janet's been doing some research on Sea Urchin. It's a very small, highly successful family-owned shipbuilder. Very high end. Everything is done by hand. These boats are considered the Bentleys of yachts. The company only builds maybe eight a year. And Roy Eugene Moseley has been involved with two Sea Urchins just in the past year."

"Okay," I said. "I guess that's a start. But how does that help us track down Moseley?"

"We don't know yet," James said. "We just know Moseley likes Sea Urchin yachts. We know he was probably thinking about stealing the *Blue Moon*, until he got sidetracked with you. And there's a possibility he had the same idea about *Polly's Folly* too. He almost had Mrs.

Findley talked into letting him take it down to Costa Rica in October. But her children got wind of the plan and put a stop to it. So he settled for fleecing her instead."

"Too bad he didn't get to steal the damn boat," I said gloomily. "Maybe he would have sailed off into the sunset before meeting me."

"Doubtful," James said. "Look, BeBe, this really is good news. Bradley's talking to the Sea Urchin folks. They have a national registry of owners of their yachts. If they'll cooperate with the police, there may be a way to see if there are any other victims. Or if he's working on somebody right now. Anyway, I thought you'd be delighted that the police think they have a way to track down Moseley."

"I'm sorry, James," I said, regretting my sour-grapes attitude. "It's just this Breeze Inn situation has got me down. I'm tired and I'm broke, and the place is a wreck, and I've been working all day, but it's just a filthy, awful stinkhole. I don't see how I can turn it around. I really don't." I felt myself close to tears, and when I went to wipe my eyes I noticed that my hand was streaked with paint, and now my face was surely just as streaked. I sniffed pitifully.

"Are you crying?" James asked. "Oh, child, don't start crying. You'll make me feel like a priest again. Pretty soon I'll be telling you to make a novena."

"But I'm not even Catholic," I said, laughing despite the tears. "And you're not a priest anymore."

"Thank the Lord," James said fervently. "But I still have my faith. And you need to have faith too. We're going to set this right. We're going to find Roy Eugene Moseley, and get your money back. And we'll get the Breeze Inn thing straightened out too. Arrendale and his Sandcastle buddies don't have a legal leg to stand on with this option thing. It's all a house of cards. You'll see."

"Hope so," I said.

"I promise," James said. "Now go take a walk on the beach. It'll make you feel better."

"I doubt it," I said. "Anyway, I can't take a walk right now. I've got a bathroom to scrub."

"Walk first, scrub later," James said firmly. "That bathroom isn't going anyplace."

I put down the phone and, despite my best intentions, found myself staring out the window at the beach. The tide had gone out, and the sand was a dull battleship gray. A flock of seabirds skimmed low over the water, and I thought I could see a sailboat, way out in the sound, but they were the only signs of life in sight.

Maybe, I thought, James is right. My scuzzy bathroom could wait. The beach was right outside my back door. Even now, developers were circling around the Breeze Inn and Tybee Island like buzzards, trying to snap up even the smallest, most pathetic piece of beachfront property. Maybe I should go out, walk on the beach and get a sense of what was such a big deal to the rest of the world.

21

I found a plank walkway that led me out over the dunes, and without giving it a second thought, peeled off my socks and sneakers.

The minute my toes hit the cold, damp sand, I started to regret my hasty decision to go barefoot.

Too late now, I thought, rolling up the hem of my blue jeans, and at the same time noting the sorry state of my toes. The jaunty red polish my manicurist had applied weeks ago was chipped and faded now, and my cheap sneakers had rubbed blisters on my toes. But a $25 pedicure was definitely no longer a line item in my personal budget.

I walked down to the water's edge and dug my toes into the damp gray sand, cringing a little, yet expecting something magical to happen.

Off in the distance, two sailboats glided across the horizon, and I could see the lights of a much larger boat, cruising in the direction of the Back River. Was it a yacht? Maybe a Sea Urchin, the kind my darling, diabolical lover preferred?

I bit my lip. Somewhere down in Florida, the suave sophisticate I'd known as Reddy Millbanks was charming some other deluded dame out of her panties. Was he wining and dining her with *my* money, while I ate canned soup and slept in a motel even the fleas had checked out of? Was Reddy sending *her* pink roses like the ones he'd sent me? I chewed at the inside of my cheek. Soon, I thought, it'll be payback time.

In the meantime, I vowed, I would take the pig's ear Reddy had left me and turn it into a cash cow. I'd done it with Guale, I'd done it with my investment properties, and I'd do it again, God willing. That last thought made me grin. Have faith, James had implored me. Might as well, since faith was currently the only capital I possessed.

The cry of a seagull suddenly echoed overhead, and I instinctively covered my head with my arms. At the last minute, the flock of birds veered away, out across the water. Maybe not getting pooped on was the only magic I was going to see that day. I turned and looked up and down the beach. To the north, I saw a black dog running back and forth along the shoreline, playing tag with the waves. I started walking in that direction.

As I walked, I marveled at how quiet the beach was this time of year. Just me, some seagulls, and one black dog. And, oh, yes, when the wind changed, the whine of a power saw and the rhythmic banging of hammers on nails. I shaded my eyes to see where the noise was coming from. There it was, a couple of hundred yards down the beach, rising just on the other side of the dunes, the plywood skeleton of a whole block of humongous houses. I counted rooftops and realized there were fourteen new houses going up on that one tiny strip of land. Four stories tall, they would blot out any bit of shoreline left on that part of the beach.

I kept walking. When I got close to the construction site, I heard a long, low, wolf whistle. "Hey, *chica!*" a male voice called out. "Whachu doin' tonight?"

"Painting!" I should have yelled back. "Wanna come over and help?" But I didn't. I kept on walking, with my head held high, acting as if I hadn't heard.

As I got closer to the dog, I realized it was the same black Lab I'd seen that morning. He had the same red bandanna tied around his neck. Sitting on a blanket spread out, with the dunes to his back, was the same old man. Mercifully, he had on a shirt now, and a pair of blue nylon running shorts. A silver bicycle lay in the sand beside him.

"Are you all right?" I called out, picking up the pace. Maybe he'd fallen off the bike. Maybe he was injured, or disoriented.

"What's that?" he asked, turning his head toward me. "What'd you say?"

The old man's face was a mass of brown wrinkles. He had a neatly clipped white mustache, and up close, I could see the ropelike sinews of muscles beneath his tight white T-shirt. For an old dude, he was pretty buff.

I blushed. "I saw your bike there, and I thought maybe you needed help."

He laughed. "Oh no, I'm fine, thanks just the same. Buddy saw a horseshoe crab in the waves there, and he stopped to investigate, so I decided to take a breather too."

"Okay, then," I said, turning away. "Have a nice night."

"You too, young lady," he said. "Haven't seen you around here before, and I know most of the regulars on the island. Especially the pretty ones. You visitin'?"

I thought about that. "Nope," I said finally. "I live here. Just moved in."

"Whereabouts?" he said, and then "If you don't mind my asking."

"I don't mind," I said. "I live at the Breeze Inn."

His bright blue eyes widened. "Really. Thought the place was all closed up. Saw the signs about the new town houses. I figured that place was being torn down."

I grimaced. "It's kind of complicated. The developers who put up that sign were sort of jumping the gun. I own the Breeze Inn, and I'm not planning on tearing it down. Not right away, that is."

He nodded. "Glad to hear it." Then he scrambled nimbly to his feet and extended his hand. His grip was firm. "Mikey Shannon." He pointed toward the water. "And that's Buddy, the mighty horseshoe crab hunter."

"BeBe Loudermilk," I said. "Pleased to meet you."

"So you bought the old place from the Reeses, is that right?" he asked. "I heard the kids wanted to unload the place, after their dad had that heart attack, but we didn't know what was going to happen until that billboard went up."

"I own it now," I said, deciding to skip over the fine points about how I'd come to be in possession of such a prize.

"Then I reckon Harry Sorrentino's working for you now?" Mikey asked.

I blinked. It was amazing how quickly news traveled on this little island. Much faster than downtown. Tybee was obviously hardwired for fast-access gossip.

"Well, yes," I said finally. "Harry's helping me with repairs and things."

"Single, are you?"

I laughed. "Does it show?"

He gestured toward my left hand. "No ring. I notice these kinds of things."

"I see that."

"Good fella, Harry. Best fisherman on the island. Shame about his boat though."

"What happened to his boat?" I asked, my curiosity piqued. Harry hadn't exactly been forthcoming with a lot of details about how he made his livelihood.

"He didn't tell you?" Shannon asked. "All the fishermen out here had a terrible time of it last season. Three hurricanes in a row, the fish quit biting, and the charter business dried up too. And right when diesel prices went through the roof. The marina got a judgment against Harry for money he owed for fuel and ice and dock fees. Took the *Jitterbug* right out from under him. It's sitting up on blocks over there at Marsden Marina with a FOR SALE sign tacked to the bow. Damn shame for Harry."

"Terrible," I murmured.

"But a lucky break you got him working for you at the Breeze," Shannon said. "He's right popular with all the local ladies," he said slyly, his strong white teeth shining in his nut-brown face. "You could do worse for yourself than Harry Sorrentino."

I blushed. "I've got my hands pretty full taking on a new business, so I'm not really in the market for romance right now."

"Smart," the old man said, nodding. "Don't get your honey where you get your money, that's what I always say. Anyway, I imagine you'll have a lot to do getting the Breeze shaped up. I heard the kids kinda let the place go the past few years. Not that it was ever anything fancy."

"It's a work in progress," I agreed. Just then Buddy trotted up and dropped a large brown horseshoe crab right on my foot.

"Oh!" I blurted out, hopping backward in a hurry. To show his appreciation for my appreciation, the dog picked that moment to shake himself dry, showering me with a mist of ice-cold saltwater.

"Buddy!" Mikey said sharply. "Sit!"

The dog sat and bowed his head in shame.

"Sorry," Mikey said. He picked up a beach towel from his blanket and started dabbing me dry with it.

"It's all right," I said. "I was about to head back up to the motel anyway. I'll dry off when I get there."

"Bad dog," Mikey said, shaking a finger in the dog's face. "You scared off the first pretty girl I've hit on all day."

"Surely not the first," I said, looking at my watch. "I saw you running on the beach early this morning. You've had all day to practice your smooth moves."

He grinned again. "It's slow this time of year. Say, what are you doing for dinner? Why don't you let me buy you a burger at Fannie's?"

"Another time," I said.

"You a vegan or something?" he persisted. "Because you can get a salad there too. Or crab cakes. Or pasta."

"I'm a red-blooded meat eater," I assured him. "But I've got a lot of work to do tonight. I'm trying to get some of the units ready to rent for St. Patrick's Day. And, as you guessed, they really are a big mess. Give me a rain check?"

"Absolutely," Shannon said. "I'll drop by the Breeze and see how it's going."

"Better watch out," I said. "I might just put you to work."

"Deal," Mikey Shannon said. He looked out at the water. "You'd better get going, if you're headed back to the Breeze. Take the Seventeenth Street boardwalk and go back along Butler. It gets dark out here in a hurry."

I nodded in agreement and headed in the direction he'd pointed. The temperature was dropping, and my feet were freezing in the cold sand. When I got to the boardwalk, I sat down and put on my socks and shoes, grateful to have them dry, if sandy, again.

The Seventeenth Street boardwalk ended at Tybrisa, a narrow road lined on both sides with a Super 8 motel, an ice-cream shop, and bars and restaurants and souvenir shops, including the ancient T. S. Chu's department store.

At five o'clock, only a few cars were parked along Tybrisa, but one of them was a ratty old wood-sided Vista Cruiser station wagon. There couldn't have been two of them on Tybee.

I walked nonchalantly past the wagon, glancing inside to confirm my suspicions. A big sack of dog food lay in the back, along with a plastic five-gallon paint bucket.

So this was where Harry spent his afternoons and evenings. I glanced furtively up and down the row of businesses, wondering which one the wagon's owner was parked inside. I looked over at Doc's Bar, whose window proclaimed "Since 1948." A little terrier jumped up and down, barking and scratching at the plate-glass door.

Busted.

A moment later, the door opened and Jeeves ran out onto the sidewalk, barking an excited greeting.

"I think he likes you," Harry said, standing in the open doorway.

"He'll get over it," I said, bending down to scratch the dog's ears.

"How's the painting coming?" Harry asked.

"Okay," I said, suddenly tongue-tied and shy. "I was just taking a little break. Guess I'll get back to it. I want to put at least one coat of paint on the floor tonight."

He nodded. "See ya."

Damnit. Why did that dog have to blow my cover?

"Hey," Harry called. "You wanna come in for a beer or something?"

"No thanks," I called back over my shoulder, picking up my pace. "Getting dark. And I didn't bring a flashlight."

"Whatever." He whistled for Jeeves, and the two of them went back inside.

While I went home to paint and fume.

22

Weezie

By whining, begging, cajoling, and making dire predictions about our future love life, I managed to get Daniel over to my house for dinner that night. I did mention that Mama was making dinner. I omitted the fact that her notorious tuna-noodle casserole was on the menu.

"Come at six," I instructed when he called.

"Six? That's barbaric. Nobody eats dinner at six o'clock."

"Mama and Daddy believe in the early bird," I said. "It gives Daddy's digestive tract more time to process things before he turns in at nine. And don't forget, bring wine, lots of wine," I whispered from the living room, while my mother bustled around the kitchen. "And dessert. Chocolate would be highly appreciated."

"What's she fixing?" Daniel asked. "Should I bring white or red?"

"Bring something that partners well with awful, bordering on inedible," I said. He sighed the sigh of St. Daniel the Martyred. "How much longer is she going to be staying there? You just barely got home before she moved in. I miss you."

"You're horny," I said, cutting to the chase. "Don't feel like the Lone Ranger. I have needs too, you know."

"Maybe you could just talk dirty to me on the phone," he suggested.

"No way. She'd probably listen in on the kitchen extension. I've got a better idea. You just show up here and follow my lead. And did I mention the wine part?"

At six on the dot, he rang the doorbell. Daniel has his own key, of course, but we were still trying to keep up proprieties, for my mother's sake.

"I'll get it, Mama," I said, meeting him on the front stoop. I gave him a long, hard, passionate kiss, with a playful little groin pat as a lagniappe.

"Don't." He groaned, pressing me closer. "I'm not a man to be toyed with."

"Later," I promised. "Did you bring the wine?"

He held up a brown-paper shopping bag. "Don't I always?"

"Hi, Mrs. Foley," Daniel said, going inside and giving my mother a dutiful peck on the cheek. "Mmm. What smells so delicious?"

She patted Daniel on the top of his head, as she always did. "Oh, stop. It's just my plain old tuna-noodle casserole. Although I did sprinkle crushed-up salt-and-vinegar potato chips on top, this time, for a little extra crunch."

"Can't wait," he said, swallowing hard.

After Mama said grace, we both made a valiant effort at pushing the casserole around on our plates, in between copious helpings of tossed salad and French bread.

"So, Daniel," Mama said, sliding a second huge spoonful of casserole onto his plate, "How is the restaurant business going?"

I gave him a warning kick under the table. He put his hand on my thigh.

"A little slow right now," he said, hiding a clump of food under a lettuce leaf. "We're uh, doing some remodeling at the restaurant, so we're temporarily closed."

"You're out of work?" She clutched her throat with a look of abject horror.

"It's all right, Mama," I assured her. "It's just a temporary thing. Daniel already has a bunch of catering jobs lined up. He'll be fine."

She shook her head and tsk-tsked. "I remember, one time, when you were just a baby, Weezie, your father had plantar's warts, and he couldn't walk his route for weeks. But the post office paid him, just the same. That's the thing about a good government job," she added, nodding her head in a meaningful way. "You can always depend on it."

"Daniel has more job offers than he can take," I said. "Skilled chefs are always in demand. He's even had job offers from Jacksonville and Charleston and Atlanta."

"I suppose," she said airily. "Now, Daniel, if things don't look up, you should give Weezie's daddy a call. He still has a lot of pull with the postal service. Anyway, the benefits for a family man are the best around. Medical, dental. And all those federal holidays too! And no night work. You could be home with your wife and babies by five o'clock every day, like Weezie's daddy always was."

"Mama!" I said. "Stop that right this minute."

"What?" she said, acting all innocent. "I spoiled something?"

Daniel, bless him, reached across the table, took my hand in his, and squeezed it. He also squeezed my thigh, while he was at it. "Well, thanks. I'll keep all that in mind, Mrs. Foley, in case things don't pan out with the restaurant business."

"Oh, call me Marian," Mama said. "We're practically family."

"I couldn't," Daniel said.

"Mama Marian, then," she said, beaming first at him, and then at me.

I decided to change the topic of conversation, and quickly.

"By the way, Daniel, I talked to BeBe today," I said, hopping up and scraping the leftovers into the garbage disposal. "She needs me to take a load of furniture out to the Breeze Inn for her. She's just about got the first unit ready to move into."

I sliced up the Mississippi mud pie Daniel had brought, and carried it and three jadeite dessert plates to the table.

"Daniel made this pie himself," I told Mama proudly. "It's his own recipe. They sell this in the restaurant for eight dollars a slice."

"Hmm," Mama said.

Daniel slid the pieces of pie onto the plates and passed them around. "It sounds like she's really whipping that motel into shape. If anybody can do it, it's BeBe."

"Daniel," Mama said, pausing between bites of pie, "did you know that Joseph and I honeymooned at the Breeze Inn?"

"No, I didn't," he said. "What year was that?"

"Nineteen-sixty," she said promptly. "But I got a terrible yeast infection that week, so Joseph had to take me to the doctor after only three days, and we'd already paid ahead of time for the whole week, twelve dollars a night too! And that nasty manager, I forget his name, wouldn't give us a refund, so then we left on Thursday."

"Mama, stop!" I cried. "You're grossing us out!"

"What?" she said. "Daniel's a grown man. He needs to understand that these things happen to a woman once she starts having intimate relations."

Daniel choked so hard I had to get up and pound him on the back.

"It's the pie," Mama said sympathetically, handing him a glass of wine. "I wasn't going to say anything, but that crust was just a little on the dry side. Next time, maybe you could pick up one of those good Mrs. Smith's chocolate-cream pies."

"Mrs. Smith's," he managed to croak. "I'll make a note of it."

Mama begrudgingly allowed us to clean up the kitchen, so while she went off to watch *Wheel of Fortune,* we dumped the rest of the tuna casserole into the trash, double-bagged it, and finished cleaning up the dishes.

"What's all this about taking furniture to BeBe?" Daniel asked.

"She really does need furniture for her unit at the motel," I said. "But I figure, if we take it out there tonight, I can just tell Mama that by the time we finished unloading, I was too tired to drive home, so I just spent the night with BeBe."

"BeBe? Why would you do that?"

"Idiot! It's all a ruse. I'll be checking into the Stipanek Sheraton."

"I like it," he said, a slow grin developing. "Just you and me and the moonlight."

"As soon as we take the furniture over to BeBe's. And set it up. And see if she needs any help."

"Help?"

"The place is a disaster, Daniel. I can't just abandon her. She needs me."

"I need you," he said, nuzzling my neck.

"But in a different way. Be an angel now, and help me load up."

At seven-thirty, we pulled into the parking lot at the Breeze Inn. Although BeBe's Lexus was the only car in the lot, the NO VACANCY sign was blinking off and on. Unit two's doors and windows were wide open and ablaze with lights.

I honked the horn, and a minute later, BeBe appeared in the doorway. Her appearance was shocking, to say the least. Her blond curls peeked out from beneath a red stocking cap, and she wore faded blue overalls covered with white paint splatters. There were dark circles under her eyes, and I realized with a start that it was the first time—ever, in all our years of friendship—that I'd seen her without makeup. Still, she gave a jaunty wave of her long-handled paint roller when she saw us.

"Hey!" she called out. "Did y'all bring your paintbrushes?"

"Better," I said, hopping out from the passenger side of the truck. "Wait till you see the darling dinette set—"

"And pizza," Daniel added, bringing out the cardboard box from Vinnie VanGo's, and waving it under her nose. "And wine. We brought you a really big bottle of wine."

"My angels," BeBe said fervently. "But about those paintbrushes—"

"Later," Daniel said. "First we eat."

"But I thought Weezie's mama was cooking dinner tonight," BeBe said.

"Exactly," Daniel said. "Which is why we stopped at Vinnie's. Here. You hold the pizza while I get your dining-room table. Where's it going?"

"Nowhere, just yet," BeBe said, grimacing. "I'm in paint hell. The walls are done, and the first coat is dry on the floors, but it's going to take at least three coats."

"Looks like the manager's office, then," I said, glancing around the parking lot. "And where is the manager, pray tell? I thought he was supposed to be helping you fix up the place."

"Mr. Sorrentino is very busy right now," BeBe said. "Warming a stool over at Doc's Bar."

23

"Your manager's sitting in a bar all day, while you're over here killing yourself fixing the place up?" Daniel asked, polishing off the last piece of pizza. "BeBe, if anybody at Guale even thought about pulling a stunt like that, you'd fire their asses. So it's simple, right? If he won't work for you, fire him, and kick his ass out of here."

"It's not quite that easy," I said. "I can't fire him. I owe him money."

"How?" Daniel and Weezie asked, almost in unison.

"He's been working here for six months, paying for materials out of his own pocket, and he hasn't been paid in all that time. This morning, he presented me with a bill for $4,800, which I don't have."

"Damn," Daniel said.

"Exactly," I agreed. "I can't get this place fixed up, and ready to re-open by St. Patrick's Day by myself, and I can't afford to hire some-body else. So I'm screwed."

"We'll help," Weezie said quickly. "I can paint and sand. And I owe you, after all the help you gave me, fixing up the carriage house for Maisie's Daisy."

"I know," I told her, giving her a quick hug. "And I appreciate that. But you and I can't do plumbing. Or wiring. For that, unfortu-nately, we need Harry Sorrentino."

"But you just said he's basically a barfly," Weezie said.

"He is," I agreed. I did a couple of deep-knee bends, and then, groaning, stood up straight again. "But I found out today that he's in a bad way financially too. He doesn't know I know it, but I found out

Harry Sorrentino needs money to get his fishing boat out of hock. Some marina repossessed it because he owes them money for dock fees and ice and fuel. So I'm going to make him a simple business proposition. The sooner he helps me get the motel open, and turning a profit, the sooner I can start paying him the money he's owed."

Daniel shook his head. "Can I give you a piece of advice?"

"Can I stop you?"

"I don't know Harry Sorrentino," Daniel said. "But I know how I'd feel if I was in his position. So don't throw the boat thing in the man's face," Daniel said. "Think about how that must feel. The guy lost his livelihood." He gave me a meaningful look. "Kinda like the way you lost yours. It's humiliating, right?"

I sighed. "I hate it when you're right. Okay, I won't bring up the boat thing. I'll just use my incredible charm and persuasive powers to bend him to my will."

"You mean you'll nag him nearly to death," Daniel said.

"And speaking of nagging," I said, picking up the paintbrush I'd left in the sink.

They followed me back to unit two.

"Oh, wow," Weezie said, peeking inside. "I can't believe it's the same place."

"Really? You don't think it was sacrilege to paint all that pine paneling?"

"Had to be done," Weezie said briskly, putting a tentative finger to the painted floor. "This is dry. And I don't think it really needs a second coat."

"But you can see the grain of the wood underneath," I said. "And the places where the floor was patched."

"Doesn't matter," Weezie said, slipping out of her shoes and walking into the middle of the room. "This is Tybee, not the Telfair Museum. The look we're going for here is funky, cottagey. You want the wood grain to show. Anyway, the furniture will cover up the patched places. Trust me, this place is going to be adorable."

"I'd settle for livable, or even sanitary. Anyway, you haven't seen the bathroom," I warned, as she headed in that direction. "Not even paint can fix that."

"But the bathroom's awesome," Weezie called, her voice echoing in the empty room. "Come look."

I poked my head around the doorway and into the bathroom.

The place had been transformed. The grungy black-and-white mosaic-tile floor sparkled. An old-fashioned brass light-fixture I'd never seen before hung from the ceiling, the walls had a fresh coat of white paint, and the sink, although still a dull grayish color, had been fitted with pitted but polished brass faucets. Gleaming brass towel bars had taken the place of the cheap plastic ones I'd seen earlier in the day, and the wooden medicine cabinet had been painted glossy black. Even its glass shelves had been cleaned.

"I had no idea," I said slowly. "I mean, Harry was working in here all morning. I knew he put in a new hot-water heater, and installed the toilet and all, but I was busy in the living room, pulling up the old linoleum and carpet. I had no idea he'd done all this."

Weezie knelt down to get a closer look at the claw-foot tub. "Looks like he took some kind of commercial cleaner to this. When you get a little money ahead, we can have the tub and the sink reglazed, babe. It'll only cost a couple hundred bucks, and when it's done, it'll be fabulous."

Now Daniel stuck his head in the doorway too. "I thought you said the guy was a barfly. This bathroom looks pretty cool. I wouldn't mind checking in here myself."

Weezie punched him in the arm. "Forget it, lover boy. It's almost midnight. We're going to get her furniture unloaded and set up, and then we're headed for your place."

Daniel caught her hand and kissed it, waggling his eyebrows at both of us. "See how it is? She can't get enough of me."

Under Weezie's direction, Daniel and I began unloading the truck.

"Get the rug first," she ordered, and he dutifully carried in a long, paper-wrapped cylinder and set it down in the sleeping nook. When he unrolled the rug, I stared down at it dubiously, trying not to look a gift horse in the mouth.

The rug was an ancient oriental, its nap worn down almost to nothing, its colors faded to soft pinks, greens, and blues. One end of it looked as if it had been attacked by a horde of angry moths, leaving the edges ragged in places.

"Now flip it over," Weezie instructed.

"Huh? Wrong side up?" But Daniel did as he was told. The colors on the reverse side of the rug were even softer, leaving the pattern with a smudged, Impressionist look.

"Perfect," Weezie said, clapping her hands with delight. "I'd almost forgotten I had this thing. My ex would never let me put it in my house. It was shoved way back in the attic of the town house."

Daniel said. "What do you want to do with that iron-frame bed in the truck?"

"Set it up," Weezie said. "The mattress is brand new, and I've had that rug cleaned, moth-proofed, and sanitized. So there's absolutely no danger of cooties besmirching your precious little tootsies."

"As if," I mumbled. But then I trudged out to the truck to get the rest of the furniture. Because Weezie was right. This wasn't a mansion, and I wasn't Lady Astor.

"Bring in the wicker rocker and the nightstands and the lamps next," Weezie called after me from the doorway.

By the time we got the nightstands, lamps, and wicker chair inside, Weezie had the bed made up with clean sheets and a plump comforter. The bed, as promised, covered up the rattiest part of the rug, which actually looked amazing on the white-enameled floor. The black iron tracery of the headboard stood out from the white walls, and with the stack of crisp white pillows, and the Tiffany-blue comforter, I had to admit the little sleeping nook suddenly looked very tempting.

"Very pretty," I said, fingering the white eyelet lace edge of the pillowcases.

"Thank God for Target," Weezie said, giving it the phony French pronunciation of Tar-zhay. "The sheets are actually pretty high thread-count cotton. And I found the comforter on clearance at the end of the summer, $9.99. You probably don't remember, but I had it on a display bed in the shop, with a little feed-sack quilt folded on top of it."

"You're a genius," I said. "And I'm a spoiled brat."

"Agreed," she said, smiling. She picked up a pebbly white lamp with a shade with pom-pom trim, placed it on the little three-legged pine table on the right side of the bed, and plugged in the cord. A peeling, dark green, square bamboo-looking table was on the left, and she put the other lamp on top, then turned on both lamps.

"The lamps are milk glass," Weezie told me. "They're not all that terribly old. Sixties, I'd say. I think Meemaw probably bought them with S and H green stamps." She placed the rocker at an angle to the bed and frowned. Then she took a piece of wildly flowered green, red, and yellow nubbly fabric from the empty Target shopping bag and covered the cracked red-leather seat cushion with it.

"Works," she said, nodding her approval. "I've been saving that piece of bark cloth for ages. I had Tacky Jacky re-cover an armchair with the rest of it, but there wasn't enough left to do much with. We still need a reading lamp here, but I've got one in the shop that will work."

By unspoken agreement, we both stepped back from the sleeping nook to take it in. I gave my best friend a hug, but she shrugged out of it and returned to her I'm-in-charge-here-take-no-prisoners mode.

"Go get the stack of pictures on the front seat of the truck," she ordered. "And tell Daniel to bring in the love seat and armchair."

"Love seat?" I asked. "Where are you gonna put something that big?"

"It's a little two-seater settee. So you just keep moving," Weezie said imperiously. "I'll figure out where things go."

"Hey," I said, when Daniel carried in the turquoise-painted wrought-iron settee. "Isn't that one of the pieces you brought back from your last buying trip to Florida?"

"So?" Weezie said, deliberately turning her back to me. "Put it right against this wall," she said, patting the window opposite my bed. "And then the chair goes right here," she continued. "And the little glass-topped table goes in between them."

"The point is, that's not just old junk from your attic, it's merchandise from the shop. I can't take good stuff you were intending to sell."

"I will sell it," Weezie said, fussing with the cushions on the settee. "To you, or somebody else, eventually. In the meantime, I brought back a whole truckload of furniture from Florida, and I don't have room for all of it in the shop right now, so you're providing me with cheap storage. Do you have a problem with that?"

"No," I said meekly. "What were you saying about that stack of pictures?"

"Bring 'em on in, and then get me a tack hammer and a yardstick," she said.

I didn't dare voice any more objections to Weezie's contributions. Maybe I flinched a little, though, when I saw the pair of gaudy pictures, one a heron, the other a flamingo, that she'd chosen to go above the bed.

Of course she saw right through me. "I *know* these are not what you're used to," she lectured. "These are just old fifties paint-by-number pictures. They're not exactly Maybelle Johns. But think of it like this—they're cute, they work, and," she added ominously, "the price is right. Besides, paint by numbers is still very hot. These babies bring fifty bucks apiece in the shop."

"You don't have a velveteen *Last Supper* in that stack, do you?" I asked.

"No velveteen," she said firmly.

Daniel came in then, carrying a rectangular table on his head.

"Over there, in the kitchen," Weezie said before following him out to the truck to bring in the last of the load.

When they came back, they were each carrying a pair of aluminum-frame chairs with aqua vinyl upholstered seats whose color matched the Formica tabletop.

"Do you love it?" she asked, walking around and around the table. "Tell me you love it, or I'll have to kill you."

"I do love it," I laughingly admitted. "It makes me smile. I haven't seen a Formica dinette set like this in years."

"Thirty dollars!" she crowed. "At the Bon Wille' on Sallie Mood."

"Bon Wille'?" Daniel asked. "Where's that?"

"That's Franglais for Goodwill," I said, catching on. "It's perfect, Weezie. It's all perfect."

"I know," she said smugly. "I have the gift, the junking gene." She tugged at Daniel's arm. "Let's go, sport. Our work here is done."

I trailed out behind them to the parking lot. "Seriously," I said. "I can't thank you guys enough. As soon as I get some money ahead, I'll pay you back for everything."

"Not necessary," Weezie said, hanging her head out the passenger-side window. "This is just the start. As soon as those other units are ready, I'm gonna junkify them too. And we'll put my business cards in each room, saying the furnishings came from Maisie's Daisy. This will be my own private showroom."

"You're crazy," I yelled at the truck's red taillights.

"Like a fox," she called back

24

I crossed my fingers and turned the hot-water faucet in the bathtub. Tea-colored water trickled out at first, but cleared up after a moment, and after another moment or two, scalding-hot water gushed from the tap.

I'd taken a stack of clean bath towels and soap from the laundry room in the manager's unit, and had even found a miniature bottle of bubble bath, so old that the paper label was yellowed with age. I dumped in the whole bottle, and sank deep into the hot froth, willing my aching muscles to relax.

Tomorrow, I thought sleepily, I would have to start all over again on the other thirteen units. More scraping, scrubbing, stripping, and sanding. But, I vowed, I would not be working alone. Harry Sorrentino, by God, worked for me, and by God, he would work with me too.

Finally, when the water had gone tepid and my knees weak with exhaustion, I toweled off and stumbled to bed, where I fell instantly to sleep.

Dazzling sunlight flooded into the room, nearly blinding me with its intensity. I yawned, stretched, and glanced at my watch. Six-thirty! Somehow, I would have to rig up some kind of curtains at the windows facing my bed.

Before my feet could even hit the floor, there was a soft knocking, and a more insistent scratching, then barking.

"Yeah?" I said groggily.

Harry opened the door and poked his head inside. "You didn't lock up last night," he said accusingly. "I came home and the place was wide open."

I blinked. "Is anything missing?"

"No. But that's not the point, damnit. You left the office open too. What the hell is wrong with you?"

Aware that I'd gone to bed wearing nothing more than panties and an oversize T-shirt, I wrapped the comforter around me and stood up, trying to summon my dignity.

"We didn't finish working here until after midnight. I was tired. I haven't had any sleep. So yes, I did forget to lock up. For which I apologize. But maybe if you'd come back at a reasonable hour, you could have given me a hand and I wouldn't have been so absolutely sick with exhaustion."

"I put in an eight-hour day of work here, yesterday, in case you didn't notice," Harry began.

"Yippee for you," I snapped. "I put in sixteen hours. I'm likely to put in at least that today too. Not that you care."

Jeeves let out a low, guttural growl. Harry gave me the human, visual equivalent of a growl.

"Just lock up, okay? I can't get anything done if my power tools go missing."

"Fine," I said, hurrying toward the bathroom, and slamming the door hard behind me.

He apparently didn't realize he'd been dismissed. I could hear Jeeves's nails clipping as he trotted around my living quarters, followed by Harry's heavy footsteps.

"Place looks pretty good," Harry called to me.

"No thanks to you," I mumbled to myself, assessing my looks in the wavy glass of the mirror. I still had flecks of white paint in my hair, which badly needed washing. I looked down at my hands. My knuckles were scraped raw, and the nail on my right forefinger was black and swollen from where Weezie had hit it with the tack hammer.

"I like the white floors," he said. "You gonna do that in all the units? It'll cut down on maintenance. We won't have to vacuum, or worry about carpet stains, and sand won't show on these white floors."

"Yeah," I called back. "I thought about that already." What I didn't tell him was that I had plenty of cheap paint, but no money for carpets anyway, or a vacuum cleaner, or somebody to run said vacuum.

"Where'd you get all the furniture?" he asked. "There's some beds and dressers out in the storage shed, but nothing this nice."

"It's on loan from a friend."

Why didn't he leave already? I needed to pee, but I didn't want him out there, listening to me.

"See you in a little bit," I called, hoping he'd get the hint.

"You got any coffee?" he called back, still oblivious.

"No. No coffee, no coffeemaker, no mugs, no spoons," I said.

"Oh. Well, I guess I could make us some."

"You do that," I said, turning on the bathtub faucets to drown out any embarrassing sounds.

"Okay."

When I'd dressed in my work clothes, with my hair covered with the stocking cap again, I marched myself over to the office, where Harry was sitting at the table, sipping coffee and regarding a heap of metal parts in front of him.

"What's that?" I asked, pouring myself a mug.

"The motor for the clothes dryer," he said, poking at it with a screwdriver.

"Shit," I said, sitting opposite him. "Can it be fixed?"

"Maybe. No promises."

"We've only got the one dryer, right?"

"Yeah."

"Then it's got to be fixed. I can't afford to replace it."

He took a pair of glasses from his breast pocket and perched them on the end of his nose, leaning in closer to examine the motor. "I know," he said. "I know all about your little problem."

I felt my scalp prickle, and my hands started shaking so badly I had to set the mug of coffee down on the table to keep from spilling it all over myself.

"Which little problem is that?"

He sighed. "Tybee's not Siberia, you know. People talk. They even talk about you. You're a pretty hot topic over at Doc's Bar."

I grimaced. "Swell. So what's the Doc's Bar version of my little problem?"

Harry reached for a tin pie pan that contained a heap of nuts and bolts. He found the one he wanted, and carefully inserted it in a minuscule hole in the motor.

"Let's see if I got it straight. You had yourself a little boy toy, some rich guy from Charleston with a yacht and a fancy car. Only he wasn't really rich, or from Charleston, and the yacht wasn't his either. And when the smoke cleared, the boyfriend was gone, and so was all your money. He sold your house, and everything in it, cleaned out your bank accounts, and blew town."

He reached for his coffee mug and took a sip. "That about the size of it?"

There was no use in lying to him. Maybe it was time to put my cards on the table. "That's about right. I wouldn't exactly call Reddy a boy toy, but when you get right down to the nitty-gritty, yeah, he cleaned me out."

"And now you've had to close your restaurant. And you're broke."

"Dead broke," I said glumly.

"And basically homeless," Harry said, ever helpful.

"Not anymore. I own this place. It's oceanfront property. Extremely valuable oceanfront property that I own outright. I'm back in the game."

"Nuh-uh," Harry said. "Sandcastle Realty Associates has an option on the Breeze. Your lawyer's fighting it, but in the meantime, you can't do squat. You're screwed, sweetheart."

"Don't call me sweetheart," I said sharply. "I don't know what all you've heard from the sages over there at Doc's. But they don't know me. And you don't know me."

"Don't I?" He picked up the motor and went into the utility room, where he dropped down onto the floor in front of the disemboweled dryer.

I followed right behind him. "You think I'm just some bubble-headed downtown ditz playing Motel Barbie, right?"

He had his back to me, so all I heard was a grunt.

"It doesn't bother me what you think," I said. "And I don't care what a bunch of winos and losers think of me either. But here's the deal, Harry. St. Patrick's Day falls on a Monday, which means we'll get a four-day weekend of guests who will basically pay anything to stay anywhere within a twenty-mile radius of Savannah. I've checked the rates at the B and Bs in town. The Gastonian, the Ballastone, the Planter's Inn? They're all booked. Have been since before Christmas. They all charge at least $350 a night at St. Patrick's Day. For three nights minimum. We can make around a thousand bucks apiece, for fourteen units. That's $14,000 for our opening weekend. So, you see, Harry, the Breeze is going to be open and fully booked by then."

He laughed. "Lady, this ain't the Gastonian. It ain't even the Motel Six. Nobody will pay those prices to stay on Tybee Island. And especially at the Breeze Inn. I'm telling you, it can't be done." He rolled over onto his back to look up at me. "You saw what your unit looked like. And that was the nicest one. The rest of 'em are ten times worse. It's not just a matter of time, either. I need materials. Roofing shingles, commodes, Sheetrock, lumber. Three of the units have rotted-out doors. None of that stuff comes cheap."

"Let me worry about the money part. I've still got credit cards.

You just make a list," I told him. "I'll borrow a truck, and meet you over at Home Depot in an hour."

"Sure," he said, going back to work.

"And there's one more thing," I added.

"I can't wait to hear it."

"No more taking off at three o'clock to go drown your sorrows at Doc's Bar. I know you've got your troubles, but drinking isn't going to solve them. And anyway, I need you here. All day. Every day."

"Fuuuckkk." He said it long and low.

He sat up. "You were checking up on me at Doc's? Is that what this is all about? Well, fuck you, lady. What I do when I'm off the clock is my own damn business. And as soon as you pay me what you owe me, you can find somebody else to order around."

"I'm aware of how much money I owe you," I said calmly. "And you'll get it back. Every dime. I swear. The police have a lead on my uh, Reddy's, whereabouts. When they find him, I'm going to get my money back. And my house and my rental properties. My lawyer is very optimistic about that. And we're working on resolving this Sandcastle Realty issue too. But in the meantime I can't pay you anything until this place is up and running."

"You're living in a dream world," he said. He put the front panel back on the dryer, stood up, wiped his hands on the seat of his jeans, and mashed the button on the dryer's control panel. We both bent down at the same time to look inside the glass door. Whompa-whompa-whompa. The big steel drum started its slow rotation. It worked. At least one dream had come true for the day.

"My hero," I said, patting him on the back.

25

Up until the day I realized that my second husband, Richard, had that unfortunate penchant for computer porn, I'd always thought of myself as somebody who was naturally lucky. My life had been mostly golden. Happy childhood, loving family, lots of friends, and a natural knack for business. There had been bumps in the road, sure, but I'd always managed to bounce back from adversity and come out slugging.

But the thing with Richard had rocked my world and thrown my self-confidence for a loop. It was all so tawdry. I remember thinking I'd been essentially living an episode of *Geraldo*. How could I have been so wrong about anybody? How could I not have seen what a sleazebucket I'd been living with?

After the divorce, I'd thrown myself into my work. Both my parents had died while I was in my early 30s, so I'd taken my small family inheritance and started two moderately successful small downtown cafes, and bought and flipped my first piece of residential real estate. I worked impossible hours, and had no social life, but I didn't care. I was thirty, and driven to prove to myself, and everybody else, that BeBe Loudermilk was fine, thank you very much.

When Guale became the hottest restaurant in Savannah, I was certain my luck was back. I was still insanely busy, but I allowed myself a little time to kick back and enjoy the delicious sensation of doing and having it all.

Now, as I stood in line at the Home Depot for the fourth time in one week, praying that my last credit card would not be maxed out with this final load of joint compound and window caulking, I had little time to reflect on how my present lifestyle seemed like such a perverse reversal of fortune.

In two days, the Breeze Inn would be open for business. That is, if Harry and I didn't kill each other first.

We'd come very close to physical violence on Saturday night. Harry had spent all day Friday and Saturday hanging Sheetrock in four of the units that were in the worst shape, and then he'd taught me how to tape and mud and sand the joints. I'd gotten pretty good at it too. But that Saturday afternoon, I'd made another run to Home Depot, and when I got back, he was gone.

I flipped. Three-thirty in the afternoon and he'd already checked out for the day. I sped over to Doc's Bar. As I went through that door, I felt like a gunslinger in one of those old Westerns. I was ready for a shootout with Harry.

The trouble was, he wasn't there. Four men sat at the bar, and all four swiveled completely around on their bar stools to take a good look at me when I walked in.

"Harry Sorrentino," I said curtly. "Where is he?"

The bartender was an elfin-looking creature with short white hair and deeply tanned skin the consistency of beef jerky. Despite her age, which I judged to be mid-fifties, and the weather outside, which was just about the same, she was dressed in skintight blue-jeans shorts and a low-cut bright orange tank top. She looked me up and down with light brown almond-shaped eyes before taking a deep drag on the cigarette dangling from her lower lip. "Harry's not here, baby. Ain't seen him since Thursday. Anything else we can do you for?"

"Any idea where else he might be?"

"You the lady owns the Breeze?" The speaker had a long, graying beard in the exact same shade as the long, graying braid that fell midway down his back. He too wore cutoffs, along with an army camouflage jacket with the sleeves hacked off, sunglasses, and a black ball cap that said "Tybee Bomb Squad."

"I am," I said.

He nodded thoughtfully. "Figures. Harry don't usually date chicks as old as you."

"And I don't usually date men as old as Harry, so that works out just fine. Do you happen to know where he might have gone this afternoon?"

He shrugged. "I ain't his mama. He don't check in with me."

The other men sniggered and turned their attention back to the television mounted over the bar, which was showing an old black-and-white John Wayne cowboy movie.

"Assholes," I muttered under my breath.

I was outside, unlocking the Lexus, when the bar sprite materialized at my side.

"Don't mind them guys inside," she said. "They're harmless. Listen, I don't know for sure where Harry coulda gone, but I was thinking you might try Marsden Marina."

"The place where they repossessed his boat?"

She looked surprised. "He told you about the *Jitterbug*?"

I shook my head. "Somebody else told me. Why would he be over there?"

"He's trying to get the money together to get the *Jitterbug* back. If he's not tending bar here, he sometimes signs on as a mate on one of the other charter boats."

"Tending bar? Here?" Now it was my turn to look surprised.

"Sure. My daughter needs me to baby-sit some afternoons and nights, so Harry's been filling in for me. Until last week."

When I issued the old ultimatum, I thought.

"Thanks," I said. "I'll check over there." There was no reason for me to confide in this woman, but for some reason, I felt the need to explain just how important it was that I shanghai Harry back to the motel.

"We're fully booked for St. Patrick's Day, and we've still got a lot of work to do before we can rent out those rooms," I told her.

"Uh-huh."

But I still felt the need to unburden myself. "The Sheetrock's up, but we need to paint yet, and there are a couple of bathrooms that have to have the tile patched, and—"

"I know, baby," she said, patting my arm reassuringly. "Harry showed me around the place a couple weeks ago, right before you took over. What a rat hole! But he says you've already worked miracles. You're doing real good. Just cut Harry a little slack, if you can. It's about killin' him, losing the *Jitterbug*. Somebody like Harry, who's always run his own boat . . . well, he ain't really used to having anybody else bossing him around."

"I'm *not* bossing him around," I objected.

"Somebody's got to run the show," she agreed. "And when it's a woman, we always get called the bitch, right?"

"Exactly," I said, smiling.

She stuck out her hand. "By the way, I'm Cheri Johnston."

"And I'm BeBe," I said, taking her hand and shaking it warmly. "Thanks for letting me know about the marina. I'll check for him over there. Where is it, exactly?"

"Right on Lemon Creek," she said. "After you cross the first bridge going toward Thunderbolt, take a left at the sign for CoCo Loco's."

"Got it," I said, and I climbed in the car.

She knocked on the window, and I rolled it down. "And don't you dare let him know I told you where he was at." She grinned. "Us girls gotta stick together."

"Amen to that, sister."

I bit my lip as I passed the motel on my way off the island. The neon NO VACANCY sign was still blinking on and off. Yet another thing to add to my endless punch list, and we only had forty-eight hours until opening day.

Still, we'd come so far.

It had been Weezie who'd insisted we temporarily redirect our efforts to the exterior of the motel. "Once people see how cute it is, they'll start calling and asking about your rates," she'd promised.

Under Weezie's tutelage, I'd painted the weather-beaten old Breeze Inn sign a fresh white, with retro turquoise lettering, and Harry had installed up-lights that cast intriguing palm-shaped shadows on the front of the buildings. Weezie and Daniel had spent a full day working around the grounds, pruning the scraggly old palm trees, planting tubs of shocking pink and purple petunias, and patching the concrete porches in the fronts of all the units. Daniel had raked a fresh load of crushed oyster shell into the parking lot, filling up all the potholes and bare spots, and Weezie had even placed a pair of turquoise-painted Adirondack chairs in front of each unit.

"They're on loan from Acey, the guy who does a lot of refinishing work for me," she'd explained. "He builds them in his spare time, and I told him it would be good advertising." She pointed out the small brass plate on the back of each chair, which did, indeed, have "Chairs by Acey" engraved, along with his phone number. "People can buy them from you, right here in the office," Weezie, ever the entrepreneur, suggested. "They sell for ninety dollars apiece, and you'll get a ten-dollar commission for each chair you sell. And then Acey will replace them with new ones."

Even I had to admit, the Breeze Inn had been transformed from a raggedy-ass dog to the picture of shabby chic charm. As long as you didn't open the door to most of the units, that is.

As soon as we'd finished spiffing up the outside of the inn— "Stop calling it a motel," I'd instructed Harry. "It's an inn now. And we charge inn prices." I'd taken color photos of the Breeze with a borrowed digital camera, and e-mailed them, along with a brief (and highly hyped) press release to a travel writer at the *Atlanta Journal-Constitution* who'd once written a glowing article about Guale.

"Great," she'd e-mailed back. "The place looks adorable! We're doing a last-minute travel planner for St. Patrick's Day. You just made it under the wire." As soon as the story hit the Wednesday paper, our phone started ringing, and by the end of that day, we were completely booked for the entire four-day weekend.

"People are nuts," Harry had said when I'd shown him the reservation sheet.

"We're the ones who are nuts," I told him. "I should have bumped the rates up to $500 a night. Not a single person wanted to quibble about prices with me."

Only forty-eight hours to go. And my staff had gone AWOL. Again.

I found Marsden Marina with no problem. It was a collection of ramshackle wood-frame buildings, including a seafood market, bait shack, and boatyard. And Harry's station wagon was definitely parked there, along with three pickup trucks and a shiny red Ford Explorer with Atlanta license tags. But there was no sign of Harry, or even Jeeves. There was no sign of anybody, much.

I finally found one person at the seafood market. She was sitting at a plastic table in the middle of the concrete-floored room, busily coloring Princess Jasmine a riotous shade of pistachio. A wall-mounted television was playing a tape of *The Little Mermaid*.

"Hello," I said, looking around the empty shop, with its trays of iced-down shrimp, blue crabs, oysters, and flounder. "Is your mama or daddy around?"

"Nope," she said, putting her crayon down to stare at me in that unnerving way children have. "Who are you?"

"I'm BeBe. What's your name?"

"I'm not allowed to talk to strangers," she said, crossing her arms over her chest.

"That's a good idea," I agreed. "Are you allowed to be here all by yourself, without any grown-ups around?"

"I'm not all by myself," she said gravely. "Jesus is with me always."

Very profound. But not too helpful, I thought.

"I was looking for my friend today," I said, finally. "His name is Harry, and he has a cute little white dog named Jeeves. Do you know Harry? Or Jeeves?"

She nodded.

"Have you seen them today?"

Another nod.

"How long ago was that?"

"I can't tell time till next year."

Right. I walked over and took a closer peek at *The Little Mermaid*. It looked to me like the movie must be close to ending.

"Was Harry here when the movie started?"

Nod.

"Right at the beginning of the movie?"

Nod. "It's Harry's movie. He just lets me watch it when he comes over."

"Do you know where Harry went?"

"He and my daddy went out to catch some bait. They'll be back right when everything in the movie gets happy."

Which should be quite soon, I thought, from the upbeat tempo of the music.

Just then, a door behind the seafood counter opened and a young woman wearing white rubber hip boots and a knee-length black rubber apron struggled through it carrying a huge white plastic bucket full of shrimp.

"Hey, Mama," the little girl chirped. "This lady knows Harry and Jeeves."

"Hi there," the woman said warily, setting the bucket down on the floor. "Can I help you?"

I gave her my brightest smile. "Your daughter is very smart. She doesn't talk to strangers, especially when she's all alone."

"She wadn't alone," the woman said. "I wouldn't leave Amber by herself. I was just out in the shed, sizing shrimp. And I could hear everything going on in here." She motioned to the seafood counter, where, for the first time, I noticed a baby monitor with a glowing green light.

"What do you want with Harry?" she asked.

"He works for me," I said, and even to me, it sounded incredibly stupid and insipid. "At the Breeze Inn."

"Yeah," she said. "I heard all about you. Like Amber said, they ought to be back any minute. My husband's got a charter in the morning, and Harry just went out to help him catch some bait. Does he have to clear that with you, or something?"

"No," I said sharply. I wished acutely that I had not come here.

We heard the chugging sound of a boat motor then, and the woman craned her neck to look out the door.

"Here they come right now," she said, flying out the door to meet them.

I stood awkwardly in the doorway of the bait shop, watching the men tie up the boat and start unloading equipment.

"Jeeves!" The little girl stood beside me, issuing a shrill whistle by putting her fingers in her mouth. The dog bounded over the side of the fishing boat, clearing the dock by barely an inch. He trotted up to the bait shop, his tail wagging happily, and the little girl scooped him up in her arms.

She buried her nose in his fur and made a face. "Shoo-eee." She laughed. "You stink!" She set the wriggling dog down and he promptly sat on his haunches, looking up at me expectantly.

"He likes you," Harry called. He was walking toward me, carrying another white plastic bucket full of fish. He was dressed in a bright yellow rain slicker and faded blue jeans. His hair was windblown, his face sunburned, and he looked the happiest I'd seen him since we'd met.

"I know," I said, bending over to let Jeeves lick my fingers, which he did with heartwarming enthusiasm. I've never been really partial to dogs, but this one, I had to admit, was starting to grow on me. "But he's kind of smelly."

Harry laughed. "He jumped into the bucket of chum we were

using. Ground-up mackerel usually is kind of smelly. What's up?" Harry asked, unzipping his slicker. "And how the hell did you track me down over here?"

"I, uh, well," I stammered. "It's getting kind of late, and I got back from Home Depot, and you'd disappeared, and we've really got to get those other units knocked out tonight . . ." I bit my lip. "And you could have told me you were going fishing. Left me a note, or something. I thought you were off drinking. So I went over to Doc's Bar—"

His face darkened. "You went to Doc's? You went in there looking for me?"

"Well, yeah. Every time you disappear, it seems that's where you end up. And you could have told me you were working an extra job. I would have understood. And this thing about your boat, I'm sorry about that too. I know what it's like to be broke—"

"You don't know shit!" he said, his voice hoarse. "You think I'm some kind of deadbeat?"

"No!" I protested. "But there's so much work to be done at the Breeze, and we've got all those bookings, and you just walked off and left the Sheetrock, and we've still got to paint—"

"I didn't just walk off," he said, his eyes narrowing. "That joint compound has to dry completely before we can paint, which won't be for several hours yet. I would have been back in plenty of time to start painting. But you just assumed I'm some falling-down drunk—"

"I didn't know," I said quietly. "If you'd just told me what your situation was—"

"My situation," he said, "is none of your damned business. I'm not your charity case. I was doing just fine with my life until you showed up. I'll paint your damned motel, and I'll finish fixing it up, and just as soon as you pay me what you owe me, I'll be out of your hair. But in the meantime, do me a favor, will you?"

"What?" I said through clenched teeth, determined not to let him make me cry.

"Stay the hell out of my way."

26

As the sun came up on Friday morning, I put the last paint stroke on the bathroom wall of unit fourteen. My knees screamed in protest as I bent down to pick up my paint pan, but I couldn't hear them over the accompanying screams from the rest of my body.

Done. Or as near done as we were going to be. I rolled up the canvas drop cloth and hobbled to the door, stopping only to take a final look around. The room glowed a soft, golden yellow. It had been Weezie's idea, of course, to give each unit a name, instead of a number, and an accompanying decorating scheme, which, of course, was dictated by Weezie and her very particular ideas about what was appropriate.

And so, what we'd been calling unit fourteen had become the Sunflower Suite. It was furnished with a pair of what looked like old metal hospital beds we'd found in the storage shed. Weezie'd spray-painted them with flat black Rust-Oleum, and pronounced them perfection. A beat-up oak dresser that had served as the shed's tool bench had also been painted black, and paired with a trio of mirrors Weezie had picked up at her favorite store—Tar-zhay. The "living area" featured a pair of wicker armchairs, from Maisie's Daisy, which were separated by a table fashioned from a stack of ancient leather suitcases that Weezie swore she'd found in the lane behind her own house on Charlton Street.

And the crowning touch came from an unexpected source: Marian Foley.

I'd been really worried about window treatments for all the rooms, fussing about how much blinds or shades or even ready-made drapes would cost, when Weezie's mother came up with the perfect solution.

"Why don't I just whip up some curtains for you?" she'd asked, setting down the dish of beanie-wienies she'd insisted on dropping off for our dinner.

"Whip up?" I said dumbly.

"Sew some," Marian said. "Just some simple café curtains. Do you have any fabric?"

"No," I said, still dumb.

"Mama, that's a great idea," Weezie enthused. "Let's go take a look out in that shed where I found the beds and the dresser. There are stacks of old linens on the shelves. Maybe we could cut up some old sheets or something."

They were back five minutes later, each bearing an armload of white fabric.

"Chenille bedspreads!" Weezie crowed. "There must be twenty or thirty of 'em out there. And they're all the same. They've even got fringe."

"Can you do that? Make curtains out of bedspreads?"

"Of course," Marian said nonchalantly. "It's all just a matter of straight seams, hems, and rod pockets. Nothing easier."

An hour later, they'd set up an assembly line, and the Marian Foley Drapery Factory had gone into business.

"They're wonderful," I said, leaning down to give Marian a hug. "And you're wonderful to do this for me. And to think I didn't even know you could sew."

"Every girl should know how to sew," Marian said, sniffing meaningfully. "I made all of Weezie's clothes until she was in high school and decided it was 'uncool' to wear homemade stuff."

"I was a brat," Weezie agreed. "But you are a genius, Mama."

And now, Friday morning, I was almost ready for business. Almost.

The last load of sheets, and towels for the bathrooms, were in the dryer, which was still, thank God, working. And I still had to get Harry to nail up the little plaques Weezie'd painted, above the door to each suite.

"Suite. Sweet my ass," Harry muttered, standing in front of the Sunflower, fastening his tool belt.

"Admit it, the place looks amazing," I said.

He ignored me, set up his stepladder, and began screwing the plaque into place.

That's how it had been between the two of us, ever since he'd stormed away from me at Marsden Marina.

He'd worked at fever pitch, done everything I'd asked of him, and more, but despite my repeated apologies, had uttered not one word to me that wasn't work related.

"You want one of these things above your unit too?" he'd asked, looking down at the basket of plaques.

"Yeah," I'd said with a sigh. "Mine is now the Surfside Suite. The concierge at the Gastonian called me last night. One of their regular guests decided to come down at the last minute, and she asked me, as a favor, to see if I could fit her in at the Breeze."

"You said we were full."

"Not exactly. I upped the price to six hundred a night for the Surfside. For that kind of money, I can sleep on the sofa at Weezie's house."

"Thought you wanted to be on the property full-time in case something came up," Harry said.

"Shit. That's right. Guess I'll have to find a place to sleep out here."

"Jeeves might let you share his chair."

"I'd settle for the sofa."

He nodded and started to go back to work.

"Harry?"

He turned around.

"I really am sorry. We got off to a horrible start. And I regret that. But I want you to know, I really do appreciate everything you've done around here. You know, I've been running my own businesses for a lot of years, and I've never seen anybody work as hard, or as diligently, as you these past few weeks. I know I've been a pain in the ass, but now that the Breeze is open, I'm going to see to it that you get the money you're owed, and that you get the *Jitterbug* back."

"It's okay," he said. "You've had a tough time. I haven't made things any easier."

I stuck my hand out. "Truce?"

"Truce," he said, shaking mine.

"Shit," he said, looking down at his palm, which was now covered with sunflower yellow paint.

"At least it's latex," I told him.

A black Dodge Ram pickup truck spun into the parking lot, sending up a fine shower of crushed oyster shells.

"Damnit, Daniel," I hollered at the driver. "You're messing up my parking lot." But I gave him a smile to let him know I was only half serious.

He hopped out of the truck cab and went around to the driver's side and extracted a large cardboard box. "I baked some, uh, muffins," he said gruffly. "I, uh, wanted to do something to celebrate you opening the motel."

"Inn," I corrected. I tipped the box's lid open and sniffed the sweet smell of warm baked goods. "The Breeze Inn. Daniel, these smell divine."

He shuffled his feet and pushed a lock of dark hair out of his eyes.

"Weezie's bringing over flowers and stuff later," he said. "But I thought, you know, maybe you could put a basket of these out for your guests or something."

I gave him a peck on the cheek, and silently gave thanks again for having had the good sense long ago to hire Daniel Stipanek as the chef for Guale. He had a true artist's temperament, and I was no pushover either, but we both knew that our differences were never personal, or lasting.

"What kind are they?" I asked, my stomach growling.

"Banana nut, orange poppyseed, and honey pecan," he said. "This is a triple batch, so you can freeze some of 'em, if they don't all get eaten right away."

"They'll get eaten," I promised him. "I'm gonna have one right now. Come over to the office with me and let me fix you a cup of coffee to go with."

"Can't," he said. "I'm catering the Hibernian Society dinner, and I've got to get busy making my desserts. Bailey's Irish Cream cheese-cake tarts."

The Hibernian Society was Savannah's oldest and most prestigious Irish-heritage society. It was all male, as were most of the old-line societies. As far as I knew, the Hibernian's main function was to throw an elaborate, black-tie dinner after the parade.

"Yum. What else are you fixing?"

"I'm doing a shrimp-and-crab napoleon for the appetizer course, then chilled oysters with a Bienville sauce . . ."

"That doesn't sound Irish to me," I teased.

"It's not," he admitted. "But Billy Hennesey is president of the Hibernians this year. You know Billy. He used to come in the restaurant all the time. He's a bona fide foodie."

"I know him," I said. "But I didn't know he was president of the Hibernians."

"Yeah. Anyway, Billy said the younger members have been bitching for years about eating the same old crap every year, and paying through the nose for the privilege, so he asked me to come up with the kind of menu we served at Guale."

"Good for you," I said.

"We're doing baby lamb chops with a garlic-fig marmalade, roast asparagus—"

"No potatoes? Daniel, these people are Irish. You gotta have potatoes."

"Gimme a break," Daniel said, looking wounded. "The lamb chops are on a bed of rosemary-roasted fingerling potatoes."

"Of course. How silly of me to doubt you."

"And for dessert we're doing a medley of tarts. Pecan bourbon, the Bailey's Irish Cream, and lemon with raspberry."

"Those old bog trotters will think they've died and gone to heaven," I told him.

"Hope so," Daniel said. "This Hibernian thing is a good gig. Lot of influential people come into town for it."

I felt a familiar pang of guilt. It was my fault Daniel was killing himself catering, my fault that he and all the other staff at Guale were out of jobs.

"How's it going?" I asked.

"Okay," he said, rubbing the toe of his rubber chef's clog in the crushed shells. "I've had some phone calls, people wanting me to hire on, but for now, I'm all right with working on my own."

"The rumor mill has it that Sherry and Kick Thibadeux are splitting up," I said, referring to a Charleston couple whose Boundary Street restaurant was the trendiest spot in South Carolina. "She finally figured out that Kick's interest in busboys is a little unnatural. So he's keeping the downtown place and Sherry is opening a new place in Hilton Head."

"She called me about that," Daniel said. "But I don't know, BeBe. I still hate to give up on Guale." He gave me a crooked grin. "Besides, the bitch you know is always better than the bitch you don't."

"You sweet-tongued devil, I didn't know you cared that much."

"You'll be back. Guaranteed. Weezie's uncle James told her the cops think they know where old Reddy-Boy is hanging out down in Florida."

"Yeah, but there's no guarantee they'll catch him. Or get my money back."

He shook his head. "Uh-uh. You'll wring every last dime out of him. You forget, I've seen you, in a tight skirt and three-inch heels, chase college kids clear down the block, just for trying to skip out on a twenty-buck bar bill. Once they find the prick, he's toast."

"Hope so," I said fervently. "In the meantime, I guess I'm in the motel business for now."

"Innkeeper," Daniel said. "You're an innkeeper. And you'll knock 'em dead. For real."

"Hope so." I crossed my fingers. He crossed his too.

27

Check-in time was two P.M. I'd carefully explained this to all the guests who'd made reservations. My whole day was built around two o'clock. Two o'clock was the finish line for the race to have the Breeze Inn ready and open for business.

At noon, I was in the shower in Harry's apartment, trying to scrub Weezie's varied palette of paint colors off my hide and out of my hair. Yellow for the Sunflower Suite, coral for the Hibiscus unit, pale green for the SeaGlass, soft blue for the Starfish. I was still going over my mental to-do list when I heard the doorbell buzzing. Once, twice, three times. This would not be Harry. He'd gone to Sam's Club an hour earlier to fetch soaps and shampoos for all the units. I toweled off hurriedly, and pulled on the black jeans and sweater I'd treated myself to on my last trip to Target. I winced as I shoved my feet into the cheap black flats I'd picked up at Payless, and mourned the darling little faux-leopard mules that were now gone, along with all the rest of my belongings.

"Yoo-hoo! Anybody home?" A woman's voice. "Is the manager in?" The buzzing started anew, and now I could hear Jeeves barking from outside too.

"Coming," I called, hurrying to the door. I glanced around the newly refurbished office area. Harry had scavenged a pile of old bead-board siding from the trash heap of a house being remodeled on the north end of the beach, and had fashioned a high front counter from the old wood. Behind it, I'd set up a real desk, with our brand-new credit card machine, a row of hooks holding room keys, and Harry's old black rotary phone. It was a far cry from any kind of hotel setup I'd ever seen before, but Weezie had assured me that guests checking into the Breeze would be seeking this kind of ambience.

"If they want a fax machine and a switchboard, they can always go to the Days Inn," she pointed out.

I gingerly touched a fingertip to the still-damp paint on the sign Harry had affixed to the front of the counter: THE BREEZE INN. EST. 1948. YOUR HOST: BEBE LOUDERMILK.

The new host opened the door to the manager's unit with a bright smile firmly fixed, and promptly faced her past.

The woman standing in the doorway was tall and willowy, with lustrous black hair that fell straight to her shoulders, flawless alabaster skin, and odd green cat eyes that took in everything and missed nothing. Just as they had all those years ago when we were both at Savannah Country Day School.

"BeBe Loudermilk? What on earth are you doing out here at Tybee Island?"

"Hello, Sadie," I said, trying for warmth, but not coming even close. "I'm the owner," I said, gesturing to the desk and the new sign. "Are you staying with us?"

"I sure as hell hope so," she drawled. "Didn't you get my reservation?"

"Come on in," I said, opening the door a little wider. Behind her on the porch stood a small mountain of luggage, and a small, perturbed little boy.

She grabbed his arm. "Peyton, sugar," she said sharply. "Come in here, now."

"No." He deftly extricated himself from her grasp and stepped backward on the porch. "I want to see the dog."

"Peyton!" Her lips pressed together in an angry red line. "Don't you dare take a step off this porch or I will call your daddy right this minute." She held a cell phone in her hand for him to see. "Shall I call Daddy in Atlanta?"

"No," he said, his shoulders drooping. Pale, skinny legs hung from gray flannel shorts that matched the gray cashmere sweater hanging loosely from his bony little frame. "I'm coming."

I scrambled to the reservation book behind the front desk, praying that she'd shown up at the wrong inn. I'd pored over the book only an hour earlier, and I definitely would have noticed if Harry or I had taken a reservation for Sadie Troy.

This same Sadie Troy had been the queen of our exclusive private school. Oddly, she didn't fit any of the usual definitions of high school royalty. Not a cheerleader, not class president or homecoming queen, and definitely not most popular. No, Sadie Troy had been more feared than popular, leading a tightly knit clique of girls who were the *it* chicks at Savannah Country Day. I'd been at the periphery of that clique, accepted because I knew how to fix my hair, how to roll the waistband of my plaid uniform skirt just so, how to scrunch down the hated and required knee socks, and most important, how to torment any girls who were not in our clique. What a relief it had been, after graduation day, when I escaped into a world not defined by the Sadie Troys of the planet.

Now I ran my fingers down the booking list. "I don't see your name."

She reached over the counter and grabbed the book from me. "Right here," she said, jabbing at the last name. "Mrs. Peyton Hausbrook III."

"Right," I said glumly. So this was the last-minute referral from the Gastonian, this was the person who'd be sleeping in my bed tonight. "Welcome to the Breeze Inn."

She looked around the office and sniffed. "Wet paint? I hope my suite doesn't smell like this. Peyton has horrific allergies. Especially to chemicals."

She turned to search for her son, who was happily sitting on the floor, his arms clamped tightly around a furiously wriggling Jeeves.

"He's allergic to animals too!" she cried, snatching Jeeves from the boy's arms and flinging the dog across the room. Jeeves yelped a sharp protest and shot out the open front door.

"Surely you don't allow dogs in the inn," she said, turning back to me.

"Well, no," I said, flustered by Sadie's sudden intrusion back into my life. "Jeeves belongs to my uh . . ."

What should I call Harry? My manager? But I was the manager now. Handyman? Such a menial-sounding word. He'd throttle me if he ever heard me using such a term.

"Factotum."

Speak of the devil. Harry himself stood in the doorway, one of Sadie's suitcases in each hand. "Which suite shall I take these to, Ms. Loudermilk?"

"My, uh, I mean, the Surfside," I said, gratefully. "Thank you, Harry."

He nodded. "Anything else?"

"Not right now," Sadie said dismissively. "I'll ring if I need you." She reached in the canary yellow Coach valise on her arm and brought out a billfold bristling with credit cards, extracted a five-dollar bill, and extended it to him with her fingertips. "Just see that there's ice. And what brands of liquor do you have in the minibar?"

"Minibar?" Such a thing had not occurred to me while I was racing to get basic plumbing restored.

"I'm just restocking," Harry said smoothly. "What brand do you prefer?"

"Stoli." Sadie said. She handed him a twenty. "Get fresh lemons too."

"Take me maybe ten minutes," Harry said, the picture of courtliness. He nodded at both of us and left.

I took a deep breath and glanced at the clock: 12:10.

"Actually," I said, "you're a little early, Sadie. Check-in time is at two."

"Two? No, that wouldn't work at all. We're due at Patti Mazzone's for tea at two-thirty. You remember Patti from Country Day. And if I don't get a hot shower in the next five minutes, I cannot be responsible for the consequences. As you can see, I'm a wreck after four hours in the car with my little man here," she said, jerking her head in Peyton's direction.

She was the farthest thing from a wreck. Her green slacks were crisply creased, the matching jacket—was it from this year's Armani collection?—tightly belted at the waist over a creamy silk blouse. She wore jade earrings and bangle bracelets, and her only ring was a door-knocker-size square-cut diamond on her left hand.

Peyton stood looking solemnly up at me, pale blue eyes unblinking.

"Were you a good boy for your mom on the drive down?" I asked.

"She is *not* my mother," the child yelled.

Sadie's cheeks flushed ever so slightly.

"Peyton," she said, clutching his shoulder. "We need to use our indoors voice."

"Well, she's not," he said, softly now, but just as insistent.

"Stepmother," Sadie mouthed the word to me.

I nodded.

Peyton went and stood by the door, his back turned to both of us.

"Impossible." Sadie rolled her eyes and sighed. "What were you saying?"

"I was saying that check-in time is two," I repeated. "I'm sorry, but we've just finished a major remodeling, and your room really won't be ready till two."

"Nobody told me anything about two o'clock," Sadie said, frowning. She reached into her billfold again and took out a twenty and slid it in my direction.

"Look, BeBe, it's been *lovely* seeing you after all these years. I'm dying to catch up with what you've been doing with yourself down here, later on. But right now it is *imperative* I get into my room immediately. I've got an important conference call in ten minutes, and I need to be someplace quiet while we close a twenty-eight-million retail mall in Jacksonville."

I pushed the twenty back in her direction, trying not to lose my temper. "The thing is, your room isn't ready."

"Then give me another room. Any room, as long as it has ice, television, lemons, and some Stoli." She gave me a smile I remembered from the dark old days. It reminded me of the smile of one of those predatory animals you see on *Animal Planet,* right before said animal devours its young.

"Check-in time is two," I repeated. "And none of the rooms has a television. People come here to get away from telephones and televisions."

I didn't feel it necessary to share with her that we couldn't afford to install such modern contraptions.

Sadie blanched visibly. "No television?" She leaned closer, her eyes glittering. "I've got a four-year-old child with me, if you hadn't noticed. How in hell am I going to entertain the little urchin until his father gets down here if I don't have a television?"

She was really starting to get under my skin. Suddenly, I realized that I was no longer as intimidated by the imperial Sadie Troy. It was liberating.

"I'll understand if you want to cancel your reservation," I said. "Maybe check into a place that is more adequately equipped to meet your needs. Of course, with our cancellation policy, we'll have to charge you for one night."

"It's St. Patrick's Day. The whole damn town is booked solid and you know it," Sadie snapped. "There isn't a vacant hotel room anywhere. I checked."

"That's right," I said sadly. "Well, maybe you could go to Patti's a little early. Or get a bite of lunch. And when you get back, after two, your room should be ready."

"I'm hungry!" young Peyton announced, right on cue. "I want a Happy Meal."

A bright pink spot appeared on each of Sadie's cheeks. "Indoors voice, please."

"With extra fries!" Peyton hollered in his best outdoors voice.

The desk phone rang and I snatched it up. "Breeze Inn," I said cheerily.

"How's it going?" Weezie asked. "Are you rich yet?"

Which gave me an idea.

"Fine!" I said heartily. And then, "Oh, dear, you're overbooked too?"

"What?" Weezie demanded. "Who are you talking to?"

"I'll see," I said. I put my hand over the receiver. "This is the 1790 Inn. They've got a guest who's desperate for an extra room. Should I tell them yours is available?"

"No!" Sadie said. She grabbed the twenty-dollar bill and stuffed it back into her pocketbook. "We're going to eat, and we'll be back at exactly two o'clock. All right?"

"Fine," I said. "Sadie, do you want to go ahead and give me your credit card to hold the room, in case you're unavoidably delayed?"

She handed over her platinum card. I ran it through the credit card machine, handed it back to her, and she stormed out, slamming the door in her wake.

"What's going on there?" Weezie asked. "Who's Sadie? Is everything all right?"

"Everything's just fine now," I said, chuckling.

By the time Harry got back with the vodka and lemons fifteen minutes later, I'd had time to run a brush through my hair, dab on some mascara and lipstick, and start checking all the rooms.

At one forty-five, the first guest checked in. All afternoon, the phone rang, the doorbell buzzed, and Jeeves barked.

For the most part, our guests seemed delighted with the refurbished Breeze.

Except for the occupant of the Surfside Suite.

At seven P.M., Sadie appeared at the front desk. "Have I had any phone calls?"

I looked at Harry, who'd been manning the phones while I snuck out for a quick sandwich. "Any calls for— I'm sorry, Sadie. I've forgotten your married name."

"Hausbrook," she said swiftly. "Mrs. Peyton Hausbrook. I'm expecting to hear from my husband. He should have gotten here by now. He hasn't called my cell phone, so I thought maybe he might have called the office looking for me."

"Nope," Harry said, not looking up from the fishing catalog he was reading. "Nobody looking for anybody like that."

"You're sure?" She drummed her fingertips on the desk. "It's H-A-U-S—"

"Positive," Harry said. "P-O-S-I-T-I-V-E."

She flounced out, and he looked up at me inquisitively. "Old school chum?"

I shuddered. "It was a long time ago."

At eight o'clock, the desk phone rang. It was Sadie. "Are you sure my husband hasn't called here looking for me?"

"Very sure," I assured her.

"Anyway," she went on, "I think you'd better send that man over here to my room. There's something wrong with the bathroom sink. Every time I turn on the faucet, it smells like rotten eggs."

"That's Tybee water," I explained. "It has a high sulphur content. It's very healthy. Full of vitamins."

"Revolting," she said, and hung up. But fifteen minutes later, the phone rang again.

"Ice." Sadie again.

"I beg your pardon?" I said.

"Where the fug's the ice?" Her words were slurred. Just how big was that bottle of Stoli Harry had delivered to her room?

"The ice machine is in the breezeway, to the right of your room," I said. "You'll find an ice bucket on your dresser."

"Fug."

More guests checked in. I fielded requests for directions to town, gave restaurant recommendations, and told at least a dozen more callers that we were, unfortunately, all booked up, with not so much as a broom closet suitable for occupancy. At ten, a man called and asked for Harry Sorrentino.

He'd been half asleep, watching ESPN, but he took the call and listened with mounting excitement.

"Yeah. Okay. No problem. I'll be right there."

He hung up. "I've gotta go."

"All right," I said.

"I've been on the clock since six this morning," he pointed out.

"I know. So go already."

"I might be a while," he warned. "You got a problem with that?"

"Not at all," I said wearily. "I wish I had the energy to go with you."

At eleven o'clock, I started to look longingly in the direction of the recliner where Jeeves snored in happy oblivion. At eleven-thirty, the phone on the desk rang again.

"Breeze—"

"BeBe!" Sadie shrieked. "Get over here! The fuggin' toilet is backed up."

By the time I got to my unit, water was streaming out from under the door. Sadie Troy, clad in red satin pajamas, sat in the middle of my bed, surrounded by her luggage, a half-full highball glass in her hand. Young Peyton, pajama clad also, perched wide-eyed on the rocker, his feet tucked up under him.

"What happened?" I asked, wading toward the bathroom.

"I dunno," Sadie said, running her hand through her gleaming dark hair. "Peyton went in there to brush his teeth, and all of a sudden, the damn thing sort of 'sploded."

I peeked inside the bathroom. Water ran over the side of the commode. A small bar of soap floated at my feet, and sodden towels swirled around on the tile floor.

"For Chrissake, make it stop!" Sadie ordered.

So I squatted on the floor and surveyed the situation. There was a valve at the base of the commode. Common sense said to turn it. I did, and the running water stopped running. But now what? Weezie would have known what to do. Weezie could rewire a house with nothing more than a dull butter knife and a roll of duct tape.

But my name was not Weezie Foley. My name was BeBe Loudermilk. I was vice president of the National Honor Society at Savannah Country Day School. I had made my bow at eighteen at the St. Cecilia's Debutante Ball in Charleston and I had a bachelor's degree in art history from Agnes Scott College, but I had no experience with plumbing.

I closed my eyes and tried to think. My daddy was not what you would call a do-it-yourself type. If something went wrong at our house when I was a child, he simply had his secretary call somebody and take care of it.

But once, I recalled, on a Sunday, we'd had a stopped-up commode. And my father had attacked it with a big rubber plunger. There was a plunger in this bathroom. I'd seen it, in the corner. So now I picked it up, put it in the bowl and pumped, up and down, vigorously, half a dozen times.

And after what might have been maybe the seventh time, I heard a loud "thwuck." When I pulled up the plunger, a hunk of pink fabric appeared. I took a close look. A very lacy, delicate, pink underwire bra dangled from the bottom of my plunger.

"Sadie?" I called, walking into the bedroom, brandishing the plunger and the bra. "Does this look familiar?"

She blinked. "Wha' the fug?" She pointed at the child, who was now cowering in the chair. "Peyton! Did you flush my bra down that toilet?"

"Nooooo," the child wailed. "I waaant my mamaaaaa."

"Peyton!" Sadie leaped off the bed, splashed over to the rocker, and thrust the bra into his face. "Tell me the truth right this minute. Did you do this?"

"Noooo," he cried, squirming to escape her wrath.

"Lying lil' fugger," she mumbled. "Wait till I tell your daddy."

"I WANT MY MAMA!" Peyton cried.

"Me too kid," I said, yawning. And I went to look for a mop.

28

*I was lolling about on the sugary sand beach at Mango Cay, the warm
sun glinting off the azure water, tropical breezes caressing my bare shoulders. Travis McGee reached for the ice bucket, where the Dom Perignon had
been chilling since our afternoon swim, pausing only to plant a hot, passionate kiss on my warm and willing lips. The champagne bubbles tickled my
nose, and suddenly I heard a sharp, annoying buzz.*

And now a banging, accompanied by more buzzing.

"Hey! Anybody home in there?"

I sat up and was acutely, painfully aware that Mango Cay was a
dream, and my reality was right here, on a motel sofa. It was six A.M.
I'd finished cleaning up Sadie Troy's flooded bathroom at around
one, trudged back here, to Harry's apartment, and fallen dead asleep
on the sofa.

"Coming," I hollered.

The man in the doorway had wet hair. He wore a white under-
shirt, drawstring pajama bottoms, untied sneakers, and an unhappy
expression. Mr. Abel, from the Starfish Suite.

"Good morning, Mr. Abel," I said, groggily. "Did you sleep well?"

"Yeah," he said unenthusiastically. "But you only gave us two bath
towels. My wife went out for her morning run, and when she gets
back, she's gonna want towels."

"Fine," I nodded. "Be right back." I took two bath towels from the
laundry room and brought them out to him, along with another
sliver of soap, as a goodwill gesture.

"All right?" I asked, handing them over.

"Yeah. Also, I didn't see a coffeemaker in our room."

Coffeemakers for all the units were on my to-buy list, but they would have to wait until we got a positive cash flow going.

"Oh," I said, trying to think fast. "I guess I forgot to tell you. We always serve coffee and muffins to our guests right here in the office, from eight till ten."

"No coffee in the rooms?" He frowned.

"You can always take it back to your room," I offered. "But this way you can meet our other guests."

"Whatever." He turned and walked away.

"And good morning to you too, Captain Sunshine," I muttered.

After putting the coffee on to perk, I took a quick shower, dressed, and straightened up the office area, since we were apparently going to have our first official coffee klatch. I knocked lightly on Harry's door, but there was no answer. I went to the window and glanced out at the parking lot. No station wagon.

Where was Harry? Had he returned last night? He hadn't offered an explanation for where he was going, and after our last fight, I wasn't about to ask, and I sure as hell wasn't about to go looking for him either.

Instead, I bustled around the office, fielding still more phone calls. I managed to take several reservations for upcoming weekends in April, and I even—hallelujah!—booked the Sunflower and SeaGlass units for a whole week apiece the last week of the month, which was apparently spring break for some schools in Atlanta. I wrote notes inviting all our guests to join me for coffee and muffins after eight, and made a quick run through the property, slipping notes under everybody's door.

By eight o'clock, I had coffee and tea ready, platters of warm muffins, and a motley assortment of mugs and cups and saucers set out.

"Helllooo." A head popped in the front door, and then another.

They were Michael and Eugene, the couple in the Palmetto Suite, who'd arrived at ten last night, exhausted from the drive down from Atlanta.

"Are we too early?" This, I thought, was Eugene, who'd told me last night that he'd just recently taken early retirement from the state department of education. He was tall, with a high forehead, thinning brown hair, and an impish smile.

"She's got coffee brewed," his partner said, sniffing the air. "And somebody's been baking!" Michael, I thought, remembering that the shorter half of the duo was the one with the thick thatch of white hair, mustache, and horn-rimmed glasses. He wore white linen slacks, an Irish fisherman's sweater, and polished loafers without socks.

"Not me," I confessed. "I do a lot of things, but baking isn't one of 'em. These are from a chef friend. And since you're the first ones here, you get your pick."

"Goodie!" Eugene said, reaching into the basket for a muffin. While he and Michael poured themselves coffee, I started greeting other guests filtering in. The mother and daughter from SeaGlass, reintroduced themselves as Judy and Sarah Murry. Sarah, sipping from a can of Diet Dr Pepper, tanned and impossibly long legged in hot pink shorts and flip-flops, was a college student. Judy was a divorced fashion designer from Florida whose pierced eyebrow gave her the look of an exotic Indian princess.

"Not muffins!" Sarah groaned. "I'm doing Atkins." Her mother popped a bit of muffin in her mouth. "Oh, Sarah, give it a rest. I'm sick of hearing about diets."

By nine o'clock, Harry's living room was full of guests chatting about their weekend plans. At nine-thirty, a wan-looking Sadie crept into the room, without Peyton.

"Morning," I said. "Did you two finally get some sleep?"

"Just barely," she croaked. "The little man woke up at seven on the dot, wanting to know why he couldn't watch Saturday-morning cartoons."

"Sorry."

"You'll never know how sorry I was," she said, pouring herself a mug of black coffee. She flicked at the muffin basket. "Croissants?"

"Muffins," I said cheerily. "From the best restaurant in Savannah."

She raised an eyebrow. "Really? What's it called? Can you get us dinner reservations for tonight?"

"The restaurant's called Guale," I said proudly. "Unfortunately, we're closed right now for remodeling. But check back with us later this summer."

"Hmm," she said, breaking off the top of a muffin with her fingertips. "Don't know when we'll get back down here again. Our schedules are impossible."

"Where's little Peyton this morning?" I asked.

She rolled her eyes. "Back in the room. He whined incessantly until I agreed to find him a McDonald's so he could have his goddamned pancakes and sausage." She shuddered violently. "His mother lets him eat any kind of crap he wants during the week, and of course, on the weekends that my husband has custody, I have to pay the price."

"And your husband? Will he be joining us this morning?" I asked maliciously.

"This afternoon. *If* he doesn't miss his flight. We've both got parties tonight and I told him I'd never forgive him if he didn't make it."

"Fingers crossed," I said perkily, moving away with rapid speed. I desperately wanted to meet the man who'd committed himself to a lifetime of Sadie.

"Miss?" A fiftyish woman in white tennis shorts and sweater came into the office, her round face flushed, her hair damp with sweat. This was Ellie Cater, a dog breeder from North Carolina. "I just got back to my room, and the maid hasn't cleaned it yet."

Ah yes. The maid.

"Sorry," I said, putting down the coffeepot. "We're a little short-staffed this weekend. I'll take care of it right away."

Two hours later, after changing fourteen sets of linens, sweeping sand out of fourteen rooms and scrubbing the last of fourteen toilets, I caught a glimpse of myself in the bathroom mirror of the Sunflower Suite. Dark circles under my eyes, hair an impossible tangle. No makeup. My mother never, ever left her bedroom without a smooth coat of Merle Norman foundation, blush pink rouge, and Maybelline mascara. She was so dedicated to Tangee "Captivating Coral" lipstick that she kept a tube of it in the pocket of every skirt, coat, and pocketbook she owned. When she died, I threw away nearly a dozen tubes of the stuff, all worn right down to the metal nub.

What would Mama say, I wondered, if she saw me now. I'd never seen her do any real housework. From my earliest childhood, we'd had a series of "girls" who kept the Loudermilk household running smoothly.

Now, *I* was the girl. I peeled off my elbow-length rubber gloves and tucked them into a side pocket on the large rolling cleaning cart left in the storage shed by the previous owners of the Breeze Inn. As I trundled it down the breezeway toward that same shed, I glanced around the half-full parking lot. Still no sign of Harry's station wagon.

Back in the office, I slathered lotion on my hands and transcribed messages from the answering machine. Most were just people looking for rooms for the weekend, a couple of inquiries for future bookings. I returned calls, took reservations, and at some point in the afternoon had a muffin and a cup of coffee for a late lunch.

When the phone rang at two, I picked it up again. "Breeze Inn."

"BeBe?" It was my grandmother. "Is that you, BeBe?"

"Yes, ma'am," I said quickly. "How are you? Are you feeling all right?"

"I'm fine," she said. "But what was that you said when you answered the phone?"

"Oh. Breeze Inn."

"What's a Breeze Inn?"

"It's an inn, Grandmama. I bought the sweetest little inn, out here at Tybee. And I'm having just the best time fixing it up and running it."

Hah! God would strike me dead sometime for telling such a bold-faced lie to my granny. "But how did you know to call me out here?"

"That friend of yours, Weezie. I saw her at the drugstore this morning, and mentioned that we haven't heard from you in over a week, so she gave me your new number. An inn? What in the world?"

"Well, it was just such a good investment, I couldn't resist," I lied. "Right on the water, down at the south end of the beach."

"That's nice, I guess," she said. "But what about the restaurant?"

"We're doing some remodeling, and I was tired of just sitting around doing nothing, so I picked this place up for a song. It was sort of a whim, you might say." Wow. The lying was getting really easy.

"Just a minute, darlin'," Grandmama said. "Spencer wants to speak with you."

"BeBe?" Granddaddy's voice boomed. "Lorena thinks you're upset with us."

"No!" I protested.

"You haven't called. Haven't come by. Been more than a week."

I winced. "I'm sorry. I'm not upset with you at all. I've taken on a new business project. It's an inn, out at Tybee Island. And it's keeping me really busy."

I could hear my grandmother's voice in the background. "Spencer Loudermilk, you give me that phone right now."

Now she was back on the line again. "He's the one who's all worried about you. I told him, 'Spencer, BeBe is a grown woman. She doesn't have time to check on a couple of old poops like us every day.'"

"You're not an old poop!"

"No, but your granddaddy is," she said, chuckling. "What's that? All right, he wants to talk to you again. Now, when you're not busy, you give us a call, you hear?"

"BeBe?" I had to hold the phone away from my ear. "Listen, there's something funny with one of our bank accounts. Now, it's nothing drastic, but next time you come over, we need to take a look at that thing."

I swallowed hard. He knew. He knew what I'd done.

"All right, Granddaddy," I said meekly. "Can it wait till after St. Patrick's Day?"

"Absoutely," he boomed. "Talk to you soon. Call your grandmother though, so she won't pester me about you."

"Spencer!"

I hung up the phone and banged my head on the tabletop. How had I dragged them into this mess? And how was I going to make it right again?

29

Somehow, I made it through the next twenty-four hours. In between mopping and taking reservations and running loads of sheets and towels and playing the smiling innkeeper, I kept an eye out for Harry Sorrentino, my errant "factotum." I alternated between being frantic and furious over his whereabouts.

Half a dozen times Saturday, and again Sunday morning, I picked up the phone to call the police and report him missing. Half a dozen more times I resolved to pack up his books and clothes and tools and fling them out onto the street. How dare he take off and leave me in the lurch like this? Was he dead or drowned? I had no idea, and no idea of how to find out.

Come Sunday afternoon, I'd convinced myself I just plain didn't care where he'd gone. I was sitting in one of the Adirondack chairs in front of the manager's office, enjoying the late-afternoon sun and sipping a glass of wine, when the old station wagon came chugging into the parking lot.

"Son of a bitch!" I muttered. With an effort, I stayed seated. Jeeves heard the car and came bounding out the office door, barking a greeting to his long-lost master.

"Hey, hey, sport," Harry laughed, kneeling down to scratch the belly the dog offered. Jeeves wriggled deliriously under his touch, then jumped up and began running in circles around Harry and the station wagon.

"Hang on there, buddy," Harry told the dog. "Let me get my stuff unloaded." He opened the wagon's hatch and removed half a dozen heavy-duty fishing rods, a tackle box, and a large cooler, then headed for the porch, where I was sitting.

He was sunburned, salt crusted, and filthy, and even with the polarized sunglasses he wore, I could tell he was glowing with good humor. The same could not be said of me.

"Hello," I said coolly.

He nodded a greeting. "Hey there. Everything go okay around here?"

"Just peachy," I said.

"Great. I'm headed for the shower," he said. And as he walked past, I got a whiff of diesel fuel and the unmistakable scent of dead fish.

Half an hour later, barefoot and dressed in faded but clean khaki slacks and a blue work shirt, he eased himself into the Adirondack chair beside mine. He untwisted the cap on a bottle of beer and took a long slug.

"Aaaah." He took his beer bottle and clinked it against my wineglass. "Here's to us," he said. "The place looks great."

"Us?"

"Yeah. We did it." He gestured around the parking lot. "Every room, I mean suite, is full. Swear to God, I never thought the place could look like this."

I clamped my lips together to keep from screaming, and clutched the arms of the chair to keep myself from reaching over and slapping the look of self-satisfaction off his face.

He took another gulp of beer and belched. " 'Scuse me," he said sheepishly, a moment later. "I've been living alone so long I forget my manners."

"Have a nice weekend?" I managed.

"Oh yeah," he said. "Couldn't have gone better. How 'bout you? Any problems?"

Was he friggin' kidding me?

"Let's see," I said, trying to sum up my list of problems. "I've been running this place single-handed for two days. I've been manager, maid, handyman, and janitor. I've unstopped the toilet in the Surfside Suite four times, fixed the dryer twice, and washed, dried, folded, and stacked approximately two hundred towels. And," I said glaring at him, "cleaned up dog poop from the breezeway several times."

"Sorry about that," he said. "Jeeves gets a little anxious when I'm gone."

"Yeah," I said. "Me too."

He took off the sunglasses. "What?"

I took a deep breath. "You get a phone call in the middle of the night, then you just disappear for two days. On our opening weekend!"

"Oh," he said. "Yeah. But you handled it, right?"

"I didn't have much of a choice," I said wryly. "But it would have been nice to have some help. I've never run a motel, I mean an inn, before."

"You did fine though. Nobody's dead. The place is still standing." He reached over and gave me a proprietary pat on the knee. "Give yourself some credit here, kid. You're a natural."

I measured my words slowly. I didn't need another fight. But I really did want to know where he'd gone and why.

"I take it you went fishing," I said finally.

"Yup."

"Do fish bite around here this time of year?"

"They do if you know where to look. And I do." He pointed toward the office. "I left you a little present in that cooler. Prettiest fillets you've ever seen. Red snapper."

This was a first. I'd had men bring me red roses before, but never red snapper.

"Thanks," I said. "But how? I mean, I thought the marina took your boat?"

"Shh." He held his fingers to his lips. "Trade secret."

"And that's all you're going to tell me?" I finally lost it. "Damnit, Harry! You've been gone for two days. I know I'm not your mother, or your lover, or any other thing. But I am your employer, and I think I deserve some explanation for where you've been and why you chose this particular weekend—the Breeze's opening weekend—to take a powder on me."

He slouched back down in the chair. "Shit, BeBe. I just thought, you know, everything was pretty much running fine around here. We got everything fixed in time to open, and, well, hell, maybe I wasn't thinking."

"Maybe?"

He glanced around to see if anybody was within earshot. Nobody was stirring. Most of our guests were either out partying or in their rooms recovering before getting ready to go back out for more partying.

"All right, I'll tell you where I was. But you gotta keep quiet about it," he said, his voice barely above a whisper. "I mean it, now. You can't tell anybody about this."

"About what? I don't know anything to tell."

He leaned forward. "I found the sweet spot."

I frowned. "Is this some kind of sex club or something? Because if it is, you can just keep the tawdry details to yourself, Harry Sorrentino. I've been mixed up with one pervert in my life already, and I don't intend to have it happen again."

"Sex? Nah, nothing like that. What I mean is, I found the ultimate honey hole."

I jumped up out of my chair. "That's it. Get your stuff and get out. I'll have to pay you what I owe you in installments, but I want you off my property!"

He grabbed my wrist. "Hey now. Slow down, kid. Get your mind out of the gutter. I'm talking about fish. I think I found a way to get the *Jitterbug* back."

"You did?"

"Get yourself another glass of wine," he said. "And I'll tell you the whole deal. Oh yeah, and could you grab me a beer while you're at it?"

"You've got exactly one hour," I told him. "The guests meet in the manager's office at five for happy hour."

When I got back, Harry had a map unfolded across his knees. I sat down in my chair, and he spread it out across my lap. Even a landlubber like myself could tell that it was a chart showing the coast of Georgia and South Carolina.

"This here," he said, jabbing with a finger at a swath of ocean, "is where I've been for the past two days. The snapper banks."

"Okay." It sounded plausible.

"But not just any spot out in the snapper banks," he continued. "See, it's too early for good offshore fishing right now. Fish are migratory. You know that, right?"

"I know that birds are migratory, but the only thing I know about fish is the wholesale price I paid for the good stuff at the restaurant," I said.

"But you don't understand how hard it is to find that great fishing hole," he said, jabbing at the map again. "All the waters in this area are charted. Every decent captain on every boat knows where the fish are. And where the fish are depends on the topography of the sea bottom, on rock and coral formations, jetties, reefs, wrecks, what have you. A wreck is a huge draw for fish. But all that stuff is charted. So everybody's fighting to get out there first, to get to the good spot before the other guy. The farther out you go, the more time and money it costs."

"To find a honey hole," I said, catching on.

"Exactly." He nodded happily at my newfound comprehension.

His eyes lit up. "And I found it. By God, I found it. And nobody else knows about it. That's where I went Friday night. I went out and fished that sucker." He patted the pocket of his jeans. "You're gonna think I'm lying. Hell, I can't quite believe it myself. But in two days' time, we caught close to two thousand pounds of red snapper and grouper. I thought the damned boat would sink under all that fish. Two thousand pounds!"

"That's good?"

"Charlie Russo's paying $3.10 a pound for red snapper," Harry said. "Yeah, I'd call that good."

I would too. Especially since I knew what I paid Russo's Seafood for the fish I bought from him for Guale.

"But how?" I asked. "You don't have a boat."

He eased back into the chair. "I sorta borrowed one. Just for the two days."

"Sorta?" I was getting a very bad feeling now. Was that how Reddy rationalized his fake ownership of the *Blue Moon*? By "sorta" borrowing it?

I shook my head. "I don't want to know any more. If you've stolen a boat, Harry, you could be in a world of trouble. And I've got enough troubles of my own right now. You're on your own with the law," I said. And then, bitterly, "Sport."

"Christ," he said. "You always think the worst of me, don't you? That I'm a drunk and a thief and a lowlife?"

"You don't give me a lot of information that would lead me to think otherwise," I said icily.

"The boat I borrowed was the *Jitterbug*," he said. "It's my own damn boat. Is that enough information for you?"

I held the wineglass up to the sunlight and swirled the chardonnay. It was pretty crappy chardonnay, $9.99 for a liter bottle at the Tybee Market, but if you poured it into a nice glass and sipped it quickly, you didn't notice the vinegary qualities. Anyway, I'd taken to serving the chardonnay and an equally crappy merlot to the Breeze guests at my informal happy hour, along with Ritz crackers and pimento-cheese spread also from the Tybee Market.

"The marina owners gave you permission to borrow the *Jitterbug*? That's pretty generous of them."

"Generous? Tricia Marsden wouldn't take the time to piss on me if I were on fire. No, I forgot to ask her permission this time."

"Forgive me for quibbling over semantics, but when you borrow something without the owner's permission, isn't that called stealing?"

"Not in this case," he said stubbornly. "Look, I took the boat because I had a certain window of opportunity this weekend. The moon was right, the tides were right. The water is warming up. And clear skies. I just had the feeling that if I could get out there, I could find the honey hole and catch me some fish. And I did. And now I can give them a thousand bucks toward what I owe them."

"Only a thousand?" I raised an eyebrow.

"I had to buy fuel and ice and bait, and pay my mate," Harry said. "And yeah, I kept some back, for my own living expenses. But the rest goes to Tricia."

I should have minded my own business. But I had to know. "How'd you manage to 'borrow' the boat without her knowing about it?"

He whistled a tuneless little ditty. "That phone call Friday night? That was a friend, letting me know Tricia was leaving to go to Florida to visit her sister for the weekend. She won't get back till tonight. But when she does, the *Jitterbug* will be right where she left it. Clean as a whistle. And what Tricia doesn't know won't hurt her."

I heard a door open down the breezeway, and Michael and Eugene stepped out of their unit, shading their eyes against the sunlight.

"BeBe!" Michael called, stumbling in my direction. "Aspirin, darlin', stat."

"Gotta go," I told Harry. "Party time."

30

On a sunny morning two weeks later, I was sitting in the office at the Breeze, frowning down at the ledger. When the office door opened, I looked up, hoping to see a carload of guests who were just dying to check in.

But it was James Foley. He carried a battered leather briefcase, and the crinkles at the corners of his eyes deepened with the smile he gave me.

"James!" I said, jumping up from the desk. "Tell me you've brought me some good news. Tell me you've gotten my house back. Tell me you've stopped those bastards at Sandcastle Realty. At least tell me you got me back my painting of Aunt Alice."

He sighed and set his briefcase down on the counter. "BeBe, I wish I could tell you all of those things today. I'm sorry, but I can't."

I managed a rueful smile. "Then at least tell me you'll take me to lunch."

"That I can do," he said. "And I'll even pay."

Since it was such a sunny day, we decided on the Crab Shack. Over blue crabs and iced tea, James caught me up on my legal status.

"It's not all bad news," he started. "The judge has enjoined Sandcastle from taking any action to sell or otherwise develop the Breeze Inn, based on our evidence that Reddy Millbanks acted fraudulently when he sold the option without your knowledge."

"Thank God," I said.

"I did," James said, twinkling. He reached over and patted my hand. "There's another reason I came out to see you today. I have news," he said, lowering his voice and looking steadily into my eyes. "I think I know where to find Roy Eugene Moseley."

It sounds hokey, but right then, I felt the hair stand up on the back of my neck.

"Reddy? You found him?"

"Maybe," James said. "Just maybe."

I took a deep breath. "Where?"

"Down in Florida. Fort Lauderdale, to be exact."

"Fort Lauderdale. Where the girls are," I said, laughing at my own joke.

"Women," James corrected me. "Roy Eugene Moseley likes women. Women with money, specifically. Anyway, it's not the money that took him to Fort Lauderdale. It's the boats."

"Boats again?"

James nodded. "Fort Lauderdale is considered the boating capital of the world."

"I didn't know that. But what about Reddy? Can the cops get to him?"

He held out a cautionary hand. "Hold on. Not so fast. Remember, I told you Detective Bradley found out that Moseley fleeced a widow in Vero Beach, right before he moved up here and met you?"

"Polly's Folly. How could I forget? I even remember that he likes Sea Urchins. So, Reddy found another rich lady with a Sea Urchin down in Fort Lauderdale?"

"Possibly," James said. "Unlike you, Polly Findley still had lots of money left after Roy Eugene Moseley skipped town. He ripped her off, but thanks to her very suspicious children, who are very protective of their inheritance, there's still lots of money to go around."

"How nice for her," I said.

"Mrs. Findley's children would like to have *all* their late father's money," James said, grinning. "Their mother, understandably, is embarrassed and humiliated by the whole tawdry affair. She'd like it forgotten. But her children, especially her older daughter, Sandra, have no intention of dropping the matter. Sandra Findley has been dogging the Vero Beach police on an almost daily basis. When the detective down there mentioned to Sandra that Moseley had victimized another woman, in Savannah, Sandra called our own Detective Bradley to compare notes."

"And?"

"Bradley filled her in on your situation, and then suggested that she contact me, which she did. We had a long chat this morning. Very illuminating."

"What does she know about Reddy, I mean, Roy Eugene Moseley, that the police don't?"

" 'Know' isn't quite the correct word," James said gently. "It's more like suspicion. But I will say this for her. Sandra Findley has two things going for her that law-enforcement people don't. One, she is very motivated. And two, she has the time and the inclination to pursue Roy Eugene Moseley. She's never married, has no children, and apparently doesn't have to work for a living."

"Lucky girl."

"She's obsessed with tracking down Moseley and bringing him to justice. I think she's seen too many episodes of *The Rockford Files*."

I gripped the tabletop with my hands. "Come on, James. Quit stalling. Just tell me what you know. Or even what you think Sandra Findley thinks she knows."

"Sorry." James's eyes did that crinkly thing. "All right. Once Sandra talked to Jay Bradley and heard that Moseley had been living aboard a Sea Urchin here in Savannah, she decided to try that angle. She called the Sea Urchin folks in Michigan, and got the name of every yacht brokerage in Florida authorized to sell Sea Urchins. There are only two of those on the East Coast. She visited each one and showed them the only photograph she had, which was a fuzzy color snapshot taken of her mother and Moseley aboard *Polly's Folly*."

"And?"

"Nothing," James said. "I told you, these are very expensive yachts. The cheapest one sells new for around eight million. According to Sandra, people who buy Sea Urchins are rock stars, CEOs of multinational corporations, that kind of thing. Very high profile. Neither of the brokers had seen anybody even close to Moseley's description."

"But you said he's in Fort Lauderdale. What makes you think that?"

"One of the yacht brokers Sandra talked to suggested that somebody like Moseley—somebody with his criminal background—probably wouldn't attempt to buy a new Sea Urchin. Prospective buyers of a yacht this expensive have to get vetted six ways to Sunday before they can get anywhere near one of these boats. All your financials are scrutinized. Bankers are called, references are checked. Not even Roy Eugene Moseley would run that risk. The broker suggested that if Moseley were going to try to buy—or even steal—a Sea Urchin, he'd do so on the secondary market."

"I don't understand," I admitted.

"In some ways, buying a yacht is like buying a car, in some ways, it's more like buying a house," James explained. "If you want to buy a yacht, you can go to a broker, who is like an authorized dealer. Or, you could go to a boatyard or marina and look around. Or you could look in the classified ads. You could even go online. Sandra did all that and more. That's how she found out about BUC."

"Buck? Like a deer? Or like a stud?"

"Neither," James said. "BUC is an acronym for a company that serves as a multiple-listing service for yachts. They publish printed catalogs of yachts available for sale, and they also have an online listing service. And that's where Sandra found the paradox."

"You mean, paradox like a fable?" I asked.

"Sorry," he said, shaking his head again. "It's a boat name. *Pair-o'-Docs*—get it? Pair of doctors. One is a plastic surgeon, the other a radiologist."

"Lame," I said. "What happened to just naming your boat for your wife or your mama like the shrimpers down here do?"

"These doctors, between them, reportedly have seven ex-wives," James said. "Anyway, this *Pair-o'-Docs* is a seventy-five-foot 1991 Sea Urchin that was listed on the BUC online site for the bargain price of four million."

"That's considered cheap?"

"Very cheap," James said. "Four million is a fire-sale price for that boat. The radiologist's wife found out he and the plastic surgeon were entertaining hookers in the yacht's master cabin. She hired a private investigator who rigged the cabin with a small voice-activated video camera, and he then took the resulting tape to her attorney, who took it to the radiologist's attorney. The wife insisted that she be given the yacht in the divorce settlement, and she then turned around and listed it for sale for four million—strictly to get revenge on her cheating ex."

I chewed a little bit on the lemon rind from my iced tea. "What is it about big yachts and cheating men? Doesn't it all seem very phallic to you?"

James blushed again, so I let it go.

"This is a very entertaining shaggy-dog story, but you still haven't gotten around to telling me how Reddy figures into it," I pointed out again.

"Reddy—or, I should say, a man we suspect is Roy Eugene Moseley—spent a good bit of time sniffing around the *Pair-o'-Docs*," James said. "He apparently saw the listing on BUC, and called the doctor's ex to make an appointment to take a look."

"Uh-oh," I said.

"He's currently using the name Rodolfo Martinez," James said. "Trying to pass himself off as Cuban."

I snorted. "Reddy? Cuban? He's the ultimate white man. I've never seen anybody who looks Waspier."

"According to Sabrina, he looks the part. Dark hair, dark tan, dark eyes."

"Sabrina? Rodolfo? Are you sure you aren't making all of this up to distract me from my own troubles?"

"You give me too much credit," James said. "The doctor's ex-wife is named Sabrina Berg. She found this Rodolfo character charming. Too charming. Remember, she'd already caught her husband cheating on her. She noticed things right off the bat. He arrived at the marina in a leased Jaguar. He never took off his sunglasses—not even when they were in a restaurant discussing the yacht. And he was quite vague about how he earned his living. It made her nervous. And it made her attorney nervous too."

"What happened next?" I asked, leaning across the table. The shaggy-dog tale had suddenly become quite a compelling story.

"Nothing," James said. "She got another offer, from a legitimate buyer, through a yacht broker, which she quickly took. She called the number this Rodolfo character had given her, just to let him know the boat had been sold, but he never returned the call. And she hasn't seen him since."

"Damn!" I said, pounding the tabletop. "I thought you said this was good news."

"You haven't let me finish," James said quietly. He took a sip of iced tea. "Remember that video camera in the master cabin?"

"Don't tell me," I said. "She has Reddy on video?"

James nodded, pleased with himself. "She's overnighting a copy of it to me. I should have it tomorrow. And there's more. The marina where the *Pair-o'-Docs* is tied up is gated, with a security shack. They write down the tag number of every car that passes through the gate. Thanks to Sandra Findley, we now have that tag number."

"Thank God for the sisterhood of scorned women," I said fervently. "Now what? The cops track him down, arrest him, and drag his ass back here and get me back my money, right?"

James looked down at his lunch.

"James?"

"I'm afraid it's not quite that easy," he said.

31

The waitress came over to refill our iced teas. I was beginning to think I needed something stronger than tea, but I've found that drinking during the daytime, while running a motel, is not a good thing. So I went a little crazy and had sweet tea.

"Why can't the police arrest Reddy?" I asked. "He's a con artist and a thief. Even in Florida, that's considered a crime—right?"

"Only if you have a victim who's willing to press charges," James said. "And Polly Findley simply isn't willing to do that. Her lawyer and her children have begged and pleaded with her, but she just won't budge. Their hands are tied."

"What about the crime he committed against me?" I asked. "I'm a victim. Why can't Detective Bradley go down to Florida and arrest Moseley?"

James laughed. "When was the last time you read the newspaper, BeBe? Or watched the evening news?"

"I don't watch the news," I said. "It depresses me. I look at the headlines on CNN so I can find out who we're currently at war with, but other than that, I mind my own business—which keeps me plenty busy."

"Jay Bradley isn't going anywhere anytime soon," James said. "He's in the middle of the Los Locos murder trial. Remember those four gang members who shot up a rival gang's apartment, over in Port Wentworth, last fall?"

"No," I said. "Should I? I don't think I've ever even been to Port Wentworth."

"You really should get out more," James said. "It was all over the news in October. Six people were killed, including a two-year-old boy and one of the gang member's fifty-eight-year-old grandmother, who was baby-sitting the child. There was so much publicity here in Savannah, the defense asked for, and got, a change of venue. The case is being tried in Macon. And each defendant is being tried separately. Since Jay Bradley was the chief investigator on the case, he'll probably be tied up for months in Macon."

"So send another cop," I said. "Savannah's not Mayberry. And Jay Bradley's not the only detective on the Savannah Police Department force."

James shook his head. "With Bradley spending most of his time in Macon, they're shorthanded. And you have to look at it the way the cops do. Moseley didn't kill anybody. He didn't physically harm anybody. And he's no longer in their jurisdiction."

I pushed my chair away from the table. "So, what? You're telling me he's just going to get away with everything he did to me?"

James put his hands on the tabletop. "I'm just telling you the facts, BeBe. And asking you to be more realistic about your expectations. We'll get the real estate mess straightened out, I feel sure. But frankly, I'm not so sure we'll ever bring Moseley to justice. Or get back the money and other things he stole from you. So I'm suggesting you get on with your life. You've got an enormous amount of talent and brains and energy. I think you can make a success of running the Breeze Inn. Concentrate on that, why don't you? Instead of Roy Eugene Moseley."

"You don't understand, James," I said, my voice low, my cheeks flaming from the heat of outrage. "It isn't just the things he took. It isn't just the money. It's what he did to me. He took my home, he took my livelihood. He stole my dreams. He made me a victim. When I found out he'd gone—I can't even describe how I felt. It was like I'd been violated. You're right. I *am* good at business. I'm smart and hardworking. And yes, I had a little family money to start with, but I built my businesses from scratch, with no help from anybody. And now I'll be *damned* if I'm going to just walk away from the life I worked so hard to create."

"What do you propose to do?" James asked.

I'd known all along what I had to do. I stood up and got my pocketbook. I put a five-dollar bill down on the tabletop for the tip. That much I could afford. I silently vowed to myself that it would be the last time anybody would have to pay for my meal.

"BeBe?" James said, getting up too.

"I'm going to go down to Florida and find the bastard."

"And then what? Assuming you can find him, what do you plan to do next?"

I stood up very straight. "Oh, I'll find him all right. But don't worry, James, I'm not the pistol-packing type. And I'm not gonna run him down with my car, 'cuz it would mess up the paint job. I'm going to find Reddy, and when I do, I'm going to do to him the same thing he did to me."

I pecked James on the cheek and gave him my sunniest smile. "All right?"

"God help him," James said, with a shudder. "I don't suppose there's anything I can do to help?"

"Well, yes," I said. "And it won't cost you a dime," I assured him. "I just need phone numbers for those two women, Sandra Findley and Sabrina Berg. And, oh yeah, I almost forgot. I want a copy of that videotape of Reddy."

32

It was late afternoon by the time I got back to the motel, but for the first time in two days, Harry's station wagon was parked in the lot, right beside a big black Mercedes with Atlanta license plates, and Jeeves was stretched out in a patch of sunlight in front of the office, so I didn't feel too bad about being gone for so long.

Jeeves picked up his head momentarily at the sound of my footsteps on the crushed-shell paving, yawned, and then went right back to sleep.

"Thanks, pal," I said, bending down to scratch his ears. "I missed you too."

I found Harry sitting at the front desk, frowning at the reservation book.

"You're back," I said. "How was the fishing?"

"Okay," he said. "Couldn't get the *Jitterbug*. I think Tricia suspects something. She's got it on a trailer now, parked right in front of a big window of the marina office. There's no way I can get anywhere near it without somebody seeing me. I had to borrow a buddy's boat. Once I'd paid for gas and ice, and given him a cut from my catch, I didn't quite clear a thousand." He shook his head. "At this rate, it'll be months before I can pay her what I owe her. And in the meantime, with the weather warming up, my regular charter customers are already starting to call to book trips, and I'm having to make up excuses for why I'm not available. I can't make any real money this way. And God, I hate asking for favors."

"Me too," I said fervently. "What's shaking around here? Whose Mercedes is that in the lot?"

"Some guy from Atlanta. He checked in an hour ago. I gave him the Sunflower Suite. He didn't have a reservation that I could find, but it's not like we're all booked up. Anyway, he paid cash for two days."

I reached over and turned the reservation book so I could see how our new guest had signed in. "John Smith" was printed in heavy block lettering. He'd listed a post office box for an address.

"You're kidding," I said. "John Smith? With a post office box? Harry, what were you thinking?"

"I was thinking, 'Hmm. Cash money.' You got a problem with that?"

I walked outside and jotted down the Mercedes's license-tag number, then came back inside.

"Will you relax?" Harry said. "So what if the guy's using a phony name? It's no skin off my nose."

"I don't like it," I said, fuming. "This is a respectable inn, not some hot-sheet, no-tell motel. I'm the owner, and it's my reputation that's at stake here. Ask yourself who checks into a motel with an assumed name and a phony address? Who pays cash, in advance? A criminal, that's who."

"Relax," Harry said. "That Mercedes out there isn't stolen. I checked."

"How? With whom?"

"I've got a buddy on the Tybee police force," Harry said, grinning a little. "He ran the tag through the division of motor vehicles for me. See, I'm not a complete idiot. I even know the guy's real name and address, if you must know."

"Write it down," I said, tapping the registration book. "If something goes bad with Mr. John Smith, I want to know who he really is and where he lives. What if he damages something in the unit? We just put telephones in all the rooms. What if he runs up some hideous long-distance bill? We don't have a credit card on file to charge him for it. There's no telling what could go wrong," I said, sputtering.

"All right," Harry said, caving. "I'll write it down. But I'm telling you, it's nothing sinister. He's just a guy trying for a little action on the side, without his wife finding out."

The bell on the front door chimed then, and two young couples walked in, each looking to rent a unit for a long weekend. Things were suddenly looking up. I registered them, ran their credit cards through the machine, then offered to show our new guests around the property.

"Gotta go," Harry said, standing and stretching. "Gotta pick up the parts I ordered for the air conditioner in SeaGlass, and then I'm gonna finish repainting the windowsills in Palmetto."

With a pang of envy, I watched Harry drive off. Right now, I was innkeeper, manager, housekeeper, and bellman. Until I could afford to hire some part-time help, I was permanently tied to the place. I'd been promising my grandparents a visit for several weeks, but had felt unable to make it into town to see them. Every time I left the property myself, I was keenly aware that I might be losing business.

For the next two hours, business was what I concentrated on. The young couples, friends from Birmingham, came bouncing in again, wanting suggestions for dinner reservations, a place to rent bikes, and directions for a place to launch the kayaks they'd brought along. I had a mound of paperwork to attend to, and when I'd finally cleared it all away, I stole over to my laptop computer, open on the registration desk.

I hadn't forgotten my pledge to track down Reddy. I got on the Internet and looked up BUC, the boat-sales site James had told me about. I found three listings for Sea Urchin yachts being offered in South Florida, including one in Fort Lauderdale. I was printing out the listing information when the front door chimed and opened.

My visitor was middle-aged, wearing dark glasses, khaki walking shorts, a golf shirt, a visor, and deck shoes. "Hey there," he said, looking surprised to see me. "I'm, uh, John Smith. In the Sunflower Suite," he added. "And who might you be?"

"BeBe Loudermilk," I said coolly. "I'm the innkeeper. And the owner. Welcome to the Breeze Inn."

He flashed a set of perfect white teeth and grasped my hand, a little too firmly, making no attempt to hide the fact that he was checking me out. "Delightful little place you've got here," he said. "Very unusual. I was wondering about a place to get a late lunch nearby. And maybe pick up a bottle of Scotch."

"It's nearly four," I pointed out. "A lot of places stop serving around three so that they can start setting up for dinner customers. But there's a list of restaurants in the folio in your room. You might try Fannie's. They serve all day. And there are liquor stores at both ends of the island."

"Great," he said. "Maybe you'd like to join me for a cocktail, when I get back."

I felt the skin on my arms prickle. Not a good sign. It suddenly occurred to me that Harry had left without writing down John Smith's real name and address.

"Sorry," I said, not feeling sorry at all. "I've got guests to check in, and paperwork to do. I'm sure you understand how it is with a small business."

"What about the guy who checked me in earlier?" John Smith asked. "Surely he can mind the store while you take care of your guests."

"Mr. Sorrentino is busy with his own projects," I said. "He was only filling in on the desk for me earlier while I was at a meeting off-site."

"All right," Smith said. He gave me a broad wink. "You know where I am, if you reconsider."

"I certainly do," I told him.

When the Mercedes was out of the parking lot, I copied John Smith's tag number underneath his registration in the guest book. Just in case.

At five o'clock, Weezie bounded into the office. "I've got it!" she exclaimed, slapping a padded manila envelope down on the reception desk. "It just came this afternoon, and I had to bring it out here with all the rest of the stuff for the last unit."

The last unit, technically, was our former storage room, which had, once upon a time, been a rental unit. But for years it had been home to an assortment of rusted-out beach chairs, obsolete plumbing supplies, and miles of rotted garden hoses.

At my insistence, Harry had hauled all the junk off to the dump and cleaned the room out, and now, Weezie was transforming it to our one and only "luxury suite."

I tapped a fingernail on the envelope. "And just what is this?"

She snatched the envelope away. "It's the inspiration for the whole suite. The theme, you might say. But no peeking. Not until I'm done installing everything in the unit."

"What if I don't like it?"

"You'll love it," Weezie said. "Did Harry finish painting it?"

"He did," I told her. "Lime green? Are you sure that's what you had in mind?"

"Margaritaville," she corrected me. "Don't you love the names of paint colors? I can't wait for you to see it. It's going to be beyond divine."

"And just when do I get to see it?"

She looked at her wristwatch. "Give me an hour to get everything in place, and I'll come get you for the big reveal. Just like they do on *Trading Spaces*."

The phone rang then, and she blew out the door before I could ask for any more information.

"BeBe? This is Janet, in James Foley's office. He asked me to call you with the phone numbers for Sandra Findley and Sabrina Berg."

"Perfect," I said eagerly, writing the numbers down as she gave them to me. "Did James say anything about a video he was expecting?"

"It came five minutes ago," Janet said. "I'm going to make a copy for our files. Shall I courier it out to you when I'm done?"

In the old, plush days, when Guale was making money faster than I could spend it, I would have easily agreed to paying the forty bucks for the convenience of having something couriered over to me from across town. Now though, I was all too keenly aware of what forty dollars could buy. And I didn't have it to spare.

"Never mind. I'll pick it up tomorrow, when I come to town," I told Janet.

As soon as I'd hung up from Janet, I dialed Sandra Findley's number in Vero Beach, but only got her answering machine. I left my number, with a request that she call me immediately, and dialed Sabrina Berg's number.

When I got a second answering machine, I nearly cried with frustration. I was tired of sitting around, tired of waiting for somebody else to find Reddy. I wanted to get on a plane, fly to Fort Lauderdale, and track him down. I wanted action. All right, I wanted revenge.

For now though, I forced myself to tend to business. Shortly after six I checked in a family from North Carolina who'd reserved the adjoining Sea Horse and Hibiscus Suites for four days. At six-thirty, while I was on the phone booking them a dolphin-watching tour for the next day, I watched "John Smith's" Mercedes roll back into the parking lot. He got out of the car with a brown paper sack in hand, and strolled toward his room.

Fifteen minutes later, the phone on my desk rang. It was our Mr. Smith.

"Hello? Who's speaking please?" he demanded.

"This is BeBe Loudermilk," I said.

"Listen, BeBe, there's a huge cockroach in my bathtub."

"Oh no," I said, cringing. "I'm so sorry. I don't understand how that could have happened. We have the exterminator spray regularly."

"He must have missed my unit," Smith said. "Christ! I just saw two more of the little fuckers scurrying across the bathroom floor. I think you'd better get over here and do something about this. Damned if I'll stay in a place that's infested with bugs. On second thought, never mind. I'm packing up and getting out."

"Don't do that," I urged him. I stood up and looked out at the lot. Harry's station wagon was parked over by the unit Weezie was working on. "I'll send the maintenance man over right now to take care of it."

"Maintenance man? BeBe, this is pretty serious. I'm calling the health department. They need to be notified of the conditions in this place."

"Please don't do anything like that, Mr. Smith," I pleaded. "I'll be right over to take care of it myself."

I grabbed a can of Raid and a plastic flyswatter from the utility room, gritted my teeth, and headed across the parking lot toward the Sunflower Suite. I knocked sharply on the door.

"About time," Smith called. "Come on in."

I opened the door and stepped into the dimly lit room. He'd closed the curtains. The only light in the room came from his bed-side lamp. The room appeared empty. "Mr. Smith?" I called tentatively.

"In here." The voice came from the bathroom. The door was slightly ajar.

"I'm so sorry," I repeated, walking toward the bathroom. "We can move you to another room if you like. This is the first bug complaint we've ever had. I just don't understand . . ."

But now, as I stood in the bathroom doorway, I was beginning to understand. John Smith was stretched out in the bathtub in a couple of inches of bubble bath, wearing nothing but the same pair of dark sunglasses he'd worn earlier in the day. He was holding a glass of Scotch in one hand, and his fully erect penis in the other.

"Hey!" he said warmly. He gestured toward his crotch. "Meet my friend."

And then he did it. He wagged it at me.

"Son of a bitch!" I screamed. I held out the can of Raid and blasted him full throttle.

He screamed, covering his face with his hands. He was choking and coughing, and trying to get out of the bathtub, but he slipped and fell backward, sending a wave of soapy water over the edge.

"Goddamnit, cut it out," he croaked. "I think I've got a concussion."

"I'll give you a concussion, you freakin' pervert," I cried, hitting him with another blast of Raid. He lunged toward me and batted the can out of my hand. I flailed at him with the flyswatter, raining blows on his head and arms before he managed to grab the swatter away from me.

He was standing up now, one foot out of the tub. "Little bitch," he said, his voice low. "Fucking bitch. I'll teach you—"

The bathroom door exploded off its hinges. Harry Sorrentino stepped into the room, and thrust a splintered baseball bat directly in my tormentor's face.

"Teach her what, Mr. Peyton Hausbrook?"

33

"**Peyton Hausbrook?** That's his real name?" My head swiveled from Harry to "John Smith," who by this time had leaped out of the bathtub and into a pair of pants, and was now sprinting, barefoot, for the door of the Sunflower Suite.

Suddenly I was shaking so badly I had to sit down on the bed, before I fell down.

"Go ahead and run, asshole," Harry called after him. "We've got your real name and address. And we're calling the cops."

"The hell with the cops, I'm calling your wife," I hollered.

A car door slammed, and then we heard the powerful roar of the Mercedes's engine as it came to life outside.

Harry ran to the door, but I could already hear the rain of oyster shells on concrete as Hausbrook spun the car out of the Breeze Inn's parking lot. When the car was gone, he sat gingerly down beside me on the bed, his face anxious. "Did he hurt you? Touch you?"

"No," I said, shakily. "He was too busy touching himself. If you hadn't busted in here when you did, I don't know what he would have done. I can't believe I attacked him with roach spray and a flyswatter. How stupid. He was enraged. A crazy person."

I was shaking all over by then, and crying. Sobbing, actually.

"Hey," Harry said softly. He put a tentative arm around my shoulders and hugged me awkwardly. "It's not your fault."

"It is," I cried. "I should have just turned and walked out. It's not as if I've never seen a naked man before. But I was so shocked. And then I got really mad. I lost control. He was coming after me. He would have hurt me. Really hurt me, if you hadn't . . ."

I was sobbing and blubbering incoherently now. "If you hadn't," I tried again, but couldn't catch my breath.

"Shh," Harry said, wrapping both arms around me now. I buried my face in the worn flannel of his shirt. "You were doing just fine without me. Assholes like that, they're not really much of a physical threat. Flashers, Peeping Toms, they like to wag their weenies at women because they're incapable of having a normal, uh, relationship."

"But he's married," I said. "Remember that awful woman Sadie Troy, and her kid, little Peyton, they were here for St. Patrick's Day? He's her husband."

"Peyton Hausbrook," Harry said the name slowly. "No wonder it seemed familiar when I wrote it down. Damn." He gave my shoulder a little squeeze. "I should have listened to you. You knew right away there was something squirrelly about that guy."

"No," I insisted. "It was my fault. He started hitting on me the minute he walked in the office this afternoon. I should have known he was a pervert. Hell, I've had enough experience with 'em. He invited me to come over here for a drink. I told him I was too busy. But he tricked me. He called the office, said there were bugs in the room. He threatened to report us to the health department. So I panicked and came running over here to placate him. God! How dumb could I be, falling for that story of his."

"Ah-hem." There was a polite tap on the open door. Weezie popped her head inside. "Sorry to disturb you two. But I heard a car peeling out of the parking lot just now. Is everything all right?"

Harry stood up abruptly. "BeBe had a bad experience with one of our guests."

Weezie stepped inside and looked around the room. Hausbrook's suitcase lay open on the luggage rack by the closet. His wallet and watch were on the nightstand, and there was a nearly full bottle of Dewar's on the dresser.

"Did somebody run out without paying their tab?" she asked.

For some reason, I found that funny. I started to giggle, and I couldn't stop. Harry looked at me for a minute, and then he started to chuckle. Pretty soon he was guffawing. Tears ran down his face. And down mine. Weezie stood there, her arms crossed over her chest, watching our little sideshow, until we both finally got ourselves under control.

"I'm sorry, Weezie," I said, finally, wiping my eyes on the hem of my blue work shirt. "It's been one of those days."

"Apparently," she said. "That guy was in some hurry, huh?"

I pointed at Harry's baseball bat, which he'd left on the bed. "He was under the impression that Harry was going to use that on him."

"Ohhh," Weezie said, the scenario starting to dawn on her. "A flasher?"

"My first one as an innkeeper," I said. "I guess that's kind of a landmark, huh?"

"Hopefully, your last one too," Harry said.

Weezie picked up one of the crocodile loafers Peyton Hausbrook had left behind. "Hey. These are Gucci. They look brand new." She went over to the suitcase and examined it too. "Wow. Louis Vuitton. And this is the real thing too, not that bootleg stuff they sell on the Internet." One by one, she picked up the items in the suitcase and examined their labels, announcing them like the lineup in a baseball game. "This tie is Armani. Slacks—also Armani. Shirts are Turnbull and Asser. English. Veddy expensive."

She looked up at us. "The cheapest thing in this suitcase is probably a Ralph Lauren couture sport coat. This guy spent some money on his clothes." She got a puzzled look on her face. "Hey. You know what's missing?"

"Let me guess," I said. "Underwear?"

"There's a week's worth of clothes in here, and not a single pair of drawers."

"Eeeewww," we said, in unison.

Harry got into the act now, picking up Hausbrook's billfold from the dresser. "Six hundred bucks in cash. American Express platinum, Diner's Club, Visa, Neiman-Marcus, MasterCard. Driver's license. And this." He held up a slim gold wedding band.

"Slimebag," I said. "Sadie Troy and Peyton Hausbrook. I would say they deserve each other. But nobody deserves a sicko like him."

Harry put the ring back in the billfold. "What are we gonna do with all this stuff?"

I made a face. "Ship it all back to him," I guess. "I don't want him calling the cops and accusing us of stealing from him."

Harry snorted. "I'll call the cops myself. My buddy on the Tybee force can put out a BOLO, and he'll get pulled over before he gets halfway to Macon."

"What's a BOLO?" I asked.

"Be on the lookout," Weezie piped up. "Don't you ever watch television?"

"No cops," I said. "They wouldn't do anything anyway."

"I'm calling the cops," Harry said, picking up the phone on the nightstand. "Look, if he flashed you, he'll flash somebody else. What if he picks a little kid next time? You want somebody's kid seeing something like that?"

"It wasn't all that impressive," I said.

"BeBe!" Weezie said.

"Sorry. I know it's not funny. Harry's right. Peyton Hausbrook is a scary guy. But, you know, it wasn't seeing his little tallywhacker that scared me, it was how angry he got when I fought back. He was coming after me. Until Harry showed up."

I shuddered, thinking again about the possibilities.

Harry put his hand over the telephone receiver. "Adam Thompson, my buddy, is out on another call. But he's going to stop by later and take your statement then. Okay?"

I nodded.

"Come on," Weezie said, tugging me to my feet. "You need a

change of scenery. And I want you to see what I've done in the new suite."

"Go ahead," Harry said, putting the phone down. "I'll lock up here. Adam may want to take a look around."

"Get him to take inventory and write a receipt for all this stuff, will you?" I asked, giving a backward glance at Hausbrook's belongings. And then I had a sadistic thought.

"I'd like to see the look on Sadie's face when she opens a package containing her husband's clothes, his driver's license, *and* his wedding ring."

"I'd like to see the look on *his* face when the cops knock on his door," Harry said. "Not a pretty picture."

34

Weezie

I waited until we were out of Harry's line of vision to ask the question burning in my feverish little brain. "So," I said, drawing BeBe closer. "What's going on with you two? You looked pretty cozy when I walked in on you back there."

BeBe stopped dead in her tracks. "Nothing! Nothing's going on with us. Give me a break, Weezie. I'd just escaped assault by this lunatic, and I was hysterical. Harry was just trying to calm me down. God! The man works for me, you know."

"I know," I said, grinning. "But the two of you have been practically living together for weeks now. It was inevitable."

"Stop looking at me like that!" she demanded. "There is nothing going on between me and Harry Sorrentino. You, of all people, should know better. He is so totally not my type that it doesn't even bear discussing."

"BeBe, when it comes to men, *everything* bears discussing. Anyway, I think he's adorable."

"He's too old," BeBe said. We were approaching the unit I'd been working on all afternoon. BeBe had her hand on the doorknob.

"He's not old at all," I protested. I clamped my hand over hers, to keep her from spoiling my surprise. "How old do you think he is?"

"I feel sure he's pushing fifty," BeBe said. "It's obscene to even think about it. Are you going to let me in there now? So we can stop discussing this ridiculous subject?"

"No," I said, blocking the doorway. "I bet Harry's not even forty yet. He just looks older because he's one of those rugged outdoors types. Not like all those pretty boys you usually go for."

"Pretty boys!" BeBe exclaimed. "All the men I've ever been involved with have been totally virile. Maybe a little on the young side—unfortunately, where Reddy was concerned. Anyway, you never met Reddy, so it's not fair for you to make any generalization at all concerning him."

"Daniel told me all about him," I said. "And if I had met Reddy, you can bet I would have warned you against him. I know his type. BeBe, forgive me for saying so, but he's the kind you always fall for. Handsome, slick, sophisticated. Style over substance. Maybe you should vary the menu a little? Considering your unfortunate history with that type?"

"I think I should just skip men altogether, after my last unfortunate involvement," BeBe admitted. "Hey, can we just look at the room now?"

"Close your eyes first," I ordered. "I want you to take it all in at once."

"Ridiculous," she muttered. But she closed her eyes anyway, and I opened the door and gave her a gentle push.

"Now open," I said.

"Oh my," BeBe said, stepping farther inside.

Her reaction was a letdown. I'd been planning this room ever since the first day I'd seen the Breeze Inn. Even before that, from the first time I'd seen my favorite Elvis Presley movie, *Blue Hawaii*.

"We'll call it the Tiki Suite," I told her. "Do you love it?"

"Wow," was all she said. "Where'd you get all this stuff?"

"I've been buying Hawaiiana for ages," I told her. "But I never had a place to put it till now. It's not the kind of stuff I can sell in the shop. It's a little over the top."

I pointed out the four-poster bed, which was made up of huge bamboo poles, nailed and lashed together with raffia strips. "Daniel copied this from an old movie still. I added the palmetto thatching on the top. Kind of my take on Tybee on the Pacific."

BeBe pinched the gauzy fabric of the bed curtains. "This is nice."

"It's the cheapest unbleached muslin I could find. I got the bolt for twenty bucks. Then I washed it in really hot water and draped it while it was still damp, so it would keep that crinkly look."

She ran her hand over the bed's hand-stitched coverlet, which was a brilliant splash of tropical color against the limeade-colored walls.

"Mama made that," I told her. "I've been buying old Hawaiian shirts for ages at thrift stores and yard sales. I think she did a nice job, even if she did claim all those clashing prints were starting to make her hallucinate."

"It's wonderful," BeBe said. "An heirloom."

"If you decide to sell the place, I'm taking that quilt back."

"Indian giver." She drifted into the bathroom, and broke out laughing.

"Honest to goodness, Weezie," she said, her voice echoing off the tile walls. "Only you could have thought of this. I love it. I really do. It's nothing like I expected. Nothing I ever thought I'd like, but I could move in here tomorrow."

I poked my head around the bathroom doorway. She pointed at the grass hula skirt I'd hot-glued to the edge of the pedestal sink. "Where on earth did you get that?"

"Thank God for Chu's department store," I told her. "I picked up all the Chinese paper lanterns in the bedroom there too. And the seashells I hot-glued around the mirror frame."

She burst out laughing again when she spotted what was hung over the bathtub.

It was a matted and framed album cover. Don Ho's *Tiny Bubbles*.

"The inspiration for the whole room," I told her. "I've been looking for it for years, and I finally resorted to an online auction. It just came in the mail today."

She gave me a hug. "I love it. I can never repay you for everything you've done around here. You and Daniel. And yeah, even Harry. You guys literally saved my life."

"I haven't even come close to paying you back for everything you did to help get me through my divorce and then that mess with Caroline DeSantos," I said, squirming out of her grasp. "And as for Harry, I think you need to relax your standards a little bit. Hell, just relax in general. That one's a keeper, babe."

She crossed her eyes and stuck out her tongue. "I am not interested in Harry Sorrentino. I am not interested in any man right now. I am only interested in wringing some profits out of this money pit so I can sell it and get back to my real life downtown."

Speaking of keepers, we could both hear Harry's voice booming from across the parking lot. "BeBe!" he hollered. "You've got a phone call in the office."

She went to the door, stuck out her head and hollered back, "Can I call them back later?"

"It's some woman who says she's calling long distance from Vero Beach, Florida. Says she's returning your call."

"I'll be right there," BeBe yelled, and she took off running with a speed I didn't know she possessed.

I walked around the room, picking up the tacky pottery tiki mugs and putting them back down again, straightening the shades of the tiki-god lamps, and just generally fluffing the place up. And then I stretched out on the Hawaiian-shirt-covered bed and yawned. I plugged in the strand of twinkle lights I'd woven through the palmetto bed canopy and smiled. Maybe Daniel and I would need to spend a night here ourselves. I could see us toasting each other with mai tais on the little porch. I drifted off to sleep thinking about my own adventures in paradise.

35

My heart was pounding as I picked up the phone in the office—
and not just because I'd raced across the parking lot to take the call.

"Hello?"

"Is this BeBe Loudermilk?" Her voice was low and raspy, and she
pronounced my name as Bee-Bee.

"It's Bay-Bay," I corrected. "This is she. Thank you for calling me
back, Sandra."

"I hear you and my mother have something in common."

I winced at her directness. "Sounds like it," I said.

Her laugh was more like a bray. "So, what can I tell you that might
help put that bastard behind bars?"

"I don't know. But I hear Reddy is down there in Florida."

"Unfortunately," Sandra said. "Mother met him here in Vero, and
now he's surfaced down in Lauderdale. It's the damned boats. I swear,
he loves the boats as much as he likes the money he steals from these
stupid women."

"Ouch," I said.

"Sorry. My mother says I have a bad habit of shooting my mouth
off without thinking. I don't mean anything by it. I'm just so frustrated by everything that's happened. The son of a bitch stole more
than three million dollars from her. And yet she refuses to do anything about it. My brother says I should just let the whole thing drop.
That's easy for him to say. *He's* got a big-deal job with the bank my

grandfather started. And his wife's money. But we're talking about my inheritance here."

"It sucks," I agreed. "And I'm just as frustrated as you. I feel like we're so close to catching him. But the police up here in Savannah don't care about catching him. And my lawyer tells me your mother won't press charges. Sooo. . ."

"So we just fold our hands and keep our mouths shut like good little girls, and let him get away with it," Sandra said, her voice dripping sarcasm.

"I've never been good at being a good little girl," I said.

Harry was sitting across the room, tinkering with a fishing reel, shamelessly eavesdropping, and when I said that, he nodded his head in agreement.

"Me neither," Sandra said.

"I'm coming after him," I said suddenly.

"What do you propose to do?" she asked. "I mean, pardon me for mentioning it, but he knows you, right? I mean, I hear you were sleeping with him. He's not stupid. If you go anywhere near him, he'll take off like a shot. He knows me too, unfortunately. Mother had him to dinner at the house several times. We took an instant dislike to each other. So what can you accomplish by coming down here?"

"I'm not sure," I admitted. "But I'll have a plan by the time I get there. I've got a call in to Sabrina Berg, the woman whose Sea Urchin he looked at down in Lauderdale. She sent us a copy of the videotape she made of Reddy looking at her yacht. He's changed his appearance, passing himself off as Cuban. Calls himself Rodolfo Martinez."

"He told us his name was Royce Milstein," Sandra said. "And that his grandfather invented the strawberry frosting they put on Pop-Tarts. Every time he came to the house, he brought this big case of Pop-Tarts. And that's why my mother believed everything he told her, because she figured where else could somebody get that many Pop-Tarts, unless their family was in the business?"

We both shared a good laugh at that inventive bit of fiction.

"Okay," she said finally. "Give me a call when you get to town. Better yet, call my lawyer. His name is Owen Techet. He's got lots of connections. Maybe he can figure out a way to help us. As long as you're not planning anything blatantly illegal."

I hesitated a minute.

"Sandra?"

"Yeah?"

"What I'm thinking—right now, I'm thinking the police won't lift a finger to help us. So I may have to try something not exactly, uh, by the books, per se."

"Hmm," she said. "Sounds intriguing. Just exactly what are you hoping to accomplish? If and when you find the guy?"

"I want it back," I said. "All of it. The money he stole, my things . . ."

"Your self-esteem," she added.

"Well, yeah," I said. "That too."

"I just want my inheritance back," she said. "I have no intention of having to work for a living anytime soon. Anything I can help you with, you just name it."

"Great."

"Seriously. Come by the house. We'll have a drink. And some Pop-Tarts."

I hung up the phone and Harry put down the reel he was tinkering with. "You planning some kind of a trip?"

I took a deep breath. "Yes. Reddy, I mean, Roy Eugene Moseley, the man who stole my money, has surfaced down in Fort Lauderdale. He contacted a woman down there about buying a yacht—the same kind of yacht he was leasing when I met him."

"What kind of yacht was that?" Harry asked.

"A Sea Urchin," I said.

He whistled. "He has expensive tastes. But why go to Florida? Why not let the police deal with him?"

"They can't, or won't, touch him," I said. "And even if they did arrest him, what does that get me besides the satisfaction of seeing him in jail? I want more than that."

"You want your money back," Harry said, finishing my sentence. "That seems to be a recurring theme with you."

"I should think you'd understand how I feel," I said. "You of all people. You had your boat taken away, and now you're working day and night—even risking stealing it—just so that you can pay off your loan and get the *Jitterbug* back."

"It's not the same thing at all," Harry said. "I don't have any kind of vendetta going with Trish. She's a coldhearted bitch, but it's not about that. It's about me being able to make a living doing what I'm good at."

We heard the crunch of tires from the parking lot, and Harry stood and looked out the window. "That's Adam Thompson. You ready to do this?"

Officer Thompson proved to be a perfectly competent, balding, big-bellied fishing buddy of Harry's. He listened without comment while I told him about how Peyton Hausbrook had lured me to his room on the pretext of killing a nonexistent cockroach. He didn't even crack a smile when I detailed the way in which Hausbrook had exposed himself to me. He did, however, nod in approval when Harry recounted the way our guest ran away after being threatened with a baseball bat. Thompson wrote it all down, took a tour of the Sunflower Suite, and even inventoried all of Hausbrook's belongings before boxing them up and stowing them in the trunk of his police cruiser.

He shook my hand, pounded Harry on the back for old time's sake, and promised to file his report immediately. "Y'all understand nothin' will happen, right?"

"What?" I demanded. "Why not?"

"No offense, or nothin', but public indecency, well, even in Tybee that's just little old nitshit stuff," he said. "It's a misdemeanor. I'll file the report, and we can swear out a warrant for him and all, but unless he shows up down here again anytime soon, that's about all that's gonna happen."

"Why can't you call Atlanta and have him arrested?" I asked.

He laughed. "They got every kind of violent criminal in the world in Atlanta and they can't do nothin' about it. So they're not exactly gonna slap a blue light on a cruiser just to go after one little old pissant pervert like this fella," Thompson said.

He looked at Harry for help. "You know how it is, right?"

"Yeah," Harry said reluctantly. "I get it, but I think it sucks." He slapped Thompson on his back then. "Thanks, buddy."

"Sorry," Harry said, as we watched Thompson leave.

"I should have kept his damn wallet and money," I said angrily.

Harry laughed, reached into his pockets, and fanned out an array of twenty-dollar bills.

"A $400 fine sounds about right to me, for the scare he put into you," Harry said. "I had an idea something like this might happen."

When we were done with the police business, we found Weezie sitting in the office, flipping through an old magazine.

"It's suppertime," she said. "I thought you could use some dinner."

"I'm not hungry, but I could use a drink," I said. "A big, fat drink."

"I'll stay, you go," Harry said. So Weezie and I walked over to Butler Avenue.

"How about Doc's?" she asked, spotting the leftover Christmas lights that were still glowing through the tavern's plate-glass window.

"I don't know," I said. "It's a guy place. I feel funny going in there."

"Why?" she asked, tugging at my sleeve. "Daniel and I go in there all the time. They actually make a pretty decent burger."

"All right," I said. "Just get me in there and get me a drink. The day I've had, I think I deserve to get wasted, even if it is only Thursday."

Doc's had a different ambience at night than it had during the day.

The last time I'd come gunning for Harry, the crowd had been exclusively male, mostly of the barfly persuasion. Tonight, almost every seat at the bar was full, with men and women both. Two women were shooting pool, their cues threatening to poke innocent bystanders sitting at the bar.

Weezie slid into a booth on the far wall, and I slipped in opposite her. I immediately recognized the woman who took our drink order, and she recognized me.

"Hey there," she said warmly. She was wearing tight black leather pants and a black leather lace-up vest. Her hair was hidden by a black leather newsboy cap.

"Cheri, right?" I said.

"And you're BeBe," she said. "What're you girls drinking tonight?"

I saw Weezie shoot me an admiring glance before she ordered. "I'll have a glass of merlot. And a cheeseburger. Medium, mustard, pickles, no onion, no lettuce."

"Jack and water," I said. "Make it a double."

"Sure thing," she said, and left to go get our orders.

When we had our drinks in front of us, and I'd emptied half of mine, I finally started to relax, or I thought I had.

"Your hand is shaking," Weezie said quietly.

I looked down and saw the puddle of bourbon on the table. "Delayed reaction."

"Perfectly normal," she said. "I'd be a basket case if I'd been through what you've been through."

"I'll be all right," I told her. "I had an epiphany today, you know."

"What? After that guy flashed you?"

"Actually, it was before that. While I was at lunch with your uncle James."

She shook her head. "He can't get used to not being a priest."

"Not that kind of ephiphany," I told her. "I just made up my mind about something. Reddy, actually."

"Uh-oh," she said, taking a sip of merlot.

"He's down in Florida. In Fort Lauderdale. So that's where I'm going."

"You taking your roach spray and flyswatter?" Weezie asked.

I smiled. "Actually, I was hoping to take you. If you're up for it."

Weezie leaned forward. "I'm listening."

"Remember that caper we pulled? Back when we were trying to figure out what that slippery antiques dealer was up to in that old warehouse in town?"

She nodded. "The outfits were my favorite part. Remember? We both had those black outfits? And I had the leopard-print scarf, and you had the catsuit with the leopard belt? Only you could look good in a catsuit. I would have looked like a trick or treater—"

"Weezie!" I said sternly. "This is not about the outfits we wore. Although yes, we did both look pretty hot, as I recall. My point here is, we knew the guy was involved in something illegal, so we did what we had to do to get into that warehouse."

Weezie nodded enthusiastically. "That was brilliant, your telling those Mexicans that you were a real estate agent, and you wanted to see the space for a client. I still can't believe the way you marched in there like that, like you owned the place."

I took a sip of my bourbon and waited for my hands to stop shaking. I was also trying to think of a way to get Weezie to sign on to the plan that was coming together in my head.

"Wait a minute," Weezie said. "Is that what we're gonna do, in Fort Lauderdale?"

"A caper," I said.

"What would it involve?" she asked. "Would I get to dress up?"

"Absolutely," I promised. "You're going to be a very wealthy divorcée. With a wonderful yacht, and a lot of money to throw around."

"Mmmm," Weezie said, licking her lips. "Resort-wear. They have some amazing vintage-clothing boutiques down in Lauderdale, I hear. How do you think I'd look in a hot pink Lilly Pulitzer shift? With maybe one of those little matching head scarves with the flower appliqués? Or no, better yet, vintage Vera."

"You'll be stunning. Reddy will eat you up with a spoon."

"Reddy?" She frowned.

Cheri came back to the table with Weezie's hamburger then, and all of a sudden, with my creative juices flowing, I discovered that I was suddenly famished.

"I'll have a cheeseburger too, please," I said. And tapping my empty glass. "And another Jack and water. And a merlot for my wealthy divorcée friend here."

When Cheri was gone, I snitched one of Weezie's French fries.

"You see, Weezie," I said, "we're going to set a trap for Reddy, or Roy Eugene, or Rodolfo, or whatever he's calling himself these days."

"And I'm the bait?" she asked. "Is that safe?"

"Very safe," I promised. "Anyway, you'll just be a part of the bait. The other part will be the yacht."

"Where are you going to get a yacht?" she asked.

"Not just any yacht. A Sea Urchin. They start at around eight million."

"That's nice," Weezie said, nibbling at her burger. "Then I can wear yachting clothes too. Maybe a blue blazer, and some silk trousers. Hey, wait," she said. "You still haven't told me where you're gonna get this big, expensive yacht."

"We're just going to borrow one," I said. "When we get down to Fort Lauderdale."

"When do we leave?"

"As soon as I line up things at the inn," I said. "I've got to make sure Harry can cover for me."

"Why can't Harry go with us to Fort Lauderdale?" Weezie asked. "He knows about boats. I bet he can help us get one."

"No," I said. "We can do this by ourselves. We're wonder women, remember?"

"What I remember is that we had a man to help us the last time we pulled a caper," she pointed out. "Daniel was the wheel man. And like it or not, I think we're going to need a man to do the heavy lifting this time too, BeBe."

"Then we'll take Daniel."

"Can't," she said. "He's in Charleston for the next two weeks, helping out at a new restaurant his friend is opening."

"Not Harry," I said, "I don't want to ask him for a favor."

"Then I'll ask," she said. She bit into her burger and juice went oozing down her chin.

36

The office doorbell chimed while I was on the phone, tying up one of the dozens of loose ends involved in trying to leave town for a few days. "Come on in," I called. "Be with you in a minute," I said, not bothering to look up.

"I can wait."

My heart fell. The voice was my grandfather's. For weeks, I'd been meaning to get over to the home for a visit, but life had gotten crazy, and to be perfectly honest, I didn't know if I could face my grandparents, aware that it was my fault they were facing financial ruin.

I stood up, amazed by how shaky my knees felt.

"Granddaddy? Is Grandmama all right?"

"Right as rain," he said, giving me a quick hug. He glanced around the office, taking in everything. He was dressed formally—an ancient seersucker suit, a carefully pressed but yellowing white shirt, red bow tie, and black loafers with a high shine. "So this is your new business venture," he said, nodding his head slowly. "Very nice."

"It still needs a lot of work," I said. "And when I get things stabilized, I'll flip it and make a nice profit. Town houses, probably. I'm thinking a gated community."

Granddaddy held up his hand. "Child, stop. I know all about everything. How that charlatan tricked you into signing away your properties. Why the restaurant is closed and you're living here, eking out a living scrubbing bathrooms and renting rooms." He shook his head sadly. "Why didn't you say something?"

I felt my lower lip start to tremble. "I just . . . I was so embarrassed. And when I found out he'd emptied your money-market account . . ." I pressed my fists against my eyes, trying to forestall the flow of tears. "It's all gone," I said. "All your money. All your years of hard work. Oh, Granddaddy, I am so sorry. I will never forgive myself. It's all my fault. But I'm going to get it back. I swear to God, I will get back every nickel he stole from you."

Granddaddy was walking around the living room, examining Harry's bookshelves, thumping the walls, admiring the wood-burning stove.

"It's a cozy little place," he said approvingly. "Not squalid at all. Your grandmother will be quite pleased. You know how she worries. From the reports we had, well, I had the idea you were living in some sort of flophouse, to tell you the truth."

"Reports?" I frowned. "Who've you been talking to?"

Granddaddy came over to the desk and sat down in the wooden kitchen chair beside it. "Think I'm blind? BeBe, I've been in business in Savannah for sixty years. I may be old, but I'm not stupid. Besides, half the fellas in my poker club are retired bankers. Bankers are terrible gossips, you know. Never tell a banker a secret in this town."

"So, everybody in town knows? My brothers? Arch? The rest of them too?"

He nodded. "If Arch knows, they all know."

"God," I moaned. "They'll never let me live this down. Not that I blame them. I was responsible for your finances. And I blew it."

"I'm responsible for our finances," Granddaddy said firmly. "Always have been. I trusted you to take care of some matters, and you did that very well, until you made a very foolish mistake."

"Foolish is putting it mildly," I said. "I was an ass. And I lost everything."

"Not everything," Granddaddy said. "That's what I've been trying to tell you. That money market you were managing, well, it was a lot of money. But it wasn't everything." He allowed himself a tight smile. "Not nearly everything."

"You're not broke?"

"Not rich, not broke," he said. "Comfortable. That's all I ever aimed for. Lorena and I have been very blessed. And very careful," he added.

"Thank God for that," I said fervently. "I could deal with losing my own money. But it was killing me that Reddy stole from you, too. I was afraid you'd lose your place at the home, I mean, Magnolia Manor. That you'd be out on the street. Like me."

"It'd take a lot more than some snotty-nosed little pretty boy to put Spencer Loudermilk on the street," Granddaddy said. He patted my knee. "So you can stop worrying about the old folks. We'll be just fine."

"No," I said. "That was your money Reddy stole. I won't rest until I get it all back. And I'm going to. You wait and see. I'm going down to Fort Lauderdale, and I'm going to get back every damn dime he took. With interest."

"That so?" Granddaddy said, looking thoughtful. "What did you have in mind?"

37

Harry drove. But I insisted on riding shotgun, so Weezie and Granddaddy sat in the backseat of the Buick, dozing all the way down Interstate 95 to Fort Lauderdale. Grandaddy snored so loudly, I couldn't believe Weezie could sleep through the racket.

While our accomplices slept, Harry and I passed the time by bickering.

"Did you show Cheri how to use the credit card machine?" I asked.

He shot me a look. "She *knows* how to use one. She works at a bar, remember?"

"What about cleaning the rooms? Are you sure Cheri's daughter understands how important it is that those rooms are absolutely spotless—every day?"

"She understands," Harry said.

"I hope she remembers about not putting too much bleach in with the sheets and towels," I fussed. "The last time, you bleached holes in half of them."

"I told her no more than a cup per load," Harry said.

"I use three-quarters of a cup."

"And your whites never look as good as mine," he said smugly.

"Cheri is a very nice person," I started. "And don't get me wrong, I'm really grateful she offered to run the Breeze while we're gone. I just hope she leaves the leather look at home. I don't want our guests thinking we're some kind of biker hangout."

"What's wrong with bikers?" Harry asked. "Their money's as good as anybody else's. We've got a Harley-Davidson club coming the last weekend of the month. They've booked every room we have."

"Since when?" I asked, alarmed.

"You took the booking," he said.

"I certainly did not."

"It's your handwriting on the reservation book. PAHLs?"

"Well, yes," I admitted. "I assumed it was some kind of civic organization. The woman who booked it sounded very refined."

"Piedmont Area Hawg Lovers," Harry said. "I guess you could call that a civic organization. They booked us for their spring ride last year too, even though only half the rooms were fit for a real hog."

"God," I said, running my hands through my hair. "What other kinds of riffraff have you booked into the place while I was looking the other way?"

"Bikers are not riffraff, damnit," Harry said. "These people are reputable businesspeople, doctors, lawyers. I know they have at least one superior court judge."

"Never mind," I told him, closing my eyes to signal that we were done with this particular argument. "No matter what I say, you're going to accuse me of being a snob."

"Because you are a snob," Harry said. "You judge people solely on the basis of their looks. Which is why we're on our way to Florida right now."

"I am not a snob," I said, turning my back to him. "I have friends from all walks of life. Bartenders, chefs, antiques dealers."

"Stuck-up downtown parasites," Harry said.

"I'm not having this discussion," I said.

"Fine," he said. "Let's talk about the plan. None of this is very clear to me."

"It's a work in progress," I admitted. "But in essence, the plan is to steal my money back from Roy Eugene Moseley, or Rodolfo Martinez, or whatever the hell name he's going by these days. And the key to that, I think, is to get ourselves a yacht."

"And not just any yacht," Harry said, "a Sea Urchin, which you yourself said starts at around eight million."

"True."

"Right. And how do you propose to acquire said yacht?"

"Well . . . Weezie is a very attractive woman."

"Thank you," Weezie said groggily. She sat up and rubbed her eyes. "Why are you handing me compliments in the middle of the day?"

"It's a fact," I said. "In a caper such as the one we're going to execute, you have to use the weapons you have. We don't have any real weapons, as such."

"I hate guns," Weezie said.

"Me too," I agreed. Then I patted the Electra's glove compartment. "Although I did borrow Granddaddy's little twenty-two for the trip."

"What?" Harry and Weezie said in unison.

"What's that?" Granddaddy chimed in. "Is it lunchtime yet?"

"We had lunch an hour ago," I pointed out. "You had mashed potatoes, green beans, fried apples, and three pork chops, not to mention a huge slab of pie at the Cracker Barrel. How can you possibly be hungry again?"

"Loudermilks have very highly tuned metabolisms," Granddaddy said proudly. "When I was a boy, I could eat a pound of bacon and half a dozen eggs for breakfast, along with grits and biscuits and jelly. I've slacked off some in that department. But I don't gain an ounce. Nossir." He patted his belly. "These pants I'm wearing right this minute I bought at Wagstaff's Department Store on Broughton Street in 1956."

Said pants had once been black serge, but were now faded to a mottled gray, with a seat so shiny you could practically see your reflection in it.

"Wow," Weezie said admiringly. "I remember Wagstaff's. There was an old black gentleman in a tuxedo who ran the elevator. When I was a little girl, I used to think he was president of the store."

"That was Ronald," Granddaddy said. "A fine man. He knew every customer who came in the store. But what was that you kids were saying about guns?"

"I was saying we brought your little pistol just in case there's any trouble. I know it's just an itty-bitty little popgun. But there's a lot of crime in South Florida."

"No guns," Harry said sternly. "Promise me or I'm outta here right now."

"As far as I'm concerned, you can go ahead and go," I grumbled. "It wasn't my idea to bring you along anyway."

"BeBe!" Weezie exclaimed. "You promised to be nice."

"This is me being nice," I said through gritted teeth.

"No guns," Weezie said, gripping my shoulders with both hands. "Promise."

"Okay," I said reluctantly.

"Cross your heart, hope to die, stick a needle in your eye," Weezie prompted.

"All right. Cross my heart, blah, blah, blah."

"Damned left-wing radicals," Granddaddy muttered.

"No guns!" Weezie repeated.

"Now, what other kind of weapons were you saying we possess?" Harry asked.

"Weezie's attractive. We're both smart, and in this one case, I have an intimate knowledge of the criminal we're pursuing. I know what he likes, how he operates."

"Do you know how to steal a yacht?" Harry asked.

"Borrow. We're going to borrow one. That's why I agreed to bring you along."

"Not for my brains and good looks?"

"Hah. We need a crew for our yacht. You're a boat captain, so it seems to me you should be able to captain a yacht."

"Piece of cake," Harry said. "Again, how are you going to acquire said yacht?"

"I'll know when we get there," I said.

"And when you get this yacht, you mentioned stealing your money back from Moseley. How?"

"Simple. I'm going to sell him the yacht."

"I thought that was my job," Granddaddy grumped.

"Right," I agreed. "Granddaddy's going to be our yacht broker. He's been practicing. He's brilliant. He could sell ice cream to Eskimoes. But this time he's going to sell Reddy a yacht. And that way, I'll have my money."

"Our money," Granddaddy said. "I still think we should just kidnap the fella and beat the living daylights out of him until he coughs it up."

"And we'll be on our way to jail for selling something we don't own. In South Florida. Where there is, as you pointed out, a helluva lot of crime," Harry said.

"No jail," Weezie said from the backseat. "Been there, done that. Have either of you two ever been fingerprinted? Had your shoes and all your belongings taken away from you? I have, and I'm not ever doing it again, not even for my best friend. Not for all the shrimp in Savannah."

"No, no, no," I said, shaking my head at Weezie and Harry's lack of vision. "It's simple. We get a yacht. Borrow one. Set Weezie up as the owner. Advertise said yacht, at a bargain price, and wait for Moseley to come skulking around. *Voilà!* I'm in the money."

I allowed myself a small smile of satisfaction at having worked it all out—and in the face of such serious negativity.

"You're crazy," Harry said, shaking his head. "This is not a plan. This is a fantasy. And a dangerous one too."

38

When we were two hours north of Ft. Lauderdale, I called Sabrina Berg's number again, and again got her answering machine.

Weezie and I had spent a frustrating ten minutes, the night before leaving, staring at the murky video she'd sent James of the mysterious Rodolfo Martinez.

"Is that him?" Weezie asked, squinting at the man in the video, who appeared to be busy opening cupboard doors in the master cabin, and pausing to admire himself, more than once, in a full-length mirror.

"I can't tell," I said, pushing the pause button on the television's remote control. "The build is right, and the hairline looks the same as Reddy's, although this guy's hair is much darker, and longer. It's hard to tell with the dark glasses and the crappy lighting."

"But you think it's him, right?" Weezie asked.

"Well, yeah. It's him. Probably."

"Probably?" Weezie said, turning to look at me. "BeBe, probably isn't a good enough reason to go all the way to Fort Lauderdale."

The shadowy figure in the video turned sideways to admire his physique in the mirror, and that's when I saw the glint on his wrist.

"Son of a bitch," I exclaimed, hitting the pause button again, and crawling toward the television until I was directly in front of it.

"Son of a bitch!" I repeated. "It's him all right."

"How do you know?" Weezie asked.

"Right there," I said, jabbing the screen with my forefinger. "He's wearing my daddy's watch. It's an antique twenty-two-carat gold Piaget. Mama gave it to Daddy for their twenty-fifth anniversary. It was in my jewelry box. That lying, low-down scumbag!"

"Ballsy," Weezie said.

"He's going to pay," I vowed. "Pay big-time."

"At least he didn't sell it. Like he did your aunt's painting."

"I'm going to rip his arm off and beat him to death with it," I told her.

Now, after a bathroom break and a stop to pick up more Kit Kat bars and chocolate milk for my grandfather, we were only an hour north of Lauderdale, and I was getting anxious to make contact with the last known person to have had a Reddy sighting.

I dialed Sabrina Berg's number again. It rang five times, but she finally picked up.

"Sabrina?" I said quickly. "This is BeBe Loudermilk."

"Hey there," she said. She had a pronounced Southern accent. "I just talked to your lawyer. He told me you might be headed down this way. I take it you think Rodolfo Martinez is the man you're looking for?"

"It's him," I said. "Positively. "Look. I'm about an hour away. I was wondering if you'd have time to chat with me?"

"Gee," she said hesitantly. "When did you have in mind? Tomorrow I've got a nail appointment in the morning, and then a lunch date, and a tennis lesson at three . . ."

I glanced at the clock on the dashboard. It was nearly three. It felt as if we'd been on the road for days.

"How about later this afternoon? I know it's short notice, and I hate to impose, but I really need to talk to you."

"Yes, that would work. I'm having dinner with a friend at the marina at six."

"The marina?" I said anxiously. "The same one where you keep your boat?"

"Kept. Past tense," she corrected me. "I sold the *Pair-o'-Docs*. To the lowest bidder." She chuckled. "My ex nearly had a seizure when he found out the price. Now I'm shopping for a new boat. Something without any nasty memories attached to it."

"Is there a place near the marina where we could meet for a drink and talk?"

"There's the Binnacle," she said. "It's at Seventeenth Street, right there on the water. Do you know the place?"

"No, but if you give me directions, I'll find it," I promised. "I'm a quick study."

Although I was good at directions, Harry refused to believe I knew where we were going. An hour and ten minutes (and two wrong turns) later, Harry pulled up to the door of a large wooden structure that looked like a Disney version of a pirate's ship.

He hadn't even turned off the engine before a deeply tanned kid wearing a white shirt, khaki shorts, and a canvas pith helmet was pulling his door open.

"Welcome to the Binnacle," the kid said. "Valet parking is seven dollars."

"Christalmighty!" Granddaddy bellowed from the backseat. "We want to park the thing, not rent a room."

Harry looked to me for guidance.

"Just let me out here," I suggested. "See if you can find a reasonable motel nearby. I'll call you on your cell when I'm ready to be picked up."

I jammed Granddaddy's floppy canvas golf hat on my head, and donned my own dark sunglasses, in the off chance Reddy might be lurking around the premises.

"Let's find some food," Granddaddy told Harry. "And a liquor store. I think I might be dehydrated."

Sabrina Berg had told me she'd be wearing a white pantsuit with an orange scarf, and that she'd be sitting at the bar. What she hadn't told me was that the pantsuit was Donna Karan, and that she was an African-American knockout.

"Sabrina?" I asked as she sipped from a long-stemmed martini glass. Her bare arm was circled with half a dozen gold bangle bracelets, and on the ring finger of her right hand she wore a huge headlight of a diamond solitaire, at least five carats.

"BeBe!" she said warmly. "You found me." She patted the empty barstool beside her. "I was starting to worry that you'd gotten lost."

"My friend took a couple of wrong turns," I said. "Your directions were fine."

A female bartender dressed in an abbreviated sailor's suit set a coaster down on the bar in front of me. "Something to drink?" she asked.

"They do a killer lemon martini," Sabrina suggested.

"I'll try that," I said.

Sabrina held up her half-empty glass. "Same thing."

Sabrina Berg was in her mid-thirties, I guessed, with glossy hair that fell softly to her shoulders. Her skin was the color of caramel, and flawless. Everything about her said high cost, high maintenance.

"Now," Sabrina said, when our drinks were placed in front of us. "What can I tell you about this Rodolfo Martinez person?"

"Everything you know," I said, looking around the room. The far wall of the Binnacle was all glass, looking out on rows of slips with a forest of gleaming white yachts and sailboats. Although it was barely four-thirty, the place was crowded with a mix of young, hip, yachting types and older, well-dressed men and women in pricey resort wear.

"I told your lawyer most of it," Sabrina said. "I got a call from this man. He said he'd seen the *Pair-o'-Docs* listing in BUC, and he was very interested in looking at it. We arranged to meet at the slip. He showed up right on time. Asked a lot of questions, and spent a lot of time in the engine room. I got the feeling he knew his way around boats."

"I couldn't see his face very well in the video," I said. "Did he ever remove the dark glasses?"

"No," she said, her large hazel eyes widening. "And that made me a little suspicious. This is South Florida, so everybody down here wears sunglasses. But his were these creepy mirrored kind. Like a redneck highway patrolman wears, you know?"

I nodded. "What else?"

She fidgeted with the catch of one of the bracelets. "I think his hair was dyed. Again, you see a lot of that down here." She made a face. "Men who think if they put a little dark color in their hair, it makes them look like Enrique Iglesias. As if! I noticed the hair on his arms was sort of golden. It didn't match up. And I was wondering why he was dying it. Certainly not to cover gray. He isn't old enough, is he?"

Now I made a face. "I'm not certain how old he really is. Everything he told me turned out to be a big, fat lie."

"Honey, I feel your pain. If I had a dollar for every lie my ex told me . . ." She laughed. "Hey! As it turns out, I do have a dollar for every lie he told. And that comes to a little over twelve million, so you know the kind of bastard he was."

"My lawyer said you two had lunch together?" I prompted.

"Right here at the Binnacle," Sabrina said. "It was his suggestion. Which isn't surprising. There are at least a half dozen marinas within a few miles of here. It's kind of a hangout for the yachting types. And not just the owners." She gestured at a group of people milling around at the end of the bar. They were all in their twenties, sun browned, the women dressed in revealing little sundresses or T-shirts and midriff-baring shorts, the men in shorts and collared golf shirts. "Those kids are all probably crews from some of the bigger yachts. A lot of them live aboard, so this place is sort of a clubhouse for them when they're in town or in between jobs."

"Hmm," I said, glancing quickly around the room, halfway hoping I might spot Reddy.

"He's not here," Sabrina assured me. "I would have called you on your cell phone if I'd seen him."

"What did you talk about at lunch?" I asked.

"The boat. Maintenace records, specs, all of that. I had a folder full of information, otherwise I couldn't have told him diddly about the *Pair-o'-Docs*."

"You didn't spend much time on it?"

She hooted. "Yeah. On a deck chair. Honey, I am just a city girl from Atlanta, Georgia. The yacht was my husband's play toy. To tell you the truth, I get a little queasy when I get too far from land. I mean, I love to cruise around and all, but I am *not* somebody who wants to spend a week cooped up in that dinky little stateroom. I mean, if I want to travel, get me a room at the Ritz-Carlton or the Breakers, you know?"

"I hear you."

"And that bitch Cissy Owens! They haven't made the yacht big enough for me to spend another minute with that horse-faced heifer. We took the boat over to Bimini one weekend with her and Chip, and that was enough for me. I told Adam, you two might be all buddy-buddy, but this is one partnership you can count me out of."

"Chip Owens?" I said. "Is that the plastic surgeon who was the partner in the boat?"

"Ah-huh," Sabrina said. "He's a boob man. That's all he does. And you ought to see the set he put on Cissy, that's the wife. Little tiny skinny-ass white girl like that and here she comes with a pair of double Ds. The child could hardly walk upright. And he had the nerve to tell Adam he could tweak me up to a C if I wanted. For an anniversary present! I told Adam, if you wanted big tits, you shoulda married Dolly Parton. Not Sabrina Daniels."

The bartender flitted past and Sabrina held up her empty martini glass. "Again," she said. "And for my friend too."

I was beginning to like Sabrina Berg.

She picked up her handbag—it was from the new Kate Spade spring line; I may be poor, but I can still read *Elle* and *Vogue*—took out a gold compact, and touched up her apricot lipstick in the mirror.

"He's sorta cute, in a plastic kind of way," she said, putting the compact away.

"Who?"

"Rodolfo, or whatever his name is. I can see how he hooked you. He's one of those men who just understand women. I mean, he actually noticed my shoes the day we had lunch. But he doesn't do it in a faggy kind of way, right?"

"Right," I said ruefully.

"He loooved the *Pair-o'-Docs*," Sabrina said. "Said he liked the classic lines, better than the latest models. He couldn't believe the price I was asking. I mean, he was amazed. I thought he was gonna write out a down payment right here on the bar."

"What happened?" I asked. "If he was that crazy about it?"

The bartender came back with our new round of drinks and Sabrina took a big slurp of hers. Alcohol did good things for her. Her eyes sparkled, her face was animated. She exuded good times.

"He wanted to take it out for a shakedown," she said. "Alone."

"And you said no?"

"Oh hell yeah," Sabrina said. I had noticed that the more she drank, the less cultured she sounded. "Some guy walks in off the street, thinks he can flash a little money at me and stroll away with a yacht like the *Pair-o'-Docs*? Uh-uh. I told him, 'Have your mechanic look at it. I'll get my lawyer to put together a crew, and you-all can take it out for an hour or so, see how it runs. But no way are you stepping foot on my boat until I see a cashier's check for fifty thousand dollars in earnest money.' "

"How did he take that?" I asked.

"Said the money wouldn't be a problem. He needed to get with a guy he knew who could take a look at the electronics, and he'd call me back and set up a time."

"But he didn't call back?"

"No," she said. "The very next day after we had lunch, I showed the boat to a couple from Maine. They were wild for it. Didn't even want to check the mechanicals. They looked at it on a Thursday, left, and then called me on their cell phone to say they'd decided to take it. We met at my lawyer's office the next day and finished the deal within an hour. All cash."

"Lucky," I said. "I'll bet Rodolfo was planning to scam you out of the boat."

"Maybe," she said. "He sure looked like he could afford it. I mean, aside from those wacky sunglasses, he looked like he was made of money. Nice clothes, driving a Jag, beautiful manners. Honey, he was wearing a gold watch, I swear, it looked like something Cary Grant would have worn in one of those old movies."

I winced. "That was my daddy's watch. He stole it from me."

"Oh, honey," she said. "He does need killin'."

I took a sip of my martini, then pushed it away. It was lovely, but I needed to keep sober and pick every bit of Sabrina's brain before she got any more wasted.

"The phone number he gave you," I said. "Do you still have it?"

She reached into her bag and brought out a business card. The card stock was heavy, and the lettering engraved. "Rodolfo Martinez," it said. No address, no business affiliation. Just a phone number with what I recognized as a Fort Lauderdale area code.

"You can have that," she said. "But it's been disconnected. I called to tell him the boat was sold, and left a message. Later, when I tried it again, I got the recording saying it was no longer in service."

"You tried a second time? Even though you'd already sold the boat? Why?"

She giggled. "You want to know the truth?"

"Absolutely."

"Shhhh," she said, holding her finger in front of her lips, smearing the lipstick in the process. "Don't tell my lawyer. He'd kill me if he knew. Adam is just looking for an excuse to rewrite our child-custody agreement. See, I knew this Rodolfo of yours was up to something. But I was just bored enough, I thought I'd try to figure out what it was. Let him make his play and see how far he'd take it. And hey, I don't have to tell you. There's something about the guy. I thought,

What the hell. I've never fucked a Cuban before. Maybe it's something I ought to try, just this one time."

"Lucky you didn't," I told Sabrina. "Or that ring of yours would be history. Along with everything else you own, right down to your gold fillings."

She grinned and winked. She really was hammered on those lemon martinis.

"Who says I didn't?"

"What? My lawyer said you never saw him again."

"Shhh," she repeated, leaning so far forward she was almost in my lap. "Lawyers don't know everything."

"Are you telling me you slept with him?"

Sabrina licked the rim of her martini glass. "Mmm-hmm. And, girlfriend, if I wasn't way too smart for my own good, I'd do him again too, that's how fine he was."

I was momentarily speechless.

"Look," she said. "My ex was doing hookers right and left. He took one of 'em to Eleuthera for a week! And the whole time, I'm living like a nun, 'cuz my lawyer says, 'Sabrina, don't give him anything he can take to court.' So, all during the divorce proceedings, the custody shit, everything, I was pure as the driven snow. And afterward, you know, I got a shitload of money, yeah, and full custody of our daughter, but when was the last time I had a little fun?"

I nodded my head in sympathy. And anyway, who was I to judge Sabrina Berg?

"Can you tell me about it?" I asked.

"You want the juicy stuff?" she asked, her eyes glittering.

"No," I said quickly. "I know the juicy stuff about Roy Eugene Moseley. Just tell me about the, uh, date. Where did he take you? Whose car did you take? Did he talk about his private life at all? Do you know where he's living?"

"Whoa," Sabrina said. "Slow down. That's a lot of questions."

"Sorry," I said. "Just tell me about the date, if you would, right from the beginning. And how long ago was this?"

She took another sip of her martini, which was almost empty. The bartender started to glide over, but I gave her what I hoped was a discreet head shake. I didn't want Sabrina to pass out before I got the story of her date with Reddy.

"Hmm. Last week?"

"That recently?" I said eagerly.

"Let's see. It was maybe, oh, a week ago Thursday. Yeah, that was it, because Chantal had a birthday party to go to on Saturday, and I took her shopping for a new dress Friday morning."

"Chantal's your daughter?"

"Most gorgeous five-year-old you have ever seen," Sabrina said proudly. "If nothing else, Adam does make precious babies. The shit."

"So you went out with Rodolfo Thursday a week ago."

"Yeah."

"How did that happen? I thought you said his cell phone had been disconnected."

"He called me," Sabrina said, preening a little. "He *said* he was just double-checking to make sure the *Pair-o'-Docs* really had been sold, but we both knew he was calling to see if *I* was still available."

"Where'd he take you?"

"To Mark's, on Las Olas. You know the place?"

"Afraid not."

"Incredible food," Sabrina said. "You really should try it while you're in town."

"Did he pick you up in the rented Jag?"

"Oh no," Sabrina said quickly. "I didn't want him going anywhere near my house, or Chantal. Adam has his little spies, and he'd know in a minute if I was being picked up for a date—especially in a Jag. No, Rodolfo suggested Mark's, so I met him there."

"What did you talk about at dinner?" I asked.

"The usual. The food. He seemed pretty knowledgeable about food and wine. Insisted on ordering for me. I had the most fabulous Hudson Valley foie gras with these huckleberries. I never even heard of huckleberries before. I thought that was a cartoon dog, you know? And then I had crab-crusted black grouper with some kind of mushroom sauce. Divine! And he knew all the right wines to go with everything, of course. And then he wanted to talk about me. He asked a *lot* of questions about my ex-husband, what kind of doctor was he, where did he practice. I'd already told him about how Adam cheated on me on the boat, and he was real sympathetic about that. Said it was a good thing I got such a nice settlement. Of course, he wanted all the juicy details about the settlement, but I just told him I'd done okay. He's a big hand-holder, isn't he?"

"What? Who?"

"Rodolfo. He held my hand all through dinner, and then afterward . . ."

"Probably trying to get that fatty diamond ring off," I said.

"Uh-uh," Sabrina said promptly. She held her hand out to admire the ring. "I had to work *hard* for this sucker. I knew what he was up to. It was like a game for me."

"Did he talk about himself?"

"He laid a line of bullshit on me, if that's what you mean. Said his family made their money in the sugarcane business. Dropped some fancy Spanish words. Look, I took four years of Spanish in a Catholic high school. And my teacher was Cuban. Besides which, I've been living down here in Havana North for the past eight years. So I know how it's supposed to sound."

"What did you do after dinner?"

"Thought you said you didn't want to hear the nasty stuff," Sabrina said, grinning wickedly.

"You can leave that part of it up to my imagination," I said.

"Like I said, all during dinner, he was putting the moves on me.

You know, holding hands, brushing my thigh with his. Very sexy. And, girl, I was not saying no. Of course, he thought we should go back to my place. But there was no way. I was up for a little sex, yeah, but no way did I want him coming around to my house, around my child. Finally, he invited me back to his place."

"You went to his place?" I felt my pulse quicken.

She shrugged. "Why not? Okay, I'd been drinking all that wine. And I knew what he was up to, but I didn't care. He didn't seem kinky, or violent, nothing like that. And I had a condom in my purse, so I thought, why not? What's good for the goose is good for the gander, right?"

"Where does he live?" I asked quickly.

"In one of those new high-rise developments overlooking the in-tracoastal," Sabrina said.

"Does it have a name?" I asked.

"Beats me," she said. "I just followed him over there in my car. It's about ten minutes from the restaurant, I can tell you that. On, like, the seventh floor maybe."

Great. I wondered how many hundreds of new high-rise condo developments there were along the intracoastal waterway in Fort Lauderdale.

"Maybe you'll think of the name later."

"Probably not," Sabrina said, chewing on a strip of lemon peel, all that was left of her martini. "It was dark. I was interested in getting laid, not in getting his address."

"Sorry," I said. "What was the condo like?"

"Fancy," she said. "Swanky. Lots of modern furniture, great art. Lots of accessories. No way was it his place."

"Why do you say that?"

"I could just tell. It had been professionally decorated. You know, with elaborate window treatments. Okay, here was one thing. The dining-room table was this smoked-glass deal, with chrome legs. Real modern. It was set! Dishes, napkins, silver, everything. Right down to a silk-flower centerpiece. You ever know a single guy who leaves his dining-room table set—with a centerpiece and everything?"

"No. Most of the guys I've dated had piles of dirty sweatpants as a centerpiece."

"Exactly," she said. "I figured it was maybe the furnished model. And then, later, when he wouldn't even let me take a shower in the bathroom—which, come to think of it, also had a silk-flower arrangement—I knew for sure it wasn't his place."

"He wouldn't let you shower?"

"Nope. I really did not want to go home smelling of some guy's essence, you know? I mean, a lot of nights, Chantal climbs in bed with me. But he made this lame excuse that the hot-water heater was broken. I mean, talk about a born liar!"

"He is that," I agreed.

"Anyway, the whole night got cut short, after he got that phone call."

"Did he say who was calling?"

"He *said* it was his stockbroker. Which was another crock. But I'd gotten what I wanted, he'd gotten, well, not exactly what he wanted probably, since I made it clear this was strictly a one-time thing, so I figured, call it a night. He walked me to my car, kissed me good night. He does have pretty manners, doesn't he? And I watched to make sure he wasn't following me. He wasn't. And that's the last time I saw or heard from Rodolfo Martinez. Or whatever his name is."

39

After calling Harry to pick me up, I walked Sabrina out to the restaurant's entry. "Are you okay to drive?" I asked, as she swayed gently before grasping a thick rope handrail. "Can I call you a cab?"

"I'm fine," she insisted. "Anyway, my girlfriend's gonna pick me up. And then I'll buy both of us a 'spensive bottle of wine and a great dinner. And then I'll go home alone, to my kid." She brightened then. "Did I tell you about my Chantal?"

"The most precious little girl in Broward County," I said.

"Forget Broward, she's the cutest thing in the whole damn state of Florida," Sabrina said, waving her arms expansively.

A little, red Miata convertible with the top down pulled through the drive then, tooting its horn, the driver, an attractive blonde, waving her arms wildly.

"There's my friend M'Linda," Sabrina said. "Hey, why don't you come with us? We can have a lot of fun. M'Linda knows all the good clubs."

"Sorry," I said, meaning it. "I've got a friend picking me up, too."

"Boyfriend?" she said, giving me a broad wink.

"Well, he's a man, but we're not romantic," I explained. Just then the burgundy Electra turned into the driveway and glided to a stop behind the Miata. Harry was at the wheel, and he was alone.

"Come with us and we'll get you a boyfriend," Sabrina said, struggling to open the passenger door of the Miata.

"Maybe another time," I said. "Thanks so much for talking to me. You were a big help. I hope everything works out."

"C'mon, BeBe," Sabrina said, collapsing into the Miata. "We'll have a blast."

"Can't," I said, pointing to the Electra. "My friend's here."

Sabrina stood up in the seat and craned her neck to get a look. "Hey, is that your boyfriend?" she said, her voice shrill.

"No," I said quickly. "He's just a friend."

"What's his name?"

"Harry. Gotta go. Call me if you remember anything else. 'Bye now." I gave her a quick peck on the cheek, and she threw her arms around my neck and hugged me tightly.

"Hey, Harry," she hollered, releasing me.

Harry had a map unfolded on the steering wheel, but he looked up now, startled to hear a strange woman screeching his name.

"Hi, Harry," Sabrina repeated. "You're cute!"

He laughed and gave her a bashful finger wave.

"Whyn't you fuck BeBe?" Sabrina yelled. "She needs a good fuck!"

"Sabrina!" her blond friend trilled. "You're shit-faced!"

The two women laughed uproariously, and M'Linda peeled the Miata out of the restaurant doing at least forty miles an hour.

I watched them screech down Seventeenth Street, sighed, and got in the Electra.

"New friends?" Harry said, putting the map down.

"The gorgeous black woman was Sabrina Berg. She had four lemon martinis," I said. "I'm thinking she was seriously overserved."

"Whatever," he said, shaking his head. He pulled the car out into traffic, at a much safer, more conservative speed, which was good, because it was a spring Friday evening in Fort Lauderdale, and traffic was thick with showy cars and showy people, out to show just how young and beautiful and carefree they were.

"What?" I said.

"Nothing," Harry said. "How'd it go?"

"Better than I expected," I said. "How'd it go with you guys? Did you find us a place to stay? Did Granddad get some Scotch?"

"Yes, and yes," Harry said. A white Mercedes pulled in front of him, and he had to jam on the brakes to keep from rear-ending it. "Damn," he muttered. "How do people here stand it?"

"You mean the fabulous weather?" It was just getting on to six o'clock, but the sun was still shining, and the palm trees that lined the street were rustling gently in the wind being blown in off the nearby ocean.

"All of it," he said. "It's all too much. Too many cars, too many people . . . too much."

He was in a mood, I could tell.

"Where's the motel?" I asked, changing the subject. "And where are Granddad and Weezie?"

"Grocery shopping," he said. "The motel's not far from here."

"Pretty awful?" I asked. "I told her we can't afford beach prices. And it's still high season."

"Not too bad," he said. "A little mom-and-pop joint. It's called the Mango Tree. I guess because there's a gnarly old mango tree in the parking lot. It's clean. We're sharing a room, though."

"Who? You and me?"

"In your dreams," Harry said, laughing. "No, I meant boys and boys. Me and Spencer, and you and Weezie. They only had the two rooms, and it's not cheap, either. Hundred bucks a night."

"Oh." I'd hoped to find something much cheaper. But with Granddad along, I didn't want to check into a really risky neighborhood.

"The rooms are efficiencies. We've each got a little stove and refrigerator. That's why Weezie went shopping. We figured we could save money by fixing cereal in the morning, and maybe keep some sandwich stuff too."

"Good idea," I said. "Although I hope we won't be here too long."

"Did you get a lead on Reddy-Boy's whereabouts?"

"Sort of," I said. "He took Sabrina to his quote 'condo.' It's in a new high-rise on the intracoastal waterway. She got the idea he's sort of squatting in a decorated model."

"Not bad," Harry admitted. "She tell you all this before she got wasted?"

"She's a nice lady," I said, feeling the need to defend my new friend. "She got screwed by her ex-husband. Sabrina is actually pretty damned shrewd. She spotted Reddy for a fake the minute she laid eyes on him."

"But she still went home with him?"

I shrugged. "He's got a way about him. That's all I can tell you."

He glanced sideways, started to say something, then thought better of it.

"Didn't James tell you Sabrina met Reddy only once?"

"Yeah," I said. "But as it turns out, she doesn't always tell her lawyer everything. She actually saw him a second time. On a date."

"Christ!" Harry said.

"Don't start," I warned. "We've got more than we had when we got here, although I admit, it's not much. I've got the name of the restaurant where they had dinner. It's called Mark's, and it's on Las Olas."

"That's the main drag," Harry said. "Expensive stores and restaurants."

"She said it was maybe a ten-minute drive from the condo. A new development, and they had a furnished model. It's better than nothing. Tomorrow we can find the restaurant and try to figure out which condo development he took her to."

"He's probably long gone," Harry said.

I knew he was right, but it wasn't what I wanted to hear just then.

Harry flipped on the turn signal and slowed the Electra in front of a narrow band of lush greenery. "This is the place," he said.

The Mango Tree Motel had seen better days, probably twenty

years ago. The concrete parking lot was cracked, with weeds growing up through patches of dirt, and the symbolic mango tree was dropping dead branches onto the ground. A sputtering neon arrow pointed toward a concrete-block cube that had been designated "Office."

"Oh," I said, getting out of the car. "For this we're paying a hundred bucks a night?"

"It gets better," Harry said.

I followed him down a cracked concrete sidewalk toward the rest of the units. There looked to be maybe two dozen in all, arranged in a squared-off U shape around a swimming pool. The pool itself was surprisingly clean, a sparkling turquoise oval set in a band of white paving stones, with fiberglass lounge chairs set around its circumference. A couple of little girls splashed in the shallow end of the pool, and nearby, a balding middle-aged man in swim trunks was grilling hot dogs on a portable grill. Salsa music spilled from the open door of one of the units, and people sat out in folding lawn chairs in front of other doors, sipping from soda cans, reading paperback novels, or smoking.

In spite of its somewhat faded shabbiness, I was surprised to find that the Mango Tree felt warm, cozy even.

"These two are ours," Harry said, gesturing toward units 14 and 15, the second and third units in from the middle of the courtyard. I had my hand on the doorknob when the door opened and Weezie popped her head out.

"Hey!" she said, opening the door wide. "Welcome to Mangoville."

The unit was approximately the same size as our units at the Breeze, maybe a little larger. A pair of twin beds with bright floral spreads had a blond-wood nightstand between them holding an incredibly ugly lamp. There was a long, low dresser with a mirror, two lumpy armchairs, and in the corner, a little kitchenette with a dorm-size refrigerator, a two-burner range, and a toaster oven. The walls were painted a virulent shade of orangeish-yellow and the terrazzo floors were bare. A window air-conditioning unit rattled above one of the beds, and a picture window opened out with a view to the pool area.

"Home sweet home," I said, bouncing up and down on one of the mattresses, which produced an alarming *spoinnnging* noise.

"That one's yours," Weezie said, plopping down on the opposite bed. "What do you think of the place?"

"It's not the Breakers," I said. "But it looks okay."

Weezie sighed. "Think what I could do with this place!"

"Maybe you could work a deal with the management," Harry suggested. "Decorating advice in exchange for rent."

"Don't think I didn't ask," Weezie retorted. "The owner manages the place. Mr. Patel. He didn't think much of the idea. Can you believe he just painted all the units this nightmare color?" She shuddered. "I'll bet all this furniture came from the same close-out place. Flophouse 'R Us."

"Is my soup ready?" Granddad stood in the connecting doorway to his room. He wore a pair of loud red-plaid swim trunks, black socks, and a blue plaid sport shirt. He'd fit right in with the rest of Fort Lauderdale's senior citizenry.

"Oh, sorry, Spencer," Weezie said, jumping up from the bed. "I was just getting ready to heat it up for you when BeBe and Harry came back."

She went to the kitchenette and opened a can of generic cream of tomato soup.

"Soup for dinner?" I asked, wrinkling my nose.

"Four cans for a dollar," Granddad said. "And I had a coupon too!" He reached in the pocket of his sport-shirt and pulled out a wad of newspaper clippings.

"Spencer here is a great shopper, BeBe," Weezie told me, dumping the soup into an aluminum pan.

"I'd of done even better if it had been senior-citizen day," Granddad said. He sat down, and clicked the remote control for the television. "How did your meeting go?"

"Fine," I said. I'd been deliberately vague about the details of my relationship with Reddy Millbanks. As far as Granddad was concerned, Reddy had simply been a "business adviser" who'd cheated me out of everything.

"The lady I met at the Binnacle was pretty helpful. Tomorrow we can start looking for the condo Reddy was staying at."

"They've got the weather channel in Spanish down here," Granddad said. "Ain't that something?"

While he stared at the television, Weezie turned toward me and raised one eyebrow. "Later," I mouthed.

Harry looked down at the pan of soup with barely disguised disgust. "Is there enough for everybody?"

"We've got four cans," Weezie said cheerfully. "And cheese and crackers."

"And canned fruit cocktail for dessert," Granddad added. "The good kind with the big chunks of pineapple. But you kids don't have to eat soup," Granddad said, flipping channels now. "Go have a nice dinner out. My treat."

With a grand flourish he produced a twenty-dollar bill from his coupon pocket. "Your grandmother made me promise to treat you to a nice dinner our first night."

"Grandmama!" I said. "Did you call her? Is she feeling all right?"

"She's fine," he said. "She was going to American Legion bingo with the bridge club girls tonight. They have fifty-cent beer, and you know how Lorena likes her beer."

"Who was driving?" I asked.

"They've got a whole busful of 'em going," Granddad said. "Can you imagine what that sounds like? A whole busful of beered-up biddies?"

"Well," I said dubiously, looking at Weezie and Harry. "I guess we could go out. We wouldn't stay late, though. We've got a lot to do tomorrow."

"I'm in for the night," Weezie announced. She held up a glossy magazine. "Spencer even had a coupon for the new issue of *Coastal Living*. I'll have dinner and a nice shower, then it's reading and lights out for me."

"We couldn't just leave you guys here," I said.

"I don't know why not," Granddad said indignantly. "Think I need a baby-sitter?"

"No!" we all said in unison.

"You guys go," Weezie urged. "Really. I'm not even that hungry. Spencer made me try one of his Kit Kat bars while we were shopping."

I tried to give her the look. The look that said "Quit trying to pair me off with Harry." She was ignoring me.

"You up for supper?" Harry asked.

"I'm starved," I admitted.

"There's a little Brazilian cafe right around the corner," Harry said. "I spotted it earlier. We could walk over and check it out. Do you like Brazilian food?"

"Don't know. I've never had any."

40

Maria's Cafe was in a grubby little strip shopping center, situated between a check-cashing storefront and a coin laundry.

"This is the place you had in mind?" I asked, looking dubious.

"Yeah," Harry said. He grabbed my hand and dragged me in the door. "Come on, open your mind. You'll love this food. It's very homey, not fancy, just plain good cooking. It's my favorite kind of Latin food."

Not fancy was an understatement. Maria's Cafe consisted of a single long linoleum counter and a few tiny tables topped with flowery vinyl tablecloths. The menu was written on a huge blackboard hanging in back of the counter. None of the dishes was recognizable to me, but the whole place was enveloped in the delicious aroma of roasting meats. My stomach growled in approval.

A young Latina girl, with streaky hair worn in a lopsided topknot, and a too-tight white nylon nurse's uniform, stood behind the counter. She was the only one in the place. The restaurant owner in me calculated how much it was costing to keep the place open. She also wondered why there was so little business on a beautiful Friday night.

"This looks great!" Harry said, standing back to study the menu.

"You eating here or you wanna take out?" the girl asked.

"Your choice," I told Harry. "I'm completely in your hands tonight."

He waggled an eyebrow. It was the single sexiest thing I'd ever seen him do, and I was completely taken aback.

"We'll eat here," he told the girl. "Can we get a cocktail?"

In answer, she pushed a laminated menu card across the counter at him. "You can seat yourself," she said. "Just let me know when you're ready to order."

Harry pulled out a chair for me, and we sat at the window.

"Can I get a glass of wine?" I asked. "I mean, I know Granddad only gave us twenty bucks, but . . ."

"Don't worry about it. This dinner's on me," Harry said, not looking up from the menu. "Are you up for the whole authentic Brazilian experience?"

"Yeah, sure. Why not?"

"Okay," he said. He called to the girl. "We're ready to order now."

She sauntered over and stood expectantly at his elbow.

He rattled off an order in what sounded to me like competent Portugese, although I recognized none of the words. She scribbled it down on a steno pad, and then disappeared behind a set of swinging doors into what I assumed was the kitchen.

A moment later, she appeared with two glasses of a milky liquid and a small plate of fried objects, which she set down in front of Harry.

He picked up his glass, sipped, and nodded approval. I picked up mine, and he gently clicked his glass against it.

"Cheers," he said.

I took a hesitant taste.

"Mmm," I said. "Sort of a turbocharged coconut milk shake?"

"You could say that. The English translation for it is virgin sweat."

We both had a good chuckle over that one. The virgin sweat was sweet and cold and potent, and I finished it off quickly.

He pushed the plate of fried things in my direction. "These are *salgadinhos*. Appetizers. This one here is little bits of fried linguica sausage."

The sausages were on the spicy side, but tasty.

"And this," he said, placing a fritter-looking object on my plate, "is a fried cod ball. It's originally a Portugese dish, but these cuisines have a lot in common."

Before we'd finished the appetizers, the girl brought out a couple of plates of what looked like American salads.

"It's just tomatoes and hearts of palm," I said, feeling relieved. I ventured a taste. "With a really yummy vinaigrette dressing."

"Brazilians love their hearts of palm," Harry said, digging into his own plate. "They sell huge jars of them in every Latin groceria I've ever seen."

He made a quick, barely discernable gesture, and the waitress reappeared at the table. He murmured something to her, and she came back again, with another weird-looking cocktail. It was like the first, but slightly different.

"Jaguar piss," Harry said, laughing "You said you were up for the whole authentic experience. Anyway, it's another variation on the co-conut scheme. You like?"

"Sure." The jaguar piss was giving me a healthy buzz. What was not to like?

After the salad, we were presented with bowls of soupy, mashed-up black beans.

"*Caldinho de feijao,*" Harry announced.

The beans were delicious, fragrant with some kind of pork. I scraped the bowl to get every last bite of the broth.

"And now the entrée," Harry said as the girl arrived back at our table with a huge tray of more food—more little fried things, this time pie-shaped objects, and a platter of skewered meat.

"I can't," I said, groaning. "I'll absolutely bust."

"You can and you will," he said, forking pies and meat skewers onto my plate.

"These," he said, pointing to the pies, "are *empadinhas*. Same thing as what the Mexicans call an *empanada*. These happen to be made with shrimp. And this," he said, pointing to the skewers, "is *churrasco*. Brazilian barbecued beef."

I nibbled at the food. It was all wonderful, but more than I could possibly eat. Harry, on the other hand, happily shoveled it all in. It was fun to watch him. He ate with undisguised gusto, licking his fingers, sopping up the meat juices with a piece of bread, smacking his lips in appreciation.

"Can I ask you something?" I asked, propping my elbows on the table.

"Sure," he said, between chews.

"How does a fisherman from Savannah know so much about Brazilian food?"

"They have fish in Brazil," he said simply. "It's a great place. Wonderful people."

I took another sip of my jaguar piss. "I want to apologize for Sabrina," I said, emboldened by the buzz.

"For what?"

"You know, what she said, back there at the Binnacle. She was pretty trashed, and it was a pretty rude suggestion."

"Oh that," he said, patting his mouth with his napkin. "I didn't think it was rude at all. Crudely phrased, yes, but not rude. Anyway, she did say I was cute. Nobody's called me that in a long time. Probably not since my mama died."

"Weezie thinks you're cute."

He put down the napkin. "Weezie is a woman of unusual tastes."

"I think she has great taste. Look at what she did with the Breeze."

Harry considered that. "But you don't share her taste."

"I didn't say that."

"*You* didn't say I'm cute."

"Cute's not the word I'd use to describe you. You're . . ."

"Tacky?"

"No."

"Cranky?"

"Yes, but we're talking about appearances."

"Then?"

"Give me a minute," I said. "I'm thinking about it."

Finally, he pushed his empty plate away.

"Dessert," he said happily.

"No!" I cried. "Not another bite. I'll explode."

"You must," he said. "I've already ordered it."

As if on command, the girl materialized at our table with two small, shallow dishes of what looked like custard.

"Flan," Harry said, sinking a spoon into the hard, caramelized sugar topping. "You haven't lived till you've had Brazilian flan."

"No," I protested, but I took a spoonful, and he was right. Rich, silky, creamy, flecked with bits of vanilla, it was divine.

"Coffee?" he asked, helping himself to the leftovers on my plate.

"No," I said weakly. "You may have to carry me back to Mangoville as it is."

The girl brought the check, and Harry laughed. "Thirty bucks, plus tip," he said, taking the money out of his wallet. "Can you imagine a meal like this for that little bit of money?"

"No," I said truthfully. "If I'd served this meal at my restaurant back in Savannah, we're talking $120, at the very minimum."

It had gotten dark while we were in the restaurant. Harry casually took me by the arm and steered me toward the motel.

The little courtyard was deserted. The pool glowed an inviting azure in the moonlight, and pockets of pale green light spilled from behind the drawn curtains of the units surrounding it.

We drifted over toward a pair of lounge chairs facing the pool and sank down into them by mutual, unspoken agreement. Tree frogs croaked from the jungle of palms and orchids, ferns and other tropical-looking plants, and a sweet, flowery scent drifted with the faint breeze ruffling the palm fronds.

"What's that smell?" I asked, tilting my head up to get a look at the stars.

"Flowering ginger," Harry said, without hesitation.

"How—"

"They have fish in Fort Lauderdale too," Harry explained. "I like to know the names of things. You know, if you buy a really fresh piece of gingerroot, and plant it, usually you'll get it to grow. If you've got the right climate," he added. "I've planted a piece behind the office, back at the Breeze. Be nice to have that smell to come home to."

"We should plant some of this kind of stuff back there," I said dreamily. "Do a little landscaping. Hibiscus will grow in Savannah. And some of these ferns and things, if we don't have a really cold winter. And you know what would be really nice?"

"What's that?"

"A pool," I said. "Nothing big or elaborate. Just a little dip pool, maybe with a hot tub at one end, for guests who come in the winter. And a beautiful little courtyard. There's plenty of room, in the parking lot. I hate seeing all that paving when you first pull in."

"A pool would be great," Harry said. "Cost some money, though."

"Yeah," I said with a sigh. "A pool, landscaping, a courtyard, all of that takes up valuable real estate with no practical return on the dollar. I mean, let's face it. A motel can't make any real money these days. Look at this place. It's a dinosaur. I hate to say it, but those Sandcastle people, damn them, have the right idea. Condos are the way to go."

Harry looked away, visibly annoyed.

"What?"

"Does it always have to be about money with you?"

"I'm a businesswoman," I said. "I don't apologize for that. So yeah, I do want a business that turns a profit."

Harry sat up and swung his legs around to face me. "Didn't you ever want to do anything just because you loved it?" he asked. "Because it felt good, pure and simple?"

Stung by his unspoken but understood criticism, I turned away.

"I loved the restaurant business," I said quietly. "I loved meeting people, serving them good food in a beautiful setting. And yes, I loved making money at it. Guale's success meant *I* was a success.

Does that make me a money-grubbing greedhead? I mean, isn't that what most people want out of life?"

"Some people define success differently," he said.

"How do you define success, Harry Sorrentino?"

"Doing what I want to do," he said promptly. "Doing it the best way I know how, without hurting anybody. Living my life so I can be with people I care about. I'm just not a very complicated person, BeBe."

Now I was sitting up too. "See, I think you *are* complicated. Very complicated."

"How?" he challenged.

"You're a mess of contradictions," I said. "You like to play the part of the salty old redneck. Yet, you're anything but. You know food. You've obviously traveled. And you read. A lot, and widely."

"Lots of people read," he said. "You think rednecks don't read?"

"What's with the law books?" I blurted out. I'd been curious about them ever since the first night I'd spent at the Breeze.

"I went to law school," he said finally.

"Where?"

"Does it matter? I've never practiced law. I never even took the bar exam."

"Why not?"

"I didn't want to *be* a lawyer. I just wanted to know how the law worked. So I went to law school."

"Did you find out what you wanted to know?"

"I found some answers," he said cautiously. "I didn't care much for the way the law works. So I found an honest way to make a living."

"Fishing."

"Fishing," he repeated. "It makes me happy. When I've had a good day fishing, I'm a success."

"What's so good about it?" I asked. "I mean it. And not in the snotty way you think I mean. Really, what is it about fishing that appeals to you?"

"Everything about it appeals to me," he said simply. "I love the physical part, working on the boat, bringing in a trophy fish, being out in all kinds of weather. Mostly, I like the challenge. Figuring out the right combination of temperature, tide, time of day, the ocean topography, matching the bait and the tackle to the species of fish I'm after. Some of it's science, some of it's art." He shrugged. "And a lot of it's dumb luck."

He yawned widely then. "I don't know about you, but I'm whipped."

"It's been a long day," I said, struggling to get out of the low-slung chaise longue.

Harry pulled me up, and then pulled me into his arms, brushing his lips on my forehead, and then briefly on my lips.

"What's that for?" I asked, too shocked to hide my surprise.

"I've been wondering what it would be like," he said.

"What did you decide?"

He kissed me again. Slowly, this time. He got his hands tangled in my curls, and then he lazily let his hands wander down my back, pressing my hips into his. I wrapped my arms around his neck and took my time getting to know the feel of him. His shoulders were knotty with muscles, and his cheeks were rough with a day's growth of beard.

Harry leaned back and considered me in the moonlight. "Pretty nice," he said finally. "What did you think?"

I ran my fingers through his coarse brown hair. "Just how old *are* you?"

41

"**How old are** *you*?" he asked, tracing my lips with his fingertips.

"No fair. I asked first."

"Too old to be called cute," he said.

"Come on," I said. "It's time for full disclosure. I'm thirty-five."

"Hot damn," Harry said, kissing me again. "Past the age of consent."

"Way past," I assured him. "Stop dodging the issue."

"How old do you think I am?"

I took a step backward, then circled slowly around him, taking a careful survey.

"Nice ass," I said thoughtfully, letting my fingertips brush against it. I squeezed his biceps. "Muscular build." I was standing in front of him. "May I?" I said, trying the top button on his sport shirt.

"Be my guest," he said. "Just so you know, it's my turn next."

"Hmm," I said, deliberately noncommittal. I took my time with the buttons. "Nice pecs," I said, trailing my fingers over his nipples. The chest hair, as I'd remembered from seeing him work around the Breeze, was salt and pepper gray. But he had just the right amount, not clean-shaven professional figure skater, and not bath-mat furry either.

"You've got gray hair," I said.

"All over," he agreed. "Want to see the rest?" He reached for the waistband of his slacks.

"Not necessary," I said, covering his hand with mine.

He kissed me hungrily, and then murmured in my ear, "Lady, if I'd known this age-guessing thing could be this much fun, I'd have stayed all day at the county fair."

"Okay," I said, holding his face between my hands. "I'm ready."

"Not as ready as I am," he said, running his hands up under my blouse.

"You're forty-eight."

"Wrong," he said quickly. "Maybe you better take some more of my clothes off and try again. Or, I could take some of yours off." He pulled me in the direction of the chaise longues we'd just vacated.

A door opened in one of the units then, and an elderly woman emerged with a tiny white poodle under her arm. "Hurry up and make tinkle, Snuffy. Mama wants to go to bed."

She set the dog down and he promptly trotted over to where we were standing and looked up at us.

"Hurry up, Snuffy," Harry urged in a low voice.

But Snuffy wasn't going anywhere. He circled us twice, sniffing at our legs, then sat down on his haunches and wagged his tail.

"Snuffy!" his mistress called.

But Snuffy wasn't going anywhere. He'd made new friends and he wasn't anxious to abandon us anytime soon.

"Go, already," Harry said, groaning.

I bent down and scratched the top of the poodle's ear, and he responded by flopping over on his back. Harry nudged him a little with the toe of his deck shoe.

"Stop," I said, laughing despite myself. "Come on, I thought you said you were sleepy. It's getting late, and I need to get to bed."

"That's what I had in mind," Harry said, pulling me back toward the chaise longues.

"No deal," I said, freeing myself and heading back toward my room.

"Hey, look," Harry called.

I turned around. Snuffy was lifting a leg on a palm tree.

"Too late," I said.

He was beside me in a minute. "Let's go to my room," he said. "You still haven't correctly guessed my age."

"My grandfather is sharing your room," I reminded him. "I don't want to give him a heart attack."

"He's eighty years old. He's probably been asleep for hours," Harry said. "We can be very quiet."

"You don't know Granddad," I told him, wrapping my arms around his neck and kissing him. "Sorry, but we're going to have to continue this discussion another time."

"You could sneak in later, after he's asleep," Harry suggested. "Take advantage of me."

"Nope."

"I could sneak into your room and take advantage of you."

"Sorry. I've got a roommate too."

"I could rent another room."

"Maybe another time. Good night, Harry," I said, opening my door. "Sleep tight."

42

Hours later, I heard the faint click of the connecting door between our rooms, and smiled groggily to myself through the mist of sleep. Prince Charming had arrived. I congratulated myself on having slipped into a vintage pink satin nightie donated to me by Weezie, and prayed that my roomie, who was one of the soundest sleepers I'd ever met, would stay asleep.

"Hey!" Granddad announced.

I rolled over and opened one eye. He stood in the open doorway, fully dressed in another pair of knee-length Bermuda shorts—this time with vivid purple-and-orange flowers—a shrunken white T-shirt that said "I (heart) NY," and white rubber zori sandals. At least he'd ditched the calf-length dark socks.

"Hey, Granddad," I whispered. "What time is it?"

"Nine o'clock," he bellowed. "I was worried you two were dead over here."

I sat up and looked at the clock radio. It was indeed nine o'clock.

Granddad strolled over to the windows and jerked the drapes open, blinding me with a blast of nuclear-grade sunshine.

"What?" Weezie jumped out of bed. "What's wrong? Is something wrong?"

"It's nearly noon," Granddad said. "I want to get some breakfast in before lunchtime. But the milk and orange juice are in your refrigerator."

"Oh." She sank back down onto the bed. "Is it really nine o'clock?"

"Afraid so," I told her, yawning and stretching. "Guess we over-slept."

"I'll say," Granddad said. "Half the day is gone. Thought we had a criminal to catch today." He opened the tiny refrigerator and peered inside.

"I'll fix you some breakfast, Granddad," I said. "Just let me shower and dress."

"I'll get it," Weezie offered, padding over to the kitchenette area. "You get showered and then I'll take my turn."

"Where's Harry?" I said, as though it was an afterthought.

"Gone," Granddad said.

"Gone where?" This time I wasn't nearly as offhanded.

"Don't know. I went in the bathroom to put my teeth in, and when I got back, he'd cleared out. Made his bed before he left, though. Nice fella, that Harry."

I went to the window and looked out. I spotted the corner of the Buick through the leaves of a huge flowering shrub. "He didn't take the car," I said, feeling relieved.

Weezie held up two boxes. "Cap'n Crunch or raisin bran?"

"Better make it raisin bran," Granddad decided. "I get a little stoved up when I travel. Lorena usually makes me eat prunes when we go on a trip."

"Good to know," Weezie said, pouring the raisin bran into a pink plastic bowl.

I hurried into the bathroom and turned on the shower. Where had Harry gone? I wondered as I washed my hair. Could he really have run off, just as things were starting to get interesting between us?

No, I decided, toweling off, and sliding into a pair of white jeans and a turquoise top that Weezie had picked up at a thrift store during her shopping tour the previous day. He couldn't get far without a car, and anyway, hadn't he been the first one to make a move the night before? If he got scared off by a little harmless kissing and fooling around, I didn't need him in my life. Hadn't I sworn off men? What was I thinking?

I took a critical look at myself in the mirror as I brushed my teeth. What was there to run from? I was a reasonably attractive woman. My hair was nearly a natural blond, I had good skin—although I tend to get a little ashy after too much sun—I had blue eyes and thick, dark eyelashes. My eyebrows were probably too dark for my hair color, but I couldn't afford to have them professionally lightened right now. My upper lip was maybe a little too full and pouty, but every man I'd ever dated claimed that was a turn-on.

So just what the hell was Harry Sorrentino's problem? And why did he have to disappear—right now, just when we needed every hand available if we were to make this scam of mine run properly?

Screw him, I decided, rubbing styling gel into my towel-dried hair. Weezie and Granddad and I would have to pull off the con without Harry. I couldn't do anything to make him stay. But I'd be damned if I'd be in a hurry to pay him the back wages he said he was owed. Let him wait.

Screw Harry Sorrentino.

I stormed out of the bathroom and into my room—and right into the man of the hour's arms. In fact, I nearly knocked him down.

"Hey!" he said, when he got a look at my tightly clamped jaw. "What's with you?"

"What's with you?" I said, in the morning's most brilliant bit of repartee. "Where have you been?"

"What, did I miss bed check?" He carefully peeled off a section of the orange he was eating and offered it to me.

"You did it again," I said, batting the orange slice away. "Just disappeared. Without a word to anybody."

He looked from me to Weezie, who was sitting cross-legged on her bed, reading what looked like a newspaper classified section.

"Did she wake up with a bug up her butt this morning, or is it just me?" he asked.

"She has abandonment issues," Weezie offered.

"I do *not*!"

"She's just not a morning person," Granddad put in. "You shoulda seen her when she was a baby. She used to howl like a stuck pig when her mama took her out of her crib every morning. Cute little thing, but mean as a snake until she got some formula in her."

"He disappeared!" I said, looking for some support from my best friend and my oldest living relative. "Doesn't anybody else find that alarming? Especially when we have so much to do and time is so short?"

"I'm okay with it," Weezie said. "He brought me the *Sun-Sentinel* want ads. I can't believe how many estate sales there are today. And a chocolate croissant!"

"He brought me some good ripe bananas," Granddad said, peeling one. "I bet if you sweeten up a little, you'll get a present too."

Harry held out a white paper sack. "This was going to be your chocolate croissant. But considering your mood . . ."

I snatched the bag away from him. "All right. Maybe I was a little hasty. Maybe I need a cup of coffee or a diet Coke."

He handed me an icy can of diet Coke. "Like this?"

"You're good," I admitted.

"I went to an Internet cafe to do some research," Harry said.

"What kind of research?"

He picked up a sheaf of papers from the kitchenette counter. "These are all the BUC listings for yachts for sale for over two million."

"Wow," I said, glancing through the papers. "This is great."

"Don't be so sure," Harry said. "There are plenty of big, expensive boats for sale in Lauderdale. All over South Florida, in fact. But there are currently only two Sea Urchins for sale in the whole state. One of them is in Fort Myers. Which is on the west coast. The other is in Jacksonville."

I took the croissant out of the bag and broke off a piece and nibbled at it while I thought. "This isn't good."

Harry sipped from a Styrofoam cup of coffee and watched me. "I also checked the boat ads in the *Sun-Sentinel*. Nothing doing. And I picked up one of those boat-shopper magazines too. Still nothing. Does it absolutely have to be a Sea Urchin? What about a Feadship? Middle Eastern sheiks and rap stars own Feadships. They had one being refitted at the shipyard in Thunderbolt last year. They're pretty swell."

"All I know is, the guy has a thing for Sea Urchins," I said. "Maybe he would flip for another kind of yacht. I just don't know where to start."

"Okay," Harry said. "Where does that leave us?"

"We still need to find out where Reddy's living," I reminded him. "Sabrina said it was only ten minutes from Mark's, on Las Olas."

"I know where that is," Weezie volunteered. "I saw it while we were driving around doing our shopping yesterday."

"The road is called Galt Ocean Mile," Harry added. "It's lined on both sides with high-rises, and it runs all the way down to Hollywood and Hallandale. There must be fifty or sixty buildings that would fit that description. We need to be able to narrow it down more than that if we're going to find the guy."

"You're right," I said, sitting on the bed beside Weezie. "We've got to go at this from another direction. Maybe just find ourselves a Sea Urchin. We know they're pretty rare. So if we find one, chances are we might find Reddy nearby."

"What are you suggesting? That we search every marina in the area? That could take days, weeks even," Harry said.

"Maybe we could just call some marinas and ask them if they've got one docked there," I said.

Harry shook his head. "You obviously haven't met too many dockmasters. They don't keep that kind of information on hand, and even if they did, they're not going to tell that to some stranger over the phone."

Granddad put his bowl of cereal in the little sink. "You kids let me know when you need me. I'm going back to my room. They're having mudslides in California. Wild-fires, floods, droughts. You couldn't pay me money to live out there."

Weezie looked up from the newspaper at me. "So. Do we have a plan of action?"

"Guess not," I said glumly.

"Okay if I take the car then? These ads have me salivating. Florida's a great place to buy mid-century modern stuff. It's really starting to take off in the shop now, and it's hard to get in Savannah."

"What's mid-century modern?" Harry asked.

"Stuff from the fifties and sixties," Weezie said. "My hip young clients, especially the ones from the art school, love the stuff. And Florida's a great place to buy it because old people come down here to retire, they bring their stuff with them and die. Eventually. That's why they call it God's waiting room."

"I heard that," Granddad said from the other room.

"Isn't that kind of ghoulish?" Harry asked.

"Not for me," Weezie said. "It's just recycling. And it keeps me in business." She picked up her tote bag and held up her cell phone. "Call me if something comes up and you need me. If not, I'll be back around noon." She gave me a quick, surreptitious wink.

I followed her outside.

"What's with the wink?" I asked.

"You know," she said, smirking. "I just wanted to give you guys some space."

"Which guys?"

"You and Harry."

"Why would we need any space?"

"I'm not blind, you know," Weezie said. "You should be thanking me, not subjecting me to this inquisition."

"Were you spying on us last night?"

"I was adjusting the drapes in the room," Weezie said nonchalantly. "I just happened to see some movement out of the corner of my eye."

"You were watching us making out? That is so freakin' creepy!"

"It was an accident," Weezie said. "An innocent coincidence."

"I'll bet," I said.

"I could have killed that stinking Snuffy," she said darkly. "Just when things were getting hot." She fanned herself. "Ooh. I'm getting turned on just thinking about it again. Remind me to call Daniel tonight."

43

Harry and I whiled away most of the rest of the morning playing gin rummy. We discussed varying tactics to find Reddy, but rejected all of them as a waste of time. Then we took a break for lunch with some tomato soup and grilled-cheese sandwiches, and in between watched two hours of cable-television fishing shows and one hour of a chef on food television whose gimmick was that all his recipes were made from Spam.

Occasionally Granddad would break the monotony of the afternoon by wandering in to update us on the mud-slide situation, or to complain about the fact that the local NBC affiliate didn't carry *Golden Girls* reruns like the station in Savannah did.

Harry and I strictly avoided conversation about the previous evening's activities. Although one time, his hand did brush mine while he was taking a card from the discard pile, and I blushed violently.

"Relax," he said in a low voice, meant only for me. "I'm not trying to get into your pants." He glanced toward the connecting door. "At least, not right at this moment."

"Weezie knows," I said, staring down at the cards in my hand.

"She knows I intend to get into your pants?"

"She saw *me* trying to get into *your* pants last night," I whispered.

He laughed. "She was watching?"

"How can you think this is funny?"

"Not funny. Amusing. And why are we whispering?"

"I do not want my eighty-year-old grandfather to know about this," I said.

"Too late."

"What?" I slapped my cards down on the table faceup.

"So that's where the Jack of spades was," Harry said, raking the cards together into one pile.

"What does my grandfather know?" I wailed.

"He knows you're a woman of strong sexual appetites," Harry said, getting up and rummaging in the sacks of groceries. "You want an orange or something?"

"He saw us? Last night?"

"Apparently," Harry said. "But don't worry, I think he's cool with it."

"Oh my God," I said, burying my face in my arms. "What did he say?"

"He didn't say anything. But there was a condom on my pillow when I got to my room last night," Harry said. "Ribbed, for a couple's mutual pleasure."

"This is the end of civilization as we know it," I said. "My grandfather and best friend spying on me while—"

"Who cares?" Harry asked. "You're single. I'm single. We're consenting adults."

"You still haven't told me how old you are," I said suddenly.

"I liked that guessing thing we were doing last night," Harry said, putting his hand on my knee, then sliding it up my thigh. "I thought we could finish up tonight."

"No!" I said fiercely, slapping his hand away. "We are not making love with my grandfather listening in from the other room."

"What about if I get us a room someplace else?"

"No! He'd know what we were doing."

"When can we do it, then?"

"I don't know. Maybe . . . after we get back to Savannah. Anyway, what makes you think we *are* going to do it?"

"Oh, we're going to do it. I've known since the first day you showed up at the Breeze Inn and started trying to boss me around that we'd end up in bed together. It was just a question of time."

He crossed his arms over his chest with such a look of smug self-satisfaction that I wanted to kill him right then.

But my cell phone started to ring, and he was, literally, saved by the bell.

"Did you get lost?" The voice was familiar, but I couldn't place it until I saw the caller ID on the phone's readout panel. Sandra Findley.

"Hi, Sandra," I said.

"I thought you were going to keep me up on any new developments."

"Sorry," I told her. "There really hasn't been much to tell. I had drinks with Sabrina Berg yesterday. She's a real pistol. It turns out she actually went on a sort of date with Reddy. He took her back to some condo he was staying at, but she'd had a few drinks that night, and she's not sure exactly where he took her. So now we're sort of spinning our wheels down here, hoping to come up with a lead."

"I think I've got something that might help," Sandra said. "Mother's accountant called me this morning. She wanted to know if I knew of any reason why Mother is paying two American Express bills."

My pulse gave a little blip and I turned to Harry and gave him the thumbs-up sign. "It's Sandra," I said. "From Vero Beach."

He returned the thumbs-up.

"When I confronted Mother about it, at first she acted as if she didn't know what I was talking about," Sandra said. "But after I showed her the copy of the statement the accountant faxed over, she finally admitted that she'd given Reddy the credit card. It was supposed to be so he could take her to lunch without having to be embarrassed by her always paying. Can you believe it? She also claimed she'd forgotten she'd ever given him the card. I don't know whether that part is true or not. She has gotten pretty forgetful. My brother and I are going to have a long talk with her about finances any day now. But I did want to let you know about it before I call Amex and have the card canceled."

"Wait," I said, interrupting her tirade.

"When I think about that slimebag, running around charging things right and left to us, I just see red," Sandra continued. "You should see the bill from Burdine's! He bought himself $800 worth of underwear. And a $300 pair of sunglasses."

"Sandra," I said urgently. "Wait. Please don't cancel the card. Not yet."

"Why the hell not? He's discovered Palm Beach too. He's been in every store on Worth Avenue. Armani, Escada, Saks, Chanel, Dior. He bought himself a $1,400 gym bag at Louis Vuitton. Did you even know Louis Vuitton made gym bags?"

"Well, uh, yeah. In my former life, I had a Louis Vuitton back-pack," I confessed. "But I bought it with my own money. Of course, Reddy's probably carrying it now. If he didn't sell it along with the rest of my stuff."

"He's got to be stopped," Sandra said. "You should see the restau-rants he's been eating at. Most of them I can't even afford."

"Just don't cancel the card yet," I repeated. "If you cancel the card, he'll figure out somebody's after him, and we'll never catch up with him. Look, could you fax those credit card statements to me?"

"Yeah, I could do that," Sandra said. "Where are you staying?"

I made a face. "A motel called the Mango Tree." I scrabbled around on the nightstand until I found the motel's laminated rate card. "Here's the fax number," I said, dictating it to her. "Just send it to the attention of BeBe Loudermilk."

"All right," she said reluctantly. "You've got two days. And then I'm canceling the card, no matter what."

"Two days," I promised. "And then you can come down here and cut it up yourself."

"That's not the only thing I'm gonna cut," she said.

I put the phone down, and then it was my turn to feel smug. "Reddy has been on a spending spree. With Polly Findley's American Express card."

"And?"

"Sandra is faxing the statements over here. So we can see where he's been and what he's been doing."

"I like it," Harry said.

"Me too."

Fifteen minutes later I strolled over to the Mango Tree's office.

The man standing behind the desk wore only a pair of bright yellow polyester slacks. No shirt, no shoes. He was nearly bald, with exactly seven strands of hair coiled sideways across his gleaming head. He had skin that looked like oiled mahogany, and black-rimmed Buddy Holly glasses. Mister Mangoville. Some kind of sitar music was playing on the radio and he was swaying along to the music, in a world of his own.

"Yes?" he said, looking up, annoyed by the interruption.

"I'm BeBe Loudermilk. In unit fifteen. Did a fax arrive for me?"

He frowned. "Loudermilk?"

"Unit fifteen. I'm expecting a fax."

"Ghita!" he shouted.

A dark-haired young woman emerged from a curtained area behind the counter. She wore contemporary American clothing—blue-jean shorts, an oversize T-shirt—but she had an exotic beauty that transcended her trashy surroundings. The man chattered at her in a language I didn't understand. She disappeared, then reappeared with a handful of papers. He snatched them from her and rifled through the pages.

"Forty dollars," he announced.

"What?"

"Eight pages. Five dollars a page transmission charge," he said.

"That's crazy. You can't do that. It's price gouging."

The music played. He closed his eyes and swayed. Back and forth. Like a snake charmer. I stared at him, but he didn't see me. We were at an impasse.

"Put it on my bill," I said finally.

"Cash," he said, without opening his eyes.

"I'll be right back," I said, stomping out of the office.

Weezie was in the room, unloading a large cardboard box. "Wait till you see," she crowed. "I hit the mother lode. Can you believe, I've been at one sale, all this time? The trunk of your grandfather's car is full. I had to stop at the UPS store to have the rest of the stuff boxed up and shipped back. And I stopped at some antique shops on A1A and sold off a bunch of other stuff. I quadrupled my $600 investment, in like, fifteen minutes."

"That's great," I said, putting my hand out. "Give me forty dollars, okay?"

She gave me the money without a question. That's the thing about a best friend. They'll spy on you one day, then loan you money the next.

I went back to the office and slapped two twenties down on the counter. Mister Mangoville opened his eyes, looked at them, and tucked them in the pocket of the yellow pants. Only then did he slide the papers across the counter to me.

Back in the room, I arranged the statement pages in chronological order across the bedspread. "Here we go," I told Harry and Weezie.

Whatever you wanted to call him—Reddy, Randall, Rodolfo, or even Roy Eugene—the man was unarguably a discriminating connoisseur of consumer goods.

All the stores that Sandra Findley mentioned were on that Amex statement, along with dozens of restaurants and shops I'd never heard of.

But it was the smaller charges that caught my eye.

"Look." I pointed at a line item of $52.80 for a gas station on

DuPont Boulevard. Five days later, there was a charge of $32.37 for the same station. And the name reappeared four more times.

"And here," I said, pointing to restaurant charges at a place called the Sand Bar. I grabbed the phone book and looked it up. The address was also DuPont Boulevard.

By now, Harry had his map unfolded on the bed.

"DuPont is actually right at A1A. And it's not that far from Galt Ocean Mile," he said, stabbing the map with a stubby index finger.

"Where else is he spending money?" Weezie asked. "This is fun."

"Two more charges to the Sand Bar," I said, scanning the pages. "Three more charges, all around twenty-five bucks each, at a place called the Beach Market Deli."

Weezie had the phone book now, leafing through the business listings. "Also on DuPont Boulevard," she said.

"He's playing golf now too," I said. "Here's a charge to a place called the Grande Oaks Golf Club."

"Again, DuPont Boulevard," Weezie said. And then she wrinkled her brow. "Hey." She leafed back through the phone book. "All these places he's been charging stuff, they're all at the same street address."

She picked up her cell phone and dialed the last number she'd looked up, the Grande Oaks Golf Club.

"Hello," she said. "Can you tell me where your golf course is located?"

She listened, nodded, and hung up the phone.

"That explains a lot," she said. "All those businesses, they're all part of the same resort. The Bahia Mar Hotel and Marina."

"Bahia Mar Marina?" I pounded the bed in glee. "That's it. That's where he's hanging out. He's nailed!"

I looked over at Harry for confirmation. But he had a weird look on his face.

"Did you say the Bahia Mar?" he asked.

"Yeah," Weezie said. "Bahia Mar. It sounds so old Florida. I can't wait to see the place."

"Bahia Mar Marina," he said dreamily. "Man, I forgot it was down here. That's where Travis McGee kept the *Busted Flush*. Slip F-eighteen. Bahia Mar Marina. Son of a bitch!"

44

I looked over Harry's shoulder at the map. "How far away is Bahia Mar? And how soon can you be ready to go?"

"I'd guess about fifteen minutes. And I'm ready now."

He was wearing baggy khaki shorts, a T-shirt advertising the Savannah Sport Fisherman's Billfish Tournament, and a battered pair of Top-Siders. He had a day's growth of beard. To my own chagrin, I had to admit the grizzled-sea-captain look was starting to work for me.

"What do you think?" I asked Weezie. "Can he go to a fancy marina dressed like that?"

"*He* can," Weezie said pointedly. "You can't. What if you run into Reddy? You'll blow our cover."

"I'm not staying here," I protested. "Anyway, I'm the only one who knows what he looks like."

"We've seen the video," Weezie reminded me. "I'm not saying you shouldn't go. All I'm saying is that it may be necessary for you to go incognito."

I looked at her. She looked at me. We gave each other the mutual high five.

She opened one of the black plastic trash bags she'd hauled into the room from her morning's estate-sale outing.

"You wouldn't believe the clothes in that woman's closet," she said, sorting things on the bed. "She was the ultimate clotheshorse. I saw flapper dresses from the roaring twenties, all the way up to a St. John suit that still had the store's price tags hanging from the sleeve. I didn't buy any of the really expensive couture stuff. But I did pick up a few things. Just in case.

"Okay," she said. "Keep an open mind. Remember, we want you to look like somebody else."

She laid a yellow-and-orange-plaid polyester pantsuit beside me. To which she added a yellow silk head scarf and a pair of thick crepe-soled orthopedic oxfords.

"No," I said, grimacing. "Not even for two million dollars am I going anywhere wearing this outfit. Especially these shoes." I held them at arm's length.

"What's wrong with those shoes?" Granddad said, wandering into the room eating a grape Popsicle. "I like those shoes. Lorena has a pair just like that to wear to bingo."

I stuck the shoes back in the garbage bag. "If I wear those things, I'll get hit on by every old geezer in town. No offense, Granddad."

"Hmm," Weezie said.

"What else have you got?" I asked.

She shrugged. "Lots of sixties cocktail dresses. But you can't go traipsing around a marina in one of those. It'll look too costumey."

She rummaged around in the first sack, and then hauled over a second one that she dumped on the bed.

"Wait," she said. "I've got it. You'll be brilliant."

She held up a pair of white cotton Capri pants. "Bobbie Brooks!" Weezie announced. "Very resort wear. And they've cycled back into style again." She tossed a ruffled turquoise crop top in my direction. I held it up to myself.

"Not bad," I admitted.

"Early Ann-Margret," Weezie said. "But that's not all of it."

She picked up the previously rejected silk scarf, and tied it under my chin, and then, alternatively, with the tie at the nape of my neck.

She shook her head. "You still look like a sixties version of BeBe Loudermilk. Wait. I left some more stuff in the car." She dashed outside and was back moments later with a Burdine's shopping bag. Which she emptied. "Accessories!" she said brightly.

She tossed me a shoulder-length black wig. "Try that on."

The wig had eyebrow-tickling bangs and flipped-up ends. I'd never had bangs in my entire life. Ever.

Weezie rolled the scarf into a headband and knotted it. "Hmm. Kinda reminds me of Marlo Thomas in her *That Girl* mode."

She dug through the assorted wigs, scarves, and pieces of jewelry until she came up with a pair of white plastic-rimmed sunglasses with frames so enormous they hid most of the upper half of my face. She added a pair of large white plastic hoop earrings.

"Yes!" she said. "We're getting closer."

I got up and peered in the mirror over the dresser.

Harry tilted his head, as if trying to make up his mind about something.

"Who does she remind me of?" he asked.

"Jackie Kennedy," Granddad announced.

Weezie circled around me, clicking her tongue. "You still look sorta like yourself." She glanced over at Harry. "If you saw her walking toward you, would you say, 'Hey, that's BeBe dressed up for Halloween'?"

"Maybe," Harry said. "Part of it's her figure." He grinned.

"I've got an idea," Weezie said, heading for the bathroom. She grabbed the pants and top, turned, and beckoned me with the crook of her finger. "Follow me."

She closed the bathroom door. "Strip," she ordered. "Down to panties and bra."

I knew better than to argue.

She handed me a handful of folded-up toilet tissue. "Stick that in your bra."

"What? Why?"

"God gave you a B cup, now me and Charmin are giving you a C."

She went behind me and with a couple of no-nonsense yanks, shortened the straps of my bra by half an inch.

"Ow!" I cried. "Now what?"

"We need these bad girls riding up nice and high," she decreed. "We need you stylin' and profilin'."

"They're hitting me in the chin," I whined.

"Perfect," she said. She slapped my butt.

"Ow. Cut it out."

"Like a pancake," she said, tsk-tsking. "But there's nothing I can do about it."

"What? You didn't buy any butt implants at that sale?"

She was humming and rifling through the contents of her cosmetics bag. "Sit there," she said, pointing to the commode.

I sat.

She ripped off the wig and headband and wrapped a towel around my own hair. "Close your eyes."

A moment later she was smearing a vile-smelling lotion on my face and neck. "I brought this stuff to put on my legs, they're so fish-belly white this time of year."

"What?" I asked, getting a little concerned.

"Just a little bronzer," she said.

I opened my eyes. "Tan in a can?"

"It takes about thirty minutes of exposure before it starts to work," Weezie said, handing me the tube. "Put that on your arms and legs now. And don't worry. I use it all summer instead of wearing panty hose."

She went to work with the makeup then, tweezing and dabbing and curling, humming the whole time. I think the tune was "I Enjoy Being a Girl."

"Get dressed," she said. "And be careful putting on those white capris. I don't want that bronzer rubbing off on 'em."

"Now the wig and headband," she said, still humming. "And a little lipstick. Coral Gables coral! Perfect."

She turned me around by the shoulders to face the mirror. "Voilà!"

"Oh my God," I breathed.

"Just one minute." She ducked into the bedroom and came back with a pair of four-inch-high screaming yellow vinyl platform heels straight out of the seventies.

"Now walk," she ordered, flinging the bathroom door open with a flourish.

I minced. Carefully. What with the reengineered breasts and the Elton John shoes, I was afraid I'd tip forward any second.

Granddad and Harry were sitting in the kitchenette area, sharing a bag of Cheez Doodles. Granddad was having what I hoped was his first Scotch of the day.

"Well?" I did a self-conscious little twirl in front of Harry. "Is it still me?"

"No," he said quickly. "Not even close."

"Great," Weezie said, beaming. "Just give me ten minutes to get myself together and we'll be ready to roll."

"I'll change too," Granddad offered. "Can't let you ladies steal our thunder, can we, Harry?"

"Guess not," Harry said. He still hadn't taken his eyes off me.

Ten minutes later, Granddad reemerged from his room. His white hair was slicked straight back from his forehead with some kind of shiny pomade. He wore a pair of yellowing cotton-duck slacks, a hot pink dress shirt, and a double-breasted blue blazer with gold buttons and wide lapels. Also a silk cravat.

"A cravat?" I said. "Granddad, I'm not sure—"

"Awesome!" Weezie said, coming out of the bathroom and clapping her hands in approval. "Spencer, you look so handsome and distinguished!" She gave me a broad wink. "BeBe, we're gonna have to watch this one to make sure some rich widow lady doesn't try to cut in on your grandmother's territory."

"Aww," Granddad said, blushing.

"Hey," I said, taking in Weezie's own outfit. "No fair!"

She'd clearly saved the best of the day's pickings for herself. She wore a short, lime-green flowered rayon halter dress, lime-green sling-back flats, and a floppy pink-and-green polka-dotted straw hat.

"How come you get to be all adorable and I get to look like—"

"Whoa!" Granddad said, bending down to examine my face. "What happened to you?"

"Nothing," I said, taking off the sunglasses. "Why?"

"It's your skin," he said. "Is it supposed to look like that?"

"Like what?" I looked down at my hands, which had suddenly turned a deep burnt orange.

I ran into the bathroom and looked in the mirror. My face was the same shade of dark copper. "Weezie!" I screamed. "What have you done to me?"

"It was just a little bronzer," Weezie said, fluttering nervously around behind me. "I use this stuff all the time. It's never done that to . . . me . . ."

She was holding up the tube of tan in a can, squinting at the label. "Oh. Here's the problem. Wow. The package is the exact same as the kind I usually buy at home. But this is X-Treme Caribe. I usually get Sun-Kist Mist."

Granddad leaned into the bathroom. "You know what you look like?"

"A crack ho!" I moaned. "I look like a crack ho who got left out in the sun for a couple years too long."

"No, that's not it." Granddad frowned. "I've seen her on that MTV sometimes. When nothing's happening on the weather channel. You know who I mean?"

"You look fine," Harry called from the other room. "Now can we get going?"

"I can't go out looking like this," I protested.

"You're just not used to being a brunette," Weezie said, dragging me out of the bathroom and toward the door. "With the black wig and the eye makeup and all, you look fantastic. Exotic, even. Doesn't she, fellas?"

"You look hot," Harry said, giving me an up-and-down leer.

"I know who it is," Granddad said, snapping his fingers. "You look like that Jennifer Lopez. Only not quite as bootielicious."

45

The Bahia Mar Hotel and Marina was some kind of wonderful. Manicured green lawns and palm trees . . . and valet parking.

"Deal with it," I told Granddad when he started to object.

We'd gone over the plan, such as it was, on the way over.

"I'll look around the marina, see if there's any kind of yacht in particular that old Roy Eugene is scoping out," Harry said. "Spencer, maybe you could hang out in one of the bars and kind of get the lay of the land."

"Sure," Granddad said. "I'll be very discreet." He glanced at his watch. "It's almost five o'clock. You think they'll have early-bird specials?"

"It's Florida," I told him. "They invented the early bird. I guess Weezie and I will hang out in whatever bar Granddad doesn't go to. And remember," I warned him. "No more than two Scotches and water. Or I'll tell Grandmama."

The Sand Bar overlooked the marina and what looked like a modern-day armada of boats, yachts, sailboats, and everything in between. Weezie and I split up. She took one end of the bar and I staked out the other. It was early Saturday evening and the place was already starting to get busy, with people standing three deep in some spots, waiting to place a drink order.

It took only about thirty seconds before I had company.

He was short and bulky, with a sunburned nose and neck. He wore a dark green polo shirt with "Grande Oaks Golf & Country Club" embroidered over the breast pocket, and had a sun visor perched low over his forehead. He edged his way into the bar and leaned forward, flashing an easy smile.

"Did you already order?"

I looked around to make sure he was talking to me.

"Not yet."

"I'm Pete," he said.

"And I'm Jennifer. But they call me Jen."

"Hey, Davey," he called. A bartender who was making a big racket with a blender turned and looked over his shoulder.

"Hiya, Pete," he said. "Whatya drinking?"

Pete gave me a questioning look. Why not? I thought.

"Lemon martini," I said.

"Two," Pete said, holding up the appropriate number of fingers.

Davey brought our drinks and Pete settled in to tell me his life story. He was in software sales, originally from Columbus, Ohio, but living in Lauderdale for the past four years. "It's paradise," he said. "But maybe not in August. How about you?"

"Just visiting for a few days," I said. "I'm from Atlanta."

"Thought I recognized that Southern accent," Pete said.

He asked me the questions men always ask women in bars, and I answered with the same mix of truth and lies women always tell strange men.

"So," I said brightly. "You're a golfer. Do you play a lot at the course here?"

"As often as I can," he said. "I'm a member. Do you play?"

"Not really," I said. "But I think a friend of a friend of mine plays here. Maybe you know him? Rodolfo Martinez?"

He frowned. "Doesn't ring a bell."

"He's sort of new in the area, I think," I said.

I gestured toward the marina with an exaggerated sigh. "I just love to look at all those gorgeous boats out there."

"Big toys for big boys," Pete said dismissively. "I've got a twenty-two-foot Ski-Nautique, but I keep it at the dock at my place. In Lighthouse Point."

"Great," I said. "Do you know a lot about boats?"

"I know my way around on the water," Pete said. "Hey, would you want to go for a little moonlight cruise? I could bring the boat up here one night, pick you up, take you to dinner. There are lots of waterfront restaurants where we can tie up."

"I don't know," I said. "I'm here with my girlfriend."

"We'll bring her along," Pete offered. "Plenty of room."

I took a long sip of the martini. Pete had nothing in the way of information to offer me. He was pleasant and harmless, but he needed to move along.

"Here's the thing," I said hesitantly. "She really is my girlfriend."

"Huh?" Harmless *and* clueless.

I leaned over and whispered in his ear. "I like girls."

He straightened up. His face had lost its ruddy hue. "No kidding?"

"Sorry," I said.

Next up was Cliff, a cute blond preppie type from Long Island who was in town for his college roommate's wedding.

"Don't I know you?" he asked, wedging himself in beside me at the bar.

I tilted my sunglasses down to get a better look. He had deep blue eyes and a yummy little cleft in his chin. The phrase "contributing to the delinquency of a minor" crossed my mind.

"Probably not," I said, with genuine regret. "I've never been to Long Island."

Against my better judgment, I let him buy me a drink. But when he nibbled on my ear and asked about the possibility of "hooking up" for the night, I had to get tough.

"Run along now, Cliffie," I sighed. "Find somebody your own age to play with."

A reggae band had started setting up on the postage-stamp-size dance floor opposite the bar. The crowd had gotten so tight, it was hard to move and harder to carry on a conversation.

I had to boost myself up on the bar rail to catch sight of Weezie. But she was still there, at the other end of the bar, deep in conversation with a guy in a straw cowboy hat.

"Buy you a drink?"

He said his name was Howard, and he was a graying stockbroker from Boynton Beach who made no move to hide his wedding band.

"Play any tennis?" he asked, checking out my X-treme tan.

"Not much," I said. "I really like boating."

"I've got a thirty-two-foot Hatteras docked right down there," he said, pointing out the window.

"Wow!" I said, as if I knew or cared what a Hatteras was. "I knew this guy, back in Jacksonville, he had a really neat boat. A Sea Urchin. Have you ever seen one?"

"Your friend must have done very well for himself," Howard said. "Sea Urchins are the top of the line."

"Yeah." I sighed. "I've never seen one since that one time."

"Take a walk with me," Howard said, smoothly putting his hand on my thigh. "And you can see another one. It's docked down on the far end of the same row as mine."

"Really?" I casually slid his hand away. "A Sea Urchin? What's it called?"

"*Reefer Madness,*" Howard said with a frown. "It supposedly belongs to some washed-up rock-and-roll guy. You believe that? A guy names an $8 million yacht something like *Reefer Madness*?"

"Where'd you say it's tied up?" I asked, hopping down from the bar stool.

"Right down the dock from mine," Howard said, resting his hand on the small of my back. "Wait till you see the sweet little cabin on my Hatteras."

"Oh," I said, making a frownie face. "I don't think so. I don't think that would be a good idea."

"Why not?" he asked, sliding his hand just slightly south, till it was resting on my not quite bootielicious butt.

"Genital herpes," I whispered. "I'm having a little flare-up."

46

At eight o'clock, the four of us reconnoitered in the hotel's front entryway.

"I found the yacht!" Weezie announced, fairly dancing with excitement.

"So did I," I said. "It's called *Reefer Madness.*"

"It's an eighty-six-footer," Harry said, handing the valet-parking attendant the claim check for the Buick.

"Fella that owns her used to be in some sort of rock-and-roll band," Granddad said, straightening his cravat. He patted the blazer's breast pocket. "I got the band name wrote down right here. Outlandish name." He produced a bar napkin and squinted at what he'd scribbled on it. "Oh yeah. Here it is. Meatball?"

"Meatball?" Weezie said. "Spencer, are you sure?"

"That's what the man said. What the hell kind of name is Meatball?"

"I never heard of a famous band called Meatball," I said.

"'Bat Out of Hell,'" Granddad said, reading the napkin. "That was their big hit. But I been watching MTV and I never heard of a song called 'Bat Out of Hell.'"

"You must mean Meat Loaf!" Weezie said. "That was the name of their first huge hit album. 'Bat Out of Hell.'"

"'Paradise by the Dashboard Light,'" Harry added. "It was a landmark piece of songwriting, not that I was ever a big Meat Loaf fan. Give me Jimmy Buffett any day."

I pondered that. "So you'd rather have a Cheeseburger in Paradise than Meat Loaf? What does that say about your age?"

"It says nothing about my age," Harry retorted. "It's all about taste in music."

"What the hell?" Granddad exclaimed. "Meat loaf, cheeseburger? You kids don't know anything about music. Now my generation, we had some great tunes. Songs like 'Begin the Beguine.' Or 'Flat-Foot Floozie with the Floy-Floy.' "

The valet-parking kid pulled up with the Electra, Harry tipped him, and we piled inside, everybody chattering all at once.

"I saw the yacht," Harry said. "And, man, that is one sweetheart of a floating palace. I bet that thing would sell for four million, easy. I wouldn't mind stealing it myself."

"Anybody see any sign of Reddy?" I asked, turning around.

"Hard to say," Harry said. "I made a couple circuits around the marina before I spoke to the dockmaster, who pointed me in the direction of the *Reefer Madness,* although he wouldn't tell me exactly who owns it. He hasn't had anybody else asking about Sea Urchins, and he hasn't seen anybody who fits our description of Roy Eugene, but it's a pretty busy operation. The dockmaster did tell me that the *Reefer*'s owner lives in Nashville, and there's a live-aboard crew of two or three."

"Reddy's definitely hanging around here," I said. "I just know it. I can sense it."

"What else did you sense, Jennifer?" Harry asked.

I stuck my tongue out at him. "I sensed I was being hit on the whole time I was in that bar. I got invited to dinner and a moonlight cruise, and two guys just cut to the chase right away and outright propositioned me for sex. I told you this getup makes me look like a hooker. What about you, Weezie?"

"Not all the guys who talked to you were losers," Weezie said, giggling. "I saw that cute young blond guy whispering sweet nothings in your ear."

"Oh yeah?" Harry said, glancing over at me with a raised eyebrow.

"He was an infant," I said. "Barely out of diapers."

"I'd be willing to baby-sit him," Weezie said.

"Could we get back to business? Anyway, I saw you getting up close and personal with at least one hot guy at your end of the bar," I pointed out.

"That was research," Weezie said. "And it just so happens that the guy you saw me talking to told me that he used to date a girl who works as a chef on *Reefer Madness*. Her name is Emma Murphey. They broke up because the boat he crews on just got back from a three-month cruise to St. Croix. He wanted her to sign on to his boat, but she didn't want to give up her job on the *Reefer Madness*. Apparently it's a really cushy job because the owner only comes down maybe once or twice a year. So the crew just lives aboard and goofs off most of the time. My guy, his name is Jason, told me Emma usually hangs out at that bar you went to, BeBe."

"The Binnacle?"

"Yeah," Weezie said. "That's the place. Another guy who crews on the boat is named Liam. I didn't get a last name."

"That's terrific." I said. "Great work."

"I know," she said, fluffing her hair. "But hey, BeBe, what is up with these guys down here? I mean, I had more adolescent-acting middle-aged married men making passes at me. I don't know how single women stand hanging out in bars like that."

"Now you know why I got married three times," I said. "Anything's better than this."

"Even Richard?" Weezie said.

"Nothing is worse than Richard," I said.

"Forget Richard," Harry said.

"Believe me, I'm trying to," I told him. "Weezie, did your new friend tell you what this Emma looks like?"

"Short, dark hair, big green eyes, long legs, big boobs," Weezie said.

"Sounds like somebody I need to meet," Harry said. He looked in the rear view mirror at Granddad.

"Hey, Spencer, I think it's our turn to go hang out in a bar and pick up chicks, don't you?"

I gave him another punch. This one wasn't nearly as playful.

"What's that?" Granddad asked, sitting up with a start.

"Harry thinks the two of you should go cruising for ladies," Weezie explained. "In that bar BeBe was at yesterday."

"Cruising?" Granddad said, blinking.

"Strictly for research purposes," Harry added.

Granddad checked his watch. "Maybe another night. It's been a pretty busy day for me. I need to check on a developing cold front over the Great Lakes. Maybe you could just drop me off at the motel?"

"Me too," Weezie added quickly. "I want to sort through all the stuff I bought at that estate sale today. Some of it I'll keep, but the rest of it I'll sell on eBay. I brought my little digital camera, so I might even go ahead and photograph some of it."

"You're doing it again," I said, a warning note in my voice.

"Doing what?"

"You know what," I said. "The same thing you did last night."

"Forcing us to spend quality time together," Harry said. "Alone."

"It worked out, didn't it?" Weezie said. "I didn't hear any complaints."

"Not from me," Harry said.

"Attaboy," Granddad said.

I turned around to face the backseat co-conspirators. "Okay, you two. No more spying. This happens to be my private life. While I appreciate your interest, I don't need cheerleaders. And," I said, directing my sternest look at my grandfather, "Harry doesn't need any coaching. Or any, uh, family-planning supplies. If you get my drift."

"Better to be safe than sorry," Granddad said, crossing his arms over his chest.

"Just out of curiosity," I said, "can I ask where you got that thing?"

"Bought it from a vending machine in the men's room at Henry's Diner," he said promptly. "I always kept it in my billfold. Just in case."

"Henry's Diner?" Harry said. "That place closed down when I was just a kid. What, twenty, twenty-five years ago?"

"Has it been that long?" Granddad asked.

"Good Lord," I said, shaking my head. "Antique condoms. Just what I need."

"Hey, Harry," Weezie piped up. "If you're not going to use it, give it to me. I'll sell it on eBay."

47

BOOM thumpa-thumpa-thump. BOOM thumpa-thumpa-thump. The heavy bass beat rattled the front door of the Binnacle.

"Place is jumping," Harry said, standing aside to let me enter.

"Holy crap," I said, squeezing inside the entryway and pulling him in behind me.

The Binnacle was an entirely different scene tonight. What had been a high-ceilinged, light-flooded restaurant on Friday afternoon was now a pitch-black, cavelike nightclub pulsating with loud music and an even louder audience.

We could see a spotlit deejay on a raised platform in front of the wall of windows, and directly in front of him, a sea of bobbing heads, which must have been the dance floor. But other than that, the room was so mobbed, little else was distinguishable.

As we inched forward we came to the maître d's stand, which was now manned by a muscle-bound Cuban guy in a tight-fitting red silk T-shirt.

"Ten-dollar cover charge," he announced in a bored voice.

"Ten dollars? To listen to canned music from a deejay?" It was my voice but my grandfather's influence.

He held up a roll of red cardboard movie tickets. "You get a free drink ticket with the cover. You staying or going?"

"Staying," Harry said, handing over a twenty-dollar bill.

The doorman ripped two tickets from his roll and gave them to

Harry, who guided me forward with a firm hand placed in the small of my back.

"How are we gonna do this?" I asked, shouting in Harry's ear in order to make myself heard. "There must be three hundred people in here. It's a zoo."

His eyes were already searching the room, no doubt for the missing Emma.

"We split up," he said. "I'll take the right side, you take the left. Meet me back at the door in, what, an hour?"

I looked at the cheap plastic watch I'd bought at a drugstore earlier in the day.

"Ten-thirty," I agreed. "And don't let me catch you flirting with any chicks unless they have big boobs and green eyes."

"It's a deal," he said, laughing and melting into the crowd.

It took me fifteen minutes to snake my way over toward the bar, during which time I had my already aching toes stomped on half a dozen times, and my butt groped at least twice. By the time I reached the bar, I was ready to concede that my mission was impossible. Every woman in the room seemed to have short dark hair and big boobs.

Ten minutes after I'd claimed a hard-fought spot at the bar, a bartender finally materialized in front of me. He was pencil thin, with shoulder-length pale blond hair, an even paler mustache, and a ruffled pink tuxedo shirt.

I handed over my red ticket with a sigh of relief. "Maker's Mark and water."

"Sorry. You only get well drinks with this," he said. "Jim Beam?"

"Okay," I said wearily.

He brought the drink and set it down in front of me.

"Is it always this crazy here at night?" I asked.

"Saturday nights are pretty wild," he agreed. "We get a ton of tourists, plus the regulars. Is this your first time?"

"My first Saturday night," I told him. "I'm looking for a girl who supposedly hangs out here a lot. She's the chef on a yacht? Her name's Emma?"

He shook his head. "Sorry. I've only been working here a couple of weeks. I don't really know any of the regulars' names yet."

I sighed again. "Short dark hair. Green eyes. Big boobs, long legs?"

"Don't know her, but I'd like to."

"Yeah, you and every other guy in town." With deep reluctance, I put a five-dollar bill on the bar. "How about any of the other bartenders?"

The bill disappeared in a flash. "What was the name again?"

"Emma Murphey. She crews on the *Reefer Madness,* tied up over at Bahia Mar."

Five minutes later, my drink was gone, and so, apparently, was my new friend. I knew I needed to keep looking, but the Elton John shoes had my feet screaming, and by now my shortened bra straps had dug deep tunnels into my protesting flesh.

With my back to the bar, I gazed out at the crowd. Every head in the room was bobbing to the same tune, "Brick House," by The Commodores.

Shake it down, shake it down, shake it down, now, the music urged. Good godamighty, my head was bobbing too.

"You're looking for Emma?"

I whirled around. Blond-boy bartender was back, accompanied by a really tall also blond person of questionable gender, also wearing a ruffled pink tux shirt.

"This is Joy," my new friend said.

"Really?" I said.

"Save the jokes," Joy said. "I've heard 'em all." Her voice was surprisingly high, given her boyish good looks. "What do you want with Emma?"

Think fast, I told myself. Think really fast. I decided to go with the partial truth.

"I own a restaurant, and I heard she's a pretty decent chef," I said.

"Who told you that?" Joy asked.

"Somebody in the Grille, over at Bahia Mar," I said. "I didn't get their name, but they said if I was looking for kitchen help, I should maybe talk to Emma Murphey."

"Emma hasn't come in tonight," Joy said. "But I heard she might be in the market for a new job. That asshole she works for has been jerking her around pretty bad."

"You mean Meat Loaf?" I asked.

Joy frowned. "Who's Meat Loaf? Emma said the guy's name is Doobie."

Ah, the young, I thought. So innocent. So clueless. Joy, I sadly thought, probably didn't even know all the lyrics to "Brick House," let alone "I'd Do Anything for Love (But I Won't Do That)."

"Do you know how I can get in touch with Emma?" I asked.

"I'm not her agent or anything," Joy said, looking annoyed. "She might be at Dirty Dan's, over on A1A. It's in a strip shopping center with a Publix and a Blockbuster."

"Thanks." I shook Joy's hand. She held it out, palm up. Expectant.

"Right," I said, extracting another precious five-dollar bill from the pocket of the capris, and shaking her hand again. The bill disappeared. Another hospitality professional.

"Only five? Are you kidding?" Joy said, insulted.

"Five," I said firmly. "It's not like you're her agent or anything."

In the car on the way to Dirty Dan's, I filled Harry in on what I'd learned, which, admittedly, wasn't much.

"Emma's boss's name is Doobie," I said. "And she's been telling people he's been jerking her around lately."

"I found a girl who knows this guy Liam," Harry said. "She thinks Liam moonlights at a Radio Shack somewhere here in town."

"Did she know which one?" I asked. "In a town this big, there could be half a dozen or more Radio Shacks."

"Nope," Harry said. "Just that he's a big gadget freak. He doesn't hang out at the bars. She says she met him at the Starbucks closest to Bahia Mar."

"A Starbucks addict," I said. "That's excellent. Once you get hooked on that stuff, nothing else will do. We can check that out in the morning. And hope he hasn't decided to buy a bag of the stuff and brew it himself back on the boat."

Five-bucks' worth of information from Joy hadn't included exact directions to Dirty Dan's. We drove up and down A1A for nearly an hour, until we found a shopping center with both a Publix supermarket and a Blockbuster and Dirty Dan's.

The bar was just a narrow little neighborhood place that smelled like stale beer and burnt popcorn. You had to pass a double row of video games at the front of the room to get to the bar. We spotted Emma right off. A young girl with short dark hair, she wore a minuscule pair of gym shorts rolled down to her pelvic bones, and a skintight white spaghetti-strap top that did indeed reveal all of Emma's publicized blessings. She was scowling down at a Golden Tee golf game.

"Shit!" she said, pounding the top of the game.

"Emma?"

"Oops. Sorry," she said. "Were you waiting to play?"

"No. Actually, I was hoping to talk to you," I said.

"Yeah, sure. Are you the lady who's looking for a chef for a restaurant?"

"How'd you know?"

She laughed. "Joy called me on my cell phone. What kind of restaurant are we talking about here? 'Cause if you're thinking about bar food, I won't waste your time."

"No—" I started to say.

"Look," Emma said, resting her elbows on the top of the game. "I may not have a diploma from Johnson and Wales or anyplace like that, but I can freakin' cook. You want French? Pacific Rim? Afro-Caribbean? I can do it. But I am not taking a job as another line cook or a prep girl, or any other crap like that."

She took a deep breath. "Well?"

"Let's talk," I said. I gestured to Harry. "This is my friend Harry. Can we chat?"

"Absolutely," Emma said. We followed her to the far end of the bar. Harry sat on one side of her and I sat at the other.

"Hey, Alton," she called to the bartender, a wizened man with a graying military-style crew cut. "Let me have a Speckled Brown Hen."

"Is that another kind of martini?" I asked.

Emma laughed. "It's a microbrew. I'm not really into hard liquor."

"I'll have the same," Harry called.

"Me too," I said.

Alton brought the beers and a bowl of bar nuts, gave us a nod, and faded away.

"So," Emma said. "What's the deal?"

"Why don't you tell me a little bit about your current cooking job?" I asked.

She ran her fingers through her hair, leaving it standing up straight. On her it was cute.

"Don't get me wrong. I love Doobie, I really do. When he's straight, man, he is just the best. Wicked funny and sweet. And he loves good food. Or, he used to, anyway. He was willing to try anything. We'd get into port on some little island you never heard of, and I'd go ashore and buy fresh fish, fruit, whatever was local. And he was game to try all of it. 'Surprise me,' he'd say, and just hand me a wad of money to go shopping. It was a dream job, you know?"

"Was? It's not anymore?" Harry asked.

She shrugged. "It's not Doobie, it's his old lady."

"Who is Doobie?" I asked finally.

"Doobie. You know, Doobie Bauers."

"Actually, I don't know him," I said.

"Yeah, I forget people know about the band, and Meat Loaf. Most people, unless they're really hard-core Meat Heads, they never heard of Doobie. But see, Doobie was there in the very beginning."

"So, he *is* a member of Meat Loaf?" Harry asked.

"*Was*. He was with them until, like, the third album, maybe? And then, when Meat disbanded the group to go into rehab, Doobie did a lot of session work. He wrote some big hits for other bands, toured with Def Leppard, even. But mostly he's famous for being in Meat Loaf."

"That's nice," I said. "But we saw the yacht, *Reefer Madness*. It must be worth a lot of money. Can an ex-musician really afford something like that?"

"Are you kidding?" Emma asked. "Hell, yeah, he can afford it. You ought to see his ranch, or whatever you call it, in Nashville. One thing about Doobie, even when he was totally messed up on drugs, he was smart about business. A bunch of his songs have been on movie sound tracks. Have you seen the new Toyota Avalon television commercial? That's Doobie's song playing in the background."

"Wow," I said, impressed. "But you said things have gone sour with your job?"

Emma took a swig of beer, then daintily wiped her mouth on a napkin. "Yeah, it really bites. I'm not supposed to know about it, or say anything yet, but Anya is making Doobie sell *Reefer Madness*. So I'm gonna be out of a job pretty soon now."

"Who is Anya, and why is she making him sell the yacht?" I asked.

"She's his old lady," Emma said. "What a bitch! If she'd just mellow out and leave him alone, everything would be cool. Look," she said sadly, "Doobie is in the music business. It's not a secret. He's had, what do they call it?" She made little quote marks with her fingers. "Substance-abuse issues.

"I mean, Doobie is old school rock and roll. There's a lot of pressure in the business. A lot of money on the line every time he goes into the studio. Doobie can't relax until he smokes some weed, or maybe snorts a line of coke. So he flies down here, we take the *Reefer* out, he drinks some Cristal, and he gets a little high. Who gets hurt?"

"Anya doesn't like that, I take it?" Harry asked.

"It makes her totally nuts," Emma said. "She won't even let him come down here without her anymore, and when they do come, she has a personal assistant go all over the boat, trying to find his stash, and trying to get everybody to narc out on Doobie."

Emma giggled. "The last time they were down, it was freakin' hilarious. Anya's running all over the place, ordering everybody around. I mean, she had me making macrobiotic meals for him. Brown rice and steamed veggies! And every time she's not looking, Doob is dipping into his secret stash and getting wasted. When we got back into Bahia Mar that last time, she was so pissed she couldn't even see straight. They had a huge fight. God, what a bitch! That's when she told Doobie, 'Either get rid of the boat, and get straight for good, or I'm outta here.'"

Emma took another sip of beer. "Personally? I think he should keep the boat and kick her bony ass out on the street. But I don't get a vote."

Harry and I looked over at each other and exchanged a tiny, secret smile.

But Emma wasn't stupid. She caught the looks.

"Hey. What's going on here? Why are you so interested in Doobie? Oh, man, you never really intended to give me a chef's job, did you?"

She'd been straight with me, so I decided to be straight with her.

"I really am in the restaurant business, Emma," I said. "But I met this man . . ."

"Yeah," Emma said, shaking her head. "Same old story. And you got screwed. Right?"

Taken aback by her bluntness, I could only laugh. "Right. He swindled me out of everything. That's why I'm down here in Fort Lauderdale. Looking for Mister Wrong."

"What's any of that got to do with me?" Emma asked. She jerked her head in Harry's direction. "And what's it got to do with him?"

Good question.

"Harry and I are . . . friends," I said. "He manages the motel I own in Savannah. And, we, uh . . ."

"We're friendly," Harry said, grinning. "Getting friendlier all the time."

"The man who swindled me—his real name is Roy Eugene Moseley—is, we think, right here in Fort Lauderdale. He's been hanging around Bahia Mar marina, we think, because he's interested in yachts. Big, expensive yachts. Specifically, he has a thing for Sea Urchins. And the *Reefer Madness* is the only Sea Urchin in the area right at this time."

"Again, what's that got to do with me?"

"Roy Eugene came really close to stealing another yacht, a Sea Urchin, from a widow up in Vero Beach last year," I said. "And we think he was getting ready to buy, but more likely, try to steal, another Sea Urchin here in Fort Lauderdale. Fortunately for the woman who owns that boat, she sold it to a legitimate buyer before Roy Eugene could make his move."

"And you think he's gunning for the *Reefer*?" Emma asked, her eyes getting big.

"Maybe," Harry said.

"Absolutely," I said. "We've been able to trace his credit card activity. He's playing golf at Bahia Mar, eating in the restaurants, hanging around in the bar."

"So, call the cops," Emma said.

"The cops won't do anything," I said bitterly. "And even if I was able to have him arrested, so what? It doesn't get me back what he took."

She raised an eyebrow. "Which was what?"

"Everything," I said. "My home, my furniture, my money. I had to close down my restaurant, lay off all my employees. He even stole my grandparents' savings."

"That is cold," Emma said. "How much money are we talking?"

"More than two million," I said, "not counting things like my father's antique watch and an irreplaceable painting that was a family heirloom."

Emma sipped her beer.

Harry excused himself to go to the men's room.

"He's cute," Emma said, as soon as he was gone. "Have you slept with him yet?"

I blushed. "Why does everybody keep asking me that?"

"Why not?" Emma said. "You're straight, right? Only thing. Just how old is he?"

"I don't know," I admitted. "He won't tell me."

It was time to change the subject to one I was more comfortable with. "If you didn't go to culinary school, where did you learn to cook?"

"Here and there," she said offhandedly. "I took some community college classes, worked in a few bars and a few restaurants. I was working at the Sand Bar when I met Doobie, supposed to be waiting tables, but I kept slipping into the kitchen, talking the chef into letting me try stuff. Doobie was in one day, and I'd fixed this red snapper seviche. He went nuts for it, and hired me on at the *Reefer*. That was two years ago."

She sighed deeply. "I knew all along it was too good to last."

Harry came back from the men's room and we ordered another round of beers.

"So," Emma said, looking from me to Harry. "You still haven't told me how I figure into all of this."

"I don't really know," I said.

We gave her a description of Roy Eugene, but she swore she hadn't seen anybody like that hanging around the *Reefer Madness*.

"When is the boat going to be sold?" I asked.

"That's up to Anya," she said. "She hasn't officially told us anything, but they let Ernie go last month. Right now, it's just me and Liam living aboard, keeping things buttoned down. As soon as I get another job lined up, I'm outta there. Liam's got a girlfriend in Boca, he'll probably move in with her until he gets another gig, but I can't afford to get an apartment right now, so I won't quit until I get something else."

"Will you work on another yacht?" I asked.

"No way," she said firmly. "I want a real job, in a real restaurant."

"Have you talked to Doobie about any of this?" Harry asked.

"Can't," she said.

"Why not?" I asked.

"He's in rehab," Emma said. "It's supposed to be a big secret. After that last cruise, Anya checked Doob into Betty Ford. Poor guy. I hear the food there sucks."

"Say, Emma," I said casually. "Maybe we can work something out."

Her green eyes glittered. "That's what I was hoping you'd say. Count me in."

48

Harry was quiet in the car on the way back to Mangoville. But that was okay, because it gave me a chance to study him more closely.

How had I not noticed before just how crazy sexy the guy was? I closed my eyes, trying to analyze his unexpected appeal. He wasn't handsome in that slap-your-mama way that Reddy had been when we first met. He didn't have the golden-boy good looks of Sandy Thayer, my first and third husband. He didn't even have Richard the Wretched's dark, smoldering sensuality.

In fact, he wasn't like any man I'd ever been with before. He was, dare I say it? A grown-up. Sneaking another peek, I thought about how much I liked the way his hair refused to lie down flat, and the fact that he refused to use any kind of product on it. I liked his clear gray-green eyes and the crinkling crow's-feet that radiated out from them. I even adored his strong chin, covered now with a half-inch of stubble.

"You're staring at me," Harry said.

"Yes," I agreed.

"Probably trying to figure out how to make your big move and jump me right here in the front seat, but without making us end up with this land yacht in a ditch."

"Not really," I said.

But I slid a little closer on the burgundy leather seat, and silently thanked my grandfather for having the foresight to keep an old eighties car with bench-type front seats.

"That's more like it," Harry said approvingly. He slung his arm over my shoulder and drew me even closer, almost onto his lap. He kissed my bare shoulder.

"What are you thinking about?" he inquired.

"I was thinking how glad I am that you agreed to come down here with me."

"Had to," Harry said. "I was afraid if you came alone, you'd kill somebody."

"No, really," I said. "I can't tell you how great it is to finally have a really experienced man in my life."

"You got that right," Harry said, letting his fingertips rest lightly on the top of my breast.

"Mmm," I said, snuggling even closer. "You're the man, Harry."

"Just wait till we get back to the motel," he promised. "I've been thinking about this all day. All weekend." He kissed my neck. "You make me crazy. You know that, right?"

"Good crazy," I said. "I've been thinking about this ever since I saw the *Reefer Madness* tied up at Bahia Mar. It's all going to work out just right."

Harry nuzzled my neck, and with his free hand tugged the wig off my head and tossed it to the floor. He gently finger-combed my flattened hair, and rubbed the nape of my neck. His touch was hard and warm and deft, and I spooned myself into the curve of him.

"You are an amazing lady, BeBe Loudermilk," he said. "You even turn me on in this weird getup of yours. I can't believe I'm having sex fantasies about a woman dressed up as a seventies go-go dancer."

"Whatever floats your boat," I said, turning to face him and slipping my hand inside the open neck of his sport shirt.

"Oh, lady," he said softly. "You are rocking my boat tonight."

"It's only going to get better, isn't it?" I asked, kissing him hard on the mouth.

"Wait," he said, his breathing getting shallow. "We're almost back at the motel. Five minutes, tops. What do you say I get us a room of our own? We'll have a whole night together. Just the two of us."

"Sweet-talking devil."

I waited by the car while he went into the office at the Mango Tree. Five minutes later, he stormed out, slamming the door behind him. His face told the whole story, but I had to ask.

"What happened?"

"No vacancies," he said, pounding the roof of the Buick. "Can you believe there's not a single vacant room in this stinking roach motel?"

I glanced over at the Mango Tree's neon sign, which did, indeed, have a blinking NO VACANCY on it.

He knelt down beside the car and took my hand in his. "I'd say we could go to another motel, but you know the deal."

I sighed, and kissed him. "Yeah. No money. And no honey."

He kissed me back and helped me out of the car.

"It won't always be like this, I swear."

"I know."

Harry glanced back at the Buick, stopped, and went back and looked inside.

"This backseat looks pretty roomy," he said, waggling his eyebrows. "Leather seats too."

"No way, Jose. We are not having Paradise by the Dashboard Light. Not tonight. Not ever. Now come on, handsome. Walk me to my door?"

49

Over a bowl of Cap'n Crunch and a cup of instant coffee the next morning, I outlined the plan that had started to gel the night before.

"I went to the Internet cafe this morning," I told Weezie and Granddad.

"Yeah, you must have gotten there really early," Weezie said. "I never even heard you leave. In fact, I never even heard you come in last night."

"I tippy-toed. But listen, I got on the Internet and looked up Meat Loaf."

Granddad peeled his banana and made a face. "If it's all the same to you, I'll just stick with cereal today, same as always," he said.

"Meat Loaf, the band," I said. "I Googled them on the Internet. You wouldn't believe how many Web sites are devoted to them. It's unreal."

"Did you find that girl last night? The one who supposedly works on the yacht?" Weezie asked.

"Yeah. Emma. She's cool. It turns out the guy who owns the boat is named Doobie Bauers. According to the official Meat Loaf biography, his real name is Douglas Jefferson Bauers. He got the nickname Doobie in high school."

"Interesting," Granddad said. "I remember a television show called *Dobie Gillis*."

"Right," Harry said. "This is different. Way different."

"Doobie Bauers cowrote a lot of Meat Loaf's big hits," I said. "And a lot of other hits. He's got, like, seven platinum albums to his credit, and two Grammys, and a ton of money. Originally, he was a keyboardist. But he hasn't really toured in at least seven or eight years, that I can see. In fact, he's kind of become a semirecluse."

"Poor guy," Weezie said.

"Here's the only picture I could find of him," I said, sliding a computer-printout photo across the dinette table toward them.

"It's an old wire-service photo from 1997," I said. "It ran with a story in *Rolling Stone* about attempts to mount a Meat Loaf reunion tour."

Weezie studied the photo intently. " 'Keyboard artist-slash-composer Doobie Bauers says "No Thanks" to another helping of Meat Loaf,' " she read.

"The story said Doobie felt at the time that his music was going in a whole different direction," I explained. "Plus, he'd ballooned up to about 340 pounds. He was even beefier than Meat Loaf."

"Oh, man," Harry said. "That's rough."

"Not to worry," I told him. "Doobie lost more than a hundred pounds right after that. And apparently gained a nasty little meth habit at the same time."

The four of us took turns turning the photo this way and that, staring at the fifteen-year-old image of the keyboard artist-slash-composer Doobie Bauers. What we saw was not particularly memorable. A middle-aged white guy, wearing a baseball cap, wire-rimmed spectacles, and a thick beard, hunched over an electric keyboard.

"I read where he never goes anywhere without a baseball cap," I said.

"Bald spot," Weezie said knowingly.

"And like I said, this is the most recent photo. The only other ones I found are from the late seventies, when he was still touring. In those, Doobie has dark hair down to his ass, and a giant handlebar mustache. He weighs maybe 130 pounds soaking wet, and he's wear-ing skintight black leather pants."

"In his defense," Harry said. "It *has* been more than thirty years. Even Mick Jagger is starting to look middle-aged."

"Mick Jagger looks older than Granddad," I retorted.

I slid another photograph across the dinette table. This one showed an attractive blonde in a well-tailored pantsuit, wearing a broad-brimmed straw hat.

"'Anya Bauers Co-hosts Children's Hospital Charity Fund-Raiser,'" Weezie read. "This is his wife? She looks a lot younger than old Doobie."

"She's Mrs. Bauers number three," I agreed. "She's all of thirty-five. Young enough to be Doobie's daughter, according to my re-search. She doesn't really come down here to Fort Lauderdale very often. She's got some kind of sun allergy, which is why she's wearing these big hats in all the pictures I found of her in the *Nashville Ban-ner*."

"Who doesn't like Fort Lauderdale?" Granddad asked, puzzled. "The sun, the sea. Early-bird specials at almost every restaurant. Senior-citizen discounts everywhere!"

"It isn't necessarily Lauderdale she hates," I said. "From what Emma says—she's the chef on the yacht—Anya doesn't like Doobie to come down here either, because when he does get down here to go out on the *Reefer,* he, uh, gets himself in trouble."

"Chasing women?" Granddad asked, chuckling. "I sure did see a whole lot of pretty women worth chasing at that bar yesterday. If I was the chasing kind, that is."

"It's not women who are his problem," I said. "Emma says when-ever Doobie goes out on the yacht, he gets totally trashed on cocaine or alcohol or marijuana or all three."

"Tragic," Weezie said, shaking her head sympathetically.

"Emma was really helpful last night," I said.

"So," Weezie said. "Last night turned out okay?"

"In some ways," Harry said, putting his hand on my thigh under the table.

I moved it away without changing expression.

"I think I've figured out how to get my money back from Roy Eugene Moseley," I told the three of them. "And I think it might even work. I'll need you two, of course," I said, nodding at Weezie and Granddad.

"Now," I said. "We can't pull this off unless we have a legitimate crew for the yacht. Fortunately, Emma has agreed to help out, and she thinks Liam, he's the only other crew member still living aboard the *Reefer Madness,* will sign on too."

"Why?" Weezie asked. "What's in it for them?"

"When Anya Bauers really does sell that yacht, and that's gonna be pretty soon, they'll both be out of a job anyway," I explained.

Weezie shook her head vigorously. "That's still not a good enough reason to risk going to jail—for a woman you just met."

"Emma's a chef," I said. "She's going to be needing a job. I have a restaurant."

"Had," Weezie said.

"And when we reopen Guale, which we'll be doing very soon, Daniel can always use good help."

"And the other guy? What's his name?"

"Liam. I haven't met him, but Emma says he'll go along. And if I have to pay him for his participation, I will. It's part of the cost of the operation.

"Fortunately," I said, "we don't have to question Harry's motivation. There is no way I could do this without somebody like Harry."

"A man of experience," Harry said smugly, sliding his hand up my thigh. "Motivated for entirely selfless reasons."

"A man who knows how to steal a boat," I agreed. "In fact, he's stolen boats lots of times."

"Hang on a minute," Harry protested. "The *Jitterbug* is my boat. And I wasn't really stealing it, I was just borrowing it."

"Better yet," I said. "Harry here is going to help us borrow the *Reefer Madness*."

"I am?"

"Yes," I said, fluttering my eyelashes at him. "And you're also going to pose as Doobie Bauers."

"But not the supersize Doobie," Harry said.

"You're going to be the trim, sexy, slightly drug-addled Doobie," I said. "And you, Weezie, are going to be the lovely, if bitchy, Anya Bauers."

"I like the lovely part," Weezie said, studying the photo.

"And the bitchy part shouldn't be much of a stretch either," I told her.

"And what about me?" Granddad asked. "Did you bring me down here just to watch the weather channel and hang out at bars all day?"

"Not at all," I said. "I am so grateful that you brought that blazer and cravat. Because you've got the most important job of all. You're going to be the yacht broker who sells the *Reefer Madness* to Roy Eugene Moseley, for, I'm thinking, $4.8 million."

"He only stole two million from you," Weezie said, frowning.

"But the *Reefer Madness* is worth a lot more than that. I checked prices on that Internet yacht brokerage site. And that gives Sandra Findley her inheritance. Besides, yacht brokers earn a ten percent commission. And that's just about what Roy Eugene stole from my grandparents."

Granddad frowned. "I hate to be an old stick in the mud, young lady, but this plan of yours has one basic flaw. It's illegal to sell something you don't own. And don't you think Doobie Bauers is gonna get pretty annoyed when he figures out somebody sold off his yacht?"

"He'll never know it happened," I said. "Doobie is in drug rehab out in Phoenix. By the time he gets out, the *Reefer* will be tied up right where he left it, at Bahia Mar. But I'll have my money back, and with any luck, Roy Eugene Moseley will be in jail."

"And if things go wrong?" Weezie asked. "If we don't get the money, and Roy Eugene steals the *Reefer Madness,* and we can't give the boat back, and the police show up?"

"Your uncle James is a very good attorney," I said. "He kept you out of prison, didn't he?"

50

Weezie

The FOR SALE signs went up on the bow and stern of the *Reefer Madness* on Monday. At two that afternoon, Spencer took his place at the bar in the Grille, equipped with a cell phone and enough money for two Scotches and a ham sandwich. And Harry and I made our debut as Doobie and Anya, the battling Bauers, that same day.

Being somebody else was fun at first. Naturally, I made a run up to the Junior League Thrift Shop in Palm Beach for my wardrobe, which I'd decided should be sort of BoHo resort wear. Bright-colored silk capris and tops, a couple of little sundresses, sandals, and to top it all off, wide-brimmed straw hats. I spent $86 for my whole wardrobe, which included $12 for the Prada sandals that put me in a swoon.

BeBe wanted to make me dye my hair Anya blond, but that was one battle I won. I'd be wearing hats most of the time, I argued, and anyway, who was to say that Anya Bauers wouldn't have gotten bored with blond and dared to go red—like the real me?

Harry was not what you'd call cooperative when it came to his own wardrobe. I'd picked him up some perfectly acceptable pre-worn Tommy Bahama tropical-print sport shirts and colorful shorts, and BeBe managed to talk him into trying them on. Briefly.

"No way," he said flatly, once he took a look at himself in the mirror in our motel room. "I look like a Hawaiian fruit fly."

"You're adorable," BeBe cooed, circling around him, touching and patting in all the right places. "You look like Jimmy Buffett. But younger."

"Hell no," Harry said, peeling the shirt off over his head without even bothering to unbutton it. "Not even for you. I'm not that whipped. Yet," he added darkly.

I held up the only photo we had of Doobie Bauer. "You're supposed to be him, remember? Not Harry Sorrentino."

"Fine," Harry said. "I've already thought of that. After I dropped you off at that fancy thrift shop, I did some shopping of my own." He held up a crumpled brown grocery sack. "At the Kidney Foundation store." He ducked into the bathroom, and when he came out, BeBe and I were amazed. The transformation was complete. And inspired.

His shorts were a pair of cut-off green army fatigues. Over it, he wore a tie-dyed purple-and-blue Grateful Dead T-shirt that proclaimed "It's All Good." On his feet he wore gnarly brown leather huaraches. His sweat-stained Florida Marlins baseball cap was on backward, and for the first time I noticed that he apparently hadn't shaved in a week.

"Oh my God," BeBe muttered. "He's found his inner derelict. The only thing he lacks is a cardboard 'Will Work for Food' sign."

Harry grinned and held up a small wire apparatus.

"Is that a roach clip?" I squealed. "Harry, you're a genius!"

He shrugged. "I found it in the pocket of the shorts."

For three days, we hung out on the deck of the *Reefer*, under impossibly sunny blue skies, trying to do whatever it is that the idle rich do. Mostly, Harry lolled around in a deck chair swigging from a seemingly endless series of Coronas while listening to selections from the real Doobie's head-banging rock CD library, while I lolled in my bikini, under an umbrella, reading one of the real Anya's well-thumbed magazines. *Vogue, O, Elle, Harper's Bazaar, Self*, and yes, even *Cosmopolitan*.

"Be a Dirty Girl!" was the headline on one *Cosmo* article Anya had dog-eared. "Sleaze, Squeeze, and Tease Him Till He Begs for Mercy."

There go twelve years of Catholic schooling, I thought, carefully tearing the article out and slipping it into my beach bag for future reference. Mama was gonna have to have some extra novenas said for my soul. Daniel, I thought, would be grateful, as always, for this kind of continuing education.

While we lazed, Liam and Emma puttered around doing what they said they always did, polishing and wiping and generally keeping the yacht ready to go to sea at a moment's notice. At noon, Emma brought us lunch trays, and fruity tropical drinks.

"I could get used to this kind of life," Harry said, that first day, after he'd polished off a grilled-grouper sandwich and before taking his second siesta of the day.

While Harry was napping, Liam suddenly materialized at my side. "Sunscreen?" he asked, squeezing out a dollop on my shoulder.

I flinched as the cold lotion hit my bare skin. "No thanks," I said quickly.

"Anya always has me do her," he said, his sleepy brown eyes lingering a little too long on my chest.

"What does Doobie have to say about that?" I asked, pulling my beach towel around me.

"Doob? Man, as long as the beer's cold and the seas are smooth, he's chillin'."

I got up and walked over to the port side of the yacht, being careful to keep the hat brim pulled down low. The marina was a hive of activity that day. Boats were pulling in and out of their slips. I could see people on the yachts nearby hosing down decks, loading and unloading gear from two-wheeled carts. As I leaned on the rail, I saw a guy on a fat-wheeled silver bike ride slowly by. His head turned as he took note of the sign lashed to the stern. He wore dark, mirrored sunglasses, and he made no effort to hide his admiration for what he was seeing. I went quickly back to my deck chair.

"Harry," I called quietly.

Nothing.

"Harry, wake up. A guy just rode by on a bike. I think maybe it was Roy Eugene."

Doobie's music was starting to give me a headache. I went over and sat down on the edge of Harry's lounge chair. He had his baseball hat covering his face, and the dull buzz of his snores made the cap rise and fall with each exhalation. I put my lips right next to his ear.

"Harry!"

He bolted upright. "Christ! What's wrong?"

"You were snoring," I said.

"It's part of my disguise. You woke me up to tell me that?"

"I woke you up to tell you that a guy just rode by on a bike and took a long, hard look at our FOR SALE sign," I said. "I think maybe it was our guy."

"Good," Harry said, lying back down again. "Wake me up when he gets ready to write the check."

"You're worthless," I told him.

"And don't call me Harry," he added

Our third day on the *Reefer,* I noticed that Harry was taking a lot longer to finish a lot fewer Coronas. After a lunch of curried lobster-tail salad, instead of taking another nap, he roamed the boat restlessly. He spent two hours inspecting the engines, emerging grease smudged and sweat soaked and awe inspired by what he'd seen down there.

"Christ," he said, sinking down into his deck chair with a tall glass of what looked suspiciously like iced tea. "Twin 750 Caterpillar diesels with 360-degree walk-around access. We could take off tonight and be in Belize by tomorrow afternoon, up to our asses in bonefish and tarpon."

I put down Anya's January issue of *Town & Country*. I was bored out of my gourd with reading about the newest options in nonsurgical facial peels, irritated with ads for "whimsical" diamond-crusted doodads that cost more than my parents' house, and truly peeved by a story about a Houston society matron who'd spent $40,000 importing orchids for a charity gala to benefit a local humane society.

"Being rich and sun intolerant is incredibly tedious," I told Harry. "I can't even get a good tan. No wonder Anya Bauers is such a bitch."

"Try being rich and stoned all the time," Harry said. "And this godawful music! My eardrums are starting to bleed. I don't know how much more I can take of it."

I saw a blur of silver out of the corner of my eye. "Don't look now," I said carefully. "But the guy on the bike is back."

"Mirrored sunglasses, white golf visor?" Harry said, barely tilting his head in that direction.

"Check."

"He's turning around and coming back for a second pass. By God, I think you could be right," Harry said. He got up, made a big show of stretching and yawning, then ambled over to the gangway leading to the belowdeck's area. "Liam," he hollered. "Bring me my bong."

"Doobie!" I screamed, getting into the spirit of the part. "Don't you dare! I'm calling your shrink."

"Fuck you, Anya," Harry said, snarling.

With my hands on my hips, I fixed him with an icy glare. "Like you could, you limp-dick has-been."

"Whoa," Harry whispered without moving his lips. "Lay off the personal stuff. I'm a recovering addict, remember?"

"Hey, Emma," he called, in a loud, lazy voice. "We're gonna need some nachos up here too. And a bottle of Cristal for me, and a coupla chill pills for my old lady."

Now I was standing up screaming down at the gallery. It was actually pretty cathartic. "Don't you dare bring him anything. Either of you! If you want to keep your jobs until we sell this goddamn tub, you stay right where you are."

Harry slumped down in his deck chair with his back to the pier. "Okay," he said. "He's moved on. Show's over."

Emma stood just belowdeck, staring up at me with her huge green eyes. "This is all an act, right?" she whispered.

"We had an audience," I told her. "And I think we just baited the hook."

"Man," Emma said. "That was scary. You sounded exactly like her."

"Thanks," I said. "If you think this was good, stick around for the second act."

Harry and I were sitting up on the deck, pretending to ignore each other, when my cell phone rang. I picked it up and listened, smiled, and then clicked it shut.

"That was Spencer," I said. "He just got a call from a man named Rory Mason, who would be very interested in taking a look at the *Reefer.* Four o'clock tomorrow."

"Good," Harry said, running his hand over his chin. "Let's get this over with. No offense or anything, Weezie, but I don't know how much more I can take of being married to you."

51

"**Game on,**" Harry said when he called Wednesday night.

I gripped the phone tightly. "You're sure it's him?"

My nerves were past frayed. Since Harry and Weezie had moved aboard the *Reefer Madness,* I'd spent the past three days pacing around the motel grounds, willing Reddy to take our bait. I'd tried watching daytime television, reading, even sunbathing by the pool, but I was too keyed up to concentrate on anything for more than an hour.

Granddad wasn't much help either. He'd been camped out in the bar at Bahia Mar, posing as a yacht broker, and he'd been having a high old time. Every night he came back to the room with stories of the people he'd met, and what he'd watched on the television in the bar.

He had a new passion too. The golf channel. After his first day as a professional barfly, he'd raced back to the motel to share his discovery with me. "Look," he'd exclaimed, pointing to the television. "That's the first qualifying round for the Masters." He jabbed at the screen with a finger. "That's Davis Love the third. I used to see his daddy when I went down to St. Simon's Island to play golf with the fellas at home."

"Wonderful, Granddad," I said. "Did anybody call about the boat today?"

"Nah," he said, waving his hand dismissively. "Just some foreign fella, says he owns a shoe factory in South Africa. I told him we already have a buyer."

"You're sure it wasn't Reddy?" I asked anxiously. "That's the kind of story he'd make up. He told me he was a Millbanks from Charleston, and that was a load of bull."

"This was an older man," Granddad said. "Not your guy at all. Anyway, after lunch today, I watched Chi-Chi Rodriguez giving a putting exhibition. Then I watched the 1998 British Open. They had a lot of high winds and rain that year . . ."

Granddad reported another call about the yacht on Tuesday. "Fella says he's in the entertainment business too. Ever hear of somebody calls himself A. T. Money?"

"He's a major rap star," I said. "He sang the national anthem at the World Series last year. Did he call you himself?"

"His business manager. Or so he said," Granddad said. "He sounded black."

"That would make sense. A. T. Money is black. You didn't offend him, did you?"

My grandfather was no racist, but he'd been born and raised in Savannah, after all.

"Hell no," Granddad said. "I just told him we had a pending contract, and I took his phone number and told him I'd call if nothing came of the other offer."

"Good thinking," I said approvingly.

Wednesday night, right after Harry called, Granddad sashayed into my room at the Mango Tree. He was wearing a brand-new hot pink golf shirt with "Grande Oaks Golf" embroidered over the breast pocket, and carrying a Styrofoam take-out carton, with a brown paper sack stuck under his arm.

"You talked to him?" I asked, pouncing on him. "You're sure it's Roy Eugene?"

Granddad set the carton on the kitchenette counter and opened the paper bag, which turned out to contain a bottle of Scotch.

Granddad said "It's him, all right. There's some dinner there for you," he said, sliding the carton in my direction. "You must be get-

ting tired of turkey sandwiches. Anyway, I thought you'd want to celebrate tonight."

The carton contained a slab of meat loaf topped with congealed
brown sauce, a mound of lumpy mashed potatoes, and some wan-
looking steamed broccoli.

"How nice," I said, leaning over and kissing his cheek. "It, uh,
looks delicious."

"Go ahead and eat before it cools off," Granddad urged. "This
was the early-bird special at the diner down the street from here. And
can you believe it was only $1.99?"

I forked into the meat loaf with as much enthusiasm as I could
muster. "Tell me about the meeting. Tell me everything. All Harry
said was that Reddy is going to take a look at the boat tomorrow at
four."

"Not just look at it," Granddad said, pouring whiskey into a
chipped juice glass and topping it with water from the faucet. "He
wants to take it out for a spin."

"No!" I said quickly. "We can't do that. It's too chancy. What if
something goes wrong with the boat? Or Reddy tries to pull a fast
one and steal it?"

"It's called a sea trial, and it's purely routine in this business,"
Granddad said, offering me the glass of Scotch.

I took a long, calming sip. "How do you know what's routine in
the yacht business?"

"You're not the only one who does research," Granddad said,
preening a little. "I stopped by a very nice establishment on Seventeenth Street on Monday, Case Marine Sales, and had a long talk with
one of their brokers. Very illuminating. They answered all my questions, and I looked at several nice midsize yachts. My favorite was a
fifty-four-foot Bertram. *The Lucy Goosey*. Beautiful. And only
$750,000."

"You're not really considering buying a yacht," I said. "You're too
old. Anyway, Grandmama would never allow it."

He sighed. "I know. Lorena barely allows me to buy flashlight batteries, even. But a man can dream. And now, I'm all set to deal with Reddy, or Roy Eugene, or Rory, as he's now calling himself."

"I can't believe you met with him," I said.

"He's very convincing," Granddad said. "Very presentable. If I didn't know different, I'd swear he really was a semiretired orthodontist."

"An orthodontist!" I hooted. "He's really getting brazen."

"Semiretired," Granddad said. "Since he invented those new invisible braces all the kids are getting these days."

"Such a liar," I said, grinding my teeth. "What else did he tell you?"

"Just that he's been in the market for a yacht for some time now, and that he'd narrowed his choice down to a Sea Urchin. He's been up to Michigan and seen the manufacturing plant and everything."

"He probably tried to hijack one from the factory," I said.

"He claims he's also shopping for a waterfront house," Granddad said mildly. "Moved down here from Charleston, and he was visiting friends who have a boat at Bahia Mar when he saw the sign on the bow of the *Reefer Madness*."

"Good," I urged.

"He asked a lot of questions. Wanted to know how long the current owner has had her, who he is, how many hours the boat has logged, why it's being sold."

"What did you tell him?"

"Told him I couldn't discuss it over the phone," Granddad said, chuckling. "That's when he offered to meet with me for a drink. Which we did this afternoon."

"And?"

"I was pretty cagey with him," Granddad said. "You'd have been proud of me. I told him the owner's name was confidential, but that I could tell him the fella is in the entertainment business. He's owned the boat for three years, bought it new, and the engines have only about four hundred hours on them."

"That is good," I said admiringly.

"He asked me point-blank if the owner was Doobie Bauers," Granddad said. "I hemmed and hawed, but finally admitted it and swore him to secrecy. And then I told him my client was selling the yacht because his business doesn't permit him enough free time to enjoy the boat properly."

"You're good," I said. "I never knew you had it in you, Granddad."

"I surprised myself," he admitted. "Never knew lying could be so much fun."

"Take my advice," I said. "Don't make a habit of it."

"Anyway," he continued. "Rory, or whatever his name is, already knew quite a bit about the boat, and about Doobie and Anya Bauers. He even knew they're currently staying aboard it."

"Good," I said cautiously.

"And he insisted that they be along for the sea trial tomorrow," he added.

"Huh?"

"Claims he's a big fan of Meat Loaf."

"No," I said flatly. "That's not possible. Reddy's not the type. He's too young to know about Meat Loaf. Anyway, Harry looks very convincing. Weezie too."

"I certainly hope so," Granddad said, leaning back in his chair. "There's five million dollars riding on this thing tomorrow."

"Five million? I thought we were asking $4.8."

"I upped it," Granddad said. "After I looked at those other yachts, it seemed to me the *Reefer Madness* should fetch a much higher price."

"How did Reddy react to the price?"

"He tried a little horse-trading," Granddad said. "But I told him it wasn't negotiable. And I also told him to bring a cashier's check for $50,000 tomorrow."

"What! Are you trying to scare him off?"

"Not at all. It's standard practice. Earnest money. Just like in real estate," Granddad said serenely. "Besides, that way, if his deposit check clears, we'll know he really does have the money. We'll be one step ahead of him."

"You're scaring me, old man."

Granddad just grinned and sipped his whiskey.

52

Weezie

At three-thirty I was having heart palpitations. My mouth was dry, my palms were sweaty, even my eyeballs itched. "I can't do this," I told Harry. "I can't pretend to be a real person. I'm not like BeBe. I'm not ballsy like her. I *cannot* do this."

"You'll be fine," Harry said, his voice surprisingly low and soothing. "You've been Anya Bauers all week. Such a raging bitch, just the sound of your voice makes my balls shrivel. Poor old Doobie," he said, shaking his head.

"That's just with you," I whined. "You act so much like I imagine Doobie does, I want to throttle you. I totally get that woman's motivation now. But I can't do this in front of Reddy. I'll fall apart. He'll never buy it. And then what? What if he's got a gun or something? I'll ruin everything and it'll be all my fault."

We were down in the master cabin of the *Reefer Madness,* getting ready for our meeting with Spencer and the man calling himself Rory Mason.

I'd put on my shortest, tightest sundress, full makeup, big flashy fake jewelry, and my showiest hat, which happened to be a hot pink Helen Kaminski number.

"You'll do great," Harry said, looking me over. "Just keep telling yourself you really are Anya. And I really am Doobie."

He leaned over the marble sink in the mirrored dressing room, wet his hands, soaped them up, and then proceeded to wipe the soap in his eyes.

"What are you doing?"

Tears ran down his face. He blinked rapidly, rubbed his eyes, and blinked again.

"Christ, that stings," he muttered.

"Oh," I said, catching on. His eyes were now totally bloodshot and red-rimmed. He rubbed his chin, which was covered with a nasty half-inch-long stubble. And then he picked up a Corona bottle and chugged about half the beer, letting it run down his chin and onto his shirt front. He belched loudly.

Today's wardrobe selection included a red Van Halen T-shirt that had faded to a dull pink. He wore shapeless wrinkled khaki shorts and no shoes.

"You really are revolting," I said admiringly.

"Hold that thought," he said, slapping me on the butt.

We went up to the galley to check with Emma to see how preparations were going for our little sea cruise.

She was whirling around in the gleaming stainless-steel space, sprinkling parsley on a silver platter of mini quiches, setting out champagne glasses, and piling exquisite little brownies on another plate.

Harry snitched a quiche, chewing rapidly, and letting the crumbs drift down on his shirt. "These are damn good," he said. "Crab?"

"Crab and avocado," Emma said. She was all business in her white chef's coat and tight white jeans. "The brownies are amaretto espresso."

I helped myself to one and pronounced it divine.

"Tell your friend," Emma said. "After this goes down, I'm gonna be in serious need of a new job."

"If BeBe says you've got a job, then you've got it," I told her. "We've been best friends for years. She won't let you down."

"Just don't let us down, okay?" Harry said. "And forget you ever heard the name BeBe."

"I never heard of her, *Doobie,*" Emma agreed. She brushed a crumb out of Harry's beard. "My God, you look more like him every day." She sighed. "Poor Doob. He hates rehab."

"Where's Liam?" Harry asked, checking his watch. "Spencer and Rory ought to be here pretty soon. We want to get underway as soon as possible."

"He went to pick up more ice," Anya said. "He'll be right back."

We heard the thud of footsteps from above deck. "That'll be him," Emma said.

"I'll go give him a hand," Harry volunteered.

My stomach lurched again, and I hurried back to the master cabin, where I popped two Tums that I found in the medicine cabinet. I promptly threw them back up again.

As I was brushing my teeth, I heard voices overhead and my stomach took another nosedive.

"Hey, Anya baby," Harry called. "Get your ass up here. We got company."

I blotted my face and reapplied my lipstick, then slipped into a pair of high-heeled sandals and put on my hat.

I could feel the yacht's engines churn to life. I glanced out the cabin's porthole, and saw the foam of water. We were underway. Showtime.

Spencer and the "client" were standing on the sundeck in the stern of the boat, watching as we slid smoothly away from the dock.

"Here's Anya," Harry called when he caught sight of me.

I walked slowly and deliberately toward them, hoping nobody would notice that my knees were wobbling and my hands were trembling.

"Anya," Spencer said warmly, taking my hands in his. "I'd like you to meet Rory Mason."

Mason held his hand out and took mine and held it just a millisecond too long.

It wasn't difficult to see how BeBe had fallen so hard and so fast for this guy. His hair was much lighter than it had been in Sabrina Berg's video. It was now a pale blond that made his golden tan look even more glamorous. He was taller in person, with pale blue eyes behind horn-rimmed tortoiseshell glasses. He wore white linen slacks and a blue silk T-shirt that just matched the color of his eyes.

"Nice to meet you," I managed to say. I was having a hard time concentrating, because at that moment I was so scared I thought I might wet my pants.

"Thanks for having me on such short notice," Rory said. He had an authentic Southern accent, upper class, educated, not too exaggerated. "I have to tell you, I've been coveting this boat since the minute I set my eyes on it."

My mind went blank. I couldn't think of anything appropriate to say. What if I blew it? Was he already figuring out what a fraud I was?

More footsteps. I turned to see Harry lurching toward us, a half-empty beer bottle hooked in his right hand, and a lit cigarette in the other.

"Goddamnit, Anya," he bawled. "Get those fuckin' heels off my teak decking. How the fuck many times do I gotta tell you—no fucking heels!"

I whirled around and looked at him, then deliberately turned my back on him, so angry I could feel blood rushing to my face.

"Excuse my husband's manners, Rory," I said evenly. "He's just distraught over facing the reality that we really are going to have to part with the *Reefer*."

Without warning, Harry jerked me by the arm and shoved me down into a deck chair. He reached down, grabbed the shoes off my feet, and chucked them overboard.

"Doobie," I screamed. "Those shoes cost $200."

"Hey, look," Harry said, turning to Spencer and Rory, who stared openmouthed at my loutish husband. "Now the bitch is just like she was when I met her. Barefoot and ignorant."

Spencer laughed nervously. "Doobie's always kidding around. Always the entertainer, right, Doobie?"

Harry shrugged. "Whatever." He took a deep drag on the cigarette, then flicked it over the side of the boat. "So, Rory. What do you think of our little floating palace?"

"Nice," Rory said, trying to sound offhanded.

He was still staring at me, expectantly. I took a glass of champagne from the tray Emma was still holding, and downed it. Maybe the alcohol would steady my nerves.

"Of course, I need to look at the mechanicals and the electronics," Rory said.

"Liam can help you with that shit," Harry said carelessly. "Right, Spencer?"

"Shall we?" Spencer said, gesturing toward the stairs to the pilothouse. "If you don't mind though, I'll stay here. My knee has been giving me the devil lately."

"Fine," Rory said, turning and heading toward the wheelhouse.

When he was out of sight, I gave Harry a quick kick. "Go with him," I whispered. "I don't want him alone with Liam."

Harry raised an eyebrow, but he did as I suggested.

"What's wrong with Liam?" Spencer whispered.

"I don't know," I said. "Probably nothing. I'm just nervous. I want off this boat. I want this whole thing to be over with."

Spencer patted my shoulder sympathetically. "It won't be long. We're just going out about three miles to a place called the Hillsdale Cut. Out and back. Keep doing what you're doing, kiddo."

I gave him a weak smile and made myself sit back down in the deck chair instead of bolting for the stateroom and locking myself inside.

Thirty minutes later, Harry and Rory climbed back down the

stairs, and headed for the bow of the boat, to inspect the engines, I assumed. Harry was being loud and obnoxious, and Rory Mason looked as if he'd like to slug him.

It was a beautiful afternoon for a cruise. The seas were calm and emerald green, and the late-afternoon sun was warm without being brutal. I was the mistress of a $5 million yacht. And I wanted to hurl.

Harry and Rory came up from the engine room and joined me on the sundeck, where Emma soon appeared with another tray of drinks.

"Appetizers in the main salon?" she asked. "The wind is picking up a little."

"Good idea," I said, getting up quickly.

"Fuck appetizers," Harry mumbled. "That fancy shit's for phonies. Bring me some tequila and nachos."

"We'll have the appetizers in the salon," I told Emma firmly. "And you can bring Doobie some mineral water. He's had quite enough to drink today."

"Bitch," Harry snapped. He collapsed into a deck chair beside mine. I got up and gestured for Spencer and Rory to follow me to the main salon.

"I want to apologize for Doobie's behavior," I told Rory, after he'd seated himself right next to me on one of the black leather banquettes in the salon. "He gets this way when he's getting ready to go back into the studio to record. I thought having the boat would help him to relax, but instead it seems to have aggravated his, um, well, certain behaviors. Which is why we've decided to sell the *Reefer.*"

"He's a drunk. A mean drunk," Rory said mildly. "And if I'm not mistaken, he's on drugs too. And yet you seem like a lovely lady. Why do you put up with it?"

I took a crab quiche and forced myself to nibble slowly, trying to think of what to say. I gave Spencer a pleading look.

"Anya is committed to helping Doobie," Spencer said. "And speaking of that, maybe I better go up on deck and make sure he's all right. We wouldn't want him getting up and falling overboard."

Rory watched Spencer leave. "Seems to me it would be better all around if your husband did take a fall."

"Don't say that," I exclaimed. "You don't know him. He hasn't always been like this. He's creative. High-strung. His therapist says he needs total, unwavering support."

Rory leaned back on the banquette cushions and looked around the salon. The pale eyes took in Doobie's framed album covers and platinum records, the plush carpet and the mahogany paneling, the flat-screen television and the cabinet full of glittering crystal and silver.

His hand brushed against the back of my neck. "You keep talking about what he needs. What about you? What about what you need, Anya?"

I swallowed hard and chewed my bottom lip. This was unreal. Was he hitting on me? Where the hell were Spencer and Harry?

We heard footsteps again. "Come on now, Doobie," Spencer said. "Nobody's mad at you. We're all friends here. Come and have something to eat. Anya's getting worried about you." Rory's hand casually dropped back down to the banquette.

Get in here, I willed. Anya is mostly worried about herself, alone with a shark.

Harry staggered into the salon and collapsed into my lap. "Hey, baby," he crooned, stroking my face. "I'm sorry. I'll buy you another pair of shoes. I'll buy you a dozen pairs of shoes. How's that, baby?"

A look of disgust crossed Rory's face as he jumped up. "I'm just going to have a look in the staterooms now, if you don't mind."

"Of course," Spencer said. "I'll show you around."

I felt limp with relief once he was gone. "Don't you dare leave me alone with him again," I whispered.

Harry straightened up immediately. "He tried something with you?"

"He would have," I said. "He's a slimeball. And he thinks you need killing."

Somehow, we got through the rest of the cruise. Spencer kept Rory busy, pointing out all the yacht's bells and whistles, and I kept as far away from him as I could.

By the time we glided back to the dock at Bahia Mar, I could tell from his conversation with Spencer that Rory had made up his mind. The *Reefer Madness* would be his.

I managed to keep a smile fixed on my face as we gathered back on the sundeck and exchanged pleasantries.

"So?" Rory said, giving Harry a cool, appraising look. "Do we have a deal?"

"Talk to Spencer," Harry said. "He's the deal maker."

"Yes?" Rory said, extending a hand to Spencer.

"Yes," Spencer said. "I'll walk you to your car, and we can discuss terms."

The men were walking toward the parking lot, looking backward at the boat, talking quietly. Go already, I thought. Leave. My nerves were shot. I was ready to collapse.

"The terms are cash," Harry bawled suddenly. "Tomorrow. No later than noon. I wanna wrap this up and get back to Nashville. Noon, you hear?"

The men kept walking without turning around. "Harry," I said. "Call BeBe. Tell her we're even. And tell her you owe me a new pair of shoes."

53

Weezie

I found Emma straightening up in the galley. "You were wonderful," I gushed. "The appetizers were just right—elegant and understated. We really can't thank you enough for helping out."

She held a champagne flute up to the light, polishing it with a soft cloth. "You're welcome. It's kind of my swan song, you know? You think he bought it?"

I rubbed the knotted muscles in my neck. "I hope so. Spencer just called. Rory gave him the deposit check. Fifty thousand dollars. It's a cashier's check, so I don't think it can bounce. Now all we have to do is get through tomorrow and we're home free."

"Yeah," Emma said softly. "I'm kinda sad about moving on. I didn't think I would be, but I am. This place has been home for nearly two years. And I'm gonna miss working for Doobie. He really is a sweetheart. Those crab quiches were his favorite. The brownies too, although, since it was you guys, I didn't use his favorite ingredient."

"I appreciate that," I said wryly. "So, Emma, what will you do now? I mean, until BeBe gets back to Savannah and gets Guale reopened? Have you made any plans?"

"For the short run," she said. "One of the waitresses at the Sand Bar is getting married this week. I can stay in her condo until they get back from their honeymoon, and I'll pick up her shifts at the restaurant too. In fact, as soon as I finish cleaning up, I'm going to her bachelorette party."

"I'll finish up here," I told her. "You've done enough for today."

"Well," she hesitated. "I guess that would be all right. I'll probably just crash with a friend tonight. But I'll be back first thing in the morning to pack up all my stuff."

"Fine," I said. "We're supposed to close the deal by noon tomorrow."

I took my time straightening up the galley. Everything fit neatly into its own tidy little compartment. Too bad life wasn't like that, I thought. I was spritzing the stainless-steel counters down with glass cleaner when I felt the hairs on my neck prickle.

I whirled around. Liam was standing in the doorway, his sleepy brown eyes taking it all in. He wore tight blue jeans, no shirt, no shoes. He was deeply tanned, slim, buff, and deeply troubling.

"That was some performance you gave today," he said.

"Thanks." I put away the glass cleaner, under the sink.

"All done," I said brightly.

"Where's your boyfriend?" he asked.

"Harry?" I started to say that he wasn't my boyfriend, but then thought better of it. "He went with Spencer, to make sure all the paperwork is ready for tomorrow."

Liam nodded. "Five million dollars. That's a hell of a lot of money."

"It's not as if we're stealing it from Rory," I said. "He stole that money from my friend. And from Spencer. Their life's savings. And he's done the same thing to other women. He's a criminal. And that money is theirs."

He ran his hand over the gleaming countertop. "But the *Reefer* ain't theirs. It don't belong to them."

I frowned. "I thought you understood. We're not really selling it to Rory. As soon as he takes possession of it, and his check clears the bank, there'll be an anonymous phone call to the cops. Notifying them that the yacht has been stolen. Doobie gets his yacht back. We get our money. All is well."

"Yeah," he drawled. "I understand the plan. I just don't know that I really want to go along with it. You know?"

I felt a chill start to work its way up my spine. "But you agreed," I said finally. "You told Emma you'd help out. Look, if you're afraid you'll get in trouble . . ."

He took a step closer and ran his finger down the strap of my sundress. "Oh, I'm not afraid of trouble. Tell you the truth, it kinda turns me on. How 'bout you?" he asked, raising an eyebrow. "You getting turned on?"

I could feel his hot breath on my neck. I took a step backward, but now I was flat against the sink, with no place to hide.

"This whole situation makes me intensely nervous," I said, telling the truth. "In fact, this conversation is really, really making me nervous."

"You're cute when you're nervous," Liam said, tucking a strand of hair behind my ear. "In fact, you're pretty damn cute all the time. What's a hot little number like you doing with an old fart like Harry?"

"Look, Liam, what is it you want from us? Money? I can talk to Harry. Once the deal cleared, we intended to pay you for your help."

"Money's good," Liam said, looking down at me through those sultry, half-closed eyes. "But y'all are expecting a big payday tomorrow, and all because I took your mark out on the *Reefer* today for a sea trial. Without me, none of that would have happened."

I took a deep breath. "Actually, we could have taken the boat out without you. Harry can run a boat. He's a charter-boat captain. But that's beside the point. You did help us out, and we do intend to pay you."

"I had a different deal in mind," Liam said. "Cutting out the middleman, you might say. Dealing directly with the buyer."

"You can't," I blurted out. "It's all set. Rory made a deal with us. If anything changes, he'll get suspicious and take off. You don't under-

stand him. He's a criminal. In fact, we're pretty sure he'll try to pull
something to cheat us."

"Shh," Liam said, pressing his finger to my lips. "You've got such
a pretty little mouth. But you're talking too much. Thinking too
much." He wrapped his arms around my waist and pulled me to him,
and then he was kissing me, pushing his tongue into my mouth, moving his hands up, cupping my breasts.

"Liam," I said, shoving him away. "Stop it."

"Come on," he said, catching my wrist and holding it tightly. "You
saying you're not turned on? You saying you haven't been thinking
this whole time about how you could cut Harry and the rest of them
out of this deal and keep all the money for yourself?"

"No!" I said, trying to wrench away from him.

He grabbed my shoulders and pinned me against the counter. "I
have," he said, breathing fast. "If anybody's gonna make any money
off the *Reefer Madness,* it's gonna be me. If anybody's gonna sell her,
it's gonna be me. Now, sweet thing. What's it gonna be? You gonna
stick with Harry and go home poor? Or are you gonna let Liam show
you the good things in life?"

"You can't—" I started.

"Oh yeah. Yeah, I can," he said calmly. "And I will. You said it
yourself, Rory wants this boat. He wants it bad. He don't care who he
has to pay to get it, or what he has to do. It'll be easy. You tell me
where Rory's staying, I'll call him tonight, tell him the terms have
changed. It's you and me he's dealing with now. No broker. No
Harry. And if he buys from us, the price is, say, half a million less."

I felt myself go absolutely cold. Here I'd been worrying about Roy
Eugene Moseley finding us out, and all the time Liam was waiting in
the wings, just waiting for a chance to pounce. On the boat. On the
money. On me.

Harry, damnit, I thought, get back here. Now.

"Whatcha thinking, sweet thing?" Liam was standing in the doorway again, his thumbs hooked in the waistband of his jeans. I could tell he was watching his own reflection in the glass of the porthole over the sink, admiring himself.

Suddenly, I started to get pissed. Oh yeah, I thought. Yeah, Liam. You are such a badass hottie. I bet girls have been telling you your whole life what a badass you are. How could anybody resist?

"I'm thinking . . . why not?" I shrugged.

"You're in?"

"Yeah."

"Allll right," he said, giving me a high five. "This calls for a little celebration." He grabbed my hand. "Follow me." He led me through the narrow hallway, in the direction of the master stateroom.

Oh God, I thought. He's gonna drag me into the stateroom and rape me.

"Where we going?" I asked, digging in my heels. "Look, I think you're cute and all, but I'm not really ready to take this to the next level this fast. And Harry's coming back. If he comes back and catches me with you, I don't know what he'll do. That wasn't all an act with him today, pushing me around. He's got a temper. And I'm afraid of him."

"Shit," Liam said. "Old fart like that? I could kick his ass up and down this boat. Relax," he said, tugging at my hand again. "Just a little party. Nothing serious. Come on, I'll show you."

He pushed open the door to the master stateroom. "In here," he said. "Hell, Weezie, I'm not gonna rape you. I never had to force a woman in my life. I just want to show you something."

Reluctantly, I followed him into the room. He pulled open a sliding door. It was a closet, full of men's clothes. He kneeled down and pushed aside a suitcase. For a moment, while he was down on the floor like that, it occurred to me, Hit him! Hit him on the head and run for your life. But before I could even look for something to hit him with, he was standing up, holding out a blue Adidas gym bag.

"What's that?" I asked.

He took the bag over to the bed and dumped it out.

"Doobie's stash," he said, turning to give me a big grin.

It was a supersize smorgasbord of controlled substances. There was a gallon-size ziplock bag of marijuana. A sandwich baggie of white powder. And a dozen bottles of pills in rainbow colors.

"How'd you know where it was?" I asked. "Emma said Anya turned the boat upside down, looking for wherever Doobie was hiding it. And she never found it."

"Who do you think got it for him?" Liam said. "He couldn't risk carrying stuff on him, flying down here, going through Nashville and Atlanta, with airport security searching all over his ass. And Anya watched him like a damned hawk. Never left him alone for a minute once they got to Lauderdale. This way was much easier. He'd give me a call, tell me they were coming down, and I'd take a little trip to the candy store."

"Wow." My mind was racing. How in the hell was I going to get out of this?

He picked up the big baggie. "Some excellent Jamaican. I scored it on our last cruise. And the coke's righteous. Doobie hooked me up with a guy who gets primo stuff. Or maybe you like 'ludes?" He cocked his head and gave me a wink. "So what's your pleasure?"

"Oh." I winced. Think fast. Say something. "Damn. The truth is, this stuff makes me nauseous. I've been like this ever since college. I smoke the slightest bit of weed, and I puke my brains out. Same thing with coke. But I wouldn't mind a drink."

"Not much of a party that way."

"I don't care what you do," I said generously. "What I'd really love is a cosmopolitan. Do you think we have the stuff onboard to make a cosmo?"

"Oh, yeah. Anya drinks 'em all the time. What a hypocrite. It's okay for her to get tight on vodka, but let Doobie smoke a little weed to relax and she freaks."

I started stuffing the drugs back into the gym bag. "If you tell me where everything is, I'll make us a pitcherful. Do you know if there's any triple sec?"

He reached out and grabbed the baggie of marijuana. "You sure you don't want any of this? It's really good shit, guaranteed to mellow you right out."

"Positive," I said. "I guess liquor's my drug of choice."

"Whatever," he said, busying himself rolling a joint. "Everything's in the liquor cabinet in the main salon. I'll be up in a minute."

I found the liquor and Rose's lime juice in the cabinet under the wet bar in the salon, right where Liam had said I would. I held the cocktail shaker up to the light. It was Baccarat, with a sterling-silver top. Very nice. I poured in the vodka, triple sec, cranberry juice, and lime juice, and added some crushed ice. After a vigorous shake, I poured myself a hefty drink for courage and knocked half of it back in one long gulp. Then I took the bottle of pills I'd palmed from Doobie's stash and poured out half a dozen blue tablets. What they were, I didn't know and I didn't really care, as long as they made Liam go nighty night. I smashed the pills with the bottom of the vodka bottle, put them in the cocktail shaker, and gave it an even more vigorous shake.

Footsteps. My hands were shaking again. On second thought, I crushed two more tablets, put them in the bottom of an empty martini glass, poured out another drink, and gave it a vigorous stir.

"Here you are," Liam said, walking into the salon. He was wearing shoes now, and an unbuttoned shirt, had a lit joint in his hand, and his eyes had gotten even sleepier, if that was possible. "Find everything you need?"

He reached out for me, and I handed him the martini glass.

"Yeah. Try this. It's kinda my specialty."

"Pussy drink," Liam said. But he took it and sipped. "Different. You put something different in it, right?"

"It's my secret ingredient," I said, giving him a wink. I took a dainty sip of my own drink and waited.

He sprawled himself out on the banquette, picked up the remote control, and turned on the television. It was tuned to MTV, and a trio of Latino girls dressed in white patent-leather bikinis were writhing around on the floor in front of a huge neon crucifix, while a menacing-looking black guy dressed as a Trappist monk sang a rap version of "Faith of Our Fathers." I wondered if Spencer had ever seen this video. I'd have to remember to ask him. If I got off this yacht in one piece.

"Come sit right here by me," Liam said, patting the banquette.

I stayed where I was.

He took another slug of the cosmo. "Come on," Liam drawled. "I won't bite. We're gonna be partners, right? You and me. Partners gotta be tight."

I picked up the cocktail shaker and perched on the edge of the banquette. "Let me top you off," I said. "Partner."

54

When the phone rang in the motel room, I regarded it with deep suspicion. Anybody who knew me would be calling on my cell phone. And then I looked at the cell phone, sitting on the nightstand, and realized I'd let the battery go dead.

"BeBe?" The voice was whispered, barely audible.

"Who is this?"

"It's me, damnit, Weezie."

"Why are we whispering?"

"I'm in trouble," she whispered. "Get over here. Now. Bring Harry and Spencer."

"They're not here," I said. "Where are you? What's wrong?"

"I'm on the yacht. Get here now."

And then she hung up.

Get there how? I wondered. Granddad and Harry had the Buick. I'd been sitting around the motel room all afternoon, going bonkers from boredom and nerves. I grabbed my purse and was almost out the door when it occurred to me: disguise. Reddy could still be skulking around the marina, watching the *Reefer Madness*.

Cursing, I called a cab. I pulled the dark wig over my own hair, and shoved some socks in my bra. There was no time for any more extensive costuming. I just barely had time to put on the yellow platform heels before I heard the cab tooting its horn.

"Bahia Mar marina," I told the driver. He turned and stared at me.

"You working?"

Oh. He thought it was that kind of business.

"No," I said, frowning. I handed him my last twenty-dollar bill. "Could you move it, please? It's kind of an emergency."

"Everything's an emergency with you people," he muttered, but ten minutes later he was letting me off at the marina.

"You want me back in an hour?" he asked, giving me a wink.

"No," I said. "My pimp's picking me up."

I clomped as fast as the platforms would take me to the end of the dock where the *Reefer Madness* was tied up. I gave a furtive look up and down the dock to see if anybody was watching, then boarded quickly.

Up close, the splendor of the *Reefer Madness* took my breath away. It made Roy Eugene's Savannah yacht, the *Blue Moon*, look like a bathtub toy. Everything was white and gleaming and smelled like money. And there was nobody around.

The sundeck was deserted. I kicked off the platforms and tiptoed around to the bow of the boat. Nobody there either. Back in the stern, I eased open the door to what looked like a living room. "Weezie?" I whispered.

"Get in here." An arm reached out and grabbed me.

"What the hell?" Weezie was sitting on a huge black leather banquette, next to a strange man who'd been hog-tied with a series of brightly colored bungee cords.

"It's Liam, the first mate," she whispered.

"What happened to him?" I asked.

I could tell she'd been crying. "He, he, was groping me. Kissing me . . ."

"So you tied him up? That seems a little extreme, Weezer."

"He was going to double-cross us!" she exclaimed. Even though it was uncomfortably warm in the room, she was rubbing her arms and her teeth were chattering. "He said he and I should go to Reddy and make a deal with him ourselves, without Harry or Spencer. And if I didn't go along, he'd rat us out to Reddy. And I was scared. He was going to ruin everything."

"So then you tied him up," I said, nodding approval.

"No. Not right away. I acted like I was going to go along with him," Weezie said.

"He wanted to party. He showed me Doobie's stash. Down in the master salon. There's a whole gym bag full of stuff, coke and marijuana and pills and I don't know what all. He wanted me to smoke dope with him, but I told him it makes me puke, which is true. So he smoked a joint, and I made us a pitcher of cosmopolitans, and I dropped in eight or nine of these blue pills I sorta stole when he wasn't looking."

I knelt down and took a close look at Liam. His eyelids fluttered. I picked up his hand and dropped it. Limp as a fish. "What kind of pills?"

"Like I cared!" Weezie said. "They did the job, okay? He drank two cosmos, then he just sort of stopped talking, and he started to teeter, and then thunk! He was out cold. And I'm petrified. What if I gave him an overdose? What if he dies? Oh my God, what if he wakes up? We have got to do something with him."

"Calm down," I said, rubbing her hands, which were icy. "His breathing sounds fine. He's got a pulse. And he's not puking up blood or anything."

"You've been watching *ER* again," she said.

"And *General Hospital.* Did you know there's a soap-opera cable network?"

"BeBe! What are we gonna do?" Weezie wailed. "We've got to do something with Liam. What if Reddy turns up and finds us here with him?"

"Show me that stash of drugs," I said briskly. "We need to figure out what you gave him, and whether it's likely to kill him."

Liam gave an almost inaudible moan then, and shuddered.

"Wait," I said. "First we need to tie him up more securely. He's pretty muscular looking. And we've gotta move him too."

"There's a locker up in the bow of the boat," Weezie said. "It's where they stow life jackets and stuff. We can stick him in there for the time being."

I hooked my arms through his and Weezie took his feet, and between us, we managed to drag-carry Liam up to the storage locker, and wedge him in between the ropes and life jackets. But the locker had no lock.

"This'll do until we find something better," I said.

"What about tying him up with some of that rope?" Weezie said.

"No, it's too thick. Let's look around for something better."

"Maybe a belt or something," Weezie said. "Doobie and Anya's closets in the master salon are full of clothes. We can look there. And the gym bag is there too."

"Holy geez," I said when she opened the door to the master salon. Everything in it was cream colored, from the carpet, to the heavy satin draperies, to the silk coverlet on the king-size bed.

"Check out the ceiling," Weezie said, running to the closet.

It was mirrored.

"Kinky," I said. "Wouldn't you think that would make you seasick on a yacht?"

She threw a blue gym bag in my direction. I unzipped it and dumped the contents out on the bed. "Whoa," I said. "Now we know why they call it *Reefer Madness*." I rifled through the pill bottles, looking for the blue capsules she'd described.

"These?" I asked, spilling some out into my hand.

"Yeah, probably," she said.

There was no label on the bottle. I held one of the pills up to the light to look for lettering or numbers. "Nothing."

"He said something about 'ludes," Weezie said, opening a vanity drawer.

"Quaaludes," I said. "That makes sense. I heard they quit making them, but some people buy them on the black market. That could be why there's no label on the bottle, or lettering on the pills themselves. If it's Quaaludes, he'll be all right. He'll just take a really long nap and wake up with a headache."

"Look at this," Weezie said. She held up a lacy black garter belt.

"Ooh, Anya," I said admiringly. "Looks like you have a naughty side."

"It's French," Weezie said, examining the label. She pulled out some more lingerie, a black lace bustier, and the tiniest thong panties I'd ever seen.

"Interesting curling iron," Weezie said, laying a black rubber wandlike apparatus on the top of the vanity. "I don't think I've ever seen a battery-operated one before."

"No, no, no, my little Catholic princess," I said, giggling. "Not a curling iron. It's a vibrator. The perfect gift for the woman who has everything."

"What?" Weezie took a closer look and her face went bright pink. She hurried over to the sink and started scrubbing her hands.

I took over her spot at the vanity. "Let me see what else is in here."

I held up a pair of sheer black stockings "We could tie his hands with these."

"They're real silk," Weezie said, fingering the fabric. "It would be a shame to ruin them."

"Aha," I said, digging down to the bottom of the drawer. I pulled out a square flat black velvet case. "I think I found the Bauers family jewels."

I flipped the box open. The lining was red satin, and nestled inside was a pair of shiny silver handcuffs with black fur accents.

"Perfect," Weezie said, grabbing them and shoving the vanity drawer shut with her hip. "I don't even want to know what else is in there."

Liam was snoring softly when we went back to the equipment locker. We rolled him on his side and clamped one hand with the cuff to some water pipes in the locker room.

"See? Just think of it as a power nap," I told her.

"Now what?" she demanded. "Do we just leave him here?"

"We've got to," I said. "We couldn't drag him off the boat now—someone will see us. He'll be all right here for the night. The guys can deal with him tomorrow."

"Speaking of the men," Weezie said, "where are they? Harry said they were going to go take care of the paperwork for the yacht sale. But that was hours ago."

"There's no telling where they are now," I said. "They've bonded."

She crossed her arms over her chest. "I am not staying another night on this boat. Not with that sex fiend. And not with that, that *thing* you found in the vanity, either."

"All right," I told her, linking her arm in mine. "You've been very brave and very ingenious. Just let me go hide Doobie's stash back in that closet. Then we'll go back to the Mango Tree and order a pizza. Harry and Spencer can hold the fort here tonight."

55

Back at the motel, we found my grandfather stretched out on top of his bed, fully dressed, including shoes and socks. Protruding from the breast pocket of his blazer was an unlit cigar and a red plastic cocktail swizzle stick that said "Embers Lounge." With each soft snore he exuded a cloud of Scotch-scented breath.

"Granddad," I said, patting his cheek softly. "Wake up."

He shook his head and mumbled something.

"Wake up," I said, shaking him by the shoulder. "Where's Harry? What have you two been doing all this time?"

He opened one eye. "Business. Been doing business." He patted his breast pocket, and brought forth a wad of paper. "All set for tomorrow. All set." And then he turned his head and closed his eyes and went right back to sleep.

I unfolded the papers and held them up for Weezie to see.

"Sales contract for the *Reefer Madness*," I said. "It looks pretty official."

A piece of paper fluttered down to the bedspread. She picked it up and held it out for me to examine. "This looks official too."

It was a cashier's check for $50,000, made out to S and L Yacht Sales.

"Excellent," I said. "He even thought to make up a corporate name for himself."

"Who's S and L?" Weezie asked.

"Spencer and Lorena," I said, without hesitation. "That was the name of the furniture store they used to own on Broughton Street. S and L Quality Furnishings. Eighty years old and he's still a hopeless romantic.

"Granddad!" I was shaking him again. "Where's Harry?"

"Gone back boat," he mumbled. "All set."

I leaned down and kissed him on the cheek. "You bet," I said softly. I took off his shoes, pulled the bedspread over him, and turned out the light.

"What now?" Weezie asked, following me through the connecting door to our own room.

I snatched the wig off my head and threw it on a chair, and pulled the socks out of my bra. "We get a good night's sleep. Tomorrow's it. The big day. We either pull off the biggest scam of the century or we go home broke. Either way, it all comes down to tomorrow."

"What about Liam?" Weezie asked, sinking down onto her bed. "What if he gets out? Shouldn't we let Harry know he's there?"

I picked up the phone on the bedside table and dialed Harry's cell phone number. It rang three times and then rolled over to voice mail. "Harry," I said quickly. "It's me. You've got a passenger tied up in the closet thingy in the bow of the boat. It's Liam. He tried to double-cross us, so Weezie slipped him a mickey. Don't let him out. I'll explain in the morning. 'Bye."

"Happy?" I asked, turning to Weezie, who was undressing.

"I guess," she said. "You still haven't explained your plan."

I went into the bathroom to try to scrub the rest of the tan in a can off my face.

"Tell you in the morning," I called. And then, "Right after I figure it out myself."

56

*Danger. Travis McGee could taste it, smell it, hear it in the buzzing
nothingness of the shimmering tropical heat. "Get down," he whispered to
the tawny-skinned blonde. In a moment, he was pressing the cold steel of the
revolver into her shaking hands. He kissed her, his unyielding warmth en-
veloping, then releasing her. He unsheathed the knife, held its glinting
metal between strong white teeth and crawled forward on elbows and knees.
The shots came without warning, spinning him down and around in a
stream of hot crimson. "Trav!" she screamed.*

"BeBe!"

I sat straight up in the bed, my eyes wild with fright.

Weezie stood over me, barefoot, in her nightgown.

"Are you all right?" she asked, yawning. "You were screaming
something."

"Bad dream," I said, echoing with a yawn of my own. "What time
is it?"

"Seven-thirty," she said, dropping back to her own bed. "I swear, I
feel like I just closed my eyes a minute ago."

"Go back to sleep," I told her.

But the phone rang. I grabbed for it, dropped it, picked it back up.

"BeBe? Did I wake you up?"

It was Harry. "No," I told him. "It was Travis."

"Who?"

"Never mind. What's up?"

"You want to tell me why you two assaulted, drugged, and detained Liam?"

"Is he awake? You didn't let him go, did you?"

"No," Harry said. "He's still out cold. I haven't touched him. About those handcuffs—"

"But he's alive, right? We don't want him dead. Just quiet. For the time being."

"He's breathing," Harry said.

"Tell me he's alive," Weezie said, palms pressed together, heavenward.

"He's alive. But sleeping," I told her.

"Tell Harry he had it coming."

"He had it coming," I told Harry.

"He groped me," Weezie said.

"He—"

"I hear her," Harry interrupted. "You drugged and hog-tied him because he had wandering hands? Is that good policy?"

"He was threatening to double-cross us," I said. "He wanted to cut you and Granddad out of the deal, just split it with Weezie. And he threatened to tell Reddy what was going on if she didn't go along with him."

"Riiight," Harry said. "Forget I ever doubted you."

"I will," I said. "What about Granddad? What did you do to him last night?"

"Me?" Harry protested. "If it weren't for me, we'd still be in that dive. The Embers. He wanted to stop by after we got the sales contracts fixed up. Some other geezer he met at the Sand Bar told him they had senior-citizen happy hour. He got happy, all right. He only agreed to leave when they jacked drink prices up after ten o'clock."

"All right," I said finally. "I think I've got everything figured out for today."

"I'm listening," he said warily.

I pulled Randall's cashier's check out of the nightstand drawer where I'd stashed it the night before. "His check is drawn on an account at Bank of America. There are two branches near the marina. One is right down the street, and the other is just a couple blocks up. As soon as the banks are open, I'll take the check by there to make sure it's the real deal."

"Good idea," Harry said.

"And I'll open an account at the same branch," I added. "For S and L Yacht Sales. The minute we get the big check from Randall, we'll race over there and deposit it in our account. Since the check is from the same bank, they won't put a hold on the funds."

"If there is a big check," Harry said.

I got a cold chill up my spine. "What do you mean 'if'?"

"He's up to something," Harry said. "I slept in a lounge chair up on deck last night. He rode by at least three times on that bike of his. Checking on us."

"Did he see you?"

"No," Harry said. "I had the chair pulled up under the overhang of the cabin. It was totally dark. There's no way he could have seen me."

I gave it some thought. "He can't take the boat from us. Not by himself."

"No," Harry said. "I won't let that happen."

"Then he's planning another scam," I said. "With the money."

"Makes sense."

"We've got to make him think he's gotten away with stealing the boat," I said.

"What?" Weezie said.

"What?" Harry chimed in.

"Get the check from him, let him think he's got us swindled, and then turn the tables on him," I said.

"How?" Weezie asked.

"How?" Harry asked.

"We need a speakerphone here," I said. "Look. I'm just thinking like he'd think. He's got to give us a bona fide check for the yacht. That's a condition of the sale. But if I know Reddy, he has no intention of paying for something he thinks he can steal. I'll bet you ten bucks he takes possession of the *Reefer,* chugs away from the dock, and then promptly beats it back to the bank to withdraw the funds before we can cash that check."

"Can he do that?" Weezie asked.

"We're not gonna give him the chance."

"Just how do we stop him?" Harry asked.

"Let him take the *Reefer,*" I said. "See to it that he gets just far enough from Bahia Mar, and no farther."

"And then what?" Weezie asked.

"I'm assuming that's where I come in," Harry said.

I turned to Weezie. "That's where Harry comes in. Can you do it?" I asked him. "Fix it so the boat comes unfixed—just long enough for us to get to the bank and put his money in our account before two o'clock?"

"He can do it," Weezie assured me.

"No problem," Harry said.

"Speaking of problems," I said. "I'm wondering what we do with Liam. If Reddy really is lurking around the area, watching, we can't just let him walk off under his own steam. Not until the deal's done and the ship's sailed. So to speak."

"Leave it to me," Harry said. "It's natural that I'd be unloading my own personal possessions from the *Reefer Madness* before it changes hands, right?"

"Right," I said.

"When Weezie and Spencer come back over here this morning, get them to stop at Home Depot and pick up a big plastic tarp. Also some beer. Heineken."

"I get what you want with the tarp, but why the beer?" I asked.

"We're out," Harry said. "A man gets thirsty. Can I ask you something?"

"Anything."

"Do you really think this crazy-ass scheme of yours is going to work?"

I looked over at Weezie, who was now sitting cross-legged on her bed, watching the *Today Show*. I thought about Granddad, passed out in the other room. And Harry. I'd been thinking a lot about Harry these past few days. About the kind of man he was, what he wanted from life. What I wanted from life. Two very different realities. And yet . . .

"It'll work," I said. "It just has to."

"Okay, kid," he said softly. "That's all I wanted to hear. See you soon."

"Not soon enough."

I was thinking about that dream I'd been having just a few minutes ago. Another chill went up my spine.

"You be careful, Harry Sorrentino, you hear me?"

"I hear you, kid."

57

After his big night on the town, Granddad was looking a little washed out. His hands trembled slightly as he fiddled with his bow tie, and his eyes had dark circles beneath them.

"Are you sure you're up to this?" I asked as he folded himself into the front seat of the Buick.

"Why wouldn't I be?" he snapped.

"I got the impression you might have been, uh, overserved last night."

"I'm fine as frog hair," Granddad insisted. "You worry about your job. I'll worry about mine. Have you got the check?"

"Got it," I said, patting the envelope on the front seat.

"Just let me do the talking," Granddad said. "I've been in business and banking a lot longer than you, young lady."

"Yes, sir," I said meekly.

When the Bank of America branch across the street from Bahia Mar marina opened its doors at nine o'clock on Friday, Granddad and I were the first customers in the door.

I needn't have worried. He marched up to the customer-service desk in the bank's lobby and held Randall's check out to the woman seated there.

"Young lady, I need to know which local branch this check is drawn on."

She took a sip of her coffee, looked at me, and then back at him.

But she took the check, started tapping on the keys of her computer, and soon had an answer.

"This account was opened at our Broward Plaza branch," she said. "It's about two miles from here. Do you know the shopping center?"

"I do," I volunteered.

"Anything else I can do for you?" she asked.

"Not a thing," Granddad said, with an abbreviated tip of his straw cap.

We drove on to Broward Plaza. Once inside, Granddad again approached the customer-service desk, which was manned by a Hispanic woman in a bright orange jacket. Her nameplate said she was "Veronica Gallegos."

"Hello, Miss Gallegos," Granddad said, sweeping off his hat.

"Hello," she said, looking up and dimpling at the sight of such gallantry. "Can I help you?"

He produced Randall's check. "My name is Spencer Loudermilk. I'd like to open an account at your bank this morning, and deposit this check."

She took the check, nodded, and started rummaging in her desk for the proper forms. "Won't you sit down?"

"Thank you," Granddad said, seating himself and gesturing to me. "This is my granddaughter and business partner, BeBe Loudermilk. We'll want to make her cosigner on the account."

"Fine. Will this be a business or personal account?" she asked.

"Business," he said. "S and L Yacht Sales."

"And will you require checking and savings?"

"Just savings," Granddad said.

She nodded and pushed some papers across the counter for him to fill out. He wrinkled his forehead and gave me a nod. "Granddad's having some vision problems this morning," I told her.

Ms. Gallegos waited until I'd filled out the forms, then sat and tapped the information into her computer. Ten minutes later, she was handing us a bank book.

I filled out the savings-deposit slip and handed it to her. "Just one other thing," I said.

"We'll be depositing a very large check this afternoon, probably drawn on the same account as that check we just gave you. There won't be any problem with the funds clearing, will there?"

She frowned. "It's a cashier's check. Funds are guaranteed, and the check you've given me is for an account opened right here at this branch. But I can check and see if there are sufficient funds, if you like."

Ms. Gallegos tapped some more keys, and then stared at the computer screen. "I should think there are sufficient funds in this account for a very substantial withdrawal."

Granddad stood up and tipped his hat again. "Pleasure doing business with you."

"See you soon," I said.

Granddad was humming softly as we drove back to the Mango Tree.

"What's that song?" I asked.

He frowned. "You don't recognize it?"

"No," I said. "But it's nice. What's it called?"

" 'To Each His Own,' " Granddad said, humming another bar. "That's our song, Lorena's and mine. It was a big hit in our day. We'd get all dressed up and go dancing just about every Saturday night. There was the Bamboo Ranch in Garden City. We used to listen to Buddy Livingston's band. Had four sisters who could really sing— Irene, Darlene, Marlene, and Earlene. And then there was Remler's Club Royale on Victory Drive. That's where we heard 'To Each His Own' for the first time."

"Funny," I mused. "I was married to two different men, and I don't think we ever had an 'our song.' Come to think of it, we didn't do too much dancing, either. Maybe at an occasional wedding or something. Or at the Telfair Ball."

Granddad snorted and shook his head.

"What?"

"Sandy was an all right person. Nice family and all. But he wasn't the right man for you. Never was. And as for Richard!"

"Don't start," I warned. "I've admitted he was a huge mistake. I think I should get a . . . what's that word they use in golf? When you take a bad stroke and it doesn't count?"

"A mulligan."

"Yeah. Richard was my mulligan."

"You know what a Silverstein is?" he asked, getting a glint in his eye.

"The people who owned that jewelry store on Broughton Street where the Starbucks is now?"

"No. In golf, if you hit an absolutely unbelievable shot, the other guy can yell 'Silverstein' and then you have to take that shot over. It's like a joke on the golfer."

"I don't get it."

"You wouldn't," Granddad said. "Me and Lorena, we'd be a Silverstein. And I'd do it all over again. Every minute of it."

At the next red light, I leaned over and kissed him. "Old softie."

He cleared his throat. "I have something to say. I wasn't going to bring this up at all, but since you mentioned the subject, I feel it's my duty to tell you something."

"Uh-oh."

"It's about Harry."

I felt my face color. "Look, Granddad—"

"He's a fine man, BeBe. An honorable man. He's decent and hard-working. Not afraid to get his hands dirty. And he appears quite taken with you. So, I just want to say that if the two of you—"

"Can we just skip this?" I pleaded. "No offense, but I'm really not comfortable talking about my love life with you."

"I'm just saying."

I started humming to drown him out. "I'm not listening."

"Don't screw it up," Granddad said. "No more mulligans."

58

Weezie

I thought BeBe's grandfather was going to have a stroke, right there in the 7-Eleven, when the clerk told him the price of a six-pack of Heineken. "Six dollars and eighty-seven cents? For beer?" He mopped his forehead with his handkerchief. "I've got suits I did-n't pay that much for."

"*Que?*" the cashier said.

"Never mind," I said, putting the money on the counter. "I'll get this."

"Absolutely not!" Spencer said, slapping his hand over mine. "I forbid it. German beer! This is what we get for agreeing to the Marshall Plan."

"Spencer!" I hissed. "Let's just pay for the beer and go. It's getting close to noon. Reddy will be at the boat anytime now. And Harry really needs this beer. And the tarp. *Before* Reddy gets there."

"We'll go to another store," Spencer decided, turning his back on the counter. "It's these durned convenience stores. Highway robbers, all of 'em."

"Never mind the beer," I said, glancing at my watch. It was after eleven. "Let's just go on over to the marina. I'll buy Harry some beer afterward."

"All right with me," Spencer grumbled, getting into the passenger seat of the Buick. "Still don't see why he needs a tarp, of all things."

BeBe and I had decided not to share Liam's fate with Spencer. We felt it might dampen his enthusiasm for the day's events. I know it dampened mine.

"I think it's a boat kind of thing," I said. "Harry understands all this stuff."

Lame! I thought.

We were halfway down the dock at Bahia Mar when we spotted Harry, hurrying to meet us. His shirt was drenched through with sweat, his face sunburned.

"What took you guys so long?" he asked. "We've got to get this show on the road. I've already seen Rory ride by twice."

"Sorry," I said, handing over the bag with the plastic tarp. "Home Depot was packed, and I got a little confused and took a wrong turn out of the shopping center."

"You know what they charge for a six-pack of that German beer you like?" Spencer demanded. "Nearly seven bucks!"

"We had to skip the beer," I told Harry. "Time constraints."

"I gotta get that guy loaded and moved," Harry muttered. "Did you leave the trunk of the Buick unlocked?"

"What guy?" Spencer asked.

"That's just, uh, yacht talk, for equipment," I said quickly. *Lame!*

"I'm gonna get one of the three-wheeled carts from the dockmaster's office to load the, uh, equipment," Harry said, turning back in the direction he'd come from. "I'll meet you guys at the *Reefer.*"

"I'll go on ahead," I told Spencer, who was strolling at a leisurely pace. "I need to pack my stuff that's in the master stateroom."

When I got to the *Reefer,* Emma popped her head out of the galley. Her face was pale. "Oh my God, Weezie," she whispered. "We've got trouble."

"I know," I said. "I didn't want to hurt Liam. Just put him to sleep for a little while so he'd quit pawing me. But he was going to spoil everything."

"It's not Liam," she said urgently. "It's Doobie."

"You mean Harry?"

"I mean the *real* Doobie Bauers," she said. "Anya just called. The real Anya. Doob went AWOL from Betty Ford. Yesterday. She thinks he's headed down here."

"No," I said. "He can't. Not now."

"That's what I said. Anya checked. He bought a one-way ticket to Fort Lauderdale." She checked her watch. "His plane should be landing right about now."

"No, no, no," I wailed. "This can't be happening."

Harry trundled the cart over the gangplank from the dock. "What can't be happening? Did Liam wake up?"

"It's Doobie," Emma said. "He's here. In Fort Lauderdale."

"Christ," Harry said, dropping the cart's handles with a thump.

"What else did Anya say?" I asked.

"She was actually asking for Liam," Emma said. "At the time I didn't realize you had him tied up and handcuffed in the gear locker."

"What's that?"

The three of us turned around to see Spencer standing motionless on the gangplank. "You've got the first mate tied up?"

"It's a long story," I said. "He was going to double-cross us and sell the *Reefer Madness* to Rory himself."

"And what's that you were saying about Doobie?" Spencer asked, joining us on the sundeck.

"He's run away from the drug rehab, and he's headed here. To the *Reefer Madness,*" Emma said. "He told his roommate that he was gonna come down here, load up the *Reefer,* and make a run for Bimini. Anya was calling to tell Liam that under no circumstances is he to let Doobie take the boat out. She's on her way here too."

The sun was beating down on my head, I could feel sweat dripping down my back, and my stomach was doing flip-flops. "We've got to get out of here," I said. "If Doobie shows up here and finds out what's going on, we'll all go to jail."

"Calm down," Harry said. "Nobody's going to jail, unless it's Roy Eugene Moseley. Here's what we're gonna do. Emma, you're the only one who actually knows Doobie. How will he get here from the airport? Does he have a car there?"

"No. Anya usually arranges to have a limo pick them up. But when Doobie comes alone, he just calls the boat and has Liam swing by the airport."

"Let's hope he does that this time too," Harry said fervently. "Stay by the phone, okay? If he calls, tell him Liam's busy, but you'll pick him up. You've got a car, right?"

"Yes."

"Great. Assuming he calls, you pick him up, and then you stall. Tell him you have to buy groceries, take him to the liquor store, but whatever you do, don't come back here until we call and give you the all's clear."

"But what if he doesn't call? What if he just takes a cab? I mean, with Doob, you never really know what he's gonna do," Emma said.

"I'll stay by the phone here," I volunteered. "If he calls, I'll just tell him I'm Liam's girlfriend, and that he's out running errands. In the meantime, maybe you could just kind of hang around out front, then you can intercept him as soon as he gets here."

"And then what?"

"Stall," Harry said. "Doesn't matter how. Just keep him the hell away from the marina. You've got a cell phone, right?"

She held it up.

"Good. Give me the number. I'll call you as soon as the deal's done. Remember, don't let him anywhere near the dock."

She told Harry her number and he punched it into his cell phone.

Emma picked up an oversize canvas gear bag. "Good luck, you guys," she said.

"Weezie," Harry said, "I've got some tinkering to do in the pilot-house, and the engine room. There's no time to waste. You and Spencer stay up here and watch out for Rory. Same thing as with Doobie. If he does show up while I'm still tinkering, you'll have to stall. Don't let him onboard until I tell you."

"How?" I wailed.

"Rory likes you, right?" Harry said. "Use your charms."

"I *have* no charms. I'm so scared, I think I might puke."

"No puking," Harry said sternly. "Spencer, you're her wing man. Keep her calm and keep Rory *off* this boat."

"Right," Spencer said, snapping a salute. But Harry didn't return it because he was already climbing the stairs to the pilothouse.

"Right," Spencer said. "Let's get busy then. You said you needed to get your stuff out of the master stateroom, right?"

"Right," I said, taking a deep breath.

"Crap," I said. "Liam! What do we do about Liam? He's still tied up in the gear locker. What if he tries to get out when Rory's aboard?"

"I'll deal with Liam," Spencer said. "The double-crossing bum. You just get your stuff packed up. Load it in this cart Harry brought down."

"All right," I said. "The sooner I get off this tub, the better."

It didn't take long to pack my stuff. I'd only brought a pair of pajamas, my overnight bag, and one of my Anya Bauers sundresses. I threw everything in the bag, then took one more look around the stateroom to make sure I hadn't missed anything.

That's when I remembered Doobie's stash. I opened the closet door, unzipped the bag, and shook out half a dozen of the magic blue pills into my hand. I put the bag back where I'd found it, closed the closet door, and went out to the galley.

It wasn't even noon yet, but I needed a drink. Just a little nerve calmer. Unfortunately, I didn't think we had any elephant tranquilizers in stock.

Instead, I fixed a pitcher of Bloody Marys. I was just adding the celery salt and Tabasco when Spencer came back. He was natty as ever today, in a pair of navy blue slacks and a white golf shirt under a pale yellow sport coat, all of which I'd picked up at the Junior League Thrift Shop.

"Cocktail?" I asked, holding up the pitcher.

He glanced at his watch. "It's five o'clock somewhere," he said cheerfully.

"How's Liam?" I asked, sipping my own drink.

"He seems a little restless," Spencer said, squeezing some lime into his glass.

"Oh God." I dumped the rest of my drink down the drain. No amount of liquor would do the trick now.

"Not to worry," Spencer said. "You girls did a fine job tying him up. He's not going anywhere for the time being."

"We've got to get him off this boat," I said, drumming my fingers on the stainless-steel countertop. "And me. I want out. I want to go home. I want my dog. I want my boyfriend. Heaven help me, I think I even want my mama."

Spencer patted my hand. "There, there. It'll all be just fine. It's almost over."

"Almost," Harry repeated, sticking his head in the galley. "I've taken care of some mechanical adjustments. I'm gonna go clean up, then I'll join you on the sundeck."

"What about Liam?" I repeated.

"Too late to move him now," Harry said. "But don't worry, we'll get him off."

"Bloody Mary?" Spencer said, holding up the cocktail shaker.

Harry shook his head no. "Wish I had a Heineken."

By noon, the three of us had arranged ourselves artfully around a table, under an umbrella on the sundeck. Harry produced a deck of cards, and he and Spencer played gin rummy as though they hadn't a care in the world.

By one, my nerves were raw. The phone didn't ring. People came and went up and down the dock, but there was no sign of Rory Mason. At one-fifteen, Emma called from the parking lot. "Have you guys heard anything?"

"Nothing," I said. "No sign of Doobie up there?"

"No. I even tried calling Anya in Nashville. She doesn't answer.

There's a flight out of Nashville that gets in here at four. Unless she took the nonstop, in which case she could be here in half an hour."

I put the phone down. "Maybe I will have a drink."

At one-thirty, Rory Mason strolled aboard the *Reefer Madness* like he owned it. He had a knapsack slung over his shoulder and a wide, carefree smile on his face.

The change in Harry was instantaneous. He slumped down in the chair. "Gawddamnit, you're late. Never mind. I changed my mind. Gonna keep the gawddamned boat."

Rory looked from me to Harry to Spencer.

"Doobie's kidding," I said quickly. "He's not used to waiting for people. I told you, he's on edge. Going right back into the studio as soon as we get back to Nashville."

"Shut up, Anya," Harry ordered. "Don't talk about me like I'm not here. Whyn't you go fix Rory here a drink, while the grown-ups get down to business. Check around, make sure you got all your shit packed up. And I mean all of it."

I got up and nearly ran for the stateroom. I picked up my overnight case, looked around, and then headed for the galley. And then Harry's words struck me. Make sure I had *all* my stuff, he'd said.

What about Liam? We couldn't just leave him in the gear locker, could we? But then again, we couldn't very well move him now, not right under Rory's nose.

I ran to the bow of the boat and stood very still outside the gear locker. It was quiet. My stomach lurched. Liam, I decided, would be Rory's problem. Just as soon as I got off this boat and out of this marina. And this state.

I was gathering up a tray with the pitcher of Bloody Marys and some glasses when the phone rang. I grabbed it. "Hello?"

"Hey. Who's this?" a stranger's voice demanded.

I put the pitcher down and took a deep breath. "This is Eloise. I'm Liam's friend."

"Well, this is Doobie. Tell Liam to get his sorry ass out to the airport to pick me up. And tell him I wanna be underway by four o'clock. No excuses."

"Uh, well, Liam isn't here right now," I said. "I'll send Emma, okay?"

"Shit," Doobie said. "I wanted Liam to pick up some stuff for me. Never mind. Tell Emma to get over here. And when Liam comes back, tell him to go to the candy store. We're gonna need a lot of candy on this trip."

59

Weezie

I patted my pocket and felt the magic blue pills. Maybe, I thought, I should take one myself. A chill pill. I could use some chilling. My hands were trembling so much I left the tray and the pitcher in the galley and just carried two full glasses up to the deck.

Rory was studying the sheaf of papers Spencer gave him. I set the glasses down on the table. "All set," I said in a cheery voice.

Harry gave me a questioning look.

"Emma called," I said. "She's going to pick up a friend at the airport. Right away."

Rory signed the papers and pushed them back across the table. "Everything looks fine."

"'Bout damn time," Harry said. "Where's the damned check?"

"Doobie!" I said sharply.

"It's all right," Rory said, chuckling. "I don't blame your husband. It's a lot of money." He reached into his backpack and pulled out a cell phone and an alligator-skin notebook. He put the phone on the tabletop, opened the notebook and extracted a check from it, and handed it over to Spencer.

He held up the phone. "You can call the bank if you like, to check on the availability of the funds. I don't feel comfortable carrying that much cash."

"That won't be necessary," Spencer said, examining the check before handing it to Harry.

"All right?" Spencer asked. His Adam's apple bobbed up and down in agitation.

Harry shrugged, as though he handled multimillion-dollar business transactions every day. "Looks fine to me."

I stood up abruptly. "Then let's go," I announced. "I've got things to do before we leave for Nashville."

Harry held up his hand. "Just a minute." He looked over at Rory. "When were you thinking of taking possession of the *Reefer*?"

"Right now," Rory said, standing up. "I've waited a long time for this. I want to take her out immediately. A shakedown cruise, if you will."

"Right now?" Harry repeated. "We've got a few things we need to clear out. How 'bout you come back in an hour or so? I can get my stuff unloaded—"

"Right now," Rory said, his voice deadly calm, his affable smile long gone. "You've had all morning to clear out your stuff. Now, we've signed the papers. You've got your check." He stuck out his hand, still unsmiling. "Pleasure doing business with you. Any of your belongings you haven't already gotten, I'll pack up and leave with the dockmaster."

"Shit, man," Harry muttered. "Nothing like 'Here's your hat, what's your hurry?'"

"Exactly," Rory said. He walked us to the gangplank. I was just about to follow Harry over to the dock when he clamped a hand on my neck. "Not you, Anya. Doobie, you don't mind if I have a private word with your lovely wife, do you?"

Harry turned around. I felt my knees start to buckle. My eyes were screaming "No! Don't leave me here!" But I couldn't even croak the word no.

"It'll just take a moment or two," Rory said, his voice silky. His fingertips massaged my neck ever so lightly. It felt like a snake wrapping itself around my throat. I wanted to gag.

"Just a minute, then," Harry said reluctantly. "Like she said, we got stuff to do."

Rory turned and led me back to the table where we'd been sitting only moments before. He leaned in so close his lips brushed my neck. "Do you really intend to stay with that burnt-out troglodyte?"

"He's my husband," I managed to gasp.

"Leave him," Rory said. "I want to show you something." He leaned over to get the backpack. In that second, my hand found the magic blue pills in my pocket. I dropped two of them in his half-empty drink, and slid his cell phone into my pocket, willing him not to notice.

When he came up, he was holding a small black-velvet box.

"The deal breaker," he said, extending it to me.

I held my breath and opened the box. Inside was a pair of gorgeous emerald earrings, each emerald surrounded by diamonds.

"What?" I gave him a questioning look. "What's this for?"

"You," he said simply. "A lovely lady should have lovely things." He jerked his head in Harry's direction. "What's he given you? Grief? Humiliation?"

I snapped the lid of the box and handed it back to him. "I can't. He may be an asshole, but he's my asshole."

"You're making a mistake," Rory said. "Don't kid yourself. He'll never change. Addicts don't."

"Maybe," I said.

"How old is he, anyway?" Rory asked, annoyed. "He could be your father."

At that point, I turned my back on him and walked briskly toward the gangplank. Off this boat. Off this dock. Outta here.

When I got to the dock, Harry and Spencer were waiting for me. I turned around. Rory stood on the sundeck watching me. I gave him a finger wave.

He shook his head, but held his glass aloft in a mock salute.

"Cheers!" I called.

He laughed and downed the drink.

"Asshole," I said, under my breath.

"Let's get outta here," Harry said. "It's ten till. I want to get to that bank before he manages to call and close that account."

"I don't think he'll be making any calls," I said, showing them the cell phone I'd just pocketed.

"What about Liam?" Spencer asked.

"Not our problem anymore," Harry said. "You heard me, I tried to get Rory to let me unload him. But he wasn't having it. So let him deal with Liam."

I had another pang of guilt. "What if something happens? He could starve to death in that gear locker. Or suffocate or something."

We were halfway down the dock when we heard the *Reefer*'s diesel engines thrum to life.

"Keep walking," Harry said. "The bank. We've got to get to the bank before he does."

"But Liam!" I said. "Who knows how long Rory will be out before he finds him."

"He'll only be out about a half hour before he runs out of fuel," Harry said. "And then he'll have plenty of time to roam around the boat and find his stowaway."

"How . . . ?"

"I fiddled with the fuel gauge," Harry said. "Can we go now?"

"Well, okay," I said. "But I should tell you I did some fiddling of my own."

"How's that?"

"I slipped some 'ludes in his Bloody Mary."

"No way," Harry said. "I was watching you the whole time."

"I did it when he called me back. He was bending down to get something out of his backpack. I was afraid it was a gun or something. And I had the pills in my pocket. For insurance. It was only a couple. That's when I took the phone too."

Harry chuckled. "Between us, Roy Eugene Moseley is going to have a short, but very strange voyage."

We were almost to the Buick when we saw a battered white Toyota pull into the parking lot. The Toyota passed us and the driver, a woman, gave us a small, furtive nod. The man in the passenger seat had a baseball cap pulled low over his face, and he was wearing dark glasses.

"It's Emma," I said. "And Doobie Bauers."

"Get in the car," Harry said. "We need to beat feet."

Spencer slid into the backseat and I sat up front, riding shotgun with Harry.

"Shame," Spencer said, looking out the rearview window. "I'd love to see what happens next."

"Later," Harry said. "After we get that check deposited in your account."

Five minutes later we were at the Bank of America. "Turn off the engine," Spencer instructed. "She burns oil if you leave her motor running too long."

Harry sighed and rolled down the windows. It was in the high 80s. Perspiration dripped down his face. I was feeling a little moist my ownself.

But Spencer was cool as ice, strolling inside with new pep in his step.

Harry and I sat outside in the car. It was 1:59 by Harry's watch, 1:56 by the clock on the Buick's dashboard. Harry fiddled with the radio, switching stations from gospel to country to oldies to classic rock.

"What did Rory want back there, on the boat?" he asked.

"He wanted me to leave you. He offered me a really nifty pair of emerald and diamond earrings too," I said. "He said you're an addict, and you'll never change."

"That's bullshit," Harry snapped. "People change all the time."

"You asked," I said lightly. "I'm just reporting the conversation."

"He's a professional bullshit artist," Harry said. "A pathological liar, a thief, a con artist. What else did he say?"

"He called you a troglodyte," I said, with a giggle. "And he said you're way too old for me. Hey, Harry, just how old are you?"

He turned and gave me a cold stare. "Not that it matters," I added. "You've got a very youthful spirit."

Five minutes later, Spencer came strolling out of the bank, whistling merrily. He opened the back door and hopped inside. "All done," he announced.

"Really?" I twisted around in the seat. "You're sure? The check's good? And you made it before the two o'clock close of business?"

"Everything's fine and dandy," Spencer said. He handed me a slip of white paper. "There's the deposit slip. I had them wire it to BeBe's account in Savannah. Five million. All nice and legal."

"Sort of," I said.

Harry started the Buick's engine and we drove off.

"Let's just cruise through the parking lot at Bahia Mar," I said. "I'm dying to see what the real Doobie Bauers looks like."

"No way," Harry said, his jaw set. "We are not going anywhere near that marina. What if Reddy already found Liam? What if he's turned right back around to Bahia Mar? We are getting the hell out of Dodge before it gets too hot around here."

BeBe was sitting on her suitcase in front of the office at the Mango Tree, elbows propped on her knees. And right beside her were three more suitcases. She jumped to her feet as soon as we pulled into the parking lot. "What happened? Did you get the money?"

"We did it!" Spencer hollered, jumping out of the car before Harry even had it in park. "By God, we did it. We skinned him good."

"For real?" BeBe squealed. "You got the money? He fell for the whole thing?"

"Hook, line, and sinker," Harry drawled. BeBe fell into his arms. He picked her up and spun her around, and there was a good deal of showy kissing.

"Come on, let's get out of here," BeBe said, picking up her suitcase. "I can't wait to get back to Savannah, and I especially can't wait to see the look on those snotty Arrendales when I kick them out of my house and make them give back my painting."

"And then what?" Harry was loading suitcases into the trunk of the Buick. "What happens after you do all that, BeBe?"

"I get my old life back," she said triumphantly. "Only better. Because I'll have you in it now."

"Oh," Harry said. He looked at his watch. "I guess we'd better hit the road then. We wouldn't want you to miss any of your old life, now, would we?"

60

"One last thing," Weezie announced. "You guys owe me. You owe me and Spencer."

"What's that?" I asked, turning around in the seat to face her.

"We've got to go back to Bahia Mar," she insisted. "We can't just leave without finding out what happens next. BeBe, just as we were leaving, Emma was pulling into the parking lot. With the real Doobie."

"What?" I glanced over at Harry. "Is that right?"

"Yup," Harry said. "Doobie ran away from rehab yesterday and flew into Fort Lauderdale this morning. Anya called to tell Emma he was on his way, and to have her tell Liam that under no circumstances was he to let Doobie take the *Reefer Madness* out."

"And then Doobie himself called," Weezie put in excitedly. "I almost died when I picked up the phone and he said he was at the airport."

"Didn't he wonder who you were?" I asked.

"I just told him I was a friend of Liam's," Weezie said. "I told him Liam was out running errands, but I'd have Emma pick him up at the airport. And then Doobie said to tell Liam to make sure he went to the candy store, 'cause they were gonna need plenty of candy for their run over to Bimini. According to Liam, that was Doobie's code to tell him to make a drug buy."

"Anya's on her way down here too," Harry added. "Her plane should have landed by now."

"The stuff's about to hit the fan," Granddad said. "Love to be a fly on that wall."

"That's why we've got to go back to the marina," Weezie repeated. "I have just got to find out what's going on."

"We can ask Emma," I said. "She can fill us in later. After we get back to Savannah. But we are not risking everything by going back to that marina."

Harry looked over at me.

"What?"

"Weezie's right. She put herself out on a limb for you. She got pawed by Liam and hit on by Roy Eugene. All out of friendship for you. This won't take long. We can just cruise by and see what's happening. Don't you think you owe her that much?"

Granddad gave me a not so subtle nod and a wink.

"Okay," I said with exaggerated reluctance. "I've been cooped up in that motel room for two days now. Let's go check it out. But if there's any sign of Reddy, Harry, don't even slow down."

"Don't worry," Harry said. "None of us is anxious to see him again."

"He did buy me some beautiful earrings," Weezie said. "Emeralds and diamonds."

"Probably phony," Harry put in. "Like everything else about him."

When we got to the parking lot at Bahia Mar, things were jumping. At the marina entrance, there were three Fort Lauderdale police cruisers parked with blue lights flashing, along with an assortment of other cars, and vans equipped with satellite television thingies. A helicopter hovered overhead.

"Wow," Weezie said, reading the logos on the vans. "CBS, ABC, NBC, and FoxTV."

"Look," Granddad said, pointing out the window. "That fella in the orange T-shirt and ball cap. He's the one we saw in Emma's car."

"It's Doobie," Harry said. "Gotta be."

The real Doobie Bauers was surrounded by uniformed police officers, and a horde of camera- and microphone-toting reporters. He was talking and making wild gestures in the general direction of the dock. As we watched, a cab pulled up to the entrance, and a petite blond woman hopped out and made a beeline for the crowd. Running right along behind her was a middle-aged man dressed all in black, with a gray goatee.

"Roll down the windows," Weezie begged. "That's gotta be Anya. I wonder who that is with her? Come on, roll 'em down. I want to hear what happens next."

Harry rolled all the windows down, but we were still too far away.

"Can't hear a damn thing," Granddad complained. He opened the car door. "I'm goin' over there."

"Me too," Weezie announced, opening the other door.

Harry looked at me and shrugged. "Just for a minute," he said, jamming a ball cap on his head. "Nobody here knows us from Adam. We're just interested bystanders."

"And unindicted co-conspirators," I muttered, but I couldn't resist either. I twisted my hair into a ponytail and poked it up under Weezie's abandoned straw hat, and donned my own sunglasses.

"Wait up," I called to Harry.

We stood at the far edge of the crowd. I'm short anyway, but it was nearly impossible to see through the mass of cameramen and reporters.

"What's going on?" I finally asked a teenager who had a minicam trained on the action.

"That old white guy in the orange shirt is telling the cops that somebody stole his yacht," the kid said, lowering the camera. "He's supposed to be some famous rock star, I heard on my police scanner at home. That's why I came over here. Thought maybe I could shoot some footage to sell to *COPs* or *Hard Copy*. But, dude, he's like, way old."

"What's his name?" I asked, all innocence.

A young woman in a T-shirt with a Z-103 Zoo-Crew logo shook

her head. "Doobie Bauers. He used to be in Meat Loaf. That's why my producer sent me over here. But c'mon. Meat Loaf? That is so yesterday." Her voice dripped disgust. "Waste of time."

I could hear a high-pitched voice now, berating the officers. I stood on my tiptoes to get a better look, but all I could see was the backs of reporters' heads. I circled around and snaked my way through the pack. Finally, I wedged myself in between a tall black guy with a long boom mike and a short brunette in a cheesy yellow linen suit that screamed recent college grad. She had a notebook and was scribbling like mad.

"What are you people doing, standing around with your thumbs up your ass?" Anya screamed, getting right in a cop's face. "A crime has been committed. That boat is worth seven million dollars. And you're just standing around."

I could hear Doobie saying something, but couldn't get the gist of it.

"What's going on?" I asked the reporter with the notebook. "Who's that woman? What's she been saying?"

"Name's Anya Bauers," the girl said, still scribbling. "And that's her husband. Doobie. Spelled D-O-O-B-I-E. He apparently ran away from the Betty Ford Center and showed up here today. She followed him down. Sort of an intervention, I guess. But now his yacht's been stolen, and she's screamin' at the cops to do something."

"Who's the guy in black?" I asked. Goatee man had an arm around Doobie's shoulder, obviously trying to calm him down, but the more goatee talked, the more agitated Doobie became.

"Somebody said that's his therapist," the reporter said. "But then somebody else said they think it's his business manager."

"I heard it's his nutritionist," a crew-cut guy in a white dress shirt and striped tie said. "His wife told the cops her husband is suffering from an electrolyte imbalance, and that's why he's been acting erratic."

Another reporter, this one wearing a headset, turned to the reporter with the boom mike. "Hey, Jack," he said excitedly. "That's the desk back at the station. The Coast Guard just radioed in that they intercepted the missing yacht, beached on a sandbar a couple miles out. Get this, the name of the boat is the *Reefer Madness*. They're towing it over to the Coast Guard station."

The little newspaper chick chortled and scribbled madly.

"Oh, man," the headset reporter said. "They've radioed to have ATF meet 'em at the dock. Apparently they found a huge stash of drugs onboard. There were warrants out on the guy who stole the yacht. They even found the boat's first mate, tied up and handcuffed in a closet. Says he was taken hostage. Let's go. I wanna get over there and get some footage of the boat before the feds get everything roped off and locked down."

I quietly inched my way out and around the crowd until I found Harry, chatting with a cameraman beside the FoxTV van.

"Hey," he said, glancing over at me. "Did you hear? They found the *Reefer Madness*. Apparently the guy who was stealing it ran aground on a sandbar. He ran out of gas. What a loser!"

"Yeah," I said with a sigh. "Don't you just love a happy ending?"

61

I must have dozed off somewhere between Daytona and St. Augustine. When Harry shook me awake, we were just crossing the bridge over the Back River. It was dark, and I could hear Granddad's soft snoring from the backseat.

"What time is it?" I asked, not bothering to suppress a yawn.

"Nearly one A.M.," he said quietly. "I dropped Weezie off at her place, but you didn't even move a muscle."

"Sorry," I said. "I should have offered to drive, but I was so tired. I don't think I've slept more than three or four hours at a stretch in the last couple days."

"It's all right," he said. "Listen. I'm going to let you drop me off at Mikey Shannon's place at Tybee Terrace, if you don't mind."

"Mikey's? Why? You're not coming back to the Breeze with me?"

"I'll be by later," Harry said. "Mikey's been keeping Jeeves for me. I called him earlier and he said he'd just leave the door unlocked for me. Cheri and her daughter are probably sound asleep in my unit, so I'll bunk on Mikey's sofa tonight, and spend some time with Jeeves in the morning. Poor old hound must think I've abandoned him."

"Okay," I said slowly. "Sounds like you've got everything all worked out."

"It's late," Harry said. He glanced in the rearview mirror at Granddad and chuckled. "That Spencer, he is really a piece of work, you know that?"

"I do now," I said. "He likes you too. A lot."

"'Cause I paid for his Scotch," he said.

"More than that," I said, reaching for Harry's hand. "He told me he approves." I blushed and looked away. "You know. Of us. He told me not to screw it up this time."

"Nice of him," Harry said. He moved his hand to flip the turn signal.

"So, this is it," he said, turning right into the single-story concrete-block bungalow village that made up Tybee Terrace. He pulled up behind a unit where a red bicycle was chained to a bike rack, and put the Buick in park.

Harry jumped out of the driver's seat, went around to the trunk and got his suitcase. He came back around to my side of the car. I rolled the window down and leaned out. The air was soft and sweet, and there was no traffic, and I thought I could hear the roll of the waves on the beach across Butler Avenue. Almost home, I thought.

"So," I said, turning my face up toward his. He bent down and kissed me, his lips barely grazing mine. "I'll see you tomorrow?"

"Yeah," he said. "Absolutely. See you tomorrow."

I watched him lope off around the back of the cottage, and when I heard the bang of a screen door, I scooted over behind the steering wheel and drove on down the beach to the Breeze Inn.

The NO VACANCY sign was lit up, which made me smile. When, I wondered, was the last time, other than St. Patrick's Day, the Breeze Inn had had a full house?

"Granddad," I said, going around to the backseat. "Granddad. Wake up. We're home."

"I knew that," he said, sitting up. "I was trying to give you kids some privacy."

"Turns out we didn't need it," I said, sliding in beside him on the backseat. "So what about it? Can you drive back to town tonight? Or do you want to sleep here?"

"Home," he said simply. "Lorena's expecting me." He got out of the car and stood gingerly, groaning as he straightened his back.

"I'm too old for this foolishness," he said.

"Never!" I told him. "You are the man. You're my hero."

He planted a quick kiss on the top of my head. "I'm proud of you too, young lady. I always have been. Of all the grandkids, I think you're the most like me. You've got a good head for business. You know what you want, and you're not afraid to go after it."

"I wish that were true," I told him. "We both know I'm a big screwup. But thanks anyway. Thanks for believing in me. And for being there when I needed you."

"Anytime," Granddad said. He opened the trunk and handed me my suitcase.

"Tell Grandmama I'll call her this week," I said. Then I blew him a kiss, and he slowly backed the Buick out of the parking lot and pointed it toward home.

The light was on in the manager's unit, so I decided to see if Cheri was still up, to let her know I was back.

Cheri answered the door before I had a chance to ring the bell. She was barefoot, dressed in an oversize black T-shirt that said "My Other Car's a Hawg," and holding a lit cigarette and an open can of Michelob.

"Hey there!" she said brightly. "I saw the headlights of the car and saw you coming in. Everything go okay down in Florida?"

"Yeah. Great," I said, wondering why I didn't feel so great if everything had gone so great.

"You found the guy who ripped you off?" she asked.

"We did," I said.

She stepped out onto the front porch, and looked around. "Where's Harry?"

"He's spending the night at Mikey Shannon's. Didn't want to disturb you this late at night."

"Hah!" she brayed. "Harry Sorrentino knows I don't go to bed till three or four in the morning. All those years of bartending, I can't get used to a nine-to-five kind of life."

"And he wanted to see Jeeves," I added.

"Right." She nodded.

"Everything go okay around here?" I asked. "Any problems?"

"None I couldn't handle," she said. "Y'all have got the place fixed up so cute, it's like playing house. Me and my daughter have had a ball running it."

"And you're full up!" I said. "I can't believe it."

"Yeah," she said. "Bunch of schoolteachers come down here from Atlanta for the weekend. I never seen women party as hard as they have. They've had themselves a good old time."

"You didn't rent my place, I hope."

"Nope," Cheri said. "I figured you'd be back before Monday, so I just left it vacant. Stephanie cleaned it good for you, though. We think it's the cutest unit out here. Hope you don't mind us taking a peek."

"Not at all," I assured her. "I can't thank you enough for everything you've done here. Harry said you'd be great, and it turns out he was right."

"Well," she said. "Harry's a good friend."

"Hey," I said. "Would you be interested in a job working here?"

She took a drag on her cigarette. "Might be."

"I desperately need help. And I can afford to hire it now. I could use you in housekeeping, and probably working the front desk too."

"I can do that," Cheri said proudly. Then she frowned.

"Wait a minute. When Harry called, he said you'd be selling this place soon as you got back."

"He told you that? What else did he say?"

"Just that you were wanting your old life back. You know, in town, and all that. He said you didn't wanna mess with nothin' as rinky-dink as runnin' an old motel out at Tybee."

"It's an inn," I corrected her. "And I never said Tybee was rinky-dink. Anyway, it'll take me a while to get all my affairs straightened out. In the meantime, I need help."

Cheri stuck out her hand. "You got it. When do I start?"

"You already have," I said. And we shook on it.

My room was, as Cheri promised, empty and neat as a pin. I stood in the doorway for a minute to take it in. It was even smaller than I'd remembered. But the enameled floor was shiny from waxing, the bed was made up with snowy white sheets and coverlet, and the place smelled of Pine Sol and bleach. Cheri had opened the window in the kitchen nook, and the cotton curtains rippled in the breeze coming off the ocean. I set my suitcase down and flopped onto the bed.

Mattresses, I thought. I would buy all new, high-quality mattresses for every room in the Breeze. My guests would never again have to endure the cheap, wafer-thin mattresses we'd slept on at the Mango Tree. I'd buy new linens too. Velvety-thick oversize bath towels. Down pillows. High-thread-count sheets. The ones we had now had probably been bought when the Breeze was built. Televisions too, I thought, drowsily, with cable hookups. And DVD players. We could keep a small library of movies in the office. And while we were at it, I'd buy an espresso machine for the office. To go with Daniel's muffins. And fresh fruit. We'd put fresh fruit baskets in every room. There would be nothing rinky-dink about the Breeze Inn, I vowed. If. If I decided not to sell. If Harry were here to help me run it. If Harry were here. . . .

62

But Harry wasn't there. By the time I got up the next morning, his station wagon was gone from the parking lot, so I knew he'd been by to pick it up. I hung around the office Sunday morning, catching up on paperwork and dealing with guests during check-out, but there was still no sign of him. I paid Cheri, and her daughter, and we agreed on a schedule that would allow them to take turns as house-keepers.

At noon, I placed the call to Sandra Findley.

"Sandra? It's BeBe Loudermilk."

"BeBe!" she exclaimed. "Where are you? It's been all over the news down here. You did it, didn't you? You caught that son of a bitch!"

"Not me," I said modestly. "The Coast Guard. All we did was work it so the Coast Guard *could* catch him. Actually, I'm back in Savannah."

"And the money? What about the money?"

"I think you'll be pleased," I said. "Where shall I send it?"

"Unbelievable," she kept saying, while giving me her banking information. "You really did it. I can't believe you conned a professional con artist."

"I had a lot of help," I told her. "And some dumb luck. And of course, without your persistence, none of this probably would have happened."

"Wait till I tell my brother," Sandra crowed. "Hey! You never did come by for that drink. I owe you that and a lot more, now."

"Another time," I told her. "For now, I've got a lot of business to catch up on."

By two o'clock, I'd drunk a whole pot of coffee, read the entire Savannah and Atlanta newspapers, had a leisurely phone chat with my grandmother, and made out a lengthy, and extravagant, shopping list.

At three, I could stand it no longer. I got in the Lexus and cruised past Doc's Bar. No sign of Jeeves, no sign of Harry. I checked Mikey Shannon's unit at Tybee Terrace where I'd dropped Harry the night before, but the station wagon wasn't there.

Screw it, I thought. I'd drive into town, treat myself to a late lunch, and drive past my house on West Jones, just to reassure myself it was still standing.

I meant to go straight downtown. But a funny thing happened when I hit the U.S. 80 bridge, and the Lexus, apparently with a mind of its own, made the turn into Marsden Marina. I didn't know whether to be glad or concerned that Harry's car wasn't there.

The *Jitterbug* was there, however, mounted on a trailer, with a FOR SALE sign on the bow. On an impulse, I pulled the Lexus up beside it, got out, and walked around.

It was just a boat, as far as I could see. Certainly nowhere near as shiny and impressive as the yachts lined up along the dock at the Bahia Mar. What was it about boats, I wondered, that made men so crazy for them? Reddy had been just as compulsive about owning a Sea Urchin as Harry was about regaining custody of the *Jitterbug*. Both of them had been willing to lie, steal, and cheat to get their hands on their respective obsessions.

I let my hand trail over the faded yellow fiberglass hull of the *Jitterbug*. How long, I wondered, would it take Harry to buy her back? He'd have the $4,800 I owed him, just as soon as he showed up at the Breeze to collect it. But from what he'd said, that wouldn't go nearly far enough toward paying off his debt to the marina owners.

Why not? I thought. Why not pay it off myself? I could certainly afford it now. And Harry was the reason I could do that. He'd gone down to Fort Lauderdale with no real promise of any kind of reward, and performed like a champ. If it hadn't been for Harry, I knew we never could have scammed a world-class scammer like Reddy. I owed Harry. I owed him big time.

I found Tricia Marsden at a desk in the marina office, elbow-deep in paperwork, her fingers nimbly racing over the keyboard of an adding machine.

"Hi there," I said, pushing open the screen door.

"Do something for you?" She didn't glance up from her calculations, which gave me a little time to get a good look. Tricia wasn't what I'd expected. A mass of dark wavy hair had been swept off her neck and into a ponytail. She was trim, tan, wearing a white open-collared shirt and a pair of pink-framed glasses that slid down her nose.

"I'm interested in the *Jitterbug*."

That stopped her cold. She looked up. I stared. Harry had told me that Tricia Marsden was a stone-cold bitch, a shrewd businesswoman. He'd neglected to mention that she was stunningly beautiful, with bright blue eyes, thick black lashes, and a full, pouty mouth.

"Interested how?" she asked.

"Interested in buying it," I said. "What's the price?"

She smiled. "You're kidding, right?"

"Not at all. It's for sale, right?"

"Oh, yes," she said, "$32,500." She raised an eyebrow, waiting to see how I'd react.

"Fine," I said, reaching for my checkbook.

"Fine?"

"That's right."

She frowned. "Can I ask what you want with a fishing boat like the *Jitterbug*? She's not exactly a sport cruiser, you know."

"I know." I looked up at her. "Do I make it out to Marsden Marina, or to you personally?"

"I've got a stamp," she said. "You don't want to have her checked out by a mechanic, anything like that?"

"Won't be necessary," I said, filling in the check. "I'm told it runs just fine."

"Who told you that?" she asked, standing up.

"Harry Sorrentino."

She sat back down again. "How do you know Harry?"

"We're friends," I said, tearing the check out and handing it to her.

She took the check and studied it. "BeBe Loudermilk. Aren't you the woman who bought the Breeze Inn?"

"I am."

"So, actually, you're his boss."

"And his friend," I said.

"A very good friend, apparently."

"Just settling a debt," I said, turning toward the door. "I'm going to take the FOR SALE sign off the *Jitterbug* now, if you don't mind. And I'll tell Harry he can pick it up, when? At his convenience?"

"The trailer's mine," she said, the pout turning sour.

"Is it for sale?" I asked.

"Not to him."

I turned back around. "Look. What is your problem with Harry? I know he's owed you money, but I should think a lot of other fishermen owed you money too, after the bad weather we had last year. You've been paid. Isn't it time to get over it?"

"My problem with Harry?" She shook her head. "Get over it? Why don't you ask him what my problem is with him."

"He told me you're not exactly friends."

"Not exactly." She laughed. "That's one way to put it. Did he happen to mention to you that we were married?"

"No," I said quietly. "He didn't mention that."

"He wouldn't," she said bitterly. "It was a long time ago. And it's not something he likes to discuss. But then, that's Harry."

"I'll let him make the arrangements to take delivery on the *Jitter-bug*," I said.

"You do that. And tell him if it's not out of here within the next twenty-four hours, I'm going to start charging him for storage."

"Bitch," I said, under my breath. I let the door slam behind me. I yanked the FOR SALE sign off the boat and flung it onto the backseat of my car, and I sped out of the marina parking lot, in the general direction of downtown Savannah.

None of your business, I told myself as I tooled down Victory Drive, oblivious to the pink and purple beauty of the head-high azaleas in full bloom. She was married to him a long time ago, I rationalized as I turned north toward downtown on Drayton Street.

There is something very wrong here, I was thinking when I turned onto West Jones. I'd told Harry all about my three unfortunate marriages. He'd been sympathetic, even understanding, but he'd failed to mention his own past with the beautiful and bitchy Tricia Marsden.

Holy shit! I stopped the car in the middle of the block, right in front of my town house. Or, technically, Steve and Gretchen Arrendale's town house now. I had to stop, because a moving van had the street blocked. The Arrendales' front door was open, and men in white coveralls were busily trundling furniture out of the house and into the back of the van.

I jumped out of the Lexus and ran over to the sidewalk. There was a FOR SALE sign propped up in the Arrendales' parlor window. And a matching one in the window of my town house.

"Hey," I called, running after the two men who were coming out of the Arrendales' with a massively ugly pseudo-Georgian mahogany china cabinet. "What's going on here?"

"Moving," said the man on the dumb end of the cabinet. He had a red do-rag wrapped around his head, and forearms the size of tree trunks.

"The Arrendales? Where are they going?"

They got to the van and started up the metal loading ramp. I followed them right up and into the van, which was half full of cardboard boxes and furniture wrapped with padded moving quilts.

"New house out at Turner's Rock," one of the guys said, grunting as he let down his end of the cabinet.

"Are they here? Are they still in the house?"

"No, thank you, Jesus," said Do-Rag. "She's already over at the new house. So she can supervise," he said, making a face about the supervise part.

I looked around the van, searching for the Maybelle Johns painting. *My* Maybelle Johns painting.

"Have you already packed up all the art in the house?" I asked. "I'm looking for a painting. It's an oil painting of a little girl."

"*She* packed up all the art," said the guy in the plain white baseball cap. "Doesn't trust us ignorant apes to touch her valuable art collection."

"But the painting of the little girl. Did you see it? Before she packed everything?"

Do-Rag shrugged. Baseball Cap shrugged. "House was full of pictures. They all look the same to me," Do-Rag said.

I climbed down out of the van, then darted inside the open door at the Arrendales'.

The place was a mess. Cardboard boxes were stacked everywhere. Rugs were rolled up, furniture was padded and taped. The walls were bare. I ran upstairs to double-check, but it had been cleared first.

When I got downstairs, I went out the kitchen door, into the courtyard garden. I let myself out the wrought-iron gate and into the lane that backed the town houses, and then let myself in through the gate that opened onto *my* garden. At *my* town house. I hauled an empty trash can over to the kitchen window and climbed up to peer inside. Empty. The kitchen was as empty as it was the last time I'd seen it.

I climbed down and went out to the Lexus. I picked up my cell phone and called James Foley's cell. No answer. I called the office, just in case. Still no answer. Out of desperation, I called Weezie.

"Hey," she said, answering after the first ring. "Are you out shopping with all your ill-gotten gains?"

"No," I said, my voice grim. "I drove over to West Jones Street. To make sure it hadn't been knocked down. But it's worse than that."

"What?"

"It's been sold again. To the Arrendales. And now they're selling it and their house."

"Why? Where are they going?"

"The movers are there right now. They said they've bought a big new house out at Turner's Rock. But they haven't seen my Maybelle Johns. I need to talk to your uncle, right away, but I can't get hold of him. Do you know where he is?"

"As a matter of fact, I do. James and Jonathan went on some kind of field trip with the historical society, to Charleston. Mama said they're not due back until tonight."

"This is a nightmare," I said. "And I can't wake up."

"Just relax," Weezie advised. "James will get it all straightened out. Go back out to the beach and kick back and relax. You remember relaxing, don't you?"

"Only vaguely."

I decided to skip the late lunch. Ditto shopping. I wasn't in the mood. And as I drove back toward the beach, I could see charcoal-edged clouds skittering across the horizon. So much for a walk on the beach.

Harry's beat-up station wagon was parked in front of the office at the Breeze. I exhaled slowly. Relax. Kick back. And for God's sake don't ask why he never mentioned being married before.

63

Harry was sitting at the kitchen table in the office, fiddling with the same outboard motor he'd been fiddling with since the day we'd met.

When I walked into the office, Jeeves hopped down from his armchair, barked a cheerful greeting, and scampered over to allow me the privilege of scratching his ears.

Harry looked up, but he didn't offer to let me scratch his ears, so I just lavished that much more attention on his dog, who didn't argue about it.

"You're back," I said. Duh.

"Yeah," he said, putting down the screwdriver he'd been using on the engine, and wiping his hands on a greasy rag. "You too, huh?"

This was some scintillating conversation we were having. Like Hepburn and Tracy. Only not.

"I went into town, to check on things," I said, sitting down at the table across from him.

He held up a bottle of beer that had been sitting near his elbow. "Want one?"

"No thanks," I said.

"How were things in town?" He went back to fiddling with the motor.

"Not too good," I admitted. "Those snotty Arrendales, the ones who bought my painting from Roy Eugene Moseley? They're moving. Their house and mine both have sold signs out front. And my painting is already gone. I looked."

"Tough," Harry said, sipping his beer and looking quizzically at an unidentifiable hunk of iron that he'd unscrewed from the motor.

"Tough? These people . . . these *carpetbaggers* have moved, they've moved my painting. And my house has been sold again."

"Buy the house back," Harry said. "You can afford it now. And buy a new painting. You can afford that too."

"We're not talking about just any old painting here," I said. "We're talking about a Maybelle Johns portrait of my aunt. It's a family heirloom, Harry. The artist—a famous Savannah artist—won't be doing any more portraits. And my aunt—it was painted when she was just a little girl—is long dead."

"Oh," he said. Not "Oh, shit." Or "Oh my God, how awful." Just "Oh." More like, "Oh, so what?" or "Oh, big, effin' deal."

"What about your house?" he said, sitting back in his chair, finally giving me his full attention. "Do you know who bought it this time?"

"I have no clue. I tried to call James Foley to see what he knows, but Weezie says he's out of town until late tonight."

"So now what?" he asked.

"I wait," I said, with an exaggerated sigh. "Waiting sucks. I'm no good at it."

"You're a woman of action," he observed.

"You say that like it's a bad thing."

"Not bad. Just true."

I stood up abruptly. "It's just that I hate being a victim. I hate feeling powerless, like I have no control over events shaping my life. *Major* events," I added.

"Nobody likes that feeling," Harry said.

He was trying to be reasonable, damn him. "But everybody, at some point in their life, does. We just have to deal with it, try to make the best of a bad situation," he said.

"Is that what you're doing?" It came out sounding nasty and hateful.

"Who? Me? I'm just trying to get this damned motor running. Mikey found an old metal johnboat washed up in the creek, and if I can get this motor running, we can do a little crabbing and shrimping now that the weather's turned."

"What about the *Jitterbug*?" I asked.

He looked surprised. "What about it?"

I reached in my pocket, brought out the set of keys Tricia Marsden had given me, and tossed them in his direction. He caught them in midair, looked down at them, and then back at me.

"Where'd you get the keys to my boat?"

"Tricia Marsden gave them to me," I said. "Interesting woman, Tricia."

"Interesting how?"

"She's spectacular looking. Not the kind of woman you expect to find running a marina."

"Is she?" He shrugged. "Not to me."

"She's gorgeous." I stated it as a fact. "And you must have thought so too, at some point in your life."

He narrowed his eyes. "Is there a point to this conversation we're having about Tricia Marsden?"

"She can't stand you."

"The feeling's mutual."

"And yet you were married to her."

"Jesus!" he said, jumping up. He paced to the other side of the room. Jeeves scampered after him, his ears twitching in agitation, but Harry ignored him, pacing back in the other direction, with the dog right at his heels.

"What were you doing messing around with Tricia?" he demanded, stopping directly in front of me.

"I went to the marina on the spur of the moment," I said, backing away from the intensity in his eyes. "I didn't plan to. I just did. I was headed into town, and I saw the turnoff for the marina, and I turned in. I thought I'd see what it would take to get the *Jitterbug* back for you."

"You decided that. On the spur of the moment."

"Yes," I said defiantly. "I owe you. I owe you a lot. For going to Florida with me. For getting my money back from Reddy. It wouldn't have happened without you."

"You owe me exactly $4,800," Harry said. "Not a dime more. That was our deal."

"I disagree," I said softly. "I paid off the boat. It's yours again. But Tricia told me to tell you she wants it out of the marina right away. She says she'll start charging you storage fees if you don't move it within twenty-four hours. And she won't sell you the trailer it's sitting on. She really hates your guts, Harry."

He went into the bathroom and closed the door.

Now what?

I heard the toilet flushing, then water running. Five minutes later, he came out of the bathroom and sat back down at the table and started fiddling with the damned motor again. If I could have picked it up and flung it out the door, I would have.

"Harry?" I sat back down across from him. I took the screwdriver out of his hand, and put it in my lap for safekeeping.

He put both palms down flat on the tabletop. "I really wish you hadn't gone to the marina today."

"But I did."

"What do you expect me to say?"

"How 'bout, 'Thanks, BeBe.' Or maybe, 'Did I mention I used to be married to Tricia Marsden? It's a funny story.' Or I don't know, maybe you could just talk to me and not act like we didn't start some kind of relationship thing down in Florida. I would deeply appreciate it if you would say any of the above."

He picked up the bottle of beer and emptied it.

"It's not a funny story," he said flatly. "It's not even interesting. But since you insist, here it is. Tricia and I were married for about ten minutes, several years ago. I don't talk about it, and I try not to think about it, because it represents a really screwed-up time in my life. I was friends with her old man, Jimmy. Tricia and I had known each other for years. When Jimmy got sick with cancer, he was worried about what would happen to her, after he died. Her mother split when she was just a kid. So we got married. Bad idea. Really, really bad idea. We fought about everything. And then we split up. It was the first good idea we'd had."

"What did you fight about?" I asked. "And why does she still hate you?"

"I told you," Harry said. "Everything. Anything. Why do you care?"

"I care about you," I said, crossing my arms over my chest. "Remember?"

He looked away.

"We wanted different things. After Jimmy died, Tricia had all these big plans. To expand the marina, build condos, a restaurant, a hotel, all of it. And she thought I should want that too. But I didn't. She thought that because I'd gone to law school, I should be a lawyer. But I didn't want that either. I'm a fisherman. It's what I'm good at. It's what I enjoy. She's still pissed about it. And I don't give a damn. Satisfied?"

"No," I said. "What about us? You've been avoiding me ever since we got back to Savannah. What's that all about?"

"I don't know," he said, running his hands through his hair. "I feel like . . . I feel like we're going down that same road I went down with *her*. I do care about you. Honest to God, I do. You're not like any woman I've ever known before. You're bossy, and funny, and infuriating, and sexy, and one minute I feel like decking you, and the next minute—"

I got up and went around the table and sat in his lap. I wrapped my arms around his neck. "And the next minute, what?"

He kissed me. And then he groaned. "Noo. This is not going to work."

"Why not?" I kissed him back. I nibbled at his ear, and whispered,

"I'm not like Tricia. I don't want you to be anything you're not. You can fish, or shrimp, or herd goats for all I care. Just as long as you let me do what I want."

He shook his head. "That's just it. We want different things. You've told me a million times, you want your old life back. I know what your old life was like. You're like that Billy Joel song, you're an uptown girl. You want the big house in town, and your restaurant and the clothes and jewelry and parties and all the stuff that goes with it. And I don't. I'm happy right here at the Breeze, just as it is. I'm happy running the *Jitterbug,* fishing, and having a beer at Doc's whenever I feel like it. It won't work, BeBe."

He stood up and dumped me unceremoniously onto the floor.

I stood up slowly, dusting the seat of my pants.

"That is just the biggest bunch of crap I ever heard, Harry Sorrentino!" I cried. "How do you know what I want? And how do you know what will make me happy, when you won't even take the time to find out if *you* make me happy?"

But he wasn't listening. He went to the closet and started pulling clothes off the hangers, throwing them into the still-unpacked suitcase he'd left open on his bed.

"Where are you going?" I demanded. "Don't tell me you're running away from home."

"I'm checking out," he said, his voice tense. "I can't stay here anymore. You don't need me anyway. You've got Cheri and Stephanie. They can work the desk. Until you sell the place to those developers."

I marched over to the bed and sat on top of the suitcase and folded my arms over my chest. "Nuh-uh. No. I am not letting this happen. I won't let you leave like this. I promised Granddad I wouldn't screw it up this time. And I'm not."

His voice was tight. "I don't want to do it this way. But you've got me backed into a corner. There are some things you just can't control, BeBe. I'm going now. There's a unit next to Mikey's coming vacant at Tybee Terrace. Just leave my stuff here for now. I'll come back and pack it all up when you're not around."

"Just like that?" I asked, watching him go.

"Yeah," he said. "I gotta go get my boat moved." Then he turned abruptly. I threw myself down on the bed and closed my eyes. I wouldn't watch him go. I couldn't. I heard the door slam. Then a moment later, I heard it open again.

"Harry?" I sat up.

"Forgot something," he said. I watched in disbelief as he strode over to the kitchen table and hoisted the boat motor onto his shoulder. He left again, without a word. I heard the door slam again, and then a sad whine. Jeeves sat erect on his haunches, ears quivering, black button eyes glittering with unspoken sadness.

I jumped up and gathered the dog in my arms, nestling my face in his fur.

The door opened. Harry, chagrined, put out his arms and Jeeves leaped into them.

He closed the door, and I heard the station wagon's engine cough and start up.

I ran out onto the porch, enraged by the injustice of it all. "And your little dog too!" I screamed.

A kid riding by on his bike slowed, then pedaled furiously away.

64

James Foley was sporting a Hollywood tan and an expensive-looking new silk-blend sport coat. His old oversize eighties-era eye-glasses—the ones that always made him look like a younger version of Mister Magoo—had been replaced with tragically hip new frames. He leaned back in his office chair and guzzled a bottle of spring water.

"You've changed," I said, looking him up and down. "Is that Jonathan's doing?"

He blushed. "And Janet's. The two of them went through my closet and purged it of everything except the tweed sport coat I bought before I entered the seminary. They said it's been out of style so long, it's come back in."

"I liked you better when you were sweet and geeky," I said. "You were unique. Gay, and yet hopelessly clueless."

"Yes, well." He coughed and tapped the open file folder on his desktop. "I called Steve Arrendale this morning, right after I talked to you."

"What did he say?" I asked, leaning forward in my chair. "Where's the painting? Will he sell it back to me? Why did they move? And how did my house get sold again?"

"One question at a time," James said, laughing. "First of all, the Arrendales have your Maybelle Johns painting. I'm sorry, BeBe, but Arrendale says he has no intention of giving it back to you."

"I'll buy it," I said fiercely. "It's my painting, James."

He held up one hand. "We'll get back to the painting in a minute. As to why the Arrendales have moved, it has to do with Mrs. Arrendale's pregnancy."

"Gretchen," I said bitterly. "Social-climbing carpetbagger."

"They've recently learned that she's expecting triplets," James said.

"Appropriate," I said. "The bitch is having a litter. I hope they all have colic. Simultaneously."

"Tsk-tsk," James tsk-tsked. "Gretchen Arrendale is currently unable to walk up stairs. And as you know, both your town house and theirs have all the bedrooms on the upper floors."

"That explains why they're selling their place, but why was my house being sold again?"

"The Arrendales had actually bought your house from St. Andrews Holdings," James said. "They'd even started knocking through the walls that separate the town houses. But then they found out about the babies, and decided they needed something more modern, and convenient for a family with three infants. They found a spec house being built in that new community out at Turner's Rock, bought it, and put both town houses on the market last week."

"So, I could buy back my house?" I asked. "And theirs too? I wouldn't have to live next door to the Arrendales anymore?"

"I think they'll entertain any reasonable offer. Jonathan says the talk around town is that their finances are overextended right now."

I sat back and let that sink in. The Arrendales, bless their status-grubbing little hearts, were offering me what I'd wanted. My house. And if James was correct, I could probably name my price. I had the money. I could do it. So why wasn't I jumping on the bandwagon here?

"I just want the painting of my aunt Alice," I said. "That's the most important thing."

"Since when?" James asked, looking over the rims of his stylish new glasses. I was pleased to see he hadn't done anything about the crow's-feet. Thank God for that.

"Since right now," I said. "There are other houses, as somebody pointed out to me last night."

"Other paintings too?" James asked.

"Not like mine," I said. "Look. Can we use the town houses as a bargaining chip? Tell the Arrendales I'll buy my house and theirs—for their asking price—if the Maybelle Johns painting of my aunt is included in the deal."

"I'll ask," James promised.

"If she sells me back the painting, I'll see that Gretchen gets invited to be on the Telfair Ball committee," I said rashly.

"I'll mention that," James said.

"Speaking of the unspeakable Arrendales," I said, "what kind of progress have you made with our injunction against Sandcastle Realty?"

"The judge granted our motion for a temporary restraining order," James said.

"That happened before I left town," I reminded him.

"There's been an interesting development while you were gone," he said. "I told you the Arrendales' personal finances are stretched thin, but I've also heard that the money people behind Sandcastle Realty are getting antsy about having so much money tied up in a project that's in limbo."

"Good," I said, smiling. "Excellent."

"They've authorized me to make you what I think is a pretty interesting offer," James said.

"Offer away."

"They'll pay you $2.6 million to walk away from your claim to the Breeze Inn."

"That much? For real?"

James nodded. "Roy Eugene Moseley paid $650,000 of your money for the place. They're offering to quadruple that, and to forgive the option money they paid Moseley. But they want an answer immediately. Ideally, they could finish construction of the first units before the end of summer. The meter's running, BeBe."

I stood up and walked over to the window behind James's desk. The sun was shining and it made even the greasy industrial water of the Savannah River look green and inviting.

A chunky black tugboat was chugging past on the river. From the name on the tug's stern, the *Barbara Jane,* I knew the boat belonged to Waymire Towing. The Waymire family had owned and run tugboats on the Savannah River ever since I could remember, and ever since I could remember, all their boats had been named for company founder Ray Waymire's daughters: Barbara, Alice, and Helen. I knew if I went outside and walked farther along Factor's Walk, I could see the Waymire docks, could see the *Helen III* and the *Alice II* tied up there too.

This was a Savannah thing. In Atlanta, bustling, maddening Atlanta, nothing stayed the same. Companies were formed and went bust, corporations transferred families in, then back out again a few years later. It all came down to money and expediency. But Savannah was different somehow. In Savannah, we cling tenaciously, foolishly, even, to a sense of continuity.

The old joke goes that it takes three Savannahians to change a lightbulb: one to screw in the bulb, and the other two to form a committee to save the original lightbulb.

I thought about the Breeze Inn. The existence of the Breeze wasn't really vital to a lot of people. It wasn't historic, wasn't a Revolutionary War battleground. It wasn't even all that attractive. I would probably never get rich running it. On the other hand, if I walked away from it right now, I'd come away a wealthy woman. I would have my old life back.

"BeBe?"

James swiveled around in his chair to look at me.

"I think I'll keep it," I said.

"Excuse me?"

"I'm not selling the Breeze," I said, firmly.

I sat back down in the chair facing my lawyer. "Can you work out the details? I can pay Sandcastle's option money back now."

He frowned. "It might get a little tricky, but if that's what you want . . ."

"It is," I said.

He nodded and wrote something on the legal pad in front of him. "I'll get Janet working on the deal right away. In the meantime, I had a call this morning from an attorney down in Vero Beach. Owen Techet."

"Techet?"

"He represents Sandra Findley," James said. "He thought you'd want to know that Roy Eugene Moseley was arrested in Fort Lauderdale on Friday. He's being held without bond on a variety of federal and state charges, including theft, fraud, burglary, forgery, and resisting arrest."

"Hmm," I said, trying to sound noncommittal. "How fascinating."

"Very," James said drily. He reached into the center drawer of his desk and pulled out a padded courier envelope, which he pushed across the desk toward me. "This came by messenger this morning."

I opened the envelope, and a thick braid of yellow gold slid into my lap. "My Daddy's watch!" I cried.

"Roy Eugene Moseley was wearing that when he was arrested," James said. "Jay Bradley sent the Lauderdale cops the theft report you filed after Moseley disappeared. Techet persuaded them that they should return it to you."

I fastened the watch around my left wrist. It hung there like an oversize bangle bracelet, but I didn't care.

"After Moseley's arrest, they discovered he'd been illegally squatting in the model apartment of a high-rise condominium project called La Dolce Vita, right there in Fort Lauderdale," James said. "When they searched the premises, they found his luggage, which contained quite a few other pieces of jewelry. Owen Techet says the Findley woman's emerald and diamond earrings were in his shaving kit, along with two diamond engagement rings, one white gold, the other rose gold, an opal and diamond ring, some pearls, and assorted other pieces."

"My jewelry," I said, twisting Daddy's watch. "Grandmama's jewelry. I never thought I'd see any of it again."

"You still haven't," James reminded me. "Techet says the Fort Lauderdale police will arrange a showing of all the recovered pieces for Moseley's victims, just as soon as all the charges against him are sorted out."

I winced at the word "victim."

"Techet tells a pretty entertaining story about how Moseley was apprehended," James went on. "He was on an eighty-six-foot yacht called the *Reefer Madness,* which he'd apparently grounded on a sandbar about a mile from the marina the boat was stolen from."

"Really?"

"The Coast Guard found the yacht."

" 'Semper Paratus,' " I said brightly.

"I beg your pardon?" James said.

"The Coast Guard motto. It means—"

"Always prepared," James said. "I was a priest for twenty-five years, you know."

"Right," I said.

"When the Coast Guard boarded the yacht, they arrested Roy Eugene Moseley, who continues to insist that his name is Rory. And after they boarded, they did a thorough search of the yacht. They found the boat's first mate, a man named Liam McConnell, tied up and handcuffed and stuffed in a gear locker. They also discovered a large cache of drugs aboard the yacht."

James folded his hands on the top of his desk.

"Should I ask any more questions about your trip to Florida?"

"Probably not," I said.

"Mr. Techet says his client, Sandra Findley, would like to talk to you, when you've had a chance to rest up from your trip."

"I'll give her a call," I agreed, standing up. "We've got some unfinished business. Is that all?"

"Just one more thing," James said, glancing down at his folder. "I got a call from a restaurant broker while you were out of town. He has a client who's looking for restaurant space in the historic district. They'd be interested in talking to you about Guale. Either leasing the space from you, or buying it outright."

Funny. For years my life had revolved around Guale. There had rarely been a day I didn't spend at Guale. I hadn't given a lot of thought to the restaurant in the past few days. But I had promised Emma Murphey a job. A restaurant job.

"I'll have to think about it," I said. Then I went over and kissed the top of James's head.

"James!" I said, drawing back. "Are you wearing hair product?"

65

Weezie

On Monday it felt so good to be home that I didn't even mind the kinds of mundane business chores that used to bore me to tears. Today, I was sorting through a cigar box full of old costume jewelry I'd bought as part of a lot at an auction the week before I left for Florida.

Most of the stuff was worthless, cheap plastic pop beads, hopeless tangles of inexpensive gold- and silver-colored chains, the kind of stuff most of our moms had in the bottom of their jewelry boxes. But I'd bought the box because I'd spotted a signed Miriam Haskell sunburst brooch in among the detritus, and now it was time to dump out the box and pick through the pieces one by one, looking for anything else saleable.

I was examining a flashy pair of rhinestone drop earrings with sterling-silver settings and Austrian crystal stones with my jeweler's loupe, looking for what I hoped would be the Eisenberg hallmark, when the phone rang. It was Daniel.

"Hey," he said breathlessly. "Can you meet me at the restaurant?"

"Which restaurant?" I asked. After all, Guale had been closed for weeks now, and he'd subbed at half a dozen other places since then.

"Guale," he said. "Meet me around back. Come now, okay?"

I picked up my pocketbook and the keys to the truck and headed for the door. Jethro, who'd been asleep on the floor under my worktable, suddenly came to life and bounded right behind me.

"All right," I told him. "But you have to stay in the truck. They have very strict rules against dogs in restaurants."

He didn't seem to mind, and when I opened the passenger-side door of my old turquoise pickup, he jumped up into his usual seat.

In five minutes, I was pulling into the lane that ran behind Guale, which was on Congress Street, in the heart of the old city market district.

As I rolled to a stop behind the restaurant, Daniel was just walking out the back door. He was wearing my favorite pair of tight black jeans, a faded black T-shirt, and beat-up Converse Chuck Taylor's.

I hopped out of the truck. Jethro stayed in his seat, content to hang his head out the open window.

"Hey," I said, greeting Daniel with a kiss. "What's the big deal that I had to drop what I was doing to run over here in the middle of the day?"

He reached in the pocket of his jeans and held up a key.

"We're celebrating," he said, his eyes dancing. "We're reopening Guale. And BeBe is bringing me in as a full partner."

"Really? That's wonderful."

"As soon as we're up and running and making a profit again, I'll start payments to buy BeBe out completely. Guale will be all mine."

"Daniel!" I wrapped my arms around his neck. "Oh, baby, that's so great. I can't believe it. But what made BeBe decide to sell out? She didn't say anything about that to me when we talked last night."

He was unlocking the fire door to the restaurant. "I got the feeling she just decided this morning. She called and asked me to meet her over here. And when I got here, she was standing in the entryway, looking around, as if she didn't recognize the place. She just said her heart wasn't in it anymore. The only provision she made on our deal is that I have to hire some chick y'all met down in Lauderdale."

"That would be Emma," I said. "She's a wonderful cook, and she'll be a great addition in the kitchen."

"We'll see," he said, sounding like the temperamental genius he liked people to think he was.

"What about BeBe?" I wondered. "What'll she do if she's not running this restaurant? Guale has been practically her whole life."

"She didn't say and I didn't ask," Daniel said.

"Just like a man."

He held the back door open and motioned me inside with a grand sweep of his arms.

"*Entrez!*" he said.

The kitchen was dark and chilly and eerily quiet. And for the first time in years, there were no delicious smells wafting from the range or the ovens. In fact, the only smell was the faint scent of Lysol.

I followed Daniel through the dark kitchen, and I jumped and had to suppress a scream when he turned suddenly and swept me into his arms.

"You're mine, Eloise Foley," he said, his voice husky. "Guale is mine, and you're mine. And we are here to celebrate this momentous occasion."

"Champagne?" I asked.

"Later," he said, taking my hand and leading me out of the kitchen. "Right now, I thought we'd check out that big leather banquette in the private dining room."

66

After I left James Foley's office, I decided to drop by the home to see my grandparents. I met Granddad at the door as he was bringing in the last sack of groceries from his trip to the store.

Grandmama was unloading the sacks and already finding fault with their contents.

"Spencer Loudermilk," she exclaimed, holding up a bottle of cherry red dish soap. "What is this vile liquid supposed to be?"

"Detergent," he said, busying himself with the *TV Guide*. I wondered idly why he bothered with it, since he had every listing memorized by heart.

"Well, it's not like any kind of detergent I ever saw," she said. "You know I always use Palmolive verdant spring."

"This kind was buy one-get one," Granddad said, snapping on the television with the remote control and settling back in his chair.

"Well, yippee-doo," Grandmama said. "Now I got two bottles of gunk I don't intend to ever use."

She went to the pantry, got a bottle of Diet Dr Pepper, and poured one over a glass of ice for me. "I have to buy this myself," she explained. "Your grandfather keeps bringing home that generic mess. Tastes like battery acid."

She motioned for me to sit down at the kitchen table, and I did as she suggested. "Now, what's this talk about a new fella in your life? Your grandfather said you seem pretty smitten with this man."

I sighed. "I was. But I don't think it's going to work out with Harry."

"Harry. That's a good, strong name. You don't hear that name too often anymore," she said. "I like it."

"You'd like him too, I think. Come to think of it, this is the first Harry I've ever dated," I told her. "Well, I don't guess we ever really did date. Except for once, down in Fort Lauderdale, he took me out to dinner."

She went on unloading groceries, putting the canned goods in the cupboard and the milk and eggs in the refrigerator. "What makes you think it's not going to work out with this Harry person?"

"He told me so. Yesterday. And after he told me it wasn't going to work out, he started packing up his stuff. He's leaving me. And the Breeze Inn."

She clucked disapprovingly. "That's a shame. How do you feel about it?"

"Mad. Hurt. Confused. I finally get this mess of a life of mine halfway straightened around. I finally find a man I like—and respect. And he dumps me."

"Did he say he doesn't like you anymore?" she asked.

"No. He says he's crazy about me. But he says we don't want the same things in life."

"That's just plain ridiculous," Grandmama declared, shaking her head. "And just like a man to make up some kind of hogwash excuse for running away. Honey, if you leave it up to this man, the two of you never will get married."

"Married!" I yelped. "Who said anything about getting married? I've been down the aisle three times already. And it never works out."

"But you're allowed a mulligan," Granddad said, strolling into the kitchen. He opened the cookie jar, reached in, and grabbed a handful of cookies.

"Put those back," Grandmama said, slapping the back of his hand.

"I'm not studying carrying you to the doctor after you make yourself sick eating cookies."

With a sheepish expression, he dropped the cookies back into the jar.

"And I saw that Kit Kat wrapper in the bottom of the grocery sack," she went on. "Don't think you're fooling me, Spencer Loudermilk."

She shook her head again and folded the empty plastic sacks into neat bundles that she stashed in a cloth bag she kept on the back of the kitchen door for that purpose.

"Enough messing around," she said finally. "Do you love this man?"

"Yes, ma'am."

"And you say he loves you?"

"So he claims."

"Then you need to get married," she said. "You're not getting any younger, you know. If you wait too much longer, those ovaries of yours will be all shriveled up, like Raisinettes."

"I'm not that old," I protested.

"You're nearly forty," she said. "I was nineteen when I had your father. And your mother was twenty-seven when she had you."

"I'm only thirty-five."

"And how old is this Harry person?"

"He won't tell me," I admitted. "But I know he's older than me. Anyway, who says I want children?"

"I do," she snapped. "We need a new baby in this family. And heaven knows, your brothers' wives aren't about to have any more. Which is probably a blessing."

"You are too much," I told her. "Trying to turn me into a broody hen just so you can play with a baby."

Grandmama slammed the cabinet door shut. "That's enough," she said. "I'm not going to sit around here listening to your sniffing and moaning about your love life. Now, if you love this fella, you go on out there to that motel of yours and tell him so."

She flounced into the living room and snatched the remote control out of Granddad's grasp.

"Go on," she said, shooing me out the door. "My stories are fixing to come on. That's enough soap opera for me."

67

The neon VACANCY **sign** was lit up when I pulled into the parking lot at the Breeze, which was appropriate, I thought, seeing Harry's Vista Cruiser, the tailgate down, backed up in front of the office door.

He was a weasel, I told myself, waiting until I was gone to clear out his stuff. Grandmama was wrong about us. It would never work out, but I didn't intend to allow him to leave without letting him know what he was missing out on.

"Damnit, Harry," I announced, barging into the office. I stalked over to the bedroom area, where I found his suitcase standing by the door. Jeeves sat up on the sofa and barked a happy greeting to me, but his master wasn't around.

"What now?" His voice, muffled, came from the utility room.

I went in, expecting to find him loading boxes with his fishing gear.

Instead, I found him sitting cross-legged on the floor, with what looked like the disemboweled guts of the washing machine spread out around him.

"I thought you were going," I said.

"I thought so too," he said, sorting through a pile of widgets on the floor.

"Why didn't you?"

He sighed and looked up. "Give me a hand, will you?"

I put out my hand and hauled him to his feet. But he didn't let go of my hand once he was standing.

"The damned washing machine is messed up again," he said, gesturing toward a mound of sopping-wet laundry on the floor beside it. "It chewed up a whole load of towels."

He held up a shredded white towel for my inspection, and the scent of Clorox almost knocked me down.

"You put in too much bleach again," I said. "It's not the machine that's screwed up. It's you."

"That's what Tricia said," he answered, wiping his hands on the seat of his jeans.

"Tricia? Since when have you started listening to what your ex-wife has to say?"

He winced at the word "ex-wife." "She can't be wrong all the time. It's statistically impossible."

"What exactly brought on this new level of understanding?" I asked.

"I went over to the marina yesterday, to move the boat. And I ran into her. She was asking all kinds of questions about you. Like, if we were only friends, why were you shelling out $32,500 to buy back my boat for me?"

"What did you tell her?"

"That it was a loan. I told her I intend to pay you back. That's when she let me have it." He shook his head. "Man, that woman cusses like a sailor."

"I'm sure your tender sensibilities were shattered," I said.

He grinned, then touched the watch hanging from my wrist. "What's this?"

I took it off and showed it to him. "It's my daddy's. Reddy was wearing it when they arrested him. The cops took it off him, and that lawyer down in Florida, the one who works for Sandra Findley, overnighted it to James. I just got it back this morning."

He turned it over and looked at the inscription, then handed it back.

"Pretty nice."

I took a deep breath. "I'd like you to have it, Harry."

"Me? No. Like you said about that painting of your aunt. It's a family heirloom. I couldn't."

I took it and slid it onto his wrist and snapped the catch.

"It's a gift," I said lightly. "Not a loan. To thank you . . . for everything."

"You bought my boat back," he said. "We're even. Only, not really. I still owe you."

"I'm not talking about the money," I told him, fighting back unexpected tears. "You taught me what's important. When I met you, I thought I'd lost everything. In a way, I had. But I'm not talking about material things. I'm talking about trust. When I came out here to the Breeze, I had to trust you. I didn't have any choice. As it turns out, I got lucky."

"No," he said, putting his hands on my shoulders. "I'm the lucky one. I got a second chance. According to Tricia, I don't deserve it. She says I'm a stubborn, pigheaded, emotional retard. She can't figure out what you see in me."

"Well," I said, taking one of his hands and kissing it, grease and all. "You're a man of infinite possibilities. And you're pretty good with your hands too."

"Not to brag or anything," he said, "but I've been told I'm the best damn charter captain on the coast. You'd never want for fish . . . if we, you know, stuck together."

I took a step backward.

"Harry Sorrentino," I said, eyes blazing. "Is that your idea of a proposal? Because if it is—"

He pulled me to him roughly, but kissed me with a tenderness that took my breath away.

When he was done, he didn't let me go.

"Just now, I literally don't have a pot to pee in. Well, I do have a thirty-five-horsepower Evinrude, and a half interest in a sixteen-foot johnboat, and a lot of expensive fishing equipment. But, you know

I'm a hard worker. I don't know anything about the restaurant business, but I'd be willing to learn. And to help out when the charter business is slow."

"I'm selling Guale to Daniel," I said. "But there's this old motel out here at Tybee that I've got my eye on . . ."

He raised an eyebrow. "What about your town house? And your old life?"

I took a deep breath. "Turns out not everything in my old life was worth keeping. I'm buying back the town house. For sentimental reasons, I guess you'd say. I think I could make a new life out here. Fixing up the Breeze. Maybe opening a new restaurant out here, buying more property on Tybee."

"It could be a great investment," Harry said.

"And a great place to raise children," I added.

"Children?"

From the doorway, Jeeves gave a concerned "YIP!"

"Eventually. My grandmother seems to think I owe her some. And she points out that I'm not getting any younger, and I have to admit she's probably right."

He nodded thoughtfully. "All right."

"That is," I said, "if you're not too old to have children."

I cocked my head and gave him the once-over, still liking what I saw. "Just how old are you, Harry Sorrentino?"

He picked me up in his arms then, and carried me out of the utility room and into the office. He set me down for a moment while he went to the office door and locked it. And clicked the dead bolt.

"One more thing," I told him. I went over to the desk and flipped a switch. Outside, I could hear the faint buzz of the NO being added to VACANCY.

"Now then," I said. "What was that you were saying about equipment?"

Breeze Inn Crabcakes

If you're paralyzed by fear of frying, these crabcakes are a winner, because they're baked in the oven, not fried. While they're in the oven, mix up a batch of Blue Breeze cocktails!

1 tbsp. butter
2 tbsp. minced red onion
1 clove garlic, minced
2 tbsp. red bell pepper, minced
½ tsp. Old Bay crab boil seasoning
3 tbsp. half-and-half
1 tbsp. spicy brown mustard
1 egg
½ tsp. minced parsley
1 lb. white or claw crab meat, picked over for shells

Topping:
½ cup bread crumbs
¼ cup grated parmesan cheese
2 tbsp. vegetable oil
2 tbsp. melted butter

Sauté vegetables in butter till limp, about 3 minutes. Add Old Bay, half-and-half, and mustard. Mix well. Add egg, parsley, and bread crumbs, mixing well. Gently fold in crab.

Form into 8 patties about ½-inch thick, or smaller, for appetizer-size servings. Stir together bread crumbs and parmesan. Pat topping onto both sides of the crabcakes and refrigerate until firm, about 2 hours.

Place patties on cookie sheet, sprinkle with oil and butter mixture and bake at 400° for 7–10 min.

For appetizer servings, place mini-crabcakes on a bed of mixed salad greens, top with spicy remoulade. For entrée servings, top with mango salsa.

Blue Breeze Cocktail

Pour into cocktail shaker:
4 ounces lemonade
2 ounces vodka
1 ounce blue curaçao

Shake, pour over tall glass of cracked ice, top with seltzer, and stir. Garnish with lime slice and 3–4 blueberries threaded on a cocktail pick.

Savannah Breeze

Mary Kay Andrews

A Reading Group Guide

HARPER

NEW YORK . LONDON . TORONTO . SYDNEY

Introduction

Mary Kay Andrews's latest novel has everything: love, a little revenge, and even two great recipes. Her lively main character, BeBe Loudermilk, has great energy and drive, but even the resourceful BeBe takes a hit when a gorgeous con man seduces her and walks away with everything she owns. Well, almost everything. All that's left is a dilapidated 1950s motel on Tybee Island. The Breeze Inn is not this former Savannah deb's kind of haunt, to put it mildly. Soon, though, with her spirit of can-do and the help of a few good friends, BeBe picks herself up and pitches in. What happens along the way, including an attraction to the also dilapidated but fast-improving manager of the Breeze Inn and some innovative decorating ideas, will keep readers staying up late. This is a delectable romp, masterfully written, and it hits all the right notes: serious, fun, and truehearted.

Questions for Discussion

1. Were you fooled by Reddy? Were there any clues that he was trouble?

2. Can you imagine losing everything you own in the world, even your clothes? What do you think that you would do?

3. Is this a particularly Southern novel? If so, what are the elements that make it that way?

4. BeBe is a woman who thinks she knows what she wants in life. How does this stand in her way?

5. What does Andrews's portrayal of BeBe's grandparents have to say about aging? Did you find these characters frustrating, charming, or both?

6. Do you believe that people can really change? How do BeBe and Harry change each other? Is this change believable?

7. On page 162 Bebe says, "Up until the day I realized that my second husband, Richard, had that unfortunate penchant for computer porn, I'd always thought of myself as somebody who was naturally lucky." Do you think there is such a thing as "natural luck"?

8. Each of the characters in this story has pride, and shows it in different ways. How do we see this, and what part does pride play in what happens?

9. Would you say that this is a feminist novel? Why or why not?

10. *Savannah Breeze* definitely has a happy ending. What is it about happy endings in general that has such a powerful effect on readers? Are there happy endings in real life?

Questions for the Author

1. *You write as if you are really familiar and comfortable with these characters. Are they based on people you know? Of course, they are fictional, but do you feel as if you have a relationship with them?*

My characters—especially BeBe and Weezie—seem like real people to me, especially since *Savannah Breeze* marks a return appearance from an earlier book. None of them is based on real people, but I'll admit a tiny bit of me is in each of my female protagonists. Usually it's nothing anybody else would recognize, but maybe my own reactions to situations presented in real life. Or sometimes, I twist around what my own reaction would be and give a character like BeBe the polar opposite reaction. And with secondary characters, I sometimes borrow from real life. For instance, in *Savannah Breeze*, Granddad's addiction to candy bars and the Weather Channel was based on my own late father's habits.

2. *Who or what have been some of the major influences on your development as a writer?*

I think my development as a writer has been a gradual evolution. I come from a journalism background, so in my early novels, which were mysteries written under my own name, I concentrated on good plotting and puzzle solving. When I started writing the Mary Kay Andrews novels, I gave myself permission to play with style and characterization, and to let my natural sense of humor come through in the books. Of course, I'm always trying to grow and change, to keep myself and my readers entertained.

3. *Do you enjoy the actual process of writing, or is it just hard work, or both?*

Writing is just doggone hard. I love the sense of achievement I get when seeing a pile of pages on top of my desk at the end of a work day. And on a really good day, I can give myself an "attagirl." And on the bad days, I stare at the computer, I stare at the ceiling, and I stare at the classifieds looking for a high-paying job that doesn't involve writing fiction!

4. *You used to be a journalist. If you were to have a career other than writing, what might it be? Designer? Chef?*

If I weren't a writer, I might have become an antique dealer, or a shopkeeper, or a beach bum.

5. *What advice would you give to someone who wants to write a novel?*

My best advice to beginning writers is to read, read, read. Figure out what you want to write. Play to your strengths. Write and keep writing. Treat your writing like a job. Approach it with dedication. And don't take yourself too seriously.

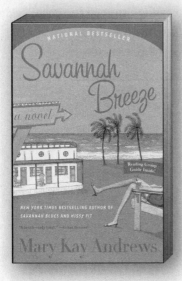

SAVANNAH BREEZE
A Novel

ISBN 0-06-056467-9 (paperback)

A brief but disastrous relationship with the gorgeous Reddy, a con man, causes Savannah belle BeBe Loudermilk to lose everything. All that remains is a ramshackle 1950s motor court on Tybee Island.

Breeze Inn is a place where the very classy BeBe wouldn't normally be caught dead, but what choice does she have? Soon Bebe has the motel spiffed up and attracting paying guests.

Then there's a sighting of Reddy in Fort Lauderdale, and BeBe decides to go after him.

"Mary Kay Andrews has perfect pitch when it comes to endearing, smart-mouth heroines."
—Anne Rivers Siddons

"Andrews lays on lots of Savannah atmosphere and Southern charm."
—*Boston Globe*

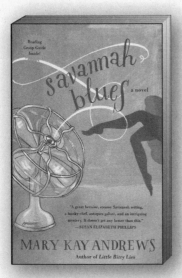

SAVANNAH BLUES
A Novel

ISBN 0-06-051913-4 (paperback)

A delightful, witty novel with a delicious revenge-against-the-bimbo-who-stole-your-ex plot. After a rough divorce, Weezie's husband is awarded their house in Savannah's historic district. Relegated to the carriage house, she must sit by and watch as her ex moves his "perfect" new girlfriend in.

"A great heroine, steamy Savannah setting, a hunky chef, antiques galore. It doesn't get any better than this."
—Susan Elizabeth Phillips